Robert lives in Alloa, Scotland, with his wife Lorna; dog Ziggy; cats Roxy, Jake and Doowood. He has a son, Jamie; daughter-in-law, Gemma; granddaughter, Maya and grandson, Cooper. He is the writer of the classic Christmas tale, *I've Got Jesus in the Back of My Taxi!*

To, Cooper Judd Ferguson, for being my wonderful grandson.

Robert Ferguson

Red Lentil Soup

Living in Another Person's Reality Is the Holy Grail of Mind Control!

Austin Macauley Publishers™
London * Cambridge * New York * Sharjah

This is a work of fiction. Names, characters, businesses, places, events, locales, and incidents are either the products of the author's imagination or used in a fictitious manner. Any resemblance to actual persons, living or dead, or actual events is purely coincidental.

A CIP catalogue record for this title is available from the British Library.

ISBN 9781398443396 (Paperback)
ISBN 9781398443402 (ePub e-book)

www.austinmacauley.com

First Published 2022
Austin Macauley Publishers Ltd®
1 Canada Square
Canary Wharf
London
E14 5AA

Special thanks to, Issa Touma, for granting permission to use his unique and brave film, *9 days: From My Window in Aleppo* in my book. The film details the nine days Issa spent holed up in his apartment filming the Aleppo war that surrounded him. Issa is a director of art festivals, a curator and director of Le Pont arts organisation. He is a renowned photographer.

Iain Overton,
Thanks to, Iain, for his assistance on explosive devices and supplying information on the after-effects of such devices. Iain's acclaimed book, *The Price of Paradise*, is a must-read and informative in detail.

Hotel Phoenicia, Malta.
Thanks to Hotel Phoenicia for giving permission to use their beautiful hotel as a home-from-home for my characters. It's a superb hotel and a firm favourite.

Special thanks to:
David Abernethy, HMP Edinburgh
The Pub, Valletta
Trabuxu, Valletta
Café Cordina, Valletta
The Cramond Inn, Cramond
Presbyterian Churches in Edinburgh, Aleppo and Valletta

The Isle of Arran

The Atholl Hotel, Dunkeld

The Dunalastair Hotel Suites, Kinloch Rannoch

The City of Edinburgh

Pitlochry and the Village of Moulin

The City of Aleppo

The beautiful island of Malta

Rhineland-Palatinate region western Germany

Agenda bookshops, Malta.

For his advice and knowledge of Malta law, I am grateful to Dr James Scerri Worley.

I would like to thank Leslie Vella, from Kappara Malta, for permitting his wonderful image of the Triton fountain in Valletta as the front cover. Leslie also helped with Maltese transliteration on many occasions. Thank you, Leslie. You are a gem!

For her fantastic artwork, used as the back cover image, I thank the talented Scottish artist, Jo Lockie.

Special thanks to Jamie Sharp for his guidance on the legalities of the Scottish Legal system.

Chapter 1
The Funeral

Graveside, Dean Cemetery, Edinburgh. The present-day. The month is June.

The day was overcast. The minister, a small, pot-bellied figure, sporting an almost ridiculous white, grey, comb-over—which hoodwinked no-one—cleared his throat before speaking.

'Earth to earth, dust to dust, ashes to ashes,' he intoned while keeping his eyes firmly closed and resting his clasped hands over a small, black leather-bound Bible, which sat fittingly on his bloated belly.

The preacher looked content, knowing this much-rehearsed routine had once again been delivered well, correctly worded, professionally served and brightly articulated. His physical performance included an elaborate rocking movement. Swaying to-and-fro on his toes, head tilted to heaven, the purist minister replayed this automatic graveside sermon from memory and notably at each funeral he attended. God belonged to the minister, and though he taught the word of the Lord, you could not have him! God belonged to him!

It was a well-rehearsed graveside service by a dutiful vicar who had devoted years of service to his white Presbyterian God, his biblical God—an older man with bushy silver-coloured hair, donning a long grey beard and wrapped in a flowing, seamless white robe.

This was one ability he offered to any bereaved family of the Scottish faith. *Professional but boring*, Bill believed.

Bill heard a few recognisable religious soundbites, as he liked to call them: *We have gathered here today*, was one ever-present funeral element he had witnessed at his parents' memorial service. And subsequently: *Jesus said, I am the resurrection and the life. He who believes in me, though he dies, yet shall live, and whoever lives and believes in me will never die*. Then finally, the predictable and ultimate religious ending—*Amen!*

The minister opened his swollen eyes after finishing the standalone service at the site of the burial plot.

Bill McKenzie was a life-long non-believer; his late wife Laura a sober, trendy, committed Christian, who regularly attended church, wherever her travels took her. When religion was the main discussion, Bill would use the same atheist quote to get his sceptic point across. *If you could reason with people who believe in God, there would be no people that believe in God.*

It was two weeks past that Bill and Laura McKenzie were involved in a severe and fatal accident; near their home in West Coates central Edinburgh. A Jaguar E-Pace SUV driver purposely drove on the wrong side of the road, aiming to hit them. Powering indifferently and erratically in the direction of Bill and Laura on their bicycles.

Bill, noticing the vehicle, reacted immediately. Gripping and pressing both handbrakes tightly, his sudden halt hurled him over the handlebars, away from the car. He tumbled, violently, attempting to land by the tuck-and-roll method a professional cyclist would use, but it didn't work. He was knocked out cold. His spontaneous reaction prevented a full impact with the Jaguar and possibly mitigated severe injury. His recently purchased e-bike slid back onto the road and was caught under the skidding front wheel. The bike received more damage than he did.

Regrettably, the car caught Laura full-on, with a violent, forceful impact that catapulted her helpless, doll-like body over the vehicle roof and threw her down solidly, headfirst on the pavement—a few yards from where the car would eventually stop. As Bill regained his senses, the SUV driver was restarting the engine, intent on departing the scene of the crime. The engine started and the wheels spun burning rubber as they gained traction on the wet, greasy ground. The car sped away.

Driving skilfully, the heartless executioner avoided oncoming traffic as he drove north up Magdala Crescent; just a few yards from Bill and Laura's new Edinburgh home.

Burnt-out remains of the car were later discovered at Eagle Rock near Drum Sands, not far from Cramond, a village and suburb in the north-west of Edinburgh. The vehicle involved in the accident was stolen. The identity of the driver was never discovered.

Bill gradually regained consciousness. As though his body was rebooting, his eyes blinked open, and his eyelids twitched and shuddered.

Getting progressively stronger, although sporadic pain surged through his tender body, he made an extreme effort to move nearer to Laura. Crawling uncomfortably through the anguish of each hurtful movement, reaching a foot or so from his wife, he screamed tearful words: “Hang on, help is coming. Everything to live for…hang in there! Laura, help is on the way…”

Blood trickled from his nose and a small laceration appeared on his forehead.

He was too late.

The ambulance was too late.

Everyone was too late.

Laura was gone.

She was pronounced dead at the scene.

Laura would now meet her God.

Chapter 2
Losing Laura

It was 10.30 am.

Laura's beautiful flame extinguished for no reason held no purpose with Bill or with the way he understood life's frugality. It was all so ineffable. If he had gotten to her in time, could he have saved her?

Gotten to her in time?…It was like catching the wind, writing on the wall, or barking up the wrong tree. Stupid, worthless clichés. No actual meaning. Bill knew there was absolutely nothing he could have done. It was pointless.

His inner mind spoke, and he did as it requested. *Look to the sky and see Laura's soul float up through the clouds.* He glanced upwards to heaven he didn't believe in. But look he did.

Her soul would go to heaven when God demanded, she would say.

Bill's agnostic views flew past a slight simmer and reached boiling point. An abusive, spiteful steam spouted from his mouth, entirely aimed at God; Laura's one true God. Her God of mercy.

His angry tears mixed with rain and blood, falling to the road; the rain would disperse and leave no clue of this accident ever occurring. Bill continued abusing Laura's God. Even though he didn't believe in Him, he felt justified venting his anger at the invisible, imaginary cruel deity. A divine spirit with no emotional connection to his creation.

"Where are you? Is Laura's belief not good enough? Why would you take her life? It is me that doesn't believe in you; I have no faith in you at all; you are despicable; how can you be a God of mercy?" Bill bristled.

He cried more profanities until he could speak no more; sobbing childlike tears as he rocked Laura's lifeless body.

"This is the thanks you get, Laura. You spent all your life believing in a nasty piece of work, a God that offers no love or kindness. Why would he take your precious life? A pitiful God, a God with no scruples, that's your God, Laura. A pitiful, scrupulous, false idol!"

He embraced Laura as an unceasing stream of rain poured down.

Groups of people began to gather at the scene, showing a morbid curiosity.

Traffic was becoming blocked at the junction of West Coates and Haymarket Terrace—and a bus at the centre of the obstruction came into Bill's view.

He looked through mournful eyes at the blue single-decker. It had two large vinyl graphic images of distinguished Scottish scientists applied to the bodywork: obstetrician Sir James Young Simpson, and chemist James Young, a colourful advertisement as a weird intrusion on Bill's misery and despair.

Most of the bus passengers were unwilling viewers of the tragic event. Many averted their eyes; others wept openly; a few watched keenly, only to satisfy their ghoulish curiosity like a vulture could sniffing out the carcass of a rat hidden under decomposing plant material. And there were the morbid life insulters, filming it all on their mobile phones.

No doubt videos and photographs would be uploaded onto social media. Hearts, likes and sad face emojis would flood the internet. Nowadays, everyone was a news reporter: One social media headlines included—'A Major accident in central Edinburgh'. Another newspaper would head the story 'One fatality, woman hit and killed by speeding car'.

Scottish TV news anchor John MacKay would say: Two cyclists struck by a hit-and-run driver. One person dead'.

And a national TV news caption would state: 'A woman has been killed by a hit and run driver.'

A female police officer, trained in trauma-processing, struggled to wrench Bill from Laura's body, her black felt police hat bundled to the ground as she grappled, with all her strength, to pull Bill from his dead wife. She used comforting words. Assistance came from a robust male colleague—possibly an amateur rugby player—but they soon managed, with considerable effort, to tear a resolute Bill away from Laura's dead body. On the cold, road, Laura's remains lay alone as the officers moved Bill from the scene. One police officer covered Laura with a blanket.

An ambulance crew took control of the situation, reassuring Bill with words of compassion as they prepared to take him to hospital, Bill continued to vent anger at Laura's God—crying out emotional abuse—as a thermal blanket was curled around his shoulders and he made unsteady steps into the ambulance, aided by a young paramedic. More police officers had arrived at the scene. The vicinity was cordoned off with black and yellow tape and police forensics took photographs of the accident site and recorded eyewitness statements. Other officers controlled the congested traffic and got vehicles moving—the bus headed into the city centre. The vinyl graphic faces of Sir James Young Simpson and James Young stared at the place of the incident until the bus left the scene.

Bill watched Laura's body being enclosed in a body bag and loaded into a private ambulance to head to the city morgue. Her trip would not have flashing lights or a blaring siren giving an infuriating and loud sound effect. This journey would be as slow as a fat kid on a skateboard.

After a full physical check-up, Bill met the police at the hospital. He gave a lengthy, confusing statement that revealed his need for medication and professional counselling. He had lost his wife. He had seen her killed.

Too many questions were asked of him.

Bill felt the police officer's enquiries become abbreviated and less informal as the day went on. For more than two hours, he was quizzed as if he was the guilty party.

"Did you get a clear view of the driver?"

"For fucks sake, how many times do I need to answer this *fucking* question. No, no, no!" Bill growled at the weary officers.

The police officers asked routine questions that would be asked of any car accident witness. Could Bill recall the vehicle type, the colour, a registration number? Did he or Laura have enemies? Anyone who would want to hurt them? Had they had any recent correspondence of hate-mail or telephone threats? Eventually, a statement was given, and now it was up to the police to find the cold-blooded killer.

Bill touched the sterile gauze pad wrapped around his head, sweatband style, covering his head wound. He had no broken bones or fractures, but beneath the gauze, there would develop a scar highlighting his misfortune. An aide-mémoire would be recalled every time he looked in a mirror. A scar of remembrance as time passed.

After a long day and a short nap in the busy A&E, Bill was directed to sit on a trolley bed in a curtained cubicle to wait for his final assessment. The police no longer felt he needed protection. They were long gone.

A young doctor, fresh out of medical school, finished the examination by shining a torch beam into each eye, determining the severity of his concussion.

"Everything seems fine and the x-rays show no damage. Thankfully…I can say you are clear to go." The doctor looked directly at Bill and added, "Just remember to return in four or five days to have the stitches removed."

As he walked from the cubicle, the doctor stopped and turned to face Bill, holding the green curtain with one hand.

"Take paracetamol or a couple of aspirin if you have any discomfort," he said. He slipped the penlight into his top pocket and fully pulled and opened the crucible screen.

Bill adjusted his clothing, noticing the blood-stained jacket and ripped trousers, he leapt from the trolley and landed unsurely on the floor. He felt an unpleasant creeping sensation in the feet, calves and thighs which caused pain. The discomfort was a mild effect after the accident. But not a serious health condition. He felt discomfort though not severe distress.

Bill was now ready to head home, but after a few enquiries, he sought and got permission from hospital authorities to visit the mortuary viewing room to see Laura's body.

He had already formally identified her body, with a police detective and his young subordinate present; but Bill now wanted his own private closure. One more look to see Laura, her beautiful self, before the funeral directors got their greasy hands on her. Beautification, he imagined, would make her look like a mannequin. And he didn't want to see her like that.

Laura lay on a cold metal table. A full-length white sheet covered her. The diener—who is a morgue worker responsible for handling, cleaning, and moving the corpse—was a tall thin man who showed little or no emotion.

This was a man who would never display kindness or divulge sentiment, especially at his place of work.

The room was small, deliberate in size, an effort to keep the visit intimate, not daunting, or depressing. It didn't work.

The medical examiner carefully lifted the cover from Laura's face, folded it neatly down over her body, just past her neckline, and stood back to allow Bill space to see his dead wife for the last time. She looked serene, in a weird sort of way. Her face peeking out from a cover around her head gave the impression that Laura had seen her God; she looked peaceful, even happy.

"Your wife died from a subdural hematoma." the diener's low evocative voice came from somewhere close behind Bill.

"She wore a helmet."

"Laura wore a helmet."

"A simple knock on the head, with or without a safety helmet, if the trauma is sufficient enough, can lead to death. It led to your wife's death."

The doctor explained. Bill remained silent and held his stare on his dead wife.

The doctor continued to give more detailed information, recording surgical procedure observations.

"The force caused blood to accumulate in the space below the dura layer in the cranium. The vascular system in the brain is powerful. Any blow to the head may rupture any of the blood vessels leading to hematoma. Even a simple knock could do this." Although the medical information was expertly detailed, Bill was still unsure of the jargon the unnerving, disturbing technician provided.

"A simple knock!" he repeated curtly as he ambled from the viewing room. "A simple bloody knock!" He curiously watched as the unsettling man pulled the sheet back over Laura's beautiful face.

"A simple bloody knock!" Bill halted at the door, turned deliberately and looked at doctor Death.

"She spoke to me."

He wasn't hoping or looking for an answer, nor a reaction. It was a remark of grief, spoken through emotional pain. The morgue technician stared back at Bill but did not speak. Not moving, not responding, unwilling to generate deliberations, he maintained a spine-chilling glower at Bill as a rebuked child would.

The medical examiner waited for the grieving husband to speak or leave. His job description didn't cover friendly conversation with clients, alive or dead.

Knowing that this man would never repeat this story, Bill unburdened himself, would probably forget Bill's bombast as soon as he left the room. But by sharing his emotions, he released himself from the guilty weight that impressed on him that he hadn't heard Laura's last words.

"I couldn't hear her," Bill confessed. "I had sound buds stuck in my ears. All I heard was George Michael singing—*A Different Corner*. And by the time I got to her, she died. She died in my arms. But she spoke three words. I saw her voice them."

Bill's voice broke. He found himself rambling incoherent details of Laura's passing.

"Maybe she told you she loved you!"

The scowl on the diener's face was a mark of this being the first—and last—time the doctor had offered such sympathy to a grieving husband. *Why did I get involved?* the doctor's visible wince seemed to ask.

But Bill didn't view the pathologist's question as unbecoming. This was the proper perspective of a caring person.

He continued, "She said something unusual. It wasn't a cry for help, or a plea, or a prayer to her God. I think she was asking me to do something. I guess I'll never know now." The metal door made unoiled juddering squeaks and screeches as he opened it, preparing to leave the room. Bill launched a hand into the air to wave goodbye and turned to look over his shoulder, not to see if the morgue assistant had noticed his farewell but to ask a final question.

"Can I ask you something personal?" he said tentatively.

The diener didn't respond for a short time—bowing his head, he accepted.

"I'm simply curious, I've never seen such an unusual name." And Bill pointed to his own chest, indicating he meant the security ID that was held on a light blue NHS lanyard around the unnerving man's neck.

The lookalike doctor took the card in his hand and lifted it, twisting it to look at the ID, at his face, it gave details of his job title, department, photograph and bar code. He let it go and it swung back to its usual resting place on his chest. "My NHS badge?" he said. And then, "My name…Dirk Alleluia is not so strange in Sweden. My proper name is Diederik Alleluia, but friends call me Dirk. The surname Alleluia is a Hebrew name. It means 'Praise the lord'."

Bill raised both eyebrows, and also his cheeks, almost closing his eyes shut. He leaned his head to one side, nodded slow nods, thrust out his chin and gave a mysterious smile. Then he raised his shoulders stretching out his arms to offer two upward-facing hands that looked like he was expecting someone to drop a parcel in them.

Maybe a Robert De Niro imitation was as good as it got at this time of night.

"Nice name!" he said, maintaining his unintended De Niro impression. repeated with the unbefitting De Niro impression. "Nice name!"

Then he waved again and left through the screeching door which flapped shut behind him. If the doctor also waved, Bill missed it, as he made his way lethargically to the exit, along a cold, dull-coloured corridor with spots of flaking paint, lit by dim fluorescent lights doing their best to flare-up the inert gases.

Bill understood their cracking noises to be aligned to a phenomenon called magnetostriction—information dredged up from something he read somewhere.

Every light was covered with layers of dust and spiderwebs, which added a chilling mood to his memory of the mortuary.

Wind and rain whipped through the open-ended corridor, the flexible PVC curtains at each end slapping the walls as they blew inwardly.

Bill spoke the first verse of *A Different Corner* to himself: all about love being magical and that love would keep them from pain.

"What a load of shit!" he snarled.

It would take fifteen minutes to walk from this part of the hospital to the A&E exit where a pre-booked taxi would be waiting. The place was as big as a holiday resort and a golf-buggy would have come in handy.

His mind needed solace, a place to hide, something to drain the trauma that flooded his thoughts, a place where he could forget today's tragic events. Aid would come in the shape of a bottle. More than one if necessary.

Moving deliberately, placing more weight on his unhurt foot, he managed to reach the taxi. Only a minute later than his booking time.

Before entering the cab, he stood to bear witness to another ambulance rushing to deposit an emergency patient with awaiting A&E staff. His attention centred on the unresponsive patient, strapped tightly to a Pegasus stretcher-trolley, wheeled to a waiting team of medical experts. A tactically astute female voice crackled over the wind to his ears.

"Heroin overdose. Discovered in a hypoxic state and given oxygen. I've administered naloxone and the patient is stable."

The female paramedic updated the hospital staff on the medical procedure administered during the ambulance journey.

Bill entered the cab, gave the driver his address and sat back. He stretched out his legs and retraced the day's events.

–

The taxi driver placed his phone in a holder on the dashboard, refastened his seatbelt and started the engine. Leaving the hospital grounds, the taxi slowly departed. Bill could still see the patient being wheeled through the hospital doors, surrounded by expert carers, all working to save another life. The taxi driver tried to hold a conversation, but Bill was unresponsive. His mind was elsewhere.

Memories of the accident came flooding back; he recalled it in exquisite detail, including the white Jaguar E-Pace S.U.V. involved in the accident that killed Laura.

The persistent police questioning had finally elicited from Bill the car's registration plate—LMD1E. A non-existent plate, he had been told, a fraudulent plate that must have been created by the driver. It was not a registered number.

Bill thought. *LMD1E? Laura McKenzie Die?* Laura had no enemies. He had no enemies. This was purely a crazy coincidence, but how could this happen? Who killed Laura?

–

Standing by the grave, Bill listened to the overconfident minister.

Bill's attention was drawn back to the low-toned communications of Reverend McAuley, whose religious extracts immersed the small group of mourners who had come to pay their final respects.

And in Bill's case, the service naturally fell on deaf ears. At the closing of the ritual, a few kind words and a firm handshake was offered and accepted, then the minister made haste to a waiting car as suddenly, a shower of rain fell. The leather-bound Bible, now a rain shield, covered the minister's head, and to some extent the coiffeur's experiment that sat unstable on it. Some flattened strands of resolute hair spread themselves in parallel stripes across the afflicted region of baldness.

It was a hairstyle all his parishioners recognised as non-successful. Everybody who met the vicar could detect the trick. Yet, the Minister with the mock hairstyle was apathetic to any criticism it received, or the trauma his barber felt. It was his choice and his design—like his God.

The graveside mourners included two neighbours, known only by their first names: Jean and Margaret; a local bartender called Alex; and Bill and Laura's fifty-something Polish housecleaner Zofia; who spoke only a few words of English. 'Zorry for yur losh,' she muttered sympathetically.

Bill considered having one more conversation with Laura, just a few words before she was covered in saturated soil, but then thought otherwise and tossed a single Damask rose into the grave. It gave a slight *thump* as it hit the coffin. The pink lover's rose was Laura's favourite flower.

A trio of bored-looking gravediggers, all smoking, stood impatiently in the background, waiting to cover the burial opening with a planked wooden board which held only one floral tribute, a wreath selection of graceful orchids, set against delicate foliage on a soft bed of moss. There was no card attached to identify the sender.

There were no family or friends to share Bill's grief or provide sympathy, someone to shore up his affective state of mind or aid his physical well-being, or someone to offer a hug or two. But Bill being Bill, he relied on his stubborn self-reliance; what he called his 'secret sauce' to get through this day and any other day for that matter.

He would find somewhere peaceful to chill-out for a few hours.

Anywhere away from this damn cemetery.

Today, shrouded by the stress of the funeral, he wanted independent comfort. He preferred his own company. He didn't want anyone to provide support or reassurance. Especially today. He was grateful there was no one here with him. No grieving relative or friend feeling sorry for him or judging him.

He headed to a local pub he knew, a place Bill visited for the occasional lunch after his recent return to Edinburgh. The regulars were familiar faces he exchanged pleasant words with, but beyond that they were strangers.

Bill's grief was straightforward. He didn't behave as mourners were meant to or as a professional mourner playacted—a moirologist—hired by families to grieve at funerals or wakes. Bill would lose the plot if anyone tried to pay homage or produce funerary notes of reassurance—his attitude lay somewhere at the other end of the funerary spectrum. He held grievances and solemn feelings but wanted to retain them and do what he thought was appropriate. His bereavement strategy was getting drunk.

Chapter 3
Bill's Childhood

Bill Mathieson McKenzie was born into a middle-class Edinburgh family.

His parents, Duncan and Moira, were successful lawyers of note, with Moira a senior advocate, working within the High Court of Justiciary's high-profile realms. Markedly renowned and remembered as the prosecutor that dealt with evil and did everything in her power to send them down.

And if the death penalty were still an option, she would certainly ask for it!

Her courtroom celebrity came attached to a notorious murder case of 1980—which became Scotland's biggest ever murder trial.

According to her peers, on both prosecution and defence benches, Moira McKenzie was zealous in her role as a prosecution advocate and was one of the most highly regarded senior counsel at the criminal bar and was always the first choice for many agents throughout Scotland. She acted in some of the country's most notorious and documented hearings and led counsel on many high-profile murder trials during her tenure.

One case, a highlight from many in a long, illustrious career, was prosecuting Finlay McColl. An evil serial killer and one of the most deranged creatures she had ever shared a courtroom with. On her early retirement in the year 2000, Moira gave her radical views on the McColl murders.

In her well-acclaimed, well-received bestseller and most frequently borrowed book of 2001, "The Uncharming Psychopath", which topped the Scottish book list the following year, she told her story of the killer she faced in court. The predator she helped put behind bars for life and more. Literary critic James Judd Smith gave a valued critique when reviewing the paperback in the Sunday Gazette Supplement.

From the first page to the last, I was in the courtroom, in the dock and in the mind of a vicious, evil killer. Not to mention the appetite for the argument from the author and QC Moira McKenzie. A genuinely great cross-examiner with extensive knowledge of the case. With her hard work, she put an evil, sadistic creature behind bars for life.

Finlay McColl, from the outset of the police investigation, was never in the frame for the disappearance of the three Edinburgh University students. One piece of evidence that McColl did not want to be mentioned in court by his legal team was the fact that the day the students disappeared was the day McColl had spent the first of three days in hospital after a minor operation. But other proof—crucially incriminating evidence—found at his home, along with verbal statements from his psychiatrist and testimony by a Church of Scotland minister was damning. Due to this proof and testimony, McColl would be sent to jail for an exceptionally long time.

Edinburgh and Lothian police questioned many serial sex offenders on the missing students, hoping to profile the killer. This action was aided by a professor of criminology who outlined the serial predator's characteristics. The profile helped the investigators look at the existing list of suspects and determine which were most likely to have committed the crime and decide how best to capture him.

"If you don't know what you are looking for, it will be impossible to find," he said to the investigating officers. "This killer will kill again and has more than likely killed many times before."

Professor Fortune Fudge—who was working closely with the police—created a team to look at the evidence and build a profile of the individual who would commit the crime in question. Helping investigators get a firm grasp on who they were trying to track down and hopefully arrest.

A profile was soon established, though no crime scene was found or forensically examined at this point; the studied characteristics were soon outlined of a killer.

This killer was organised. His crimes were premeditated and carefully planned with little evidence typically found. According to the classification scheme, this killer would be antisocial but distinguished right from wrong and was not insane and would be a person who is incapable of feeling remorse. Based on past patterns, organised killers are more than likely to be above average intelligence, married or living with a partner, employed, educated, skilled, logical, cunning and measured. They have some degree of social refinement, may even be captivating and often exchange dialogue and seduce their victims into being captured.

Each of the sexual deviants the police questioned, not one talked.

The students had vanished without a trace, most likely abducted from the three-bedroom 2nd-floor apartment they shared on Thirlestane Road in the Bruntsfield district of Edinburgh. An area commonly associated with University students. Numerous eyewitnesses, including fellow students, had witnessed the girls drinking at regular student haunts earlier in the evening, mostly in and around the Grassmarket area.

Later that evening, from their shared accommodation, an elderly dog walker, a neighbour that knew the girls, believed she saw them leave home around midnight, possibly heading to a nightclub, in what looked like a black cab. The girls were in a jovial, drunken state but looked unharmed. The eyewitness recalled they held a lengthy conversation with the driver before leaving the street as his passengers.

Fifteen months passed. No clue ever arose, no bodies were found and justice gently simmered in wait. No Edinburgh taxi company had a booking for this address at the time noted by the witness.

Chapter 4
Meet Finlay McColl

Finlay McColl, the cold-hearted serial killer and murderer of three young women, would stand trial in a case that would be commonly recognised and remembered as *The Tie-dye Murders*. All credibly associated with each victim tied and bound with strips of dyed cloth. A sexual trait McColl obsessed, which later would connect him to two other missing girls in Northumbria and possibly four unsolved crimes in the Greater Manchester area. One long-term missing woman, Veronica Broughton, a 21-year-old Bradford estate agent who disappeared on New Year's Day in 1981, was soon identified as the person found buried in a shallow grave. Her skeletal remains were discovered in woods near Anthorn, on the Solway Coast in January 2008 by two Forestry workers. The victim, the police believe, had been abducted, most likely raped, then brutally murdered.

The severe damage to her skull, sixty-two fragments of bone, would never allow facial reconstruction or identification, due to the frantic, frenzied attack by blunt force trauma, identified as occurring at the time of burial. A forensic examiner stated that the pulverised head damage was done antemortem. And the destruction to the skull he described as a porcelain jug dropped to the floor and stood on repeatedly. Fragmented and destroyed.

Thankfully, with the inclusion of DNA profiling, the remains of the young woman were identified. Her family could at last have closure and bring her remains home and give her a proper religious burial.

Evidence showed her wrists had been tied tightly in a handcuff knot—a form of two loops on a length of rope—and secured at the centre and used as makeshift handcuffs, bound tightly with one or two overhand knots for added security. Another helpless victim with no voice. Another victim of Finlay McColl. It was a crime he would never confess to. A crime he would always deny any involvement in.

The day before his arrest for the murder of the students, McColl had left HMP Edinburgh after serving twelve months for aggravated assault on a work colleague. McColl had worked as a delivery driver for an Edinburgh-based parcel delivery service, and over a monetary argument, threw his colleague through a plate glass window, causing severe lacerations, but not life-threatening injuries.

Gordon Leitch, a psychiatrist of trust to McColl, had received a full confession from McColl to the murder of all three missing students during this jail term. After McColl's release, Leitch went to the authorities and informed them of McColl's revelation, a disclosure that McColl would boast in a malignant way on regular occasions, divulging the method he used to kill the girls. Now, the police were actively taking a full statement from Gordon Leitch.

The doctor recalled openly, elaborate details of each murder. A full journal of facts proved every aspect of McColl's declared disclosure. How McColl abducted the young women, the terrible, evil injuries he made them endure and the disturbing nuances he discovered from the killer; that only inflated McColl's disturbed mind more.

Leitch recalled and revealed the horrendous, difficult facts of McColl's brutal crimes that sadly, will now forever be embedded in his mind. Remembering these facts made him dry retch when recalling the sickening events.

It was observed that McColl transported the girls on country roads south of Edinburgh, and deep into the Ettrick Forest, by using off-the-beaten-tracks. A large area of moorland located in the Peebles area in the burgh of Peeblesshire.

And the crude, yet irreverent burial and the primary method associated with all the murders, tying the victims' wrists with a dyed cloth. And, affirming McColl's words, *blasting* their heads with a single-piece club hammer. Until they no longer stared at him. He wanted to smash their skulls in to remember their last smile as a personal gift.

Psychiatrist Gordon Leitch feared for his life. A doctor-patient relationship was less critical than revealing the truth of heartless murders at the hands of a monster. And more than likely endangered his own life. During his regular meetings with McColl, he noted willingly submitted facts in a diary.

There was growing and compelling evidence at McColl's places of death and destruction, but Gordon Leitch kept his proof safe until more details were revealed. Although Leitch knew the events he held may be false and part of an elaborate game, played from the disturbing, unprocessed mind of an insane individual. The evidence was secretly concealed, which he hoped one day would serve justice. Only when McColl had left the prison would Gordon Leitch reveal his secrets.

He saw a new Finlay McColl from that day on as a deranged, mentally unstable, evil psychopath. This was the last day he would meet or visit him.

The graves of all three women were soon discovered in the area that the doctor's evidence specified. He proved with precise and further valid facts, by supplying an actual grid-reference for the burial plots which McColl gave voluntarily and had scrawled untidily in the doctor's diary.

"Playing games with the law."

McColl would declare boastfully, speaking close to the psychiatrist's face, spitting saliva as he drivelled, "I like playing games with them!"

Circling the coordinates with contemptuous, mocking words:

"Seek, and they will find. Revealing my treasure," he added disturbingly.

https://osmaps.ordnancesurvey.co.uk/55.39984,-3.15289,12/pin

During McColl's first term of confinement at HMP Edinburgh, Doctor Leitch befriended him. As part of a working association—trying to understand the detainee that *threw* his work colleague through a plate glass window and an individual whose character style of interacting involved continual, maladaptive aggression. Which provided the doctor with further quantitative analysis of McColl's account of violence and aggression within the prison.

Leitch became a regular visitor to the prison for suicide risk assessment and psychotropic management for the inmates, both on remand and sentenced.

Finlay McColl was identified as such a case.

Both men shared similar likes in music and hobbies. Leitch had gone out his way to offer Finlay McColl a book on element collecting, a hobby McColl had loved since he was a boy. He was overjoyed that his new friend also adored and appreciated his favourite pastime. Element collecting is the hobby of accumulating chemical elements. Many element collectors simply enjoy finding peculiar uses of chemical elements. Others enjoy studying the items' properties, possibly participating in amateur chemistry and merely collecting parts for no good reason. Or simply enjoy finding peculiar uses of chemical elements. With this gift, McColl enthused and gladly accepted Gordon Leitch as a close and reliable confidant. McColl boasted of owning eighty-one elements in his collection.

Talking about elements such as technetium, promethium, thorium and uranium, which are radioactive, raised his spirit, but understood these elements were nigh on impossible to source or are comparatively expensive.

But after McColl's release after his twelve-month sentence, Gordon Leitch decided to drop the doctor/patient confidentiality in such a way as to help the dead girls' families have closure. No matter how many strategies he used to make a memory less prominent; he did not know how to erase the deeply rooted disturbing testament from his memory. He had to live with it unless he wanted to redo the whole thing.

He knew McColl was a danger to the public—everybody that knew him did—the man was a total psychopath, a killer with no scruples or integrity. He fully recalled and gave an accurate account to the police on McColl's revelations. Over many months of open confessions—which he had full access to—he would record and store every word the mad man make known to him.

"Let's get McColl behind bars and get the girls home!"

After his arrest, McColl, when interviewed about the murders, spoke the one and only time:

"I did more, I did many more, more than you could ever imagine.

Now, as I have given all the details to my shrink, you can talk through the leech. The fuckwit Gordon Leitch. He has the information you want.

He has all the facts.

I gave him the grid-reference for the burial sites.

I told him Everything!

He is my voice now. So, fucking charge me, and do your fucking best!"

Finlay McColl was not a man of words. At least not to the police. He was stubborn, he liked playing games with the law and would offer no more assistance. Like his doctor, he would listen to others, but not the law, and depending on his relationship with fellow inmates—if they asked pertinent questions about his crimes—he would never reciprocate.

In fact, several times, he did harm to those that asked.

Finlay McColl provided emotional testimony to his doctor and the police knew this, but McColl's silence was undeniably beyond contempt when questioned. The detective-in-charge, officer John Hogan, bit his bottom lip, forced himself to sit upright, removed both hands from the interview table and placed them on his legs to wipe away the sweat. He hadn't come across such an oddity in his days of policing. There were many more questions to ask, questions he knew McColl wouldn't answer, and in the end, with the quality of the evidence obtained, and the degree of proof of guilt, Finlay McColl was found guilty on all charges. He began the process of charging the accused. He read out the charge.

"Finlay McColl, I am arresting you on suspicion of the abduction, rape and murder of—"

McColl boorishly interrupted the interview by banging both fists, rhythmically, loudly, upon the interview desk and attempting, with success, to be louder than the officer's voice by booming, deafening table hits which suffocated the detective's words. BANG! BANG! BANG!

Some comments were heard through the din, but Officer Hogan hollered louder, making sure he finished the statement; as the repellent, obnoxious, human scumbag sitting opposite played his final act of defiance. The police officer embroiled in a war of noise with McColl continued to vocalise his well-used right to silence narration.

"You are not obliged to say anything but anything you do say will be noted down and may be used in evidence. Do you understand?"

McColl hit the table louder and louder, screaming vulgar abuse. "Fuck the police! Fuck you! Fuck you!"

Keeping control of the situation, the officer ran through the whole statement again. Making sure McColl heard the names of his victims. His voice was louder than before. Much louder.

McColl used his hands to cover his ears and mumbled under his breath in a childish manner to stop hearing the words.

"*Carol Hughes! Gabby Law! And Hazel Harkins!*" Detective Hogan held his sanity. Making sure his wording was precise, absorbed and recorded, or fully understood by the creature that shared the same room. Satisfied that the charge had been delivered and audio-recorded over the annoying, savage din McColl had produced, it delighted him knowing that this evil deviant is facing charges and will have to answer for his actions. McColl stood suddenly, kicked the chair from beneath him, clenched his fists tightly and indignantly pounded the table repeatedly, until his knuckles turned white, then red, with blood spraying droplets on the table and floor. The noise was deafening and uncomfortable. Angry and bitter, spitting and kicking, McColl was removed by force by two keen, determined officers who were more than willing to get involved in a struggle with the killer; with excessive force, they threw him headfirst into a cold, damp cell.

"*Let the show begin*!" were the last words McColl mumbled as the cell door was closed then locked.

Edinburgh High Court

McColl's never-ending toothless smirk and leering devilish looks gave everyone in the courtroom, a feeling of revolt, and not one, at any time, would provide eye-contact or play the game he forever wanted or wished for.

His evil glower scanned the courtroom looking for a willing participant. Staring without blinking, McColl would find a person to prey on. Stare in a continual focus—a game where two people stare into the eyes of each other until one person blinks, or looks away, then the game ends.

Not one person in court would play this game with McColl. A few tried, but they soon looked away in disgust.

In a letter, which his barrister would read in court, McColl had the last chance to deliver a meaningful statement. The letter was written by his own hand, hoping to define any sense to a world that loathed him. This was his opportunity to share his state of mind. His mind, he felt, was fresh and clean, it was the world that was distasteful and revolting. A world that doesn't deserve him.

Finlay McColl's advocate rose and spoke.

"Your honour, members of the court, if I may, I would like to read a letter from my client Finlay McColl." Feeling embarrassed but obliged to offer the necessary evil by reading the declaration. And her professional responsibility to her client.

Lord Waverley gave authority. "You may continue." The judge's eyes raised above his spectacles, head bowed, as he sat in the high throne of his bench, before returning his gaze to a file of paperwork in front of him.

McColl's counsel, Advocate Hilary Gray, looked apprehensive, she knew the letter's contents and how troublesome they were. She also knew her job.

She reluctantly began to read McColl's statement of fact:

I, Finlay McColl, being of sound mind, write this letter to the judge, jury and people interested in injustice and for those that need to be reminded of true love.

Dear Judge, your horror!

Lord Waverley raised his eyes in astonishment, he understood that when hearing the word horror, which is a typically used as an alternative word and utilised on many occasions by belligerent criminals to deride the authority of the court.

The Judge's eyes raised in surprise. He removed his spectacles and played the stare game with Finlay McColl but gave in after a moment.

Advocate Gray spoke loud and clear.

You may think after all the allegations put against me, I was going to write a letter to confess my guilt; far from it. I enjoy killing. The killing process is unique, it raises the soul to a greater height of self-awareness and far away from the nadirs of guilt, and further to the heights of glory than anyone here would expect. Killing enlightened me!

The Advocate stopped and supped a long sip of water. The strain of delivering such an objectionable message showed severely on her normally serene features. She found the account strenuous and challenging but continued to read Finlay McColl's scribbled rants.

If it pleases you, your horror, I would like to take a step back for a moment, to mention my first and most beautiful target.

My first kill was a lovely girl called Mary.

She knew me. She knew me well. Mary would smile and offer mannerable retorts when I spoke to her. But, as typical with someone that has no grasp on the lessons of love, she became distant. Avoiding me.

This I could not accept. I am full of romance and love, that's why I lay all my cards on the table. I am a hopeless romantic…but can always stand my ground. Love is exceptional and incomparable, but if someone ignores my love offerings, they should be dealt with. Mary refused my passion and this could not be tolerated.

It was then that I killed for the first time. My first kill was thrilling because I had embarked on the career I had chosen for myself—the occupation of murder. I wanted bloodied hands!

Stuff the sixth commandment. My law would be sufficient.

Murder was better than I thought it would be. I released the girl from her anger and her fear of love. I could not allow this concern to spread among the masses. Many girls have this anxiety, they cannot cope with polite and mannerable advances from someone offering love. Someone that cares for them.

They must learn the apparent signs of true love, not ignore it. I soon knew that control management was desirable. It was similar with all my girls. I enjoyed strangling the life from my beauties. They stared back at me as I tightened the cloth around their necks, but devotion to me came too late, especially when they were dying; but there it was, pure love, staring back into my eyes. Even in death, they looked pleased. Their eyes told me so much about love, even in death they loved me.

I am sure they were delighted with my work. As love can be the deepest interpersonal affection, it can also be considered a virtue representing compassion. I am a true believer in kindness, unselfishly loyal and have a benevolent concern for my lifeless beauties. I cared for them after death. All my girls sleep...They sleep silently...Together, they rest in peace.

Advocate Gray mumbled under her breath. But she did use the words McColl wrote to bring the tirade to a conclusion.

Up yours!
Finlay McColl.

The courtroom was silent. The stenographer's fingers paused and hovered motionless above the keypad, to add to the silence and tension that filled the room. The middle-aged typist stared daggers towards McColl, an icy contempt at the man that had destroyed many lives. He didn't see her looking.

Everyone found the letter challenging to understand the rants of a psychopath, at least giving him the opportunity, through his lawyer, to voice histrionics of his malevolent background. The court found it difficult to hear or bear the burden of this man's disgusting actions.

The judge brought life back to the high court when the hardwood gavel struck three-times against a sound block also made from the same hardwood to enhance its sound qualities. The courtroom was now alert.

A break for lunch was called, and probably the perfect time to call it. The bailiff spoke in a loud voice as Judge Waverly stood, "All rise."

"He is an arrogant, wicked, low-life human being." One grieving, angry relative expressed outside the court to a reporter on Scottish Television News.

"The death penalty would be too good for him." A middle-aged woman with bleached blonde hair added as she stepped into an awaiting car.

The trial was easy to conclude. The verdict, although a formal finding of facts made by a jury of members of the public, found the evidence of guilt against the accused being undefendable.

The defence stated vigorously that McColl had a fundamental right to remain silent, which added time and extreme difficulty to what already was a complexed affair; both defence and prosecution calling experts to aid the case. McColl's defence needed the best possible assistance, and their client was not for talking. All experts held a superseding duty to support the court and not to the party instructing them.

QC McKenzie found loopholes in the defendant's evidence and ripped up the rule book. She intelligently played to the jury and set loose her prolific legal talents, so the jury was in no doubt, they were unequivocally clear, that Finlay McColl was as guilty as sin. "And the wickedness this man committed"...pointing to the accused, the QC dealt blow after blow to the weak and broken argument of defence. McColl remained silent and smiled. He showed no remorse.

McColl, in his cunning ways, played this legality to its utmost ruling. By continuing silence. Sitting still, mocking his audience, smirking and leering at people in his peripheral vision. Answering no questions or accusation put to him or responding to his lawyer's whispered advice. He never spoke. Believing silence was a tool of control.

McColl's endless sneer gave the impression that he expected a full media trial of his design, and all his own making.

It was his choice to incriminate himself, provide self-evidence to his psychiatrist, have a church minister point the finger fully on him, easily find conclusive proof of evidence and allow the authorities to take legal action, which the police did. It all worked the way he wanted it to happen. QC McKenzie unveiled these facts to the jury.

- Discovering the black Renault scenic people carrier in Finlay McColl's garage, which was a similar type of car they searched for.
- DNA that matched all the girls, was found in sufficient quantity.
- Further evidence included a bloodied hammer, 9-inch kitchen blades, a reel of pink curtain material, and a box of dyed fabric created and designed by himself.

'McColl produced strips of material for each of his special clients,' Leitch recalled facts that McColl had provided him with. 'Each of his victims would have a unique strip of cloth prepared and used on them. He called this his "personalised touch"!'

During the trial, an Edinburgh based newspaper wrote: "The accused does not speak, he looks settled with all the allegations thrown at him, his demeanour remains stoic and charming to a point."

Charming!

Where on earth could any human being, with a slight grip on ethical morality, ever view Finlay McColl as charming? Moira McKenzie QC ended her closing speech with suitable words.

"The accused deserves a BAFTA for his silence, but his guilt..." She paused and looked observantly around the courtroom. Waving a raised forefinger. "His guilt...which is as clear as a sunny day, deserves a full, guilty verdict for all charges put against him.

"If anyone in this court needs reminding, the defendant sitting in the dock before us; as a local newspaper recently stated: 'McColl's demeanour remains stoic and charming.' I can assure the writer of this blurb that Finlay McColl is not charming; he is as far from charming as anyone could get.

"I would ask everyone, when they have time, to look up the adjective: 'Charming'. Let me help with this. I took time this morning to look up this word, and please indulge me one moment."

The QC picked up a dictionary from the table, opened it where the page marker was located and read through the spectacles that rested on the tip of her nose.

She read as if a teacher was reading a story to a class of interested pupils.

"The word charming is an adjective. Charming can also mean, delightful or attractive. Another example would be 'a charming country cottage'."

The QC spoke to all in the courtroom. Using her legal awareness as an actor would utilise skills to perform narration on stage. Staring at the jury, turning to the galleries offering facts of McColl's guilt. Everyone listened attentively as she explained all the facts.

"A few synonyms such as delightful... pleasing... friendly... agreeable... likeable or endearing. None of which, your honour and members of the jury, is a suitable way of describing the man that sits before us today."

She purposely removed her glasses and laid them carefully near the dictionary she had placed back on the table.

"However, you will see that the word charming not only has references to strong attraction but to spells and magic; which says more about McColl than any other peculiarities, which the insensitive, apathetic newspaper journalist felt obliged to share in print. In closing, I would say that if an adjective of charming is applied to Finlay McColl, then, without a misgiving in my mind, the word Evil is proper and fitting to describe him. The evidence against this man is powerful and compelling. Furthermore, the accused has shown no remorse whatsoever and has tried to disrespect the Scottish judiciary process with his fanciful charade of perpetual silence.

"I trust the jury members will hold these facts and recall the terrible, atrocious, ghastly actions that this man did to those young women when making a collective decision. There is no doubt, Finlay McColl is guilty!"

The defence crumbled. The defence accepted the ruling with no argument. A result McColl expected. He sneered at her every word.

No evidence would ever be found to clear McColl's name. This killer was heading to jail.

'McColl was guilty as sin. And sin was his middle name', a reporter in the gallery wrote on his notepad.

The day after the judgement, the same insensitive newspaper reporter that had labelled McColl charming would describe him now as 'perverse and depraved'. Much nearer the mark! And wondered if the reporter had been drunk, possibly paid or looking for a slither of fame, hoping to sell a newspaper, or plain stupid with free-thinking; when the word 'Charming' was initially used to define a sleazeball like Finlay McColl.

The jury took twenty minutes to find a unanimous decision on Finlay McColl's guilt. On all charges. Abduction. Rape. And murder.

McColl would serve three consecutive life sentences for the abduction, rape and vicious murder of Carol Hughes, Gabby Law and Hazel Harkins.

In his final statement, Lord Waverley said: "Your value of life is undeniably low; the depraved events these young women endured is beyond the moral realms of any normal human being. You are a dangerous predator, who can sink to the nadirs of wickedness.

"I do not intend spending any more valuable time or words on you. You must also understand there is only one course of action I will take, and that is to pass a life sentence for all three murders, all to run consecutively. For all three charges, I sentence you to life imprisonment to run from today, and I fix the sentence at 35 years."

Several British newspapers published claims that McColl was responsible for many unsolved cases of missing women in the UK. Police believe McColl's murderous splurge could have started as early as the 1970s.

Finlay McColl would serve his sentence at HMP Edinburgh. Also known locally as Saughton, a suburb of the west of Edinburgh. Dr Gordon Leitch, the practising psychologist who would be remembered as the doctor that helped send a vicious killer to life imprisonment, and to the media, the untrusting doctor that breached patient/doctor of confidentiality however good his evidence disclosed.

He would return to work his practice in Morningside, an affluent district of Edinburgh, but soon after, would leave Scotland within a month to set up a practice in a foreign land. A place where he was no longer scrutinised or harassed.

There would be no more meetings between Doctor Leitch and Finlay McColl, they would end up a thousand miles apart, only a final letter, a statement from the killer was received on the morning the doctor departed.

Dear Doctor Leitch,

I do not feel animosity toward you, I want you to know that I will remain thankful for your help with this matter. And you, my friend, will help me retain my notoriety in the future.

It reminds me of an obnoxious rock star. They become so fucked-up in their belief that they are so renowned with their false identities bringing them worldwide fame; that when the spotlight fades, then extinguishes, their overinflated egos pop like a gas-filled balloon.

To compensate, they take to drugs and over-indulge with alcohol and physically abuse their partners. Me, I don't need any drugs to fuel my ego.

It is how God made me.

Doctor Leitch. Let the game begin.

Your loving servant,
Finlay McColl.

The letter was given to the police. It had been sent from another place, and not HMP Edinburgh as the investigators discovered. But whoever posted the correspondence, the law understood McColl was the source behind the threat. It was what one would expect from a psychopath—a killer suffering delusions of grandeur and a person profoundly disturbed and damaged.

The police knew that the three yellow-faced emojis with open eyes and a zipped mouth conveyed a secret that someone will keep. It may also be used to tell someone to stop talking!

Thankfully for Doctor Leitch, he moved to one of the Greek Islands soon after, well away from McColl and his weird idiosyncrasies. And maybe his dishonest accomplices.

After mental evaluation by other psychiatrists, it was found Finlay McColl did not appear competent, or capable of undertaking the murders he was accused and sentenced for, or any abhorrent crime for that matter.

But what do shrinks know?

He was a deluded individual represented by Antisocial Personality Disorder, which was agreed by any observer that ever met him, including the specialists that observed him.

However, he generally displayed callous behaviour with little regards to others.

Sociopaths are often challenging to identify until psychiatrists are familiar with their response. Sociopaths are often manipulative, they frequently lie, lack understanding and have a weak morality that allows them to act aggressively, even when they know their behaviour is wrong. Finlay McColl was diagnosed as a sociopath. McColl voluntarily completed a psychopathy checklist, a 20-item inventory of personality traits and behaviour indicators.

All done under a suitably qualified clinician, scientifically controlled and licenced, in reliable surroundings, where each of the twenty modules is given a score of 0, 1 or 2, founded on how well it applies to the individual being tested.

A prototypical psychopath would obtain a maximum score of forty, while someone with absolutely no psychopath qualities or inclinations would receive a rating of zero. A score of thirty or more qualifies a reason for a diagnosis of psychopathy. People with no criminal circumstances usually score around five or six. McColl scored lower than most with a grade of three.

But this killer had revealed self-incriminating evidence, admitted by letter, offered testimony to his psychiatrist and recorded by the police as confessing to many more murders. Not the atypical serial killer, but a psychopath, nonetheless.

Chapter 5
Arran Honey

Most couples retire together, and Bill's parents were no different. Once their collective legal business was finalised, they settled near a small community called Corriecravie on the south-west coast of the island of Arran. An elegant white cottage with a straw-thatched roof and a white picket fence surrounded the rectangular rose garden. The extended plot was just over four acres of land.

The bungalow radiated a feeling of space and isolation, and was within easy reach of the village amenities and only a fifty-step walk to the nearest beach; with stunning panoramic sea views and spectacular nightfall over the Mull of Kintyre.

Five hives produced 165lbs of golden honey in the farm's first year. At first, selling locally, the delicious *Arran Dandelion* became popular almost immediately among locals and day-trippers and vacationists.

Sadly and unexpectedly, Ian and Moira McKenzie died within a month of each other in 2014. It became Bill and Laura's responsibility to run and operate the farm, or sell up and move on, whatever choice they made. Their mutual interest in beekeeping was more than a keen one, and their enjoyment in producing honey was palpable.

Initially, seeing the bee farm as a leisure activity, the couple found keeping a bee farm of native black bees an ideal pastime. A hobby they would indulge with effort. Despite the stress of high office and demands on their time, there are plenty of examples in history of people who pursued hobbies.

Winston Churchill was a proficient watercolour artist; Will Smith, the actor, enjoys fencing. Steven King likes nothing better than a brisk walk, or Vladimir Putin and his widely known martial arts skills are the stuff of folklore. Thanks to a steady stream of flattering exposure from Russian state media.

Bill and Laura spent several extended holidays on Arran, examining his parents' business and its value and reviewing the feasibility of a long-term business plan. Checking this feasibility thoroughly, and under the watchful eye of the successful Glasgow business Guru, Gordon Alexander Morton from the contemporary and highly regarded IT business, Progressus Trium, it looked good to go.

Within a month, the upgraded business tools were set in motion, mainly through website design, search engine optimisation, digital marketing and marketing strategies; a new virtual way of doing business forward for Arran Dandelion.

The business was now fully connected by e-commerce and its significant benefits it brought. In addition, Bill wanted an experienced leader to further the company's development.

After assessing the large file of potential applicants and challenging interviews, one candidate, who possessed a combination of skills and experience they required, stood out. At fifty-four, David Carson, a Hutton-le-hole born business maestro, one of those rare, tactical people who can see the end from the beginning, was installed as CEO.

Although diligent and authoritative, he was highly charismatic. His twenty years' experience working in the food industry for one of the UK's top-selling coffee brands, gave a surge of leadership qualities at a time when it was needed most. With his inspirational guidance, extensive knowledge of brand awareness, and Bill and Laura's financial support, he successfully took control of the company.

He headed an initial management team of ten and a workforce of forty. Over the next year, he led a once small cottage industry with no more than local aspirations to an apiary of one hundred hives.

Apart from honey and business, cricket was David Carson's great love, especially Yorkshire cricket. As a twelve-year-old boy, in 1977, his father took him to Headingly to see his hero Geoffrey Boycott score a century in his comeback match—his 100th in first-class cricket—against Australia in the 4th test. And as a special surprise, after the game, he got to meet his hero, who allowed a photo opportunity. Shaking his trembling hand, he handed him the willow cricket bat; the bat that had just performed magic like Merlin's wand. Watching the 'Thatch' bat his most prolific strokes, off the back foot through the covers, his forte, and the on-drive were majestic in their power and placement. In a wooden-trimmed glass case that sat wall-mounted proudly behind his office desk, this iconic piece of cricketing memorabilia was his pride and joy. And one that any cricket fan would wish to own.

Today, Arran Dandelion exported goods worldwide. They purchased quality honey from other bee farmers in the UK and intensively around Europe.

The company had an extensive range of products. Including honey soap, mead wine, bee pollen, gourmet black coffee, lip balm, propolis, ointments and candles and a surplus of merchandising materials, among many more branded products. They now ran a farm shop in Brodick, selling all these items and online sales send products worldwide. All with a smile and energy, as the company slogan promoted: *Good day, honey!*

Chapter 6
Laura's Childhood

Laura, like Bill, was an only child. Her parents owned and ran the independent Pitlochry wine shop, quirkily named 'Moulin Rouge'. Not named after the infamous Parisian landmark, but to the Redstone cottage her father Graham was born in, in the summer of 1946, in the small village with the same name—Moulin—that sits on the edge of Pitlochry, and the settlement can be dated back to the early bronze age.

Selling, among other alcoholic beverages, an extensive range of exciting wines from everyday drinkers to unique high brands from exclusive vineyards. A stock that included old-world classics such as Chardonnay, Pinot noir, Barolo, Amarone and Riesling, to new world produced wines out with the traditional winegrowing areas of Europe, from Australia, New Zealand, Chile, Argentina, South Africa and California. Locally brewed ales, craft beers and ciders, with an impressive selection of spirits such as Vodka, gin, rum, brandy, cognacs, liqueurs, and a vast unrivalled assemblage of whisky…and the finest malts.

Laura's childhood was happy. Full of love and never-ending laughter. By the age of six, she had already ridden horses, played junior golf, fished with her father, took twice-weekly ballet lessons, swam with dolphins in Florida, played 4th grade piano and read classic Scottish books weekly. Her favourite and her all-time best novels were *Treasure Island* by Robert Louis Stevenson and his collection of poems: *A Child's Garden of Verses* as a remarkably close second.

"Life has a nasty habit of patting you on the back one minute, then slapping your face the next," her father told the fourteen-year-old Laura after she fell at the last fence, beaten by one point, to lose her title as Junior Showjumping Champion to her closest rival. But this phrase would come back to haunt her even more. And a time no more consequential than Boxing Day 2004, when her world changed forever.

On the south coast of Sri Lanka, her parents were spending their 30th wedding anniversary at Shangri-La's Hambantota Resort and Spa. A holiday they both had saved hard for. Flying first-class with British Airways added extra luxury to this month-long break, a time of building endearing memories that would last well into their retirement, a one-off memory, a holiday of a lifetime, to relax and unwind in a tropical, exotic paradise.

An American tourist staying at the resort, Eric Deveaux, a history teacher from Squirrel Hill North, Pittsburgh, Pennsylvania, met and became friends with Laura's parents during their stay. Deveaux was forever wary of waves and water after the dreadful experience of 2004. Just before the disaster struck, he was strolling on the beach, where he met Laura's parents, and after a few minutes of conversation, they parted ways.

It was his last encounter with them.

As the sea retreated from the land, he realized that this was no trial or practice session, but a real event. Time was not on his side, it wasn't on anyone's side. He did everything he could to help others, pleading with people to move from the beach, taking valuable time to assist an elderly German woman who used a wheelchair to the nearest hotel and carrying two young children to safety. Although both waves were over three stories high, a massive and even more devastating surge of water reached the resort. This wave battered Sri Lanka and southern India, destroying fishing villages and coastal towns and as many as 31,000 people died on the east of Sri Lanka.

Eric Deveaux managed to escape to the village's outreaches where he shared a ride on the back of a moped. Deveaux was the only survivor that bore witness to the last ever sighting of Graham and Jean Smith, seeing them "sipping Mai Tai cocktails from a coconut shell, and walking barefoot on the golden sands beach, close to the hotel."

He repeated this story to every reporter that asked the question.

That day, a day Laura and many millions more would never forget. When, on 26 December 2004, at 09:20 am local time, the first in the series of waves hit the region.

The tsunami that hit Sri Lanka produced the most prominent disaster in recorded history of the island. Both the east and southern coasts were hit the hardest. Death numbers in the south were excessively high because population masses are high there.

Laura's parents have never been found.

Eric Deveaux's decision to move inland with other English-speaking tourists saved his life. He returned yearly to pay homage to the many killed in the disaster, and laid a floral tribute on the beach to the lost souls of his two Scottish friends.

It was with a heavy heart and strong will that Laura visited her parents' home in Pitlochry. She arrived five days after her parents' disappearance—having accepted their deaths and the impossibility of ever recovering their bodies—and it was the day before New Year—Hogmanay, as it's called in Scotland. Clearing the house of furniture and items that meant so much to her parents. Then she spent hours drinking instant coffee, eating teacakes, and looking through old photos; reminiscing about happier times. But selling her parent's home , two cars and the multi-seater hot tub was her primary goal.

The wine shop business, on the other hand, was a different proposal. Laura's young cousin, Jane, had worked in the shop alongside her father since leaving school, and felt a need to keep the wine shop open. Allowing Jane to run, operate and manage the shop as she saw fit, a belief she thought appropriate for Jane and the community, by keeping a family connection rooted in Pitlochry. Not that Jane needed any incentive to keep her job, Laura made sure she was now an equal partner in the business. A fresh start and a new beginning for both.

On 26 December 2012, eight years to the day since the catastrophic tsunami, a leather wallet was washed ashore on the Arcadia Beach State Recreation site in Oregon. The wallet contained three items: a UK driver's licence, a young girl's photograph and an old threepence piece. A thruppenny bit as it was called.

The driver's ID proved the wallet belonged to a victim of the Sri Lankan tsunami. Graham Smith, a shop owner from Pitlochry, in Scotland.

It is believed that one may hear the "singing sands", a squeaking or violin-like sound on the beach at Arcadia.

Chapter 7
The Marriage of Bill and Laura

The wedding was a spectacular occasion by any standards. It took place on Saturday, 10 June 2000.

Bill and Laura McKenzie exchanged their vows at the beautiful Church of Scotland Kirk in Pitlochry.

Laura looked stunning in a classic romantic gown that featured an off-the-shoulder dress; a lingerie lace corset bodice with a soft net, A-line skirt, adding a touch of dainty elegance to her natural beauty. As everyone would expect, Bill was dressed in a Prince Charles jacket and waistcoat with matt black Ghillie shoes and a McKenzie tartan, the regimental tartan of the Seaforth Highlanders raised by Mackenzie, Earl of Seaforth in 1778.

Wearing historical attire, Bill and his father gladly promoted their family heritage. The traditional dress was finished with wool-fringed, fly plaid swung over his left shoulder and held in place by a Clan McKenzie brooch. Engraved with the clan motto: "Luceo non-uro" (I shine not burn).

As the bride and groom appeared at the hotel, the wedding party waited with cameras ready to snap. Laura's father opened the door of the horse and carriage as it drew to a stop.

His gleaming face shone with pride, as he took his daughter by the arm, as she cautiously stepped down from the footplate: feeling the gravel chips beneath her flat sandals, as she took centre stage before the eager guests. A proud moment he would never forget—a gratified moment for all in attendance. Even the horse turned its head to look at Laura, and it made a whinny noise before the coachman took control. All guests stood with their mouths agape, with their starry-eyed breaths taken away, at the natural glimpse of the Perthshire beauty. Not flaunting her attractiveness in any way, Laura was not only physically perfect but she also radiated strength and light from within her soul, and her intelligence was full of wisdom.

A lone piper played the haunting lament 'The flowers of the forest' that had guests searching for handkerchiefs, as tears of joy ran down most cheeks.

The Atholl Palace hotel had welcomed guests since the middle of the 19th century. Today was the wedding reception of the lovely young couple, Bill and Laura McKenzie. Food and drink, speeches, cake-cutting and photographs, music, dance, and fun and laughter as the night drove on until the wee small hours.

Guests were saying goodbyes as taxis sat patiently on the main driveway; some remained as residents in the hotel, others booked in local accommodation, but Bill and Laura had the best suite in the hotel.

A suite, beautifully decorated ornate room, high up in a baronial tower with splendid views of the Perthshire countryside, and far away from the party that endlessly carried on, till the license, or senior management, revoked their joy.

Chapter 8
The Wonderful Flight

Bill's first visit to Malta was when he was aged twelve, in 1982, and would return annually for the following six years until his eighteenth year. Travelling on his own was quite an adventure for a young boy, but Bill's parents were too busy working in the Scottish legal system and beating the bad guys to take a long summer holiday.

A full two-month holiday, spent with Uncle William and Aunt Beth, was an adventure any young boy would willingly accept—and the beginning of the best learning process any child could ever wish for. A procedure and development made Bill McKenzie the man he became; all started in Malta, spending many enlightened holidays with his eccentric, but loving, Uncle William.

William senior was a retired British Consul and ex-serviceman and a World War 2 hero, a Spitfire pilot who flew and fought on the island during the siege of Malta in 1942. Living in a 3-bedroom apartment in Archbishop St, Valletta, just ninety-four steps away, sober; and thirty-six steps up one-floor, sober. From his daily drinking den and his beloved and legendary waterhole, *The Pub!*

The number of steps would fluctuate regularly or as Uncle William would state: Plus and minus 10%, depending on how much alcohol he had consumed.

Uncle William called this place: "My favourite haunt and fit for any bloody spitfire Pilot," or his TPVM! The Pub Valletta Malta.

The history-making Spitfire pilot stood most days, near to four pm as possible, somewhere near the bar. Dressed in khaki shorts and a khaki short-sleeved shirt, bare feet under dog-eared desert boots, with a full head of greying-waxed hair swept back from his forehead.

A tiny pencil moustache was barely seen between his mouth and nose, and a tongue that used profanity at any critical point of any heated debate or argument.

"I'm sure you are fucking wrong…but I guess it's open for fucking discussion. Get the drinks up and we can argue this shite later!"

His diction was as polite as a BBC announcer most of the time, with a low-brogue, Edinburgh accent, that was more of a sexy Anglo-Scottish hybrid, and no one that knew him; if they didn't guess or held facts of his past; would ever think he was Scottish. An Edinburgh-born middle-class boy with degrees in English Literature and Political science from Edinburgh University, and remarkably; the same young man that fought for Britain and Malta during the 2nd world-war; where he received the Distinguished Flying Medal and Bar.

Rather than known as a Scot, he was always noticeably thought of as an eccentric bank manager type; from somewhere like Chalfont St Giles in Buckinghamshire.

When intervening in conversation, or making his point heard, using a strong Edinburgh vocal, he would extensively use the term: 'Aye…but yer a long time deid'. On most occasions, he gave him immediate access to the current tete-a-tete with participants, leaving them speechless, trying to understand what was said, giving him time to wedge into the discussion, where he could control any situation from that moment onwards. His noticeable intelligence was immense, yet he always remained modest and would chat with people from every walk of life and would never make judgements on them. He was known for his discerning views on the arts, music, books, and any form of expression in human society or culture; he was a happy drunk who trusted his judgement on most topics. The man that could complete the Times crossword in 17 minutes and 54 seconds; noted and witnessed as a record, but never officially proved or recorded.

Young Bill, however, would remember him with great fondness as the elderly uncle marked with a 3-number tattoo on his left arm, inserted with indelible bluish ink and another number tattoo of '249'. Which young Bill imagined was the number of steps from his local pub to his home in Edinburgh. But it was a more critical promotion of something much more noteworthy: it was in honour of his old squadron: 249—based at RAF Ta Kal, where he flew Supermarine Spitfires in the 2nd world war.

Near the end of 1941, following participation in Britain's Battle, Bill and his squadron were posted to Malta. Bill, in later life, would recall his uncle's memories in glorious terms.

As the erudite pilot, the professor of everything, the unrepentant cruciverbalist [the dictionary term for a person proficient in constructing or solving crossword puzzles], the drunken lecturer of the whole-enchilada…or as he will always fondly picture and remember him; as the man with a wide-open, gap-toothed grin, as a gentleman and a scholar, and a gin-infused Terry Thomas lookalike; an English comedian and character actor who became internationally known through his films throughout the 1950s and 1960s.

What young Bill did know, yet many didn't, was the fact that his uncle held and organised, every 25th of January, a Burns supper in Valletta. In celebration of the birthday of Scottish bard Robert Burns. As young Bill's father said: 'The only time his Scottishness would surface, when full of the water of life, he would recite many of Burns poetic works; his Scottish tone was as broad and abrupt as a drunken Market hawker in the Barras market in the east-end of Glasgow. Or as Burns would call him; a Chapman Billy; an old Scottish term for a market pedlar.'

His very first holiday at Uncle William's was remembered as the best time he ever had, and looked forward every year, with enthusiastic anticipation, to jet off to increase his alternative education with his favourite relatives: the McKenzies of Malta.

It was the school summer holidays in 1982, when Bills parents, reluctantly but necessary, due to demanding legal cases; could not spend any valuable holiday time with their son over the summer term break. A long-distance phone call to Uncle William later was all systems go, and the beautiful holidays would begin and continue for many years to come.

His small frame strapped-in securely on a padded seat of a Boeing 707 jet plane, dangling feet just reaching the floor, for his first-ever flying experience and a great adventure was due to commence. Young Bill wore a Biggles type flying aviator hat with goggles, a recent present from his father.

'You can be a flying ace-like Uncle William', which his father hoped would abet any phobia he may have about flying. He would carry his uncle's tradition of McKenzie airborne adventures over the skies of Europe. Young Bill received regular updates on the aircraft's location from the flight attendant and was given a small, scaled-down replica of the plane he had been on.

A thoughtful member of staff sought permission from the Captain for young Bill to visit the cockpit. The cabin crew treated young Captain McKenzie as a VIP guest throughout his first-ever flight, with a further reward; he obtained a pilot's wings badge, pinned on his jacket by the senior officer on arrival at Malta. The crew would salute young Captain McKenzie as he left the aircraft.

Destination Malta concluded. Holding a Hermes travel bag full of clothes and footwear, he arrived at a climate of heat he hadn't experienced too regularly. In the photographs, the man stood waiting at arrivals as young Bill walked awkwardly, his hat and goggles unmoving on his head, visibly struggling to carry the outsize luggage; viewing with suspicious open eyes the strangeness of these foreign surroundings.

"Welcome, young man, it's good to see you again. You were just a baby when I saw you last!" said the stranger who Bill would now regard as Uncle William. Young Bill didn't know they had met beforehand if he were just a baby, how could he remember?

A giant hand gripped his hand firmly as it moved erratically like a kite swept by a tornado. "Great to have another McKenzie on the island."

The drive was short, all packed like sardines in a mini cooper, driven by a drinking friend of Uncle William: David Gillies Porter, a fellow Maltese resident. A retired English airline pilot, an unpublished writer, a trying yet doggerel poet, a watercolour-artist of the highest incompetence; but a generally loveable guy that liked football and all-things Maltese. He was known to his friends as Dulux. Although the truth is uncertain, the fact that he only had one coat may have contributed to this name of endearment.

His enthusiasm was relentless, and endless, all the way to Archbishop St in Valletta.

Incessantly enthusiastic about Malta's recent win over Iceland played on neutral ground in Messina, with Malta winning 2-1; with Ernest Spiteri Gonzi and Leli Fabri's goals in a match as part of the qualification group for Euro 1984.

William senior, wearing his Scottish hat, could recite Robert Burns poetry at the drop of the same hat, or every time he safely managed the glorious one-hundred-and-twenty steps home. Depending on how many drams filtered through the noticeable gap between the two upper front teeth, flushed over the tobacco-stained tongue, passed his gin-infused tonsils and into a liver, which Bill senior named his grain store; he could rattle off rhymes with the best of Scottish voices. Pulling his vowels and consonants, joining syllables in words and dropping "g" endings; turned into an actor of a high Scottish drama. But when Uncle William wanted an extension to his day, he would play and listen to music till the birds sang as dawn broke over the city. Keeping young Bill out of bed was not a problem. No one would tell his infuriating parents, especially Uncle Bill. His first-ever night in Valletta ended this way.

“Let’s play some classical music, Bill!” (The first time he was ever called Bill, and he liked it.) As his young nephew sat unaware of what CD, in a library of thousands, Uncle Bill would take. Watching intently, young Bill watched his uncle carefully remove the silver disc, hold it with one finger inserted into the small central hole, then wipe it clean with a pre-prepared cloth. Inserted softly into the indented tray, which was made to measure for all discs, then pressed close. Now it was the music system that took over; a motorised dish sucked the small-circular album into the depths on the electronic device: as a monitor lizard would flick its forked tongue at its prey and recoil both back into an eagerly, welcoming mouth.

William pressed play. ‘Let the music begin!’ he said, rubbing his hands.

Young Bill expected haughty, most elite hogwash, department store *Muzak* to pulsate through two floor-positioned, large box speakers. Possibly Rachmaninov, Chopin or Debussy; music his parents annoyingly played regularly. Or more than likely; Brahms, Bach or Beethoven?

What type of music does a spitfire pilot listen to? Glen Millar, Bennie Goodman; maybe!

Then, a wave of sound struck the 12year-old boy unexpectedly; as pulsating music filled the room. The loud noise of an aircraft landing on a runway, the thrusting noise of engines powering down, and burning rubber wheels screeching loudly overheated tarmac, as brakes were applied…then…the singing started; accompanied by guitars and drums, filling the sound.

It was the Beatles’ cold-war rock song. The narrator supporting their return to the USSR.

Young Bill was mesmerised by the fun-filled occasion. His cunning uncle listened to The Beatles, not Beethoven or Bach, and he had heard this song before, so he joined his uncle in singing it. And by the time young Bill returned home to Edinburgh, with the exciting vacation over, he became an expert on the best group ever, including their solo albums and Paul McCartney’s Wings hits. Every song the Beatles recorded, he became an expert fan, a mastermind on their full catalogue. Though young Bill’s all-time favourite—Uncle William possibly rated the vinyl record as a 7 out of 10—was Paul McCartney’s Red Rose Speedway album. Lenny Kaye said in a Rolling Stone review of the album: *Still, despite expected hits and misses, I find* Red Rose Speedway *the most overall heartening McCartney product given to us since the demise of the Beatles.*

Young Bill read the review and agreed with some parts of it…but miles off the true evaluation of the record.

"That is why you should never listen to a critic! You must decide for yourself!"

He was giving a reasonable opinion to his nephew. He provided excellent advice.

"Every person has a right to disclose why each song has a particular meaning to them. It is the way an individual perceives music.'

Uncle William knew everything about the Beatles. He knew every song in their complete songbook, their musical style and development, the highly controversial issues that shadowed them. And even revealed to young Bill a story that the Liverpool boys played Alloa, some thirty-seven miles from Edinburgh, as the Silver Beetles at Alloa Town Hall on 20 May 1960. Their first ever professional gig. He would make a plan someday in the future to visit Alloa Town Hall. He hoped there was a wall-mounted brass plaque or some kind of memorial promoting this fact.

Uncle William had detailed information on people and bands they influenced, awards and achievements collected and a full Beatle history (all of it) attached to the Fab Four. They, as William would say, 'are the perfect creation and result of everything that rock and roll mean and encompasses the world of popular music.'

Uncle William would arrive home from the pub when the time suited, or if the bar were closing. And the only song he would ever try to dance to. He would kindly ask young Bill to get his song ready to play. 'Now let's get dancing…Play our song, Billy boy. Play our song!

Uncle William would stand as a child waiting on a gift, a bar of chocolate to be unwrapped and offered, or a present from Santa; rubbing his hands excitedly and in preparation of the music to begin.

Then it started. Beginning with a full drum fill, then a blues progression with guitar and bass double riff. McCartney's voice boomed out the lyrics of The Beatles song, *Birthday*. "You say it's your birthday…" adding that it was his birthday too!

Uncle William stood playing imaginary drums and hopped around weirdly in the motion called dancing, singing along to his all-time best happy song.

The hilt was the level his intoxication could reach, Bill always joked.

Uncle William always preferred to share his moment. A time when his audience was invited to watch a lousy dance machine control the floor (hips don't lie) as the night rolled on until the fuel in his engine ran out. An important message was always delivered at the end of the song, *Birthday*. He would jokingly state: *The queen has two birthdays. I...on the other hand...have a birthday every day!*

Aunt Beth, Elisabetta Giada Alessandra Cancio, from Messina, a harbour city in northeast Sicily was 20 years old when she married William McKenzie; some 20 years her senior. Her father raised her. Her mother, Isabella, was killed by RAF strategic bombing; or carpet bombing as we now know it, in 1942; officially, the attack was to lay the way for Allied landings. Intended to destroy anti-aircraft batteries, military bases, railway stations, war storage factories and port facilities.

Isabella died on the first night of this bombing campaign. Beth was two years old when her father reluctantly moved her from the exposed city to Mortelle, his hometown, about 10 kilometres to the north. Here, he worked in his father's bakery business, baking an assortment of Sicilian bread. The Mafalda, with its golden crust and distinctive taste of sesame seeds, was the best bread ever. The baker's shop survived the war, and Beth's father, Giovanni, remarried in 1949; he fathered two sons who followed the family tradition by baking bread. *Cancio Panettiere*, by 1960, would expand to five shops throughout the island.

Aunt Beth would not join in on the fun and dancing, she would sit on a tatty old leather armchair, listen to The Beatles, tap her feet, clap her hands in rhythm and oblige William and Young Bill; as a guest judge in a talent show. She would always applaud their efforts.

While she never drank as much liquor as Uncle William, she always said he consumed more fuel than the Spitfire he once flew and had a temper as tough as a flying machine in battle; nevertheless, both remained happy and passionately in love.

Chapter 9
Bill and Laura's Honeymoon
June 2000

The city of Valletta appeared stunningly elegant in the afternoon sun as the couple stepped out of Malta International Airport; which serves the whole country. Choosing a taxi from many that sat on Triq San Tumas road; all eagerly waiting to transport new arrivals to various accommodation standards, dotted around the beautiful archipelago in the central Mediterranean. They were soon on their way to the hotel.

The hotel room, a junior suite, was more than generous in size. A large double bed took up much of the space. The room was beautifully decorated in a Mediterranean style. Light blues and pastel colours covered the walls and woodwork. Two bedside tables sat neatly at opposite sides of the bed frame; a large wicker chair sat in one corner, a desk and small stool, with a table lamp, sat anchored below a full-sized illuminated mirror. A few black-and-white photographic prints endorsed old Valletta and ornamented two opposite facing walls. Refreshingly, a small, two-seated balcony gave superb views of Valletta. A bath and shower combination provided a wash-down choice, with the usual sundries of tea and coffee making facilities, air-conditioning, a TV, telephone and minibar.

"Welcome to Malta!" Bill said to his wife, Laura, as they both jumped onto the large, comfortable, welcoming bed.

Relaxing by the pool for a few days, swimming and sunbathing, taking leisurely walks, trying new restaurants, drinking exotic cocktails or reading books: two books, most assuredly impulse purchases. Just a few minutes before boarding at Edinburgh Airport, Laura grabbed and took hold of the book with an intriguing cover, thinking it may be a good read: *Girl with a Pearl Earring* by Tracy Chevalier.

And Bill's must-have craving: *Angels and Demons* by Dan Brown.

Being a fan of Dan Brown, Bill had waited patiently, as many million others did, on the follow up to the techno thriller *Digital Fortress*. The *Angels and Demons* paperback became his poolside companion and Bill would read Brown's intriguing maze-like plot, on his newfound hero, the claustrophobic symbolist Robert Langdon until he completed the book a few days later.

In the evenings, cold drinks were a way to relax and unwind after dinner. The waiter placed two gin and tonics as well as a bowl of bar nibbles on the small circular table in front of them. The Club bar, an emotional connection to Malta's colonial past, began to fill. General chit-chat broke out, and the soothing background music seemed to all but fade under the din of loud conversation. Some guests were in dialogue, others in debate, a heated argument between two drunk women, and assumed consultation between business people and general palaver; with a few dirty jokes thrown in for good measure, made a small group laugh to the highest sound level. 'The more drinks took, the louder people's voices become.' Laura explained to Bill.

They moved to a quiet spot out on the terrace.

The evening air was crisp and refreshing, where dozens of nocturnal hawkmoths chased the flickering flames at each candle on every table.

As the sun went down, Valletta's city lights switched on and created the mystical illuminated skyline of many unique architectural designs. Highlighting the classic towering fortifications built by—the order of the Knights of St John—and showing many limestone baroque buildings; that silhouetted under a purple-tinted sky. Many contrasting historical grand palaces shone brightly in-all-their-glory. Out-stretching church spires fought for the right to reach heaven first. St Paul's Cathedral, tower topped with a 200ft spire, kissed each passing cloud: sitting stably, as Excalibur did, wedged in the dense, unyielding stone.

Other stylish neo-classical cultured theatres of collaborative live art forms, sitting uniformly in shape; all inspiring to create the Valletta jewel; sitting peaceful, prominent and forever sensual, as a model posing in the background.

"Would you mind if I take a seat?" said the pleasant looking, perhaps middle-eastern gentleman, knowing that the seat looked like the only available chair on the terrace. He placed a large glass of whisky on the table.

"Of course, please!" Laura spoke, moving their drinks nearer to give the gentleman's glass additional space.

"Thank you," he said, pulling the chair back from the table to give himself room. He made himself comfortable. Sitting around a foot or so from the table, with ample space to cross his legs.

A white linen shirt and white loose-fitting trousers were his choices to wear. Tanned, sockless feet and legs perched perfectly in light brown loafers. With deep-brown, dark, sunken eyes, grey swept-back hair, prominent moustache, and racketeer kind of looks, so ever like Omar Sharif; he looked wealthy. A Patek Philippe 18k white gold perpetual calendar chronograph wristwatch, held by a light brown leather strap that matched his shoes, sat tightly around his left wrist. A man of wealth, Bill thought. And a man, he was sure, owned many more ludicrously expensive timepieces and just as elegant as the accessory he currently displayed.

"I take it from your accent you are Scottish?"

"Yes, and you are Egyptian?" Laura retorted.

"I guessed hearing your voice, but you could never imagine my country of origin from mine…I spoke in English, which would pass for an American drawl. So how did you guess?" He sat forward, placing both arms on his knees and smiled, waiting on Laura's instinctive response.

"The tattoo on your arm." She offered more. "The Ankh symbol is a cross shape with an oval loop instead of an upper bar. It's an Egyptian hieroglyphic symbol, most used in writing or art, to signify the word "life". And, a symbol of life itself." She felt pleased with her deduction. Bill was happily amazed by Laura's detailed answer; his look showed it.

The gentleman smiled. He was rubbing his fingers over the tattoo, not showing his like or dislike of his ink-stained arm.

"Ah! Sharp-eyed and 100% correct. A juvenile indulgence I'm afraid. A small identity mark I had done before my move to New York to continue my studies. Take a bit of Egypt with me." He added, "You know the symbol well?"

"I have an MA in archaeology and ancient history from Edinburgh University. Egyptology was always my main attraction."

"…and was Hieroglyphics a major part of your studies?"

"Hieroglyphics was only a small part. Although I did put a lot of work into the subject. I do love ancient history. However, the Ankh has two characteristics: The cross, a symbol of life and a circle representing eternity. As a result, we get a symbol representing the immortal, the man who was able to resurrect himself in eternity. Was that your reason for the tattoo?" Laura added her clear and educated opinionated view.

"Wonderfully put! A real expert in Egyptian culture if I may say so. Very impressive indeed, and yes, it is the 'life' symbol tattoo. It was the foolhardy rationale behind the excruciating pain I had to endure just to show-off. And, to be honest, I only knew part of what you said about immortality and eternity. But that was for the Pharaohs and not for a student from Cairo. I can assure you it is just a simple piece of body art. A Christian can be identified with a crucifix, a Celtic cross or even the eight-pointed Maltese cross; though neither would denote the person's country of origin. I guess the Ankh is simply an Egyptian thing…but nevertheless…well spotted."

Emad changed the course of the conversation.

"Oh! I'm sorry…how rude." He stood and offered his hand to Bill. "My name is Emad Ammon Naguib, from Cairo, and I am here on business for the next few days."

His hand reached Bill, which he accepted.

"I'm Bill McKenzie and this is my wife, Laura."

"I'm pleased to meet you both. Are you on holiday?"

"Honeymoon!" Bill and Laura said in tandem. Grinning, they expressed friendliness.

"My God, here I am intervening on your honeymoon…I should not be so intrusive; I will leave you both to enjoy the remainder of the evening.

"No, not at all…" Laura let Emad know that he was more than welcome to stay and join their company.

"Can I buy you a drink?" An offer from Bill that clarified Laura's thoughtful statement.

"That's so kind…I will have a whisky over ice. Your choice of a brand, obviously, and being a Scot, you will choose the best," Emad asked politely.

Bill drew the attention of a waiter and placed an order for a full round of drinks. A healthy conversation grew on many topics, forming a direct relationship; laughter and humility came in abundance; as the night drew onward. An hour or so passed, Emad gave his excuses.

"Now…please, Bill and Laura. It is your honeymoon, and I have imposed myself on your time long enough. Please excuse me. I must bid you both a good evening."

Clasping his hands under his chin as if praying and nodding his head.

"I bid you both goodnight and hope you enjoy the remainder of your honeymoon. It has been a real pleasure meeting you both." Then he left. Making his way, like a sidewinder snake, through a maze of busy tables, bunched-up people standing in groups and determined to avoid collision with busy waiters, jostling for the same free spaces. At the same time, they carried full trays of empty glasses till he reached inside.

Bill and Laura would people watch. A game from their student days. When in a pub, they would pick a person, or group of people, attach a label to categorise each individual or company, then count to see how many different Huppets [(human puppets]) could be found and identified. It took seconds to find their first victim.

The age gap: An elderly, stocky-built man, gleaming under the thick boorish gold neck chains, and several fingers covered in outlandish sized rings of the same bright metal. Stood, with his partner, a leggy young model-like beauty. She was forever smiling, impish and childlike actions, stuck firmly to his shoulder. Money-orientated.

The Mockingbird: The two mouthy bitches, eyeing every woman in view, giving sarcastic, cynical opinions of their enemy's dress-sense and style. They were judging others with false perceptions: negative thoughts they would never wish on themselves.

The Oddities: A middle-aged couple desperate to be part of the scene but just didn't quite fit in. Limited social skills or general ability to publicly mix with others, didn't help their cause. They tended to rely on their low standards of people socialising by smiling rather than communication. But being with the in-crowd made sense.

The Peacock: Always the bloody show-off. The centre of attraction, a forty-something was wearing a creased two-piece suit, flip-flop sandals on his feet, and supporting a hideous ponytail, attached to the rear of a balding head. Appearing to dominate a dull debilitating conversation, to a group of four women and two men; all portraying serious interest; though every face showed a look of 'Why should we pretend to be interested, or care when we don't give a damn; or even like the bastard?'

This pretentious control-freak was so transparent you could see through him! His talent to bore will eventually burn out his audience, and when his plan backfired, he will seek another simple, gullible assembly to control.

The Spectator: A Nordic-looking, possibly German (Arisch Deutsch), bespectacled gentleman; sitting alone, babysitting the same glass of non-alcohol drink for an hour. Just there to observe and listen to others chat. Watch and make conclusions. Maybe a spy?

The Magician: One minute they were there, the next they were gone. Listening to a conversation or exciting story, or whatever held interest; they disappeared. Bored or not, with either the communication, too-much alcohol, or the general atmosphere; the apparition tended to vanish without notice.

The Loner: The one-person waiting on a date. Eyeing each woman that passed him and hoped she might be the date he was waiting or possibly receive a smile to return his attempted compliment. His facial impressions showing hope, then despair all in one movement. Will his date turn up?

The Pervert: This guy leered at women. No matter her age or size. He never hid his antisocial skills whatsoever. Denied of class, this man may be dull in conversation and uninteresting to meet, but his demeanour never changed. He was not there to talk. He was there to perv! Often, this person regularly sported a black eye, a red nose or a swollen lip. Or all!

A barman, possibly in his thirties, with many years of service to his trade, glided carefully through a now fuller, compact crowd, that filled the north-facing terrace, overlooking the start of the long, delightful, well-turned garden, of this classic hotel. Clutching high and gripping firmly, a tray holding a silver ice-bucket, containing a bottle, and two ornate glass flutes balanced next to it.

"Madam, Monsieur, courtesy of your friend, this is the finest 1982 bottle of Dom Perignon Champagne."

The barman held the uniquely shaped bottle. Using a starched-white-linen napkin wrapped methodically around it, he placed the ice bucket on the table. A small knife from his apron pocket cut the foil under the cufflinks at the bottle's neck and removed the foil cap. A paper napkin cleaned the bottleneck to remove any loose debris or dust. The corkscrew, chrome with wood handle, was centred, turned, and inserted fully into the cork; a small lever was actively pulled upwards till the cork came free, and a subtle bursting noise blasted out. A fizzing sound erupted; as a universe of bubbles flew from the bottle mouth.

The waiter offered Laura the mushroom-shaped cork, not as a present or a memorable gift, but to smell the aroma from the 18-year-old champagne. She did smell the cork and kept it as a unique gift.

The fizz was poured gently till the bubbles reach the top of the glass, then pouring stopped. Watching as the bubbles decreased, and when the foam reduced: it was then, the pouring action restarted; till the glass was full. The other glass got the same treatment. "Bubbles up, bubbles down," the waiter murmured under his breath.

Bill noticed the way the barman filled the glasses, not a drop overflowed. Always letting the first flow of bubbles decrease, then add the remainder of the fine wine slowly. The fizz, somehow, in this state, the bubbles in the glass would counteract against the bubbles poured. "Bubbles up, bubbles down." *Something to remember*, the idea crossed his mind.

Bill heard another guest, possibly one of the mockingbirds, catch the barman's attention; by calling him, Ivan.

–

A full-indulgent breakfast of eggs benedict, with smoked salmon and chives, smothered fully in a creamy hollandaise sauce, all ingredients stacked neatly on a hot buttered muffin, tasted splendid. Fresh fruit and banana yoghurt followed. Warm croissants with Maltese fig marmalade were inclusive, and a steady supply of *Pellini Bio Arabica Coffee* satisfied their morning appetite. Bill and Laura left the dining room and approached the seated area near the lobby. The reception desk was busy. The courteous, well-attired staff smiled naturally and delivered high-quality, interpersonal skills needed to provide exceptional face-to-face contact, as one would expect in a hotel such as The Phoenicia. Always finding solutions for difficult challenges. People checking-out, new guests arriving, answering the continually ringing phone, with one receptionist liaising with housekeeping to see if the room was clean and ready for early arriving guests. And unsure residents hoping for tourist information on cultural activities that weren't on their radar.

Emad sat at a table in the Palm Court Lounge with its comfy sofas and pleasant décor, perusing a table full of files.

A piping hot pot of French press coffee and half-filled cup rested near the documents. While he was deeply absorbed in thought, he caught a glimpse of Bill and Laura approaching. Removing his spectacles, placing them on top of several laminated cardboard sleeve folders: he stood and greeted both.

"Good morning, my friends." Looking pleased to meet them again; he shook Bill's hand and kissed Laura's cheeks. "Please join me for coffee; or are you heading off for a morning walk?"

"No…nothing planned…" Bill responded kindly but looked as though his pre-planned trip had dissolved before him. His game plan could wait a while longer.

"I have a bit of a quandary…and hoped you guys might help me out…"

"Sure, if we can." Hoping it wasn't illegal (the thought crossed Bill's mind, and Laura surely thought similarly).

"It's nothing unlawful…I can assure you!" Emad was guessing that his strange proposal may sound weird.

"We didn't think it would be…" Laura is keeping her stare from Bill as not to show a look of guilt.

"Good…"

His waving hand caught the attention of the waiter and he ordered fresh coffee and water. Bill knew he had more than enough 'Pellini Bio Arabica' at breakfast that would keep him awake and alert most of the day.

"I have a proposition for you both. My youngest son, Achmed, has just turned twenty-one and I want to give him a present, but I do need assistance choosing the correct one. Laura, yesterday when we first met, you amazed me with your knowledge of Egyptian culture, facts that most of my friends are completely inerudite with little or no actualities of my country's historical past. I am lost and do need assistance, and that's where I hoped you guys could help me?"

Bill filled a cup with hot coffee and took a sip.

"In what way?" Laura eyed the files on the table wondering if the facts lay there in the pile of documents.

"All I want from you both…is for you to select the best present from three. I have three gifts, and one of the three must be chosen for my son!

"Why can't you choose? I'm sure you know your son better than anyone. So much better than Laura and I…If you excuse my rebuttal." Bill hoped he didn't sound negative or upsetting to Emad's simple request.

"I understand, Bill. But I am 63 years old, and the younger generation has a different look on modern life; my son Achmed is no different. Of course, we agree on business, sports, our country, among other things…but…recent cultural changes are not…as the Americans say…not in my ballpark. That is why I would hope you could help?"

"In what way can we help, Emad?" Laura inquired.

"I have three new yachts berthed in the Grand Harbour in Valletta; I would like you to inspect them all, survey, observe the quality and advise me which one I should purchase for Achmed?"

"I don't know anything about yachts, Emad. My education doesn't allow me even a little knowledge of yacht design standards or qualities, I'm afraid!" Bill said, wiping his lips with a napkin. "They would all look good to me, I'm sure!"

"You explained last evening when discussing the best whisky in the world. We discussed the merits of the cheap foreign brands, the lesser supermarket brands.

"The standards of Japanese classics and blends, American, Canadian, and Irish offerings…and…of course; the finest Scottish malts. I asked your opinion, and you responded with…and I quote you: 'Quality is never accidental, but the result of intellectual effort. On that basis alone…Scottish malts are without doubt; the world's best!'"

"It's not my quote…it's one I have heard…or read somewhere."

"Yes, but you said it with full knowledge that this quote should at least be a set standard. Am I right?"

"Yes…em…"

"Well, that is good enough for me. Also, Laura made a genuinely magnificent deduction on my worn-out tattoo…that proves to me…you both have an eye for quality. That's all I ask of you both."

Emad Ammon Naguib put his trust in Bill and Laura. It seemed he wanted an outsider, a trustworthy advocate, even though they just met, his feelings were strong and felt justified in asking for their impartial opinion. He wanted a relationship built on mutual trust and respect, and with Bill and Laura, he thought he already achieved this. In his position, his family, aides and staff would more than likely agree with whatever decision he made, and never disagree with him, however bad his judgement was.

He knew this young Scottish couple would speak the truth and promote an honest view.

After all, his wealth allowed him to play games such as this. Even though it was above-board and non-corruptible, he was willing to let two total strangers make a family business decision; a transaction that must suit and be accepted by his son. With his instant yacht brokers' choice, he was prejudging a deal before the game starts, allowing outsiders a free run in deal-making. Better to hang back on the victory party until it was done and dusted.

Emad added, "I have full trust in you both. Please, do this small favour for me. I have a car waiting outside, and all I ask is for you both to give a truthful judgement of which yacht meets with your standards—no objections from me at any time. I give you a free hand to conclude your choice. And, on your decision, I will purchase the yacht you finally select." He offered his hand which Bill shook firmly, then Laura added hers to the process. "As you, in the UK say, no strings attached! Just visit the yachts at the harbour, enjoy a few trips around the island and have fun!"

Bill and Laura stood together, looked directly into each other's eyes and passed a slight subtle smile—hardly observing two-slow nodding heads moving in agreement. Indicating a deal had been decided. Whether they would identify the perfect yacht or make a complete hash of it all, time would tell. At this time, they would briefly become fledgeling yacht inspectors; in fact, they were not high-flying birds, both were only two warm eggs tucked unmoving in a business nest, as far as dealmakers go; they were amateurs. Enjoy a few hours at sea in luxury cannot be scoffed.

"Good, that's terrific news. Please feel free to enjoy the yacht experience. Each Captain and crew, for all three yachts, are at your disposal throughout the day. So please, feel welcome to sample food and wine each has to offer. It is a little gift from me to say thank you for assisting with this favour. I genuinely appreciate your help with this matter."

Chapter 10
Yacht Inspection

The black limo glimmered in the sunshine. "Polished enough to see your face," Laura quipped as she entered the back seat, having the door held open by the chauffeur, a 6 foot 4 inch giant, dressed immaculately in a slim-fitting grey suit and a grey Denton chauffeur hat sitting smartly on his head.

"This is the high life, Bill," she said while admiring the luxurious car interior.

The brand-new Mercedes E-class 2.6 Limo had all mod cons. Air-conditioning, cruise control, alarm, computer, electric windows, in-car entertainment (radio/cassette) and full leather upholstery. The summer song *Maria Maria* by Santana, featuring Product G&B, played softly in the background.

"Well, here we are. Inspecting yachts for a multi-millionaire and I don't have a clue what I'm up against," said Bill, unsure of what lay ahead. He continued, "What is it my lecturer always said…Suck it and see!" He slid back into the comfortable seat and clasped both hands at the back of his head.

"Our yacht picking days have only just begun!" he said wistfully, with a relaxed smile bearing witness to his pleasure.

"All we need to do is survey each yacht, make a full comparison, then decide…that should be the best and simplest way to go," Laura said, taking hold of her husband's hand.

"High-five." And both hit the mark by slapping each other's raised palm. (It has been recorded that the source of this physical congratulatory statement was between Glenn Burke and Dusty Baker of the LA Dodgers in 1977 though others have also claimed credit for this famous hand gesture.)

"What if Emad has already picked a yacht for his son?" Bill raised an honest question. "Maybe he wants us to sugar-coat this experience with our feedback. Maybe he is looking for affirmation, not honesty!"

"I'm sure he has already decided. He wants to see if we are working on the same lines of perception as he is. It's a free roll of the dice with no strings, Bill. What the hell. Let's enjoy the day. It's not if we have anything organised today. Apart from being on our honeymoon, that is." Laura, shrugged her shoulders, showing indifference to the challenge.

Bill remained silent.

"If Emad has already decided, and I'm sure he has. He may want us to confirm his course-of-action is a correct one and give a different perspective on his choice. The old-chestnut of right-or-wrong can't be laid at our feet, Bill. The probable outcome of our verdict may differ from his, then it is his move, whether our opinion is best or worse. Surely, he can decide if our choice is preferable or not. Let us enjoy the day out. All expenses paid!"

Laura removed lipstick and a round compact mirror from her small purse and applied a deep red glossy colour to her pale lips while staring at her reflection and pressing her lips together. "I think I'm going to like this adventure," blowing a kiss to Bill.

They listened to the remainder of the catchy song *Maria Maria*—with its fresh Latin sound infused with Carlos Santana's guitar playing, and as someone once said, the guy that played a billion notes over everything.

The music got louder and could be heard by pedestrians and vehicle drivers alike when they left the most beautiful splendour of Baroque architecture in Malta. The black limo moved smoothly along Great Siege Road heading toward the harbour at Birgu, some 7.5 kilometres away. The drive was relaxing and smooth. Both of them nearly fell asleep.

How unprofessional would sleeping be? Laura yawned and smiled instantaneously at the thought; a facial impression showed a look as if she had just bitten into a juicy lemon. She decided to stay awake. The song finished. An upbeat voice of a male DJ announced muffled information, on an up-and-coming pop concert in Malta. Which acts were taking part and how to win free tickets by phoning a dedicated hotline number; the driver switched him off mid-stream and allowed Laura's mind to soak up the remainder of the restful drive to Birgu.

–

As the limo came to a stop near Fort St Angelo in Vittoriosa, the heat was already approaching 29 degrees and revealed the swollen heated tyres in need of downtime. Birgu is an area in Malta referred to as the three cities—which also contain Senglea and Cospicua—three fortified cities built in close proximity to each other around the Grand Harbour. It's situated across the water from Valletta, facing Malta's capital city's Southern side.

The driver was first to jump out the car and open Laura's door as the couple exited the same side.

"That is some sight!" Laura was impressed on viewing luxurious yachts berthed neatly in a row. All were floating gracefully, all immaculate and flawless, primed for inspection, quietly waiting for Bill and Laura's scrutiny.

Each boat had a Captain standing near the boat slips of the similar-sized yachts—all wearing different coloured skip hats. The driver intervened their studied observation and offered Bill three folders. A yellow one, a red one and a blue one; which he soon realised why each Captain wore a coloured hat.

It merely distinguished one yacht from another: all folders containing specific plans, drawings, schematics and general specification of each superyacht. Emad had provided every detail they required and had noted, and delivered, the understood points; a layman, like Bill, would realise the necessary information supplied, hopefully?

Each file included cabin configuration, length, beam, draft, displacement, gross tonnage, built, construction, engines, cruising speed, builder, exterior design, and interior design.

All double-Dutch to Bill, but nevertheless, he could crossmatch information to highlight any subtle differences that would make one yacht stand out from the others.

Laura chose boat 1. The yellow one. The yacht nearest the car.

Captain Luigi Gallo, a forty-something experienced seafarer, welcomed them onboard. With visible greying stubble, which was perfectly groomed short, with areas outside the growth clean shaved, and a yellow baseball cap perched tightly on his head, holding down a long quiff of jet-black hair; he looked forever classic.

They were given free rein to inspect at leisure. Offered a glass of champagne which they kindly refused, but accepted a small, cold bottle of still water, as the temperature again rose, and would increase to 32° around mid-afternoon. As Bill and Laura sat comfortably on the sundeck, they examined the yellow-boat file, enabling them to take notes and view and compare the other paperwork later.

"Who would believe we would be involved in such a game? It's crazy!" said Bill.

The superyacht set off on a 40-minute trip from the grand harbour heading to Dragut point, racing beyond Font Ghadir, for Julien Bay; to sit motionless a few hundred yards of Torri ta' San Ġiljan; a historical 17th-century watchtower, for 10 minutes, before returning to Vittoriosa.

The same route would be repeated twice more before the day was out. During each trip, every possible space was inspected. Fixtures and fittings checked and quality of artistry examined.

When asked for data, Captain Luigi Gallo, or Belgian Captain Lucas Peeters or indeed, Swedish Captain Oliver Olsson gave full facts to all questions. They were professionals at the top of their game.

Captain Gallo gave knowledge on the condition of electrics, engines and machinery, hydraulics and safety equipment, the worthiness of a short sea trial—which included details of sea condition handling—also updated engineering certificates on the status of the hull "above and below" the waterline and superstructure.

Laura ticked off an item checklist that gave her a listed condition report of all the accommodation areas.

Bill and Laura McKenzie went from one yacht to the next, taking the same enthusiasm onboard each vessel, keeping in mind the standard of design and specification would all be near the same; checking and reviewing their notes was a priority. Put a value against a value; it had to be matched by their hard work, effort and, hopefully, proper observance to realise a perfect gift for Emad's son, Achmed.

Laura whispered in Bill's ear, "Let's keep our integrity intact and detach ourselves from any negative emotions. All we need to do is choose the right yacht for Achmed. The one…we believe is perfect." Slurping a large mouthful of water from the bottle she resealed the cap and laid it into a universal cup holder that was attached to the table. Wiping sweat granules from her red, moist forehead with the back of her hand, she spoke, "It's like choosing a kitten or a puppy, you know what I mean? the lonely one with sad eyes."

Tilting her head sideways and raising both shoulders with both palms facing upwards. "We have nothing to lose, Bill."

Bill thought for a moment, then spoke, "I'll take the kitten. You take the puppy!"

A few hours later, with every minute, within that time, being spent inspecting luxurious and preposterously, expensive yachts; they found no faults. They soon realised that one constant always remained steady and unchangeable; that was the high standard of each craft. No flaw, however small, could be found. Not a blemish discovered, not a speck of dust on the Italian carved oak furniture. Neither a smudge nor a scratch could be seen on any mirror or glass, and no cushion was out of place—and a galley with top-range kitchen utilities that any high-end boutique hotel would be proud to own.

"Time to stop looking for faults. It's time to look for quality!" Laura gave favour to a new way to find the best yacht. "Let's get factual!" She threw in as an afterthought.

Still scribbling notes, Bill tried hard not to use a glossary of boating and yachting terms, when later, they would give a justified presentation to Emad.

The Captain said, as he and Laura prepared to board the 'yellow' yacht, "Please mind your step on the Passarelle!" He soon discovered the proper name, which the folder identified as the passageway you walk on from the dock to the yacht. Often incorrectly called a gangplank. As Bill rudely called it.

Chapter 11
Return to the Phoenicia

Time seemingly flew by. The last yacht inspected, checked and noted. All matched each other in every department. "How on earth can a choice be made, if there is not one boat that sticks out. Is a guess, with a plausible lie, enough to dupe our friend Emad?" Bill asked.

The limo was waiting to return to the hotel. Bill and Laura entered and settled.

"Well, that's it. I've read over the notes and for the love of me, I cannot pick one over the other." Still staring at the three folders that sat on his lap. "Should we just pick a colour, or toss a coin?"

"Let me do the presentation and I'll prove the yacht has already been chosen, even though we had a 33% chance of guessing correctly, it was blatantly obvious when we first arrived. The tours became laborious, but admittedly, it was rather fun. And I just enjoyed the ride."

Laura laid back and, this time, closed her eyes.

"What was obvious?" he asked. Bill didn't have any idea whatsoever. 'What on earth does she mean she knew which yacht to pick. Did I miss something?' he muttered to himself.

Laura didn't reply; she was sleeping.

The mid-day traffic was substantial and caused by many alternative problems. The major roads had multiple roadworks—with inadequate mass transit options—stationary or slow-moving vehicles, local buses, trucks, business delivery vans, and, many, many taxis.

And plagued by a continual stream of holiday tourist coaches, as the limousine drove gradually through the congealing traffic on its way back to Valletta.

Bill watched drivers cutting each other up and saw several accidents on the same large roundabout in Marsa. Angry voices on the street, although close, sounded muffled from inside the comfortable sedan.

Bill sat securely behind tinted glass, and he smiled and felt he could laugh as loud as he wished, and no one would hear him. The heated argument stopped momentarily as the contenders in the street-scuffle openly stared at the passing limousine. Bill noted people with lesser attention to automotive enthusiasm would gawk, pay homage and go to the classic car passing. As soon as it left the area, shouting once again erupted, and waving hands and fists flew aggressively, with a woman smashing a laptop over a man's head after a profanity-filled rant; the limo picked up haste, as it motored ahead on a clear road to Valletta. Bill saw and heard a police car speeding past, in the opposite direction, which he guessed was hurtling to the battle scene in a view to rectify the bitter road rage.

Approximately one hour later, and according to the driver, the journey was short for that time of day; they were greeted by a smartly dressed, extremely polite and mannerly doorman near the entrance of the Phoenicia hotel. Laura awoke without persuasion. She fumbled through her handbag for the supplies she needed, and half a minute later, her face was ready.

Chapter 12
The Meeting

The suites in the Phoenicia were grand; Emad Ammon Naguib's suite was no exception to this rule; primarily housed in a building with the traditional architectural style of this prominent establishment. Sitting in the hotel's corner on the 4th floor, it offered breath-taking views of the Grand Harbour and Marsamxett. Due at 8 pm, the meeting gave Laura and Bill a few hours to nap, shower or swim in the outdoor pool. A nap and a lukewarm shower was the shared choice.

It was 8.00 pm exactly when the couple entered the suite. A cream Canali cotton suit hung favourably and fitted well over Bill's lean, 6ft frame. His footwear looked comfortable; designer canvas white espadrilles that held his fashion statement perfectly. He hoped that a look would achieve, attract attention and show other people the type of person he was; that worked to some degree.

However, though most of this was accomplished and observed, his beautiful companion stole the show. Laura looked stunning and glamorous in a black, Shein tiered halter bodycon dress and four inch-high, Gucci black sandals, helped raise her to Bill's shoulders. They developed a surprisingly healthy glow from spending time at sea, which added a brown tint to their skin. Bill's short black hair was combed to one side, his sharp facial growth partnered his movie star look.

On the other hand, Laura had her jet-black hair pulled away from her face and held tightly in a ponytail style; which showed even more beauty to a much more visible face. Her almond-shaped eyes, her perfect brows, her high cheekbones, and her full lips all held flawlessly within the look of an angel. Other guests observed and agreed on her perfection as she floated around the room as a catwalk model would during Milan fashion week.

"My friends, you look wonderful." The voice of Emad affectionately greeted them, and a firm handshake gave Bill a welcome. A kiss to each of Laura's cheeks concludes the greeting.

"Please, take a seat." Pointing to a red leather 3-seater-suite, possibly Italian, in a Chesterfield style, they sat down comfortably. The room had three other guests waiting in anticipation of the result, the scrutinised decision the Scottish couple had made and what their outcome would bring.

A young man in his twenties sat near French doors that opened to a balcony. He wore a classic Oxford navy blue jacket, open-necked white shirt, cream chinos and brown brogue footwear.

This must be Achmed, the son receiving the expensive gift Bill predicted in his mind. A stout, elderly tanned man, sweating profusely and embarrassed by it, his dress sense made him look as though he ran a bookmaker's shop in Cairo; his multicoloured tie lay loosely a few inches from where it ought to be and a tattered straw hat lay on the floor next to him. Around 5ft 6 inches in height, loose wearing cotton trousers were held unstably by a brown leather belt that struggled to contain his fat tummy. The shirt, a colourful celebration that was more suited to a Beach Boy or Californian Surfer, which was a few sizes too large, enclosed him like a half-wrapped Xmas present. A multicoloured Detective Columbo, where clothes were a necessity rather than a statement. Balanced on his lap was an open executive briefcase. Legal documents, Laura observed. More than likely Emad's lawyer. Or a travel agent? Bill's thought made him smile.

Both Bill and Laura soon saw "Columbo's" black leather footwear as Prada Punta Ala; one of the most popular high-end sneakers ever produced. Bill also thought one of the ugliest pair of sneakers ever! His substandard attire made him look much less capable of attracting the opposite sex, but a possibility of attracting bees, butterflies and a host of insects attracted to light. Or like a moth to a flame. His shirt added colour to the room.

And the chauffeur, a young George Clooney lookalike, stood near the door—as a bodyguard would do—but the intent and obedient driver, awaiting his next order, stood motionless, holding his cap tightly over his stomach, the colour of the hat matched the designer jacket.

Sitting opposite, on a similarly designed suite as the one they sat on, Emad sat cross-legged, stretched both arms out and laid them on plump, coloured cushions and relaxed as a well-fed lion would. A waiter offered drinks, cold champagne sparkling in crystal flutes, which they all accepted.

Before any other words were said or a chance given to introduce each other, Laura stood and walked near a dining table; which sat a few feet away. With the eyes of the room following her. Her glass was laid down next to three coloured folders sitting on a small pile, where she laid her right hand, flat on the bundle.

"This, Emad (tapping the files), this concluded survey has been a pleasure to do. Bearing in mind, we are not experts on yachts, not by a long chalk." Picking up the glass and using the ample floor space to conduct her pitch. She had the attention of the audience. It was her turn to role-play and dictate the scenario her way. Let's sort these boys out with womanly guile!

"Bill and I enjoyed the journey. In fact, in all honesty, it was a real thrill to have been on such luxurious yachts and spend time at sea on each. But, I am here to say that there is only one boat that you require me to choose; and that is the yacht for your son Achmed. A birthday gift!"

Sipping from the glass, a mouthful of fizzy bubbles accelerated through her mouth with escaping suds using her nasal passage as an escape route, which tickled her nose, though a polite cough cleared her throat.

"You know what I am about to say, Emad, that the plain and simple truth is, all yachts are as good as each other. I am not here now to decide which yacht to pick, I am here to choose the yacht you have already purchased."

Bill looked between Emad, the chauffeur, his lawyer, then Laura, looking for reactions to her statement. He didn't see one. Laura continued with her narration.

"Ok, here is my choice. And why I came to this decision. If I may be slightly brash and to the point. The winner, if I can say this, is the blue yacht. Pure and simple!"

Emad made a loose attempt to talk. But Laura promoted her stance.

"Please let me continue with my pitch, and I will soon clarify my findings, and why I chose the blue yacht.'

Emad showed no emotion and relaxed back into the comfort of the couch. An extremely, hardly noticeable, slow nodding head movement gave a slight notion for her to continue. She may be on the right track.

Laura resumed with the speech, and without looking at the paperwork, she rattled out facts and figures that had Bill sit up and take notice.

"It has a length of 94 metres, gross tonnage of 3229, speed 15 knots, accommodation for 20 guests with 30 staff catering for everyone's needs. But you know too well that none of this matters, it's never been about specifics or technical abilities, has it, Emad?"

The room remained silent. The professional waiter with a laissez-faire attitude poured more champagne, which Bill swallowed almost immediately. Bill never had a clue why Laura was confident with her information. He was dumbfounded, the fact that she strung out so much information without reading from one of the folders or how she had managed to come to her conclusion.

"I noticed something when we entered the last yacht. The previous surveys showed the two captains dressed similarly and immaculate, but the blue yacht Captain was different.

"While the other Captains had plain white buttons sewn on their jackets, Swedish Captain Oliver Olsson didn't. He had highly polished embossed monogrammed tunic buttons. Three letters: A.A.A. and the inclusion of the Egyptian eagle of Saladin etched above the text led me to believe that this boat, however fanciful my deduction skills are, pointed in one direction only; that this boat was Achmed's."

No one person responded one way or the other. Laura had to give more proof to her theory and watched Emad retain the same seated posture but folded his arms and sat upright. Still keen to hear more. In between Laura's speech, the air-conditioned motor purred gently to add a rhythmic mood to her performance. Bill thought he was a character in a Dan Brown book. He was the person that didn't have a clue what is going on!

"Another clue, hidden in plain sight, and for me, a straightforward one to reveal. My background in ancient history did help surface this unconcealed fact; I processed it logically. The truth revealed itself.

"Firstly, the yellow yacht, named Nut, who was the daughter of Shu and Tefnut. Is considered one of the oldest divinities among the Egyptian pantheon." Moving around the room as an actor on stage, Laura walked again, holding the audience in her grip. "This is no boat for a young man, Emad."

She once again took the seat next to Bill, still working on her presentation. Ready to complete her stylish performance. She pulled her dress over her knees and gulped bubbly.

"Inspecting the red yacht, well…my observation soon caught sight of another vinyl sign stuck prominently on either side of the hull. The name Maat came to view. And recalling distant memories from my studies of ancient Egyptian religion; Maat is the embodiment of truth, justice and the cosmic order. Another female superhero.

"So not a name a male would use for a ship."

Emad and his guests were transfixed by Laura's beauty and intellect. She talked more.

"When I inspected the ensuite in the main bedroom of the blue boat, I found a bottle, which looked like Baccarat crystal. I'm sorry at this point to admit I sprayed the perfume and the fragrance was glorious. It was clear from the brand mark on the bottle that this fragrance was among the most expensive in the world; Clive Christian's Imperial Majesty, for men."

Laura had everyone hypnotised and captivated with her intelligence, holding her nerve with confidence. She stood now and headed to the main door, close to where the chauffeur stood; still, straight and silent as a Buckingham Palace Royal guard, held his stare on Laura.

"My nose discovered this next clue, I love perfume; it's a girly thing. It was the only other time I smelt this beautiful fragrance, which I believe is a blend of cedarwood, cardamom, mandarin orange, and additional alluring notes when we boarded the car this morning. I asked myself. How could a chauffeur, however luxuriously kind his boss is, and how high his wages or allowances are, could afford to purchase such an elegant brand worth thousands?

"I skip this part as I don't know the actual cost, but thankfully the hotel concierge had knowledge of the fragrance and where it can be purchased and had a ballpark figure of a price; an expensive cost at that!

"My inquisitive nature tells me that my friend standing here is not a chauffeur, but your lucky son Achmed; who has just received a superyacht as a gift. The blue one!"

Emad stood and applauded with enthusiastic energy as Laura delivered a logical case; that a proven Baker Street, consulting detective, would be proud.

"How observant, Laura. And yes, I purchased the yacht two days ago. And also, you guessed that my son…unwillingly, I must add, played the part perfectly as the driver. I should say; near perfectly!" Pointing his forefinger at his son—the chauffeur who already had removed the jacket, disregarded the black-tie, unbuttoned the first three-top buttons on the shirt, and sat down taking a glass of champagne with him; nodding in agreement to Laura's skills. "Yes, very well done." Achmed agreed.

"I have been here in Malta for over a week now—setting up this new business. I charged myself the policy of interviewing all the potential clients, of which no one was suitable or held each strength I needed.

"Though one man, with a diploma in boat retail and brokerage just came up short. His failure was due to terrible communication skills. But generally came high on my list of potential candidates. Another three obvious choices came close, all with the same superb academic qualifications; BA in Marketing and Public Relations with honours, but for some reason or other, I just couldn't hit it off with any of them. Neither stood out.

"My top choice was a young woman from Florence. An observant, articulate, and charming girl; with a wry sense of humour; a very confident person with immense capabilities with highly recommended references. She had an MDT—a master in corporate tax law from Bocconi University in Milan. A suitable candidate, indeed. But, as luck would have it, an hour or so after our meeting, she returned to confirm that she had received a phone call offering a job in mainland Europe. An interview she had taken over a month previously. A career as a team manager for a Swiss tax group based in Geneva—one of world's leading comprehensive providers of reinsurance, insurance and other ground-breaking forms of insurance-based risk transfer—was an offer that was too good to refuse.

"There was one other candidate that shone. A person that didn't apply with academic qualifications or with excellent references but ticked every box on my want list—every damn one! Talk about finding the perfect employee!

"This person was intelligent, dependable; creative; committed; accountable and consistent; motivated yet humble and sincere and excuse my male chauvinist frailties; beautiful and funny. And that, my dear Laura…is you." He added more words quickly, "Excuse me, Bill. I don't mean anything, untoward. It is all complimentary, I assure you."

"No apology required, Emad. I thought the same. Laura does, and I agree; tick all those boxes, and much more!"

"Thank you for the compliments. But my sales pitch was generally amateur dramatics with a hint of rebelliousness." Slightly embarrassed with the occasion now. She sipped champagne slowly from the warm glass.

"Look, Bill and Laura, I will gladly offer you both a 50/50 partnership deal to join me in the Yacht Broker business right now.

You don't need any money to accept this share. It is an offer of a lifetime and genuine. I have already got the shop fitted and ready to go, and more importantly, I have many clients lined up and waiting."

Laura and Bill didn't respond. They listened, and Emad continued, "My lawyer,"—using the palm of his left hand to identify the man wearing the beach boy shirt (which clarified their initial assumptions)—"Mr Bengay Fakhry can set up legally binding documents. I was looking for a manager, but with you both, I feel so comfortable in offering you a full half share."

Both tried to talk; neither could find the words. Was this a dream? How, or why, would a stranger offer half of a business with no strings attached? It doesn't make sense, but there would be nothing to lose, no money involved to be part of the firm. It seemed straightforward and the legalities could easily be checked, so what was the problem? This may be the only chance they would ever get to accept an offer as big as this.

"Please…take as much time as you need before responding. I understand there would be a major overhaul of your lives and it would be a radical departure from what you had been doing."

The young man sitting near the French doors remained silent. Sitting still, watching with eager eyes, the business pitch, and business proposition, unfurl before his eyes. He responded to a signal given by Emad. As he struggled to rise from the comfortable chair, his legs numb with sitting too long in one position, he stood and tightened his tie into place and ran his palms over his jacket front; hoping to remove any unsightly creases.

Emad stepped closer. Raising and putting his left arm around his shoulder and pulling him ever so slightly into his own body, made him narrowly suffer the loss of his balance. His face turned red when he attempted to smile.

"This young man is Joseph Azzopardi, Valletta born and bred. He is already hired and been busy setting up the communications at the office. He is more than passionate about his work, as I have witnessed. Azzo, his nickname, is a computer tech genius. He will work and maintain the computer network and office management systems to the highest level. And help to coordinate any technical work required."

A double palm tap on his chest confirmed Emad's trust in him.

"Please think this offer over…"

"We will, Emad. It is an amazing offer for two people that have never worked in the yacht business before. Or…hold any experience in this field…" Bill was polite and courteous to his potential mentor as he could be.

"The job you both did today told me so much about the qualities you have. All I will say is take some time to consider my offer?"

Bill and Laura were already wealthy. Bill had received all his uncle William's estate, which was worth millions. So why work?

Chapter 13
The Apartment

"Tonight, I am taking you to a special place, Laura," said Bill, as they both walked down the steps of the Phoenicia Hotel. A short leisurely walk of fifteen minutes, walking past the Tritons Fountain located near the City Gate of Valletta, strolled unhurriedly through streets named Republic, Melita and Merchant, before arriving at his secret destination; on Archbishop Street.

"This place is special…" said Bill with a joyfully smile covering his face and a possible tear in his eye.

"Where are we? Is this?" she stopped mid-sentence. "Is this?" She looked upward at the tall apartment building seeing the ornate Maltese Balcony, jutting out proudly, from the wall. Laura had only seen photographs of the old apartment.

"Yes…this is my uncle Bill and Aunt Beth's home, where I spent so many wonderful holidays."

Breaking from his daydream, he took a bundle of keys from his pocket, inserted the sizeable cast-iron key into the old lock, and turned the bow key clockwise once, and it clicked open.

"Welcome to the surprise, Laura. Welcome to your new holiday home, Mrs McKenzie."

Bill lifted Laura as she screamed and giggled, and carried her up the thirty worn-out stone steps, to another sizeable wooden door, a door he remembered so well. This entrance, the entry point that would always cause problems for his inebriated uncle. The barrier that kept him a prisoner from his own home, or the unbreakable obstruction his uncle William could never pass; especially when intoxicated beyond a reasonable limit of alcohol. On these occasions, nigh on nightly, he could never gain access past this point. Too sozzled to insert the small Yale key held securely on a Supermarine Spitfire pewter keyring—a gift from young Bill; he would fall at this last hurdle. The key was still attached to the spitfire keyring.

He was always reminded by his uncle to keep quiet and make vain attempts to keep the noise levels as low as possible, not to waken Aunt Beth. Young Bill, on each occasion, was the saviour. Emerging at a crucial time to save the day, staying awake long enough to allow his loveable-gentle-giant of an uncle, access to his castle. "Brilliantly done, young Bill," he would say entering the hallway, with his boots in his hand. Patting Bill's head several times, and as always; bearing gifts of an assortment of sweets. "Thank you for your help, my little gatekeeper," he would whisper when covering his closed lips with his forefinger. Followed with a 'ssshhhh!' as he walked high on his tiptoes, heading to bed; yet, as always, to be greeted with a verbal storm from Aunt Beth.

In conclusion, his drunken uncle's wobbly stripping skills were less than amusing; as he hit nearly all the bedroom furniture in his attempt to remove his clothes in preparation for bed. Bill remained in the hallway to hear the conclusion of the final act; had, as usual, to control his laughter. Pushing a clenched fist over his mouth and the other hand clasped tight over his private parts; just in case he couldn't prevent his humour; hoping his Inspector Gadget pyjamas would remain dry. The last words, at this point, and repeated without fail, came from his uncle William.

His inebriated voice, less than constrained, losing its linguistic competence, although it contained a happy built-in tone, wafted slurred words through the closed bedroom door.

Just loud enough for young Bill to hear the glorious, and funny pronounced words. In a strong Scottish accent.

"Dinnae be daft, wummin. Yer a lang time deid!"

Then silence. As young Bill would hold his frozen stance, listening keenly, gripping the same parts harder than before, then it happened.

The gaudiest and most awful sound his uncle ever produced, possibly shaking the building's foundations, as he let rip a fart. Considerably more comparable to the tearing noise of a Spitfires four 0.8-inch, 20-mm; automatic cannons. Then a loud, unstoppable belching fit began. Acid reflux by too much alcohol-producing this irritable.

When the time was right, she would cry a few obscenities at the actions of her nauseating husband.

Young Bill's body shook uncontrollably, as a spasmodic fit of giggles influenced his delicate nervous system. He was desperately holding every part tighter than before until he could no longer accept the continual build-up of hilarity flowing through his body. It suddenly became crucial, and he needed to run. The toilet beckoned. And run, he did. He ran so fast, in a muddled-headed way, that made him slide on the hallway mat, that glided over the varnished wooden floor, working hard to stay upright; he smashed forcibly through the bathroom door and operated the string light-switch as he floated past, all in one movement.

It was cartoon-like as he came suddenly to a stop at the appropriate landing-place; the WC; sighing with relief as he peed and laughed simultaneously, with grateful pleasure, as he filled the summoning white toilet bowl, with no time to spare. A genial look of relief shone over his tiny grinning face as he completed his evening ablutions; for a second time.

"I love the photographs," Laura said, staring at both walls in the long, high-ceiling hallway, which were covered with framed photographs. "That's you! The boy with the flyer's helmet and goggles." Bending over to see the picture clearer.

"That's me, all right. My first holiday here." Bill wasn't too sentimental; he saw this time as a new venture, a time when Valletta could be a summer retreat once again. He would store these happy childhood memories and retrieve them when required. Malta was a new beginning. Laura didn't notice several black and white photographs taken at The Pub; sat a few yards up the street. Oliver Reed and Uncle William sharing a joke and a dram or two. In one picture, both stuck out their tongues and gave rude hand gestures. All signed by Oliver Reed and Uncle William as...Ollie and Bill, the pub!

The McKenzie apartment had been redecorated. New windows in place, completely re-wired, new subtle lighting installed, a full collection of white goods surrounded the outer kitchen walls; with high-spec wall-cupboards mounted securely above them. Each of the two fully tiled bathrooms had a state-of-the-art, concealed waterfall shower, dominating a significant portion of space; married with porcelain sanitary wear, with decorative hand-made Maltese cement floor tiles completing the stunning look.

Sizeable comfortable bedding for all three bedrooms, a 36-inch box Trinitron television took up an entire corner of the main living room. An ultra-modern central heating/air-condition combination system worked its valuable wonder by purring gently, dehumidifying and cooling, each room with fresh air at a perfect

78° Fahrenheit setting. The flat, now looked ultra-contemporary, except for Uncle William's stereo and music agglomeration that held its place covering an entire wall; which could still rock central Valletta. Aunt Beth's worn, black leather art-deco chair, retained the same prominent room position as it always did, yet never looked out of place amongst the present-day fresh furniture, or in vogue wallpaper hangings.

Bill made regular visits during his University years, ensuring the apartment's well-being and condition he had been the beneficiary. Aunt Beth died several years before his uncle, in 1993, with Uncle William departing his free-spirit life on 11 June 1997. Strangely enough, this is the very day the battle of Malta began 47 years to the day.

The property and the belonging were Bills. Included with the apartment was a bank account totalling £2,680,000. Unknown to Bill, or anyone else, his uncle was a lot more than a Times Crossword oracle; in fact, his potential to buy and sell stocks and shares was just as convincing; if not better.

A local estate agent kept the property clean and aired-well over the years during the refurbishment upgrade, always prepared and ready-to-live-in, at a moment's notice. And that time was now. They stayed the night.

When morning arrived and a waterfall shower instilled fresh momentum to both, they gathered many thoughts and scrutinised the excellent job offer. Eating a Continental breakfast at a nearby café filled a morning craving.

And this time was incorporated with a phone call home to his parents; to explain in detail, their decision to accept and take up the offer of becoming equal partners with an Egyptian businessman they only recently met. Though primarily, this proposal still surprised his parents, and a few seconds of silence confirmed this; nevertheless, they felt no need to deflate their son, or his wives' ambitions, or dampen their enthusiasm for this once-in-a-lifetime, opportunity. Bill further explained the full story to his mother and found the proposal strange but wonderful if legitimate. But Bill's mother being a solicitor, she offered advice, 'Before you sign, anything, get the contracts and fax them to me!'

Forever the lawyer. But it also made sense. If Bill's parents didn't understand the deal's international legalities, they guaranteed they knew someone who did. A short meeting with Emad and his legal team was amicable. Sending contract copies by fax to Scotland was not an issue; it was imperative and professional, and Emad encouraged this. He wanted Consensus in idem: consent to take the same; or parity of the minds; to be precise, a business deal and handshake was always active, but a full signed contract was the glue that held it all together.

A phone call 20 minutes later, his mother concluded all was fine with the agreement, she wished all the world's success and promised to visit Malta soon.

Living in the apartment on Archbishop Street, they ran and operated the company from a small harbour-fronted office close to the Roland marina.

Chapter 14
The Roseburn Pub, Edinburgh
The Present Day

Bill sat alone on a high stool in a quiet bar. A few regulars took their usual places, supping beer or checking the racing form of today's races. At the far end of the room, a TV broadcast a news channel, but the volume was low.

The barman looked like a twenty-something ex-student; hair shaved back and sides, with a long black floppy quiff flowing over his brow, that neatly met a skilfully trimmed black beard. His job gave him the role of a keen listener during quiet spells, especially when the customer had clearly been at a funeral. Showing respect was a regular part of a barman's job; listening to the man sitting before him wearing a black suit and tie, he felt eager to listen and understand. Not knowing the stranger's loss, or whether he was mourning or not; he played the caring barman, the keen listener faultlessly.

"It's on me." A blended whisky was poured into his near-empty glass to refill the anaesthetic sedative that Bill knew was doing its job.

"Cheers, Frank," he said, looking again for confirmation at the name badge on his waistcoat. A name he got when buying the first drink. 'Can I tell you a story? A story my uncle told me many years ago.'

He was leaning against the bar playing with his whisky glass. The bar was still quiet, so Frank nodded with interest and Bill started his story.

"Sure!" His friendly, approving face gave Bill the green light to continue. As he ran the palm of his right hand down over his beard, as if to confirm its tidiness.

Bill took a drink, his mind going over the story, making sure he got it correct and did not screw up. He hesitated at first, but it all came out as he wished.

"This was a long, long time ago, way back in the Middle Ages, or maybe before that, in a land called Mecorra. King Hakan, an obnoxious bully of a ruler, had won battle victories all over neighbouring lands and held unrivalled power, over a vast area, and held a grip of fear over many territories and fallen kingdoms. His dominance was unique."

Frank leaned in, getting genuinely interested in Bill's fanciful tale.

"All of his victories, whether on land or sea, had one special additive. Not an enthusiastic general looking for advancement, nor a son wanting his father's favour, not even a royal confidante offering secret information from his main adversaries. No, none of this. This one-man, aided every successful campaign his king fought and accepted no glory or fortune for his remarkable effort.

"This man was no military genius, no strategist or tactician. Mithral de Savea was a seer. A person gifted with moral and mystical insight; he was a wise person; or, a sage. He possessed intuitive powers. Over the years, he accurately predicted that the King would father four sons and one daughter, seize victory over a neighbouring dominion, which had previously devastated his late father's land and property. And would destroy all opposition and would be revered by his subjects and feared by his enemies. That is…until the last battle fought."

Another gulp of whisky flew down a treat as Bill revealed more of his story. By now, Frank was intent on hearing the end of this intriguing tale. Bill handed him the empty glass which Frank filled with more of the golden liquid. Putting Bill's fiver in the cash register, and placing the change in a white saucer.

Bill swallowed half the whisky and continued with the adventurous fiction.

"In other words, the insufferable King, a King that didn't give a toss for anyone. Not for anyone that sat in his court; including his family; far less a debilitated soothsayer, finally lost a battle; a battle against a nemesis; his archenemy—a stubborn King in a nearby land.

"All the previous years that had passed, he had made accurate predictions: falling into line, one after the other, he couldn't fail to appease his King. But this one loss, a severe forfeiture to his biggest adversary, was far too much to take. And with this unagreeable disappointment, was a defamatory insult to the King's standing. So, what would he do? He would act as he usually did when anyone let him down; he threw the old prescient into a dungeon and had him beaten severely.

"However, the old prophet was wise. He heard and saw from his jail window, a wooden structure—more than likely, a Hangman's Gallows—being built; which he knew too well would be his place of death, his finality from this earth, would happen here. The next day, the seer was pulled from his cell, carried roughly to the King's court and thrown to the ground, to the merriment of all in court, including family, barons, lords, church bishops and army generals, all competing for the King's favour.

"The room fell silent as King Hakan stood and faced the godforsaken older man. Approaching the frail bag-of-bones bundled before him; he spoke loudly, so his roared voice echoed, hit every wall through the grand hall, and hit the ears of all in attendance. 'Tell me, fortune-teller. Can you advise me, and my friends, details of when you will die?' Laughter circulated the room. Womenfolk held lace handkerchiefs against their mouths to nullify laughter. Then the King spoke again, 'I said, soothsayer, pray to tell me when you are going to die!'

"The old man adjusted his position to turn slowly and raise his weak body with one arm, to face his King.

The King elevated a hand, informing his courtiers to remain silent. His once-trusted advisor was about to speak. King Hakan bent over ever-so-slightly, placed a cupped hand to his ear, mocking the older man as he struggled to move. The seer could not be heard. His voice was soft, and his words mumbled were ineligible; due to severe head injuries received at the prison guards' hands. 'Speak up, man. We are waiting for your wisdom,' the King shouted louder.

"Blood was spat from the older man's mouth as he used every bit of energy he had remaining to voice his answer. The room was silent as he spoke, 'I know exactly when I will die, my King. The very hour, the day, and the way death delivers me to my maker.'

"The King smiled to his courtiers; some laughed, some didn't; some remained intrigued at how the mighty had fallen and wondered if they could find themselves in a similar predicament in the future, so they remained stone-faced. 'Can you divulge this information you predict to me?'

"The King remained adamant that he was destroying his once trusted ally by breaking his spirit and making his very being evaporate before him. 'Yes…your majesty,' said the Seer, 'and fortunately for me, my Lord, I die the day before you. That is why I cannot divulge the date of my death; It would allow you disturbing information that you would never wish to hear.'

"The room remained silent. The Sovereign had his guards clear the room of everyone, including his Queen. At this instance, King Hakan of Mecorra had a change of mind on killing the old man. He no longer wanted him dead. He was a scared rabbit. Wondering if the seer had the talent of future seeing, and because of one small mistake, that, of course, could and must be forgiven, but to what end? From that moment onwards, the older man became family; given the best lifestyle anyone would wish, live in grandeur and opulence, receive a full pension and pardon, and given Royal privileges and have the welcome use of the king's doctor and surgeons.

"Now, did the King keep the seer alive only to save his own life? Whether he trusted the older man's knowledge or not, he certainly didn't trust his own. Strangely enough, two years later, heading into another war, King Hakan died after being thrown from his horse and was dead before the battle started. But, as seers do, the older man gave Hakan's eldest son this valuable information, the would-be-new King two days before the event. He also predicted King Faulco's first decisive victory at the Battle of Crawkish Hill the following day; just as the oracle predicted, and gave King Faulco years of prestige and glory, as he continued to work alongside his trusted, and reliant confidante.

"In the end, the prophet stated he would die the day before the King, but the truth being, he didn't say which King!

"Frank, you must wonder what the moral of this weird story is. Well…I can tell you. When life is smelling of roses, and everything in the garden is lovely and sweet. Life…has a nasty habit of kicking you full-on, in the bollocks. Right on the target!"

Bill stood unsteadily but remained upright and sorted his balance. He swallowed every drop of whisky and placed the glass neatly on the bar top. Wished Frank the very best of days, slapped down a £20 note next to the tumbler, adjusted his untidy suit, tucked his shirt into creased trousers and left the pub. Frank watched him go and nodded at the enjoyment of the story.

It was a short walk home, although a bit longer than it usually took, checking traffic more than he should, trying to instil care into his inebriated movement while struggling to cross a busy road. Drivers repeatedly sounded their disgust by pressing their car horns. Offering abuse to the well-dressed drunk that staggered and tip-toed through the substantial stream of traffic; holding a hand in the air as a police officer would do, stopping oncoming vehicles and pressed his forefinger to his lips for all drivers to keep silent. Stop! I'm coming through no matter what—missing the pedestrian crossing that sat a few yards further ahead.

A new retirement home, a place to spend our winter years together, Laura said when they recently purchased the Penthouse apartment: housed on the crescent at the old Donaldson's Hospital grounds in West Coates. This well-appointed 3-bedroom residence has expansive space both indoors and outdoors.

Set in a serene and peaceful environment close to the city centre, it gave Bill and Laura an ideal place to hideaway or a beautiful place to entertain friends. They liked both ideas.

Bill stood with both hands, steadying his drunken stance, on the expansive Kitchen island light-brown marble worktop that centred the room.

Staring bleary-eyed through floor-to-ceiling windows at the far end of the room highlighted the old black and grey Gothic style building—Donaldson's Hospital; designed by Edinburgh Architect William Henry Playfair. "Ah, stuff it!" he said, throwing a drunken jelly-like, a not-caring, right arm at the grand view his blurry vision attempted to focus on.

Still in position, looking intently around the kitchen, he suddenly had a pang of hunger. A thought of cooked food engulfed his muddled thought-processes. Maybe a cheese toastie, a pizza, a jam sandwich, order Chinese; but none of that gripped his pleasure more than another drink. A bottle of Single malt caught his eye, as it stood as a dutiful soldier would, waiting on command, on the work surface near the sink.

"You will do for me, my friend," Bill said, opening the bottle and swigging a mouthful.

A staggering short walk took Bill to an L-shaped couch which he managed to slump crudely on its edge. Twisting the metal cap from the bottle he threw in the air and managed to kick it, it hit the window; somewhere between long purple velvet curtains draped at either end. "Goal!" he shouted. He was pouring a few accepted gulps direct from the bottle into his waiting mouth.

Bill had a drunken conversation with his dead mother about the frailties of life; it lasted till the bottle was empty, the talk lasted twenty minutes more; then he started to realise defeat to the awakened was close, and the king-sized bed was his new-found conviction. He knew he overindulged; he had planned it this way.

Inebriation overwhelmed his brain activity. His bodily functioning and senses began to strain, a snapshot of the bed formed a picture in his head, as swirling images spun before his eyes.

Walking barefoot to the bedroom, the last of his balance accomplished a safe landing of the bottle on a bedside table, skilfully undress half his clothes; before giving up hope, he flopped on top of the mattress. Out cold.

–

Bill's body lay motionless on the bed. He was not moving, for love nor money. Immobile as an impertinent mouse in a crowded cattery. His heartbeat, eye movement and respiration all began to slow; and his muscles relaxed and occasionally twitched, as brain activity leisurely slowed down from their wakeful state. As if his body had switched off and set itself to standby. The sleep cycle continued. Body functions began to slow further. His core temperature dropped, eye movements stationary, any brain waves at this stage of sleep are virtually non-existent, with only a few short bursts of activity; then he was in a deep sleep. His heartbeat and breathing slowed as his muscles relaxed.

Even a loud noise at this stage of a deep sleep, he would find it difficult to awaken. Bill was now in slumberland, a place of self-hypnosis, or alcohol-induced hibernation; or Delta sleep as it is also known. This stage of sleep can last from 50 to 90 minutes.

In a flash, a dream began. A vision as clear as day, it opened as bright as a movie in a darkened cinema. It was if he saw the world through another person's eyes. This was no camera lens he looked through; this was a person's vision that gave a realistic view of life. He was using this foreign body like an unwanted parasite, which made him feel guilty and awkward. He heard non-English speaking voices and saw unfamiliar faces around him. The weather was hot, and he felt the intense heat and how uncomfortable it was.

Incredibly, he knew where he was, as logic began to unveil information through his thought processes, the language he heard momentarily evolved into English. As a badly overdubbed b-movie, where the movement of the mouth and the pronounced characters struggle to match, although the words emanating from the man opposite his host sounded English. Still, somehow, these words didn't coordinate with his mouth movements, which reminded Bill of a ventriloquist dummy pronouncing a 'bottle of beer'…but this is a dream after all, and dreams do this.

He knew there and then, he was in Al-Aleppo, Syria. And the date was Thursday, 19 July 2012. There was a common link between Bill and his host. Brainwave sensors actively transmitted data to each mind, as a smart device would do via a wireless connection. Both knew they were held in this strange situation, sharing intentional and cognitive states and processes between them. Together as one: Bill McKenzie and Farid Aboud.

Bill soon understood the person opposite him, sharing food and tea, was Hasan Rahal, a school friend of Farid Aboud, who at the same age as his host, looked older and carried too much weight for his thirty-eight years.

Hasan Rahal was the highly regarded, and well-renowned cheese shop owner in this district of Aleppo, selling a cornucopia of artisan cheeses; sitting at the opposite side of the square—Wafarat aljabn or in English, "Abundant Cheese".

The rooftop restaurant in the Al-Jdayde Hotel in Al-Hatab square was in the Al-Jdeideh district of Aleppo and renowned for its narrow winding alley's. Old Arab-styled houses and mansions stood nearby, churches of mixed-faith catered for the varied diversity of religious settlements, and an abundance of silver jewellery shops that became synonymous in this district were on every street. Al Hatab Square is the beating human heart of the neighbourhood. His friend, Hasan, chatted non-stop about current Syrian affairs and the severe problems that will soon affect everyone in the country. Not just here in Aleppo.

Hasan was speaking, "Farid, my friend, our country is going to hell very quickly. My young cousin Ali, only twenty-four-years-old, was shot dead in Damascus this April, just for demonstrating. Assad's forces are already bombing in Homs; it's now known that rebels killed many soldiers in Al Quneita." He looked around to see if any stranger heard his rant, no one did, but he continued to speak with a softer tone.

"Many security forces died in a roadside bombing in the south of the country. Al-Arabiya is claiming five soldiers dead in the village of Karak.

"My friend, police stations are being attacked with groups of men with assault rifles. The present trouble is not just a civil war. We are now about to be involved in Armageddon."

He resumed the one-way conversation and occasionally ladled spoonfuls of Ful Medames into his mouth (a stew of cooked fava beans with vegetable oil, chopped parsley, garlic, onions, lemon juice and chilli pepper); in between his long-extended speech about the state-of-affairs in Syria.

Ripping a sizeable piece of flatbread, he dipped it into the stew, as a fisherman's net would scoop a shoal of fish; a handful of soaked bread filled his mouth. He still tried to finish his sentence with mumbled words. Besides this, he swirled his hand as painting imaginary circles with his forefinger. Believing this action helped to pause his communications, and hoped his hand movement, for some weird reason, allowed him to swallow the food more quickly.

Many people were lunching in the open-air restaurant.

At the restaurant's big table, a birthday party was taking place among six excited, enthusiastic children. A glorious, designed birthday cake decorated in many colours depicting the Aleppo Citadel; looked delicious and delectable. Personalised pink helium balloons with the name 'Fatima'—embossed on both sides of the natural latex inflatable; were suspended at either end of the table. After the celebrations finished, each child could get their tiny hands on a shiny, stylish foil, fluttery confetti balloon; to carry on the journey home.

One mother and her profoundly deaf daughter stared intently into the eyes of each other. Mummy's lips mouthed each word perfectly although her daughter was still learning to lip read; they communicated skilfully with Levantine Syrian sign language. Whatever her mummy transferred with a technical finger alphabet; the girl laughed uncontrollably; then hugged her mother.

A table of four young men discussed life in general. They were talking about football teams. One wore an Inter Milan football top; the others dressed in jeans and wore trendy T-shirts. Two of the teenagers wore black Hugo Boss beach shirts, and the tall skinny guy telling a funny story sported a Tommy Hilfiger shirt; with the name printed across his chest with *New York 1985*—written below the brand name. The boy eager to listen to all the stories, but not willing to input his thoughts, drank mineral water and rubbed Misbah prayer beads held loosely in his right hand. One of his friends, the shortest in the group, the guy wearing the Inter Milan top; had a Samsung Galaxy 2 with the phone screen facing his friends' eager expressions, each one waiting in anticipation to view the unique photograph he boasted about.

The clear picture of himself and his hero was clear, and both embraced, with an arm around each other's shoulder. It was none other than Abbas al-Noury; taken at the arrivals hall at Damascus Airport. The famous Syrian actor, writer and director, known for his role in the memorable TV series Bab al-Hara. Loud oohs, and uhhuh's with some handclapping showed their approval. A few businessmen argued amongst each other as plumes of blue cigar smoke hovered above them. Waiters moved around serving hot food, lifting empty plates, refilling empty tumblers with cold freshwater, and offered professional menu opinion to any customer willing to listen.

A glance to his left arm showed a timepiece stating 12.45 pm. He suddenly felt he had been a regular customer, as the surroundings and nearby buildings became evidently recognisable. Not déjà vu; but being part of the person that he now jointly viewed life.

Farid wasn't aware of another living entity sharing his neurological processes. As the mind intruding guest slept and dreamt, he had awakened into Farid's life in far-off Syria. Seeing the world as he did, feeling fear and love in equal parts; joined in a high-tech simulation; and perceived the condition as if wearing a head-mounted device that provided virtual reality for the wearer, but he didn't; all of this was life in real-time. The organism was also a human being. A good man. A man of morals. And like himself; a paid-up atheist.

Farid felt a strange feeling surge through his body. An inner feeling of a unique relationship that felt as though a twin would connect—endowed with seemingly telepathic qualities that each knows when danger or disaster threatens the other, even when they are separated. Like a close genetic connection. But Farid didn't have a twin. Just an inclination of a pairing.

His friend, Hasan, continued talking and eating, and Farid occasionally nodded his head and smiled, which gave Hasan the green light to expand his argument.

Their expansive view overlooked the old square. Farid and Bill's minds fastened together, witnessing a typical authentic day in Aleppo, as ordinary people went about their daily lives. Farid observed reality, yet Bill saw Farid's realism as a living dream. But he was there, sharing an experience with him. They were viewing existence as an actuality.

Farid's view of Al Hatab square revealed several school children behaving unruly. A small group of elderly-retired men sitting under an evergreen canopy of an Aleppo pine tree playing Banakin, a rummy-style card game popular with Syrians, and many women window shopped. A force of delivery vans of all shapes and sizes buzzed in-and-out the square—delivering whatever goods their vehicles carried and a mixture of people sat at different alfresco coffee houses that were scattered around the square.

Some men read newspapers on the atrocities that the country has recently witnessed, a student studying academic books showed real focus and set aside no distraction, a grey-headed man sat with a laptop balanced on the table and sent and received emails.

A tourist, with a Canon camera, held on a branded lanyard that swung around his neck and laid tight against his chest: he drank a sweet coffee made from sugared water and bit into a slice of H'risseh—a Syrian semolina and nut cake; which he ate heartily. He soon took photographs of his surroundings. Two aged men sat on stools near the entrance steps of a ceramic shop and shared a Hookah.

Aleppo and coloured Damascus dishes hung on a display wire on the limestone brick wall behind them. An elderly couple carried two hefty shopping bags each.

Stopping every few yards to catch their breath and to lessen the tension to their limited muscle capability and worn joints; the likely hood of osteoarthritis; the degradation of joint Cartledge. An eager young police officer checked each car was parked legally. A moped driver drove on the pavement to pedestrians' annoyance, with a taxi driver flicking a lit cigarette in his direction hoping to hit him. It hit his head, but he didn't stop. A large chase-obsessive dog barked incessantly while pursuing a small whimpering mutt.

Both ran past a sleeping cat that paid no attention to either of them, but soon his furry paws decided to ramble from the square to head home, his long-awaited meal is overdue. So much passion begins at the city's outdoor food markets. The stalls were full of fresh fruit and vegetables.

Garden radishes much larger than apples sat in rows. Akkawi cheese bobbed in milky white brine; black and green olives were in glass jars. The cuisine is the creation of productive land and location—along the Silk Road, an ancient trading route.

Street vendors set up colourful stalls selling these fruit and vegetables. Two-sided park benches were covered with circular flatbread as several women used this apparatus as a makeshift device for sun-drying bread. The cheese shop belonging to Hasan Rahal was busy as usual. A flutter of Eurasian sparrows and the ever opportunist pigeons, were always willing to sample a variety of human food; fighting for territorial rights to feed first; at each roadside café on the square. Every crumb that became available would battle out victories and defeats every passing minute, coming to blows over dropped or gifted leftovers.

Hasan still talked incessantly, his plate was clean and required a waiter to clear the table. Coffees arrived which Farid hadn't seen delivered but did hear his friend offer more political news. He gave views that were informed and intricate. This former university graduate held meticulous details of his countries current standing. As a Professor of Current Affairs would lecture his class, he spoke fluently and expertly on the subject. He intentionally kept his voice low to avoid unwelcome listeners from hearing his political outburst. As Benjamin Disraeli once said, 'Talk to a man about himself, and he will listen for hours.'

But Farid knew his friend had done his homework. Hasan added, "Assad's army is going to smash any political dissidents with brutal force. They are ruthless. Just like a rabid dog, they will kill indiscriminately with no fear of repercussion. Once they grip your ankle, these bastards won't let go. Assad will allow his militia to use any force they see fit. That means death and destruction. The Russians and Iranians are backing the despot with troops, weapons, technical support, and financial backing.

"Already there is a force being structured from pro-government authorities, the Shabiha…mostly drawn from the Alawite group. Assad is using them to enforce laws and break up protests in agitated neighbourhoods. Also, and as bad as it already is…Hezbollah is seemingly involved fighting Islamic extremists. There is thousands of Shia Militia—Liwa' Fatimiyun (Fatimiyun Brigade) which in my mind, makes this civil war, a holy war among our people. In abundance, and growing daily, Is extreme Islamic groups such as Ahrar ash-Sham, Al Nusra front, Suqour al-Sham, Al Tawheed and Al-Qaeda…all with their own, political, and religious agendas. Of course, there is transient local warlords and corrupt officials, and the inevitable contribution of local gangsters all biting the heels of anyone that gets in their way. Farid, this is hell, and it's about to get worse."

Farid looked at his friend and understood and agreed wholeheartedly with his friends' views, but each other held a different stance on moving forwards.

"I only want peace, my friend. Like you, I worry about the future. I can take no side in this conflict. If anything, the side I pray for is the side of peace. I will only help the innocent."

"Farid…there are people in this world that will never wake up and smell the coffee. That's the way life is. But I can tell you now, I am getting out!" Farid and Bill listened further.

"My wife and daughter are staying with friends in Antioch. Usually a 2-hour journey; which will be more like 12; I am guessing. The roads are busy with fleeing evacuees. These people know what's coming, Farid. You should follow me and get the hell out of here before the shit hits the fan.

"You are leaving today for Turkey?" Farid inquired.

"After I finish here."

"What about your shop?"

"Stuff my shop. My cousin was one of the first killed in the troubles, and he will not be the last. I have cleared my accounts. Yara has enough money to purchase an apartment, so there is enough to start a new life. My house, my belongings are no longer important. Life takes the lead overall material things. My family always comes first, my friend."

"I cannot leave my home, Hasan. Too many people rely on my service."

"You are a firefighter, Farid, and a brave man, I can confirm, but there will be far too many fires for you, and hundreds more like you, to extinguish the firestorm that is about to engulf Syria."

Hasan stood and laid more than enough Syrian pounds and a handful of coins to cover the meal and give a substantial tip for the waiter that appears first at the table. He tapped his forefinger on the paper money.

"This will be worthless soon. Paper money never pays for favours. It's gold, silver, diamonds…luxuries will be the set course on every menu. If you want out of this difficulty…this is the only currency the devil and his helpers will accept. Even this may not be enough." Hasan moved to Farid who had pushed his seat back and stood to greet him. A big man hug and back-patting said more than any words.

Hasan added, "I hope you reconsider, my friend. Leave everything behind and get out of this hell hole. You can stay with us in Turkey till you sort yourself out. But believe me…you would be wise if this is the only advice you get, to take it. Goodbye, my friend. Allahu Akbar."

Al-Hatab square remained busy, as Farid looked down from the rooftop restaurant. Farid watched as his friend Hasan moved along Sheik Al-Kayyali street until he was gone. His view distracted, then forcibly drawn to a group of three black vehicles parked in shared spaces, facing inward to the public ground, to the right of the square, straight ahead from his position. A large, well-built, well-dressed man about forty years stood protecting the vehicles. Immaculately attired in an Italian tailored two-piece grey suit, short, groomed hairstyle, clean-shaven and sporting a pair of police security guard TAC polarised sunglasses. He looked and promoted himself as a security officer.

Standing near the vehicles, he touched a press-to-talk button clipped on his suit lapel. The visible coiled tube emanating from his ear gave Farid knowledge that this man would more than likely be MID (Military Intelligence Directorate…) Shu' Bat al-Mukhabaratal-Askariyya. A highly trained, highly skilled, security agent working for Assad's government. Protecting a government minister would be the likely reason he and his colleagues were here. Watching and protecting the government-issued vehicles, while sending regular analysed reports to his superior; who would always remain close to their asset.

The agent looked agitated. Looking to his left, a hundred feet or so in the distance just passed the junction of Sheik Al-Kayyali Street; he became visibly perplexed by the movement of a large vehicle reversing in the direction of his place of security. Where he was the solitary lookout. The truck had arrived soon after the businessman had settled in his meeting. It may be a coincidence, but his training taught him otherwise.

The vehicle stopped and two workers jumped from the cabin and loitered close to it.

One of the workers, the boss he presumed, was permanently on a mobile phone. Possibly receiving orders.

The operative showed repetitive, purposeless, and unintentional behaviour. These movements, the security guards believed, were signs caused by anxiety. There was a violent storm brewing and is going to be bad, he felt it in his bones.

The other worker, no older than a boy, looked like a scared rabbit caught in a beam of dazzling headlights, disregarded an unfinished cigarette to the pavement and twisted his foot to destroy the remnants. They both re-entered the vehicle.

The security guard would professionally defend the place where he stood and protect passionately with his life if need be. His pay grade was good, but without a written contract of employment, he ultimately knew, in printed words or not—that his life was always on the line.

Incoherent two-way conversation between his microphone and his team on the ground became lost in the decision-making process; too much radio traffic initiated inaudible information overload; he was on his own. Take command of the situation. No one in the team had legitimate proof of any pre-emptive hit, or valuable intelligence that this was the case. Individual players in Assad's regime reported the possibility of an attack a few days earlier; although there was no real credibility to the threat; nor did they provide credence to their source of legitimacy. No coded phone message was received; as this was the acceptable parlance nowadays. An encrypted word being the preferred option when violent groups send threats.

He took slow, tentative steps closer to the heavy Isuzu truck. His heartbeat rose, and beads of stress sweat appeared on his forehead, as he reacted to emotion; noticing the lorry reversing in the wrong direction on the one-way system and coming his way. It's unique, totally irritating white whistling sound—ssh; ssh; ssh;—of the reversing alarm, played continually; as if a cruel type of calling card was personally delivered. Still, twenty feet to go, the back-up-beeper remained to play the same unwelcomed tune, as the enormous mechanical beast moved closer to its destination. A blockage that would prevent the curators' convoy from leaving and upset the protection officer on duty. He must react now and stop this truck from getting anywhere near his protection zone.

Farid saw another well-dressed man from the corner of his eye, with a dull purple tie that fluttered over his left shoulder, as he was led in the direction of the convoy.

A team of six agents whirled around him, screaming erratic words of panic. Flawlessly ushering their asset as a sheepdog would pen sheep, to the safety of the Maserati Quattroporte. Analysing every face, they passed. Staring at windows for a stranger with a sniper rifle—or a moving shadow behind a curtain. Or possibly a suicide bomber weighed down with HE devices strapped around their upper body.

Maybe a professional hitman paid to take their client out, or a terrorist bent on killing for an arbitrary reason or just hell-bent of creating havoc for their selfish cause. They avoided two fighting dogs as they moved closer to the safety of the armoured cars. A pigeon flew in front of their path, making a few hearts miss a beat—screaming instructions into microphones.

This secured vehicle has ballistic-proof body shields that would defend the minister. Once inside, the luxurious interior hid the fact that this fortress was built to withstand bullets, bombs, and other means of a violent attack.

Safely on board, engines started, and on the move, but only moved a few yards, stopped around 10mtrs from the street blockage; the reversing truck. The agent on the ground, in response, shouted and offered violent action, if neither man took up his appeal. Now Agents from the other two cars got involved, making hasty exits from the vehicles' safety. As they moved closer to the disturbance, they mechanically lowered Heckler and Kock MP5 9 x 19mm parabellum submachine guns; held strapped across each of their chests. Now a hand was wrapped around the handle with a finger ready—as training taught them—on the trigger and ready to fire; as they joined their colleague still attempting to clear the route ahead. As both workers refused to respond to any action the security men offered, the young officer pulled his weapon; a Glock 9 x 19mm pistol from inside the chest holster and pointed it directly into the cab, aiming at the driver. "Move the vehicle! Harak alsayara!" he repeated by holding a firing stance. "Harak alsayara!"

Inside the Maserati Quattroporte, the curator looked calm and unnerved. The meeting had gone so well. He wanted to return to the museum as quickly as possible. He spoke to the personal bodyguard who sat next to him.

"Get this convoy on the move, please. Can you sort this mess out? I'll be late for my next meeting!"

He was scared. He didn't like the way things were going.

Both sanitation workers, dressed in a full orange hi-visual cotton overalls, jumped from the Isuzu 500 truck cabin and calmly proceeded to pull long Damascus hunting knives from their working garments. They plunged violently as wild animals would, at the scared protection officers standing a few meters away; although each of the guards carried fully automatic weapons. Their aggressive action took the shocked protectors by surprise. The security officer fired his gun as the knife wielding aggressors drew nearer. Two precision headshots took both men out; they slumped helplessly, as a thrown rag doll would fall; smashing facedown onto the tarmac; twisted and contorted bodies lying in strange positions. People were frantic and scared. Screaming voices alerted others. Those already active ran from the scene, many others took solace in neighbouring shops.

The young officer did his duty. He protected his client.

"They must have had a death wish!" one security officer said.

"There may be others," another said.

Farid and Bill both witnessed the shooting incident. Farid wondered if he should have taken Hasan's information at face value. This place is not safe!

Bill wanted Farid to hear his voice. Shout aloud if need be. Get a message to him.

"Get the hell out of here!"

Farid threw himself to the ground, stretched out with face on the floor, expecting more shooting to erupt. Staying flat until the gunfire passed, some Mothers took their children and huddled in a safe corner of the restaurant, waiters assisted the elderly and infirmed to their feet. They offered cold water or hot sweet tea as a suitable comfort. The concerned hotel manager was eager to point out that the incident was trivial, and the police was dealing with the matter, and everyone would be safe.

Shaken and disturbed, scared people began to resurface, back to the normality of several minutes before. They were making short steps from shops or the place they found solace. A curious crowd had already gathered near the shooting as curiosity washed over their recent fear. Only interested to see dead people. Two dead extremists. Both are lying where they fell, motionless on the road, martyrs for an unknown cause, as a profuse amount of black blood leaked from fatal head wounds that solidified in pools; of dense, drying body fluid near their defiant corpses. The agents were ready to react, move the obstacle, clear the fundamentalists' remains, and get the hell out of here. Sirens were loud and visible as police, army; ambulance services rushed to the scene.

"What the hell is going on? Get the men back in here. We need to move now!"

The curator was not so sure about the situation he found himself. Nervous and shaken by events, he sought closure. His nerves stretched to the limit. The driver, a suited, balding, stout, middle-aged man, with an almost comical bushy moustache; thought his look gave him a feeling of power; replied promptly, "Yes, sir." Picking up his mobile communications—supposedly to contact one of the growing numbers of security officers attending the shooting; with one member already boarding the truck, ready to move the vehicle off the road to allow a safe route of safety.

Instead of using the two-way radio microphone fixed to his suit lapel, he used his mobile phone to interact with an unknown source. Having located and confirmed the contact, he turned to face the passenger who was already talking to his wife on his mobile phone.

The Minister was speaking on his phone.

"I have been held up but should be moving soon. One more meeting at the Museum and I'll be home shortly after—" The conversation with his wife stopped mid-sentence when he caught sight of the driver who was pointing a gun at him?

The curator was scared, he dropped his phone that fell to the floor, his wife's faint voice dissipated from his hearing range as she repeatedly called her husband's name. "Alem…Alem…"

The driver did not speak; he just smiled at the thought of violence.

Pointing a Ruger .22 LR pistol with an integrated silencer at the petrified curator, he fired one shot into his forehead; TAP! Which killed him instantly, and another shot into his chest; TAP! Alem Najjar lay slumped awkwardly against the side window. Blood splattered the rear window and cabin roof, with blood particles dripping over the seat and floor. The superfluous pistol had done its job. He threw it onto the back seat next to the corpse. A professional hit, by a man that must meet his destiny. To meet God, Allah.

A curious agent standing close had witnessed this assassination; he saw blood spray on the rear windows. He struggled to open the door to the Maserati by tugging the handle. When this didn't work, he fired shots at the driver's door and more at the windscreen as bullets bounced off the metal frame and security glass. The fat driver prayed, wiping his hands over his face, hoping that traces of mercy come down to his hands with prayer, then conveyed to his face by a wiping action. The guard recognised the prayer, and the driver prayed for forgiveness and mercy.

He repeatedly shot bullets at the car window.

Knowing the glass was military-grade bulletproof material too well, he kept trying. Disregarding the empty clip, clipping a new one in place, then continuing with the same erratic action, where the result would remain constant. No damage!

Only stopping his endeavours when the killer held a mobile phone near the window for the officer to see; showing his ultimate intention as a poker player's face would highlight the fact that he held a Royal Flush. By curling the corners of his mouth up a little in an expression of subtle amusement. There can only be one winner, and that isn't you!

Keeping his finger on the call button; ready to phone the number, the driver sneered at the officer, showing a missing central incisor on the top layer of tobacco-stained teeth. The guard dropped his pistol and voiced a prayer himself.

"Allahu Akbar!" The chauffeur screamed at the top of his voice. Then pressed the chosen option and made a connection to the detonating fuse that triggered the weapon. The sewage truck exploded.

BOOOOOOOOOOOOOOOOOOOOM!
WWWHHHOOOSSSHHH!

A mammoth blast on an unimaginable scale, set off other explosions from cars, and other vehicles situated around the square, as their fuel tanks added to the destruction of everything near the vicinity. Every window over 200 meters away was smashed. The Aleppo Sheraton Hotel, over 800 yards from the epicentre, lost several windows and anxious residents reported feeling the building shake violently.

The sewage lorry held over 3000lbs of high explosives. A simple, yet dangerous concoction of ammonium nitrate fertiliser, mixed with fuel oil, was the selected choice of extremists' ingredients when making bombs. Quickly produced, and everyday materials were readily available. Inside the vehicle's cylinder tank, a series of daisy-chained oil drums (IEDs) functioned as the primary payload were welded into position, then sealed inside the container. Which, in regular use, would hold ten-thousand litres of sewage. A multitude of various items added to the explosive mix gave the desired effect the killers wished. Included in this list were nails, scrap-metal, dead rats, vomit, human excrement, nuts and bolts, and ball-bearings; as the killers sought to cause chaos and confusion, by adding insult to injury, to post-blast infections for those unlucky to live. A mobile phone is a popular remote trigger for an IED as its signal can be transmitted up to a mile away. But this time, it was five metres away.

Soon, emergency services were on their way and added to vehicles' gridlock, blocking all primary access routes to the Square. Around the perimeter of ground zero would be jam-packed with reserve services: including vehicles from military and government agencies; and what confronted all of them was an outpouring of unexpected suffering. The injuries at the scene are the type of trauma seen in major battles. Doctors and nurses are not tenable with anticipation like a military medical unit on a war foundation. The medical trauma teams would soon find some of the wounded near death, many suffering from severe chest wounds, although lacerations were the most common injury. Those who didn't die immediately, the ones that were close enough to the blast would suffer most. Not the dead! They were fortunate.

–

There are four mechanisms of blast injury: Primary, secondary, tertiary and quaternary. All were visible and accountable by this explosion.

Primary blast injuries are exclusive to high order explosions, with the injuries caused by the blast wave moving through the body.

The blast wave causes damage to air-filled organs, resulting in barotrauma affecting the lungs, auditory organs, the eye, brain and intestinal tract. The eyes also being ruptured, and belly injury is due to bleeding and perforation; also causing harm to organs and testicular rupture.

Secondary blast damage will account for the bulk of injuries from an explosion and debris displacement; triggered by fragments that infiltrate or interact with the body—the strength of the blast wave projecting wreckage over a vast area on the materials used in the construction of the bomb. Some may show no injury whatsoever, as a small wound could be hiding a shocking injury underneath. Injuries can include fractures, amputations, scalping, lacerations, dislocations and any soft tissue injury.

Then there is tertiary blast injury.

When blast forces carry a person through the air and impact another object by energy or a building collapses and causes injuries. The subsequent injury can be blunt force trauma due to impact or piercing injury when the striking structure enters the body. Quaternary blast injuries are the fourth category in such incidents. These are caused mostly by exposure to fire, smoke vapours, radiation, biological agents, dust from the rapid combustion of fine particles, toxic substances, environmental exposure and the event's psychological impact.

First response medical staff on-site struggled to stay upright as they clambered over dangerous levels of unstable rubble from fallen buildings, or by-pass burning vehicles and structures, as fire crews heroically battled the flames; risking their lives, attempting to save others. Injuries were horrific. People are dying where they lie; some because of extensive pulmonary damage, with pulmonary haemorrhage causing suffocation. Numerous more were degloved; having a ribbon of skin ripped from their body that severed the blood supply, which amputation would be advised or required in some cases.

Victims with ruptured spleens caused when the capsule-like covering breaks open and poured blood into the abdominal area; creating internal bleeding. 89% of the surviving victims from the secondary blast sustained ocular trauma. With blast force injury to any eye or orbital; open globe injuries, adnexal lacerations of the lacrimal system; containing structures for tear production and drainage, eyelids and eyebrows hold most injuries in this group. Many wounded had broken, or missing mandibles as the blast wave caught opened mouth casualties.

Some more severely damaged victims had human body projectiles implanted into their bodies. These victims with blood and bony fragments infused within them and immediate care providers would receive prophylaxis against hepatitis B virus and action taken against HIV and hepatitis infection. A mobile group of survivors managed to walk away from ground zero; distressed and frantic, and unaware of the gravity of their injuries; in a concussed and confused state, they acted in a bewildered manner.

Walking as a zombie would, or a reanimated corpse, they snarled and slurred incoherently and fought for every breath of fresh air available; as they shrugged off any assistance that came to help them.

The Al-Hatab VBIED a (Vehicle-Borne Improvised Explosive Device) set down a marker for every faction fighting for territory in Syria now, and in the future; in what would be the ever-growing Syrian Civil War.

A crater of a forty-foot round by thirty-foot deep appeared where the truck once sat. Every building in Al-Hatab square was unrecognisable. The buildings near the blast disappeared, as did the people.

The old men playing card games were gone. As were the coffee drinkers; the American tourist and his camera; those that ate cake at the StreetSide café; the dutiful policeman checking illegal parking—evaporated; the browsing window shoppers; and the poor struggling disabled pensioners carrying hefty food supplies; all gone.

As they now became minuscule particles of once-living beings, dispersed by the blast, caught on the forceful wind, air-borne ions, becoming clouds of the dead.

When every deceased soul released from the payload of life; taken and scattered over hundreds of metres—wafting slowly down—like confetti at a wedding; lying as dust on the reluctant streets and buildings below.

And unwillingly, against their will, inhaled into the lungs of the living. Death a motive, death the result, death now the taste on the tongues of living souls.

Chapter 15
The Previous Day, Wednesday, 18 July 2012

The National Museum of Aleppo is located at the centre of the northern city on Baron Street. It's only a short walk away from Bab al-Faraj Clock tower and the famous Baron Hotel; the hotel where rooms 202 and 203 respectively, at one time in history, had distinguished guests such as Lawrence of Arabia (T.E. Lawrence) as Agatha Christie and guests. Lawrence is held in notoriety as the famed visitor that left without paying his bar bill. On the other hand, Agatha Christie allegedly wrote part of the novel, *Murder on the Orient Express*, in room 203.

The 2nd-floor office lay within the museum's interior, where it overlooks an internal courtyard that displays giant basaltic statues of ancient Hittite and Roman mythological characters; and a prominent third-century mosaic figure. The out-dated, out-of-style office looked like it was a sizeable unused storeroom.

Grey painted walls gave the room a dreary appearance. A large full-length, two-hundred drawer index-filing cabinet sat to the left side of the room. On top of the drawers, was an antique rotating black carousel ink stamp holder, clutching six rubber stamps; sitting on a bundle of discoloured brown paper files. Two empty wooden museum packing cases sat in a corner, one on top of the other; with stencilled black arrows pointing to the floor, with upside-down words easily recognised as "This way up!"

On top of the packing cases sat a 1970s Metamec; Faux Marble Battery Mantel clock, propped up on an empty shoebox; an empty tea cup covered in fungus was stuck firmly to the cardboard lid. The clock was working but was reading three minutes slow.

Next to the plywood cases, at the far-away wall, was an Art Deco drinks trolley; of nickel-plated metal with polished black glass. The table looked dirty.

And the wheels had stuck firmly to the Persian rug it sat on; it also looked as though they wouldn't turn even if oiled. On top of the trolley sat old Schweppes Glass Soda Syphon accompanied with six dirty crystal glasses. It bore the Royal Cypher; "By appointment to Her Majesty The Queen." Above the trolley, a drink tray that time forgot, hung an Ali Ferzat framed print.

A caricature of a figure wearing an opulent military uniform, spoon-feeding his subject from a large cast-iron pot, brimming with medals. In 2011, Ali Ferzat won the Sakharov prize; an award that honours people and groups of people who have devoted their lives to the defence of human rights and freedom of thought. It's Ali Ferzat's way of expressing his peaceful thoughts through cartoon profiles.

Low soft light in this part of the room, originated from an old-fashioned copper floor lamp that deprived the cartoon of illumination. It was a motionless trolley and its few immobile glass companions; that gained a minuscule smidgen of a dull orange glow; from its feeble radiance. A formidable four-shelf bookcase, the top and bottom shelves specifically, were laden with an assortment of history books. The two middle ledges were makeshift holders of a variety of bric-a-brac and curiosities of all sorts.

In amongst the debris of the gathered keepsakes, there settled a full jar of Nescafe Gold coffee, sugar in a container promoting the same name; and four merchandising coffee mugs endorsing the Museum. 'The National Museum of Aleppo—the past is our future'. On the wall near the workstation, there was a detailed wall map of Syria. A 2012 calendar, with a coloured photograph of the Citadel of Aleppo. Some dates on the calendar were marked red, and some days circled with blue ink.

The desk was more business-like. A computer was turned on, and the screensaver displayed a full-frontal image of the museum.

For internal use only—a telephone was black and had a digital screen, a plastic container of pens, pencils, and a small ruler—added to the list of useful implements on the desktop. A floor-standing ashtray was full of spent cigarette stubs, and used matches stood within range of the person occupying the desk. Well within reach of the user. A plastic seat with chrome legs was the uncomfortable seating arrangement for the office participant. The desk was flanked by two other armchairs. They looked more comfortable than the plastic one.

The Museum's current director, Dr Jamal Alfassi, PhD, opened the door to the office and held it ajar to allow two other men to enter first. With him was Alem Najjar, the curator of archaeology in Aleppo's national museum and Kamal Al-Maleh Syria's Director-General of Antiquities and Museums responsible for all of Syria's museums and historic sites. He had arrived from Damascus the previous day.

"Director-General, please take a seat," Dr Alfassi said as he closed the door slowly behind him. Making sure it was firmly closed.

The men made themselves comfortable. Alem Najjar looked slightly overawed, and his looks portrayed this. Being in the company of The Museum's director and his countries Director-General of Antiquities made him feel somewhat intimidated in their presence.

Both guests relaxed.

"Please excuse the room, Director-General. As we agree, this small room is not my main office; this is my playpen of sorts. I use it as a storage room, and if I urgently need time to myself, I use this space. And safe from any intrusion or electronic bugging as you requested." He offered relevant information on the shelter of the room they were using, as he joined the men in pouring a cup of dark coffee. He sipped some which he didn't like. Laying the cup on a white saucer, he waited for the Director-General to speak. The Director-General had requested the meeting and it was to be kept secret, what information he had, had to remain confidential.

He removed a folder file from a leather briefcase which he returned, locked, to the floor.

"Gentlemen. We have a problem!" he said without looking at either man. Although both Dr Alfassi and Alem Najjar fidgeted uncomfortably, believing they were in trouble, possibly something had gone wrong somewhere along the line with internal workings, and they were at the head of the list for punishment.

Kamal Al-Maleh produced photographs, one for each participant, the Director-general offered a full A4 copy which they both accepted. They gave intense concentration to the images. There was a brief description of the artwork on each image: The Nativity of Christ; Christ the Redeemer; and the Holy trinity. And their size: 142cm by 114cm.

He offered details.

"These three images show orthodox Christian icons that were stolen last year from a private collection in Jableh. The owner will remain anonymous.

Although, and as you would imagine, he would like these items returned. I have information that a gang from Aleppo stole the paintings. Our current information has yielded positive lines of enquiry. With this knowledge, I would like you," he said, looking at Dr Alfassi conceitedly, "to oversee this operation. According to my close associates, this gentleman is a local mafia militia; generally known as the Ghosts, or as you may have conceivably heard them called the Shabiha. Notorious for smuggling commodities such as cars, drugs, and guns between Syria and Lebanon at the command of our President's family.

"One thing is clear my friends, that is crucial in all of this, that I dare say you will fully understand. Our discussion today can never be spoken or repeated outside this room. This meeting never happened. With due diligence, I have had you both systematically checked, and understand where you stand politically, and how you both view our current situation here in Syria." Alem Najjar was about to speak, whether to kowtow to his new master or explain his views in a completely different way or squirm with fear. He decided not to.

"You are more concerned about the safety of your families and the protection and concern for our national heritage than any violent conflict, or Bashar Hafez al-Assad's unfortunate government policy's—that have driven our country to the brink of civil war." Neither man responded. "I have £100,000 in British notes in my briefcase. The amount we have agreed with our contact. In turn, he will provide these items' location, so we can hopefully retrieve them safely. I have organised a meeting tomorrow where I need you curator, Najjar, to attend this meeting. Your knowledge of religious iconology is essential and imperative; you must scrutinise the sample that will be brought to the meeting."

As Alem Najjar looked at him, he addressed him directly. "Just make sure the icon you examine is not fake!' This statement made both men sit upright. Alem Najjar wiped both hands from his cheeks, over his dry mouth and left them positioned as if praying. Director-General Al-Maleh continued, "I have installed a private security firm to provide safekeeping to and from the journey to the meeting. The time and place will be tomorrow; noon at the Beit As-Sissi restaurant in Al-Hatab Square, some six minutes' drive from here. I assure you, gentleman; this meeting is safe, and the security detail is purely precautionary, However, if their services are needed, they are top professionals. My contact will supply you with precise information where these stolen items can be found.

"Your point of contact will have one of the artefacts with him, and he will show more detailed images of the other two icons, and detailed proof that these objects are the original Icons stolen from our benefactor. Do you have any questions?"

Dr Alfassi spoke, "If these icons are real—"

He was interrupted before finishing his question by a slightly nervous, yet curious mindful employee, Curator Alem Najjar.

"If these images are of true religious icons from centuries past, then they will surpass many discovered artefacts in recent years. Let's say they are real, and if that is the case, then all three icons have been lost to history for hundreds of years. I couldn't be 100% sure until under a controlled situation in our lab, and after they are analysed, if authentic; these items are priceless." Alem Najjar spoke with courageous words. Although he didn't want to be involved in this job, it was way beyond his pay grade, and he would rather be anywhere else than here.

Dr Alfassi leaned forward and put his arms on the desk. His arm nudged the mouse that activated the screensaver. The frontal view of the Museum again lit up the dull lit room.

Alem Najjar further added and used the print of the icons as a presentation tool. He pointed to them and spoke,

"These items are mid-to-late 14th-century; all painted by a method known as Tempera. Layers of gesso, a mixture of size and chalk, are applied to a wooden surface to smooth it out. Tempera is an egg solution of water, egg yolks or sometimes whole eggs, occasionally mixed with milk, honey, or a little glue. This painting method superseded the encaustic painting method. If these icons are painted by who I believe painted them, then priceless is not the word I should have used. The value of all three paintings is unimaginable."

"Who is the artist, Curator?" The Director-General asked curiously.

"I believe, although; until they are all subjected to a full forensic analysis. I would use infrared reflectography, woods light, a stereoscopic microscope, IR spectroscopy and other instrumental techniques. And a thorough evaluation of the physical properties; I would say that these icons are the work of the most noted of all medieval Russian painters of orthodox icons and frescos. None other than the 14th-century Russian monk, Andrei Rublev."

"Andrei Rublev!" Dr Alfassi said aloud.

"Yes, I do believe so. It may seem far-fetched, even improbable, but I will say with conviction that these icons are the work of Andrei Rublev. I first saw them twenty years ago; I enjoyed doing appropriate tests with a dear friend, Professor Alexander Urusov from The Museum of Fine Arts in St Petersburg.

"The results were conclusive. 100% verified; by the world's leading specialist in Russian Arts; these icons is the work of the great man himself, Andrei Rublev."

"Gentlemen, what we seek are no forgeries but actual authentic Andrei Rublev originals. And to quote you, Curator Najjar; incalculable worth!" he further added. "My client marked each wooden panel itself—the DOSKA, with invisible ink. His initials should be visible. If not…then they are fake. You need to see the letters E. A. N.

"If the initials are visible, Mr Najjar, spend the money and get the details I require. I will take care of all business when the icons are proven originals. If we can return these historical pieces of art, in the future, we will be granted a lengthy period of a loan to this museum. The private collector has permitted this agreement. So, let's get these icons returned to safe hands."

The Director-general picked up his briefcase, laid it on his lap, pulled eyeglasses from his top pocket, turned the three-numbered combination lock till the required numbers were in sequence; then pressed the button which lifted the locking latch, and the lid popped open. He produced a sturdy brown envelope from inside the attaché case, placed it on the desk and removed two mobile phones.

The briefcase was closed and returned to the floor.

The phones were identical in type, except that one had a circular blue sticker and the other a red sticker to differentiate between them.

"Gentlemen, these devices are burner phones, as I've been informed. These prepaid devices cannot be traced; keeping our identities anonymous and our privacy intact." He handed the phone with the blue sticker to Dr Al Fassi and the red one to Curator Najjar. Both men looked at each handset as if they had never seen one before. They were scrutinising every part of it.

"The phones are fully charged and ready for use. Please take care of them as they will play an essential role in our quest." He continued to speak, "Curator Najjar, once you receive the information from our contact. You will, in turn, give him the £100,000 of cash. Only when you are back into the car's safety, text the code word 'THREE' to the Director's phone and send. There is only one number on your phone, so this should be easy enough." He gazed at the curator, hoping he understood the role he was about to play and now offering his attention toward

Dr Alfassi. “Once you receive the message, Director Alfassi, you will text me with the same code; again, there is only one contact on your handset. Once I establish a connection, I will call you within the hour. Then, as the name suggests, burn them. Or break them up, whatever you deem necessary.”

“How will you find the icons by this method?” Dr Alfassi intelligently asked.

“The information shall be given verbally, not via text or any written statement. Curator Najjar will have all the evidence I require. My contact has agreed with the plan.”

“Can your contact be trusted?” Dr Alfassi asked.

“He is known to my associates. He will not betray my authority.”

The Director-General lifted the brown envelope, opened it and removed two smaller parcels and gave one to each man. Both men studied each other and wondered where this farce was going next. Scared and vulnerable, they both felt ill at ease in the predicament they found themselves.

“What I’m about to say now is factual and to be taken seriously, and I won’t repeat this; please do not ask questions until I have finished. Just listen very carefully, let the information sink in and trust my generous offer to you both.

“There is money, flight tickets, hotel accommodation for you and your families in each package, along with a letter of approval from my office, certified and signed by me, which will allow you all to attend the Berlin festival of art. With the flight leaving next Wednesday. Now, before you offer any disagreements, or explain in detail how this cannot be organised at short notice or find a lame excuse to thank me; but gracefully decline my kind offer, I will explain a little further.

“Let’s say I have friends in exceedingly high places. These friends have informed me; that within weeks, or possibly days. By viewing intelligence as a tool of power, and by its means, on this occasion, it has, by some crazy fluctuation; came to benefit the three of us sitting having this conversation. To put this as blunt as I can. If you don’t leave next Wednesday. It is highly likely, some of your family, if not all, will be murdered. Your wives and daughters raped then stoned to death. Your sons shot or integrated into a radical group; although that depends on which faction captures them. Or all shot where they stand, or possibly detained and tortured.

“This beautiful museum and its wealth of Syria’s history will be crushed into a million pieces. Only because it does not hold water with whatever violent assemblage that enters here first. Or maybe it will be caught in a bomb blast.

Gentlemen, our government is already in discussion with Vladimir Putin to bring military forces to our land. Gunships, fighter planes, armoured vehicles, and enough weapons to win two wars. This crisis is not a game; this calamity is real.

"I have already made my decision. I know where my loyalties lie, and that is to preserve my family. Gentlemen, I thank you for assisting with this last effort to save precious artwork from destruction. Many more valuable antiquities will be destroyed in the months to come and that I do not doubt."

He stood and shook both men's hands.

"Gentlemen, I will be leaving shortly to catch my flight to Damascus. My family will also be on the flight to Berlin next week, and I hope to see you there." He looked at each man, stared into each of their eyes. In silence, staring for a few seconds holding the stare. He added, "Do not speak any of this. Not to your family. Explain, there is an invitation to a festival in Berlin. Treat it as a working holiday. But do one more thing for me." He hesitated.

"Do yourself and your family a big favour and be on the flight next Wednesday."

The conversation ended. Director-General Al-Maleh walked to the door and turned the doorknob preparing to leave the room when he stopped. Turning his attention to the cartoon print hanging on the wall.

"I also appreciate the talent of Mr Ferzat. I admire his criticism of corruption, bureaucracy and hypocrisy within the government and affluent elite. Although, I would not leave it in place, or keep it as a possession; because when the fight begins, it may be a tenure to which side you stand or where you place your loyalty. Director Alfassi, when the trouble escalates, and it will, trust me. Whoever enters and empties this museum, whether it is government forces or not, you will be held responsible for promoting anti-regime ethics. That, my friend, would not be a wise move." The Director-General opened the door fully, left and closed it behind him. He was gone.

Leaving the Director and Curator to mull over their thought processes of the objective they were about to be part of and how on earth would it play out.

The Director-General prayed that it would go as planned.

Neither man wanted any involvement with this activity, but if the country was about to implode in on itself, they at least had a way out. Both were agreeing to do as they were requested. Get the meeting done, deliver the cash, get the information the Director-General needs, and get the location where the icons were stashed and leave the rest to professionals. Send the message—send another message. And complete the business. It was as simple as that.

It would take a week to organise their move. It had to. Keeping a closely guarded secret from colleagues would cause suspicion, but they had to promote that they were looking forward to the trip. Even boast about it; to a certain degree. Being upfront and honest about their invitation to Berlin; maybe a way to hide in plain sight, by staying visible and act as normal as they could. And that included family knowing one thing about their pre-planned escape from a country that was about to implode.

Leaving behind family heirlooms, furniture, friends, close associates and colleagues, neighbours and their hard-earned properties left to an unknown future, and in the hands of forces that held no morals. But they soon agreed to make this schedule work. They would prepare to move. Taking care and attention that none of their moves showed weakness. Act reasonably always. Behave in a manner that Museum staff and others that knew them would expect.

They are all lucky to be going on a fantastical family-cum-busman's holiday to Berlin, far away from the violence that was moving their way. Treat it as such. Get the hell out of here!

Chapter 16
The Art Deal Thursday Morning, 19 July 2012

The forty-four-year-old curator Alem Najjar looked elegant; dressed in a two-piece, slim-fitting, grey suit, a white linen shirt and well-polished black brogues covered his feet.

But what let his stylish-look down badly was an ugly purple and black polka-dotted necktie. In addition to that was his feeble attempt to tie a Windsor double-knot; that failed somewhere along the line; as the flowing large V shape tie swung over a double Gucci leather trouser belt to highlight a further mistake. As a proud family man of four children, Najjar worked every hour required of him and many more. His modus operandi was a 10hr day, six days a week, and a mountain of paperwork to complete on Sundays: little or no family time, but a loving and doting father all the same. Standing at 5'10" in height, he stood straight as a pin, on the steps of the museum, waiting for the professional security team to deliver him safely to the meeting.

Innately proud of his position at the National Museum, and the crucial job he was about to undertake for Syria's Director-General of Antiquities and Museums. He felt overwhelmed; he wanted these precious items returned; it was his duty to do so.

The security detail arrived on time, approaching to where he stood. Three black saloons glided effortlessly to a stop, with a Maserati Quattroporte his transportation on this journey. Flanked back and front with BMW X5 Armoured Security Vehicles (ASV'S) All security guards were armed, giving him a sense of relief. Just so long as they don't need to use them. He felt like a famous Syrian movie star heading for lunch or a high-ranking government official on duty.

A stout, balding, middle-aged driver, suited and booted for the job, still looked unkempt; had already departed his seat from the air-conditioned car and opened the back-seat door, allowing entry for curator Najjar. Maybe he could handcuff the briefcase to his wrist, but that was fiction and this work. His ultimate mission was to save valuable art pieces and his family. The curator smiled at the man who held the door open. Settled and comfortable, with the attaché case sitting square over his thighs, he wrapped both hands around it, like he was travelling on a busy train journey and protecting the money with his life.

A few slurred words emanated from the man with the bushy moustache as the door gently closed. Words were indistinguishable; did he hear him say, "Allah?"

Did the driver believe this to be a dangerous assignment? Or did he pray to God every trip he made? These confused thoughts went through Alem Najjar's mind.

A moment later, the other rear side passenger door opened, and in stepped a leggy six-foot-tall agent wearing wraparound sunglasses, as he held; and spoke into; a small microphone attached to his jacket lapel; completing words of instructions to his team. The journey would take six minutes. Primarily an uneventful drive; although a foolish teenager overtook all three convoy vehicles, zig-zagging passing any car that got in his way; in a rundown battered black and yellow Piaggio Vespa sport scooter. Clipping and breaking the Maserati wing mirror by executing an outrageous wheelie-trick to add insult to injury, which infuriated the driver.

As the kid on the motorcycle laboured close behind the leading car, the driver behind him wanted nothing more than to accelerate, use his front bonnet to clip the Vespa's rear-wheel; and knock the little shit off the road. But he was on a business trip. He was working. His now preferred action was to use the heel of his palm to pump the horn hard; right on the trident logo located centrally on the steering wheel; which he beeped four times. The exasperated driver lowered the car window and leaned his head out, which scrambled the few hairs remaining on his head to fly in one direction, backwards. With a flailing arm extended further out into the traffic, he gave a rude hand gesture of a thumbs up; and shouted at the top of his voice: "Ebn Al-sharmoota" (son of a bitch), followed by "Manyook" (Fucker!)

Maybe real life is not like the option like button on Facebook, as in parts of the Middle East, this gesture is highly offensive. Its western counterpart uses the middle finger.

The scooter swayed left, then right, went left again, then right, playing the ignorant fool hoping to antagonise the baldy prick behind him. As he gambled his driving skill also, he saw an opportunity to overtake the BMW lead car, skirting unpredictably, a smooth well-worked manoeuvre, enabled him space to pass; at full throttle, he left the scene and returned the compliment. "Manyook."

Buzzing off in the distance, the little Vespa irritated more road users; just as its Italian name suggested—the wasp!

More car horns sounded loud; echoing profanities filled the Aleppo air, as the teenager on the motorised wasp twisted snakelike through the morning traffic.

The personal protection officer, sitting next to the curator, opened the glass security screen that divided the driver from his passengers and shouted, "Stop fooling around. Just get us to our point of extraction." Then he slammed closed the screen. A raised arm from the driver indicated an apology of sorts, although the bodyguard didn't see the evil eyes he gave to the rear mirror; the curator observed his hateful glare. The motorcade abruptly turned left onto Al Mutanabbi Street. The road ahead was clear, and they reached their destination shortly afterwards.

Alem Najjar had worked for several years at the Directorate of Antiquities and Museums Branch of Homs. The museum contains a collection of stone statues, granite coffins and other various antiques. As curator of Archaeology, his remit was to catalogue acquisitions, plan and organise exhibitions, and research objects and collections; which he did to the highest standards. Najjar Is also fluent in Aramaic and would often translate texts. His PhD in religious art was a notable addition to his skills, and his services were frequently called upon to identify or prove provenance; of many stolen paintings.

He famously examined a fourteenth-century orthodox icon depicting the Crucifixion of Christ. After many detailed forensic tests, he found the picture fake. Although, in his report, he found it to be a master-level forgery. A highly skilled painter can paint beautiful works of art and 'produce age' to the finished icon. Possibly fooling lesser art experts, but Alem Najjar wasn't too easy to fool. He was an expert in his profession and never left any stone unturned when defending art.

Al-Hatab square was busy as the nose-to-tail vehicles moved into the enclosed space. The lead vehicle forced its way through crowds of disgruntled pedestrians, and pigeons fluttered and squawked as they flew in all directions away from the intruders.

These guys meant business. They looked mean, and in their job, they carried firearms.

It was two minutes to twelve when the party stopped near the Beit As-Sissi restaurant entrance.

The security team leader, the curator's close protection officer, shadowed Alem Najjar to the square where a small lane called Sissi leads to Sissi House, where the restaurant is. Four other specialists did likewise. They were stopping at specific vantage points to secure and protect the area if they had studied it, checked plans and drawings, knew what to do and when to do it; all highly organised specialists.

The focussed and aware drivers drove the custom-built armoured personnel carriers to the square's far side, where parking cones had been placed earlier in the morning, providing ample space for all vehicles. One agent would patrol and secure this zone. Although the security team had hi-tech communications in place, there were times that hand signals relayed details in the event of losing verbal contact capabilities.

By crossing his arms over his chest, it informed his colleagues the area was safe and secure.

The agent with a neck like a bull mastiff dog, his shirt tight as a balloon skin around his muscled frame, protected the restaurant entrance; spoke into the microphone; reiterating the message verbally to the team leader. "Area secure."

As if planned, prearranged knowledge was in motion; the team leader knew where to go—taking many steps down, over stone stairs, until they reached a hidden level of the eatery into a space that looked like a cave or a grotto. Passageways and chambers hand-carved from a beige limestone located under the streets of Aleppo and suitably lit with yellow and white lights that gave a mystical feel to the environment. Some shoddy attempt at carving images on parts of the walls didn't enhance the amenity appeal, nor did it create an aged sense to the place. Several small metal tables with a glass tabletop were placed around the room. Long red cushioned pads covered rock-cut pews offered comfortable seating. A few framed unbefitting photographs of Hollywood greats hung suspended on one wall; which looked so out of place and added no glamour whatsoever.

A short, skinny man, in his mid-40s, wore jeans and a T-shirt. His snake-like eyes were covered by round metal-rimmed glasses, he had arrived 25 minutes earlier than Najjar. His companion stood alert at the foot of the stairs. Alem Najjar imagined he was the skinny man's backup; but guessed if his own protection officer sneezed, he would get weak at the knees.

"I am here to offer the return of the icons," said the skinny thief. He made his way to a seat, lifted a holdall and placed it on one of the tables. He opened it. The two security men gave each other the eye until the gangster lost faith in his defiance. He coughed, giving a reasonable excuse for losing the stare game. The PPO gave a smile that filled his stern face. His opposing foe didn't have the nerve to play the stare game. Not with this man. He was out of his depth if he thought he could match him.

Curator Najjar sat near the skinny thief when he produced a small package from the Adidas holdall—removing several layers of hessian material from the icon. Handling it without care or attention made Curator Najjar squirm at his reckless disdain for an object so valuable. If the thief threw the art onto the table, Najjar, not a violent man by any means, wanted to hit him as hard as he could; his protection officer would do the rest.

He held it up with both hands.

"Money!" was the only word the skinny thief said. It made Najjar place the icon gently on the glass tabletop away from the hands of the scumbag, lift the briefcase, open, and remove two items. He was leaving the cash for the thief to count.

A 10X loupe, a small magnifying glass device used to see little details more closely, would allow the curator to do a visible check and a compact torch-like black light, a UV light source that can see any invisible ink marks.

Curator Najjar was astonished by what the thief produced from the holdall. It was a banknote counting machine.

Ripping the currency paper straps that held them neatly packed in bundles of fifty-pound notes—a simple paper strip that showed the cashier's stamp and initials; was crumpled then thrown to the floor. He placed one bunch of notes at a time into a machine that counted and scanned them to identify potentially counterfeit banknotes. He was kept busy, working on twenty stacks of 100-pound British banknotes.

At the same time, Curator Najjar got to work on the test, not a controlled experiment in a suitable environment, but one he could satisfy his boss with. The simple proof of finding the three initials. Najjar did simple checks first by checking the panel's nature, the overall style, and the subject. Christ, the redeemer, was the icon he held in his hands. He felt sweat appear under his armpits and his forehead. The noise of the counting machine flickered onwards—18 bales of paper notes to go.

The ornate loupe fitted his right eye, and by raising his cheek, the magnifier sat static as a bionic fixture. Looking at the artwork, he knew there was no way to prove authenticity by looking at it with a loupe or checking the wood. He needed a lab to do this. But he could use the black light and hopefully find three initials—15 bundles to go. The notes were zipping out of the machine, put into paper bags, and thrown haphazardly into the Adidas bag.

Keeping the loupe in his eye, he turned the icon to face the wood panel. The torch emitted a purple light. If the initials were there, they would certainly be noticeable. He looked carefully through the magnifying loupe, straining to focus over the wood panel and holding it closer and scanning every corner. And there, in one corner, text not more extensive than a grain of rice. It would possibly be the minor legible text globally if it were a computer font.

No writing or ink mark could be found without using a loupe. It was clear, in his focus, one of the stolen icons he held in his hands was a 14th century Andrei Rublev masterpiece. He felt humbled and proud to have recovered one of the artefacts, and this game, a game of intrigue had gone much better than he imagined.

Five more piles of Bank of England notes to go through the counting machine.

The skinny thief nodded his head to his watching partner in crime. And his reaction was for him to reach to his back pocket; making Najjar's PPO go for his gun. "No…no!" said the thief facing him, raising both hands showing open palms, in the air. "Mobile phone, mobile phone." Moving as in slow motion, turning his back to reveal to the agent, a Nokia 7200 flip-phone sticking out from his rear pocket. Soon he offered a mobile phone held between his forefinger and thumb. "Mobile phone only."

He repeated, "Mobile phone only."

The PPO relaxed. Only slightly. He was still preparing to shoot. He would like to shoot this prick; he thought—no waste to humanity whatsoever. The amateur made the call.

A buzz tone rang, heard as it was held in the air for all to hear. It rang three times: Brrr. Brrr. Brrr. Then the person at the other end of the call answered. The counting machine spat out the last few notes, gathered, bagged, then put them inside the holdall, as was the currency counting machine. He zipped the holdall closed.

As a voice emanated from the mobile phone, the henchman held it up to his ear and spoke.

"Yes, sir." Holding the phone high, with his other arm similarly raised, he stepped gingerly to his partner, staring at him. He perceived his eyes looked double the size as the leader glared through convex lenses that appeared to magnify his eyes.

The personal protection officer oversaw every movement.

The lame head was out of his depth professionally but carrying out orders to the letter. He looked scared, as did Alem Najjar. The bandit-in-charge pulled the phone from his partner's hand. He held it to his ear and stared directly at Alem Najjar; the curator felt anxious. Those staring eyes can see through walls.

"Hello." He listened further. "Aah, aah," was the open-mouthed response to whatever he agreed to.

He had a look that reminded Najjar of a character he once saw in a classic movie, when spending a brief holiday, during his student days, in London in the 1990s. A vintage 70s American adaption of a French story. A film about a penal colony on Devil's Island in French Guiana was an autobiographical novel written by Henri Charrière; the prisoner known as Papillon. Najjar could not get the look of Dustin Hoffman's character from his mind. Not just the sharp thick lenses that magnified the criminal's bulging eyes, nor the open razor cut hairstyle with uneven tuffs sticking outwards.

The noticeable balding patches appearing around his skull; even the black and messy grey stubble implanted over his face and the man's similar physical stature that sat before him. Two rows of rotten teeth emerged every time he talked. Like an ashtray full of spent brown cigarette stubs, lurking from his thin-lipped gaping mouth. All which added fuel to this carbon-copy image; of the convicted counterfeiter, Louis Dega. The likeness was incredibly accurate. Both sad little men. But highly intelligent, just the same.

Louis Dega's lookalike listened to the voice on the phone. A constant string of information flew purposefully at him. He would need to remember the details. The conversation lasted three minutes exactly.

A low-toned guttural male voice finished talking; then hung up.

The Dega lookalike spoke.

"We need to remove the guards." His finger pointing at both security men.

"Of course. Could you leave us, please?" Advising his PPO to head upstairs to await new instructions. "Just wait upstairs." His security officer allowed the empty-headed villain to lead the way. In a few seconds, they had gone, although the PPO was still ready to act if required.

"You must remember these words. I will not repeat them." The Louis Dega thief spoke as if he had rehearsed the words for a one-person play. He recalled and categorised the words to suit his oratory diction and pronunciation, Immersed with data. Insert the details into a shape his client would understand. Broken down and put into a sequence that the curator should remember without much memory. A very efficient employer. You can't tell a book by its cover is often used as a measuring tool, but in this case, it was wrong, this man was intelligent and articulate. He was no amateur. He would speak slowly, and usually, those that talk like this are perceived as slow-witted or overly pedantic, this man wasn't. This man had just heard a conversation, memorised it and now offered the same words to the man that needed to grasp the words he relayed.

"Listen and remember what I am about to say. All icons are buried under the temple of the storm god in the Citadel of Aleppo. Near the Souk Al-Mahamasin, you will source the Al-Zaki soap factory which as you will see, is easily recognised—located in the northern part of the basement a passageway that will lead directly to the citadel. Eventually, you will find three tunnels facing you. The one to the right is the option you must choose. Follow this road until you see an opening. There are several openings along this road, but you only enter the one with the Storm God's carving, Haddad; engraved on the wall.

"You will know which carving is Haddad, as he is holding a lightning bolt. Enter here. There are many steps down. The vault will be full of wooden cases. Look for the small box at one end. It is light, so move it to reveal another short shaft. Before you creep through this space, make sure you cover the entrance with the box. Do not leave any clues you are there. At the end of this move, you will find the Icons. Then, my friend, it is up to you to find a way out. Take a head torch but use moderately. Only when you feel no one is near—use it. It is dark down there, so don't be seen. Keep calm and collected. Because if you don't, you will more than likely lose your head, literally!"

A door at the far side of the room creaked. It moved, just a few inches, then it slammed closed. Both men shuddered with apprehension, to the fact that someone could be listening to their conversation. An intruder!

Najjar and the criminal both voiced their attention to the threat by screaming for assistance. The first bodyguard skipping down the stone steps was the Curator's PPO, already holding a Glock handgun in his right hand. The only place in the room where activity could cause interest was the plain wooden door at the far wall, to the door marked 'Alhamam'—Toilets.

Cautiously, he pushed the door open: The entrance to action, in police or military terms, is called the 'Fatal Funnel' for a good reason. It's the channel by which we need to pass but is also the likely focal point of any potential challenger lying in wait. Walking in watchfully; looking for any movement, he saw two doors facing each other. One on the left saying 'Rijali', the other 'Nisa': Men and Women. The main door closed behind him.

The other thief stood and guarded the stairwell. He was scared. His fear showed that he was not up for this job or any situation that involved violence. He improvised and played the part of a gangster, a very scared gangster.

The door into the men's room was forced open, and it flew wide and made a knocking noise as it suddenly hit a floor stopper, but wide enough for the agent to hold his foot against it, to prevent it closing. The room was small and lit with a fluorescent bulb. Two cubicles facing him were empty, as were the four vacant urinals to his left. Inside, he proceeded slowly, skilled and prepared to shoot. Inside the lavatory, he saw a row of sinks with a cracked mirror on the wall above them. This room was empty.

Single, sure steps took him to the side of the door of the women's restroom. A massive flat-foot kick took the wooden entrance off its hinges as it fell hard to the floor and slid several feet across the white floor tiles. All cubicles and sink area was clear of people. Not a soul here.

There was one door left to check at the end of the corridor.

He needed to keep his tactics as simple as possible, especially in a stressful environment; his decisions were his to take.

His hand grabbed hold of the handle, twisted it a complete turn and opened it ever so slightly, just enough to see outside—the Glock just under his view, pointing in the same direction as his one-eyed stare. Some 20ft up the narrow lane stood a small girl, possibly around five or six years of age. She faced the man. The agent holstered his gun into his chest holder and opened the door fully. He returned the stare to the girl when an older woman materialised next to the girl, the girl's grandmother, the agent presumed.

"Raca, Raca, come here." The frail voice spoke as loud as her weak vocal cords allowed. "Come, come!" she added and knelt as low as her body permitted. Holding both arms outstretched, the girl turned and ran to her. They left soon after.

Heaving the door shut, the guard slid the rusty bolt closed, and locked down the only exterior ingress to the cellar. *Why was this leaky access point not checked by the gang of thugs*? he thought.

He made his way back to the meeting place, only to stop and pick a small child's book he found lying on the floor of the corridor which he had missed earlier. It must be the girls book.

The square book had a colour drawing of a beautiful ginger tomcat, with his tail held high in the air, strolling soft-footed along Aleppo Citadel's entrance. He hadn't seen this book before, not that he remembered.

He didn't have children.

The title was: 'Mayathiranaan, Alqat almufadel lieasifat allh'. (Mithra, the favourite cat of the storm God.) Once back into the room, all faces promoted an anxious state. "Where were you? Did you find anyone?"

The PPO answered assuredly.

"A small girl used the back door to use the toilet." Walking to the curator and handing him the book. Najjar looked bewildered as he stared at the book's front cover, then further confused, and puzzled; when he read the book title. He turned the book to look at the back cover. It showed another drawing of the same ginger tomcat, wearing a gold crown.

"It is safe now." The security guard added.

Curator Najjar asked if there was any more business. The short, bespectacled man shook his head to respond no. He picked up the holdall and left without speaking with his equally repugnant partner. Climbing the stone stairs at pace, they left the building. The PPO had informed other agents of this move.

"We may be compromised. There is a breach of security." The recognised voice of the vehicle guard spoke calmly. But urgency appeared in his tone. Other agents recognised this and acted swiftly.

“Ok, let’s get the client in the floating box. I need agents to meet at the extract point now,” he spoke as he shuffled Alem Najjar in the direction of the main entrance of the eatery.

The curator looked scared and felt vulnerable.

Curator Najjar had watched western movies. And any time he heard the term ‘Floating box’, it meant only one thing; it’s a method of constant surveillance, where a team of agents establish a containment box around the target wherever he goes. Protect at all costs; until they reach the safety of the super-secure convoy.

A team of six agents whirled around him, flawlessly ushering their asset, herding him to the safety of the Maserati Quattroporte. Analysing every face they passed, staring at windows of surrounding buildings, watching for an assassin with a sniper rifle—or a moving shadow in an alleyway.

They soon reached the safety of the vehicles.

Chapter 17
1 Hour After the Bomb Explosion

1 hour after the blast. All that remained of Al-Hatab Square was debris. The Jdaye Hotel was gone, as were all other buildings and life.

Farid came around, he had been unconscious. The noises he heard were muffled, distant and unrecognisable. A whooshing noise was the only emitted sound he heard, among the din of white noise. Continuous high-pitched whistling filled his ear canals. Indeed, he knew his eardrums were perforated. He had ruptured an eardrum when he was a child. Due to a middle-ear infection, that resulted in the accumulation of fluids in the middle ear. Pressure from these fluids caused his eardrum to rupture. It took many weeks to heal.

As he twisted his body in the confined space, he realized both legs were pinned under rubble. His feet and toes moved without pain. And the pulsating headache he felt was as if his head was stuck in a vice.

With some effort, Farid managed to pull with his right arm from his side up to his face.

Bill, back in Edinburgh, had now joined Farid's real-life reality once more. He could feel the relentless heat, and sense the suffocating smoke, and could see the flames a few feet away; and felt the same pain as his host. This dream was authentic. Living in another man's mind; seeing what he sees; feeling his emotions and being part of his journey was still hard to define or accept. This odd reverie kept rolling further and taking Bill on a ride where he knew no end. Or where he was likely to go. Aleppo was his dream voyage, but was it the final destination?

"Why are we connected?" Farid struggled to offer any words. Bill, deep in his conscience, remained silent. This sleep hallucination was getting weirder by the minute.

"I know all about you, Bill," Farid said aloud.

"I am as lost as you in all of this. I sleep, then I dream, then I awake to this weird reality. I am just an ordinary man like you, Farid," Bill spoke to Farid through his sleep connection.

Farid responded, "I thought you could tell me because I have no answer. I can hear your voice, but you cannot read or hear my thoughts. That is why I need to communicate verbally."

"You see me when you dream? And know my past?" said Bill.

"Only once! It was if I viewed a synopsis of your life. I know so much about you, but I feel that is all I will ever receive of your life. It was an offering, a full picture for me to acquaint myself with the person I was sharing my life with.

"It is the unique link we now have that will define our futures. Since the blast, I have drifted in and out of consciousness several times. It was just after the explosion that I got a message. That's why I thought I had died. But as strange and weird as this sounds; my late father appeared in my sub-conscience. And he died in 2008. You will understand why I thought I had passed over. Seeing my deceased father looking to offer me hope is a difficult one for me to accept. He wasn't a doting father in life, nor was he loving or caring. But here he was, in death, giving me advice and telling me how a Scotsman, while sleeping, would help and assist with my future. I'm sure I laughed at this point."

"Whether it is down to brain damage injury or not, only when I am out of here, and in hospital, will I know what the hell had happened. But till then, I will let you know about the crazy situation we find ourselves.

"My father told me that you are a living being, and would be an active presence, a full dynamic force within my spirituality. Although, something that I don't understand is, that like you Bill, I am also a long-serving atheist. I can feel your scepticism in my veins flowing through me—a fully signed up member of the non-believers' club. You are, as you say in the UK, a doubting Thomas? And you, unlike me, can shout from the rooftops to vent your anger against all things religious.

"I cannot promote or speak out on my birth religion's abandonment with all my inner beliefs. Atheists here in Syria will suffer persecution if facts of their lost faith are made public. There is a reported statistic that many activists approve of the death penalty for those non-believers. My journey is a rocky path to take. Especially now. This country is going to war with its self. And I will be easy picking," Farid added.

"I could see my father as clear as day. As if he was standing among the whiteness of a fluffy cloud. And I was standing before him."

"With the obstinate nature my father had in life, how could I believe a word he had to say? But I listened to his offering. There he was, my stubborn father, appearing to me in my mind proposing me to help with something supernatural. A paranormal vision of my dead father, telling me that a sleeping Scotsman would see life through my eyes, and together, we will save a life, or possibly more, and benefit the lives of many others. It is peculiar in its purest form. So my father talked, and I listened. I had no choice.

"He told me to trust you. I was to join forces with you to save lives. Which, as a fireman, I already spent my working days preventing the loss of life. It is my job. Though I still don't understand how you can assist me in saving lives. If I am here, in Syria, and you are in Scotland, I find this difficult to believe or find a plausible understanding of how this teamwork will work. At not one time did my father mention the 'G' word or mention religion until his last words. He said: Farid, never leave a void that is hard to fill, and a legacy that is hard to match. As he walked further into the cloud, he turned and said Insha'Allah."

Farid's weak voice tapered off. A lack of strength forcing him to stop talking, he was exhausted and in pain; he coughed blood, and his head dropped an inch to hit the dust and rubble. In no time, he was unconscious.

Bill woke as if he had awakened from a night terror. A horror-movie nightmare, believing linked to the recent passing of his wife, Laura. Full of fear and in a state of panic, he tried to remember the terrifying sleep visions, but these meagre notions of remembrances, slowly dissipated; the more he tried to recall the event. Something about being trapped under rubble.

He sat up. He leaned against the headboard of the six-foot super-king bed. The sheets and duvet were wet with his sweat; the bedsheets crumpled as if he fought a long battle with them. The pillow his wet head lay on, now stuck behind his back, reminded him of a Lilo swim lounger floating in a swimming pool. The bed was cold and uncomfortable to lie on, or sleep in; or sit upon. He still wore yesterday's clothes. He did not remember going to bed.

Like a sledgehammer, forcibly crashing against his skull, it soon became apparent he had drunk too much whisky the previous night. A throbbing, pulsating, alcohol-induced headache materialised. Followed by the uncontrollable fluctuation of double-vision, an overpowering nauseous feeling erupted into his frail body. Alcoholic poisoning being the reason. His balance would be wayward if he stood, the bedroom swirled wildly. Like the same image repeatedly flickering, over and over; that made him flop back down onto the soaking wet bed. He didn't feel the dampness. He was sound asleep when his head hit the duvet.

Footsteps. Nearby footsteps. Soft little steps walked carefully over loose and dangerous debris. The noise of concrete pressing against metal, plastic tables parts shifted by a kicked foot, closer, getting closer.

Farid Aboud was awake, and Bill soon joined the realism. He wasn't drunk in this lifecycle. He was alert as his host.

But, in tandem, they were both aware to the fact that someone walked close to where Farid lay trapped. Can Farid shout for help? Bill wondered.

His right hand was still free.

He moved his arm to the blockage, all grey and dust-covered wreckage, a foot or so from where his head lay and pushed at the jam with the only strength he had. And that was limited.

A portion of remains fell quickly. Dropped and allowed sunlight to invade this contained privacy, although it was more than welcome. Too much relief, fresh air followed. A full breath of air, containing minuscule dust particles, flew into accepting lungs and added strength to an already chaotic, weakened body—a glimmer of hope they both thought.

He dug more, pushed debris away from space before him. There were more faint footsteps. Someone was close.

"Help! Help!" his voice managed to project words to call for help. His lungs were full of fresh oxygen and disturbed dust particles.

Both men listened together. The sound of movement could be heard, and it was getting closer. It was then when a little girl knelt and shoved her dirty face into the opening.

"Hello, I am Farid, can you help me please?" His eyes were black, his face covered in hardened dust. Unrecognisable as himself if he could only see his messy image. He asked another question, "What is your name?"

In a cute little girl voice, she answered, "My name is Raca. Raca Sleiman and I like cats, and you can call me Sana if you want. It's my other name."

"I like cats too…Is there anyone with you that can help me…someone to get me out of here? I'm stuck and can't move." The only words that came to mind.

This girl was potentially the only hope he had of surviving this ordeal. He needed her to understand.

"Do you have a cat?" the girl asked, smiling as she conveyed her question. Her face was filthy. But she looked healthy otherwise.

"I have two cats. Brothers, called Fairuz and Ruwa. Sana, I need to get home and feed them. They will be hungry." He was polite, but the pain was the main cause of his anxiety.

"Would you be able to get someone to help me escape? I need to feed Fairuz and Ruwa?" he pleaded to a scared young girl.

Her face disappeared. Farid begged for her to stay or hoped she would seek assistance. "Get help. Please!" he was losing hope. "Please!" his faint voice offered one more word.

Just then, two small brown lace-up boots, taking up much of the space he regarded as his only escape route, appeared; when a little hand reached down into his grave and dropped a wooden cross, held on a leather strap; well in reach of his right hand.

"It's for you, Farid. I will go and get help," said the cute little voice. Farid and Bill were both relieved. Grateful to Raca. But what good will a religious cross be to an atheist, or two?

Chapter 18
The Edinburgh Apartment
The Present Day

An irritating alarm sounded loud. The iPhone ringtone spat out ting; ting; ting; ting, like four bells hit in sequence, then fading to a soft noise; then it starts again. With a loop of four relentless tings! An unyielding sound, the annoying invention of some audible crazed creator. Its annoying tone could awaken the dead. Bill sat up in his bed. Lost and confused, he hoped to gain some form of alertness. His focus held on the audible ringtone. As Bill recalled, the ringtone, the Moantone, a name Laura gave the unsuitable wake-up call. It was called the RADAR tone, he reluctantly remembered. The sound ran shivers down his spine.

Once he gathered his thoughts, he slipped off the bed, and his feet hit the plush deep-woollen carpet, and strolled unhurriedly to his phone; it was still flashing a low-level light and vibrating erratically, he stared at the screen through intoxicated eyes. The problem was solved by pressing the red button.

New, fresh thoughts brought hot coffee and food to mind. "Some food sounds good," Bill said aloud. He was hungry, and he also knew that eating a healthy, nutritious breakfast, and rehydrating were vital components, especially being hungover, and Bill fell into this category.

He took a few steps from his bedroom and into the large living room, kitchen combination. He had a terrible sleep. Tossing and turning, dream after dream, nightmare after nightmare, all disturbing lost memories. But something was apparent. And that was a sleeping terror. Something weird happened in his nightmare, but all knowledge of the events have long disappeared.

The cold-water tap was fully turned on, and it poured gushes of freshwater before Bill found a clean cup or glass to fill; eager to hydrate his body after losing so much perspiration fluid while sleeping. Having read somewhere that approximately two to four litres of water should be consumed per hour.

His bed held way over this amount; the sheets were soaked wet with his sweat. An opened twelve-inch pizza box sat on the worktop next to him and had defrosted two uneaten toasties, still sat in the panini grill showing dripped cheese, now a substantial mess stuck to the work surface. An empty bottle of whisky and an open bag of melted ice lay lifeless in the sink and another on a bedside table. There was no sober meaning to remember any of last evenings capers. Still, behind the strangeness, it was pass marks to remember turning off the electricity supply to all appliances. Thankfully, he did—he had no memory of doing any of this.

Pulling one of the top chrome handles protruding from the 4-door silver-coloured, Metallic Smeg fridge, a black brogue shoe sat on a glass shelf. Sitting among items such as cheese, a punnet of strawberries, oatmeal milk, margarine, an unopened solid pack of Italian corn polenta, different fruit yoghurts, a full bottle of Moet and Chandon and a black-tie wrapped tightly around a bottle of slimline tonic water. Artistic efforts of a drunk man! An empty green bottle of wine caught his toes as it spun in circles and moved a few feet across the wooden floor. It hurt, and it made Bill lift his foot to rub it. He swore.

After ripping the bedsheets from the bed, packing all the bed covers into a liftable bale, Bill took them to the utility room and tossed them on the floor. A shower, a shave, clean clothes, a coffee and a brisk walk was the order for today.

Bill found solace in a park he knew well. Walking energetically, he made good time covering the distance in fifty minutes. But this hard-fought inebriated journey, only took him to the edge of Corstorphine Hill, a woodland walk, that had many steep ascents, and descents with beautiful views to boot. A youthful favourite. A healthy mid-morning saunter returned many lost reminiscences that had lain dormant in his childhood memories.

A further hour of walking, he reached Cramond Beach; a beach he remembers well from his youth. A place he always loved. He took a seat on the stone harbour wall, his legs dangling childlike, aiming at the mud banks and the rocks below, that shadowed the incoming tide on either side of the inlet. Keenly watching the water splash against moored keelboats, and a few fancy-coloured motorboats with unusual names waited on the water flow to rise high. A wayfarer boat had a Scottish flag stuck on either side of the hull, with the boat name: 'Sana Miracle' in blue, self-adhesive boat vinyl; an inch or two below the flag. The owner waved at Bill, and he returned the favour.

Bill reminisced as he scanned the surrounding landscape with white-washed three-storey buildings behind him. All houses stand proud along the pier, indicating a time gone by and a time Bill seriously missed. He saw Cramond Island, sitting around 1.6km out to sea, looking east. At low tide, it was reachable by a causeway. The secure crossing is best taken two hours on either side of the low tide.

Bill had been marooned there twice with his uncle Bill.

The eager sailor on the Sana Miracle was heading out to sea, and he acknowledged Bill by strangely saluting him as the boat headed out into the Forth estuary. Countless gulls searching for a titbit gave Bill's looks of disappointment when the white object taken from his pocket was a handkerchief, not an available snack. He was glad he didn't have a sandwich in his hand or a bag of salt and vinegar-soaked chips like Laura had when the aggressive birds attacked. Attacking gulls have applied this pressure to him many times before.

Laura was struck on the forehead by a greedy seagull that swooped and snatched her cheese and pickle sandwich. Thrust from her hand, in seconds, then taken to the air; with other screaming birds chasing down the reluctant thief, hoping to fight for a share of the spoils; somewhere on the water.

But that was four weeks ago.

Laura had visited Cramond for the first time then. She saw Bill's beach, his Dad's local pub: The Cramond Inn; his dad and Uncle Bill's 'home from home'—when Uncle Bill came for a holiday. Laura loved the old schoolhouse. She would like to have purchased it instead of the city centre apartment. But it wasn't for sale. Bill said a mountain of happy memories still lay hidden there, seeped deep into the late 19th century's brickwork, a house that James Robb designed.

One year, when young Bill was spending his summer holidays with his uncle Bill and Auntie Beth, in Malta; his parents had packed up and sold his favourite house to move to a large Georgian townhouse in Edinburgh's New Town. The move was mainly for business reasons, rather than an emotional change. Nearer to their place of work; the Edinburgh courts.

It took over a month for young Bill to come to terms with his new life in Edinburgh.

His love of the village way-of-life had been thwarted by a new, accessible city doorstep. Everything a young boy wished for: record shops, cinemas, sports venues, swimming pools, theatres, and museums; all close by, a walking distance, a bus stop or two away, and he could be in neverland; without leaving Edinburgh. He grew to like city life.

But life being life, the old schoolhouse was never far from his thoughts, just a look at it made his heart flutter.

He stopped to glance at it with Laura a few weeks before her death. He was proud to show his boyhood haunts in Cramond. Even selfies snapped at the numerous spots Bill had a strong affiliation. They were together smiling with the old schoolhouse photobombing behind them. On the first attempt to take a selfie at the house, Laura stuck her tongue out. Bill hasn't the heart, or the need, to look at the pictures on his mobile phone. Maybe someday he will have the courage to see the photographs and not feel heartbroken. But that is so far away from where he is at present.

A sumptuous, and creamy mac n cheese, with a forced pint of lager, was his tasty lunch at the Cramond Inn; that gave ample justice to his appetite. He felt so much better. Being in the Inn again flooded more memories his way, he enjoyed the peace until several ramblers walked in discussing the ancient Roman fort that is situated in the village.

As Bill walked uphill away from the beach, he neared the whitewashed harl covered building, located on Cramond Glebe road. The old schoolhouse of his childhood. Reminiscing of; family parties, playing with his pet cats on the expansive manicured lawn, whacking the winning run at junior cricket with his friends; and Uncle Bill playing umpire. His grandfather Peter could keep a soccer ball up in the air using both feet and his grey-haired head; without it touching the ground (keepie uppie, as it's known in Scotland), he could reach 100 touches and more if he needed.

In his youth, his grandfather had played for his local club in Dunfermline and had trials for his boyhood team, Glasgow Rangers. But, being from a scholarly family, his sporting endeavours would always remain a love, rather than seeking success in a sporting profession. Of course, his education paid off big time, at his peak, he became one of Scotland's top post-war architects. He was designing some of the most famous buildings in Scotland. Power stations, university annexes, theatres, museums, and private builds. Awards came fast and furious for this footballing architect.

Bill would often ask his grandfather if he could design a football stadium for Dunfermline FC or Rangers FC. And he did. One Christmas, as a special treat, Bill opened a present of two picture frames covered in gold wrapping paper.

One was a unique designed stadium for Dunfermline, and the other futuristic project for his favourites, Glasgow Rangers. The paintings now hang above his bed in Valletta.

To complete the recollection of his childhood, the same journey he had taken only a few weeks ago with Laura, this one was tough to embrace. It was heart-breaking. He felt so alone. The Cramond Kirk gate was open, and he decided to look around the graveyard; it sat opposite the old schoolhouse, his parent's first house. Walking among the graves, names of long-forgotten people that time had absorbed and wrapped into the shawls of eternity. He took a seat at a wooden bench he discovered on the opposite side of the graveyard. Resting and stretching his legs out over the pathway, he felt content. It was so peaceful and quiet here. He observed many olden headstones carved with skulls and crossbones and others enhanced with angels and cherubs.

There was table and slab stones covering and securing a number of burial plots from unscrupulous grave robbers of times past. Gravestones with weathered round top with round shoulders, half-round and oval, gothic and sandstone memorials, littered the ancient village graveyard, but in their day; these tombstone types were all the rage in Scotland. Also, the introduction of Cast-iron grave markers added another enhancement to decorative art. His mind was wandering into a relaxed state. Peaceful and comfortable within himself.

Something soft brushed under his legs, which wakened him from his daydream. "Hello, what's your name?" he said to the ginger tomcat rubbing his pointed nose, his forehead and his cheeks over Bill's leg; as a welcome sign of affection. Bill thought about the question he had asked. He always inquired using the same problem to every strange cat or friendly dog he met; and not for one moment did he expect any animal to answer. The ever so friendly cat jumped and joined Bill on the bench, looking at the gravestones as Bill had done. He purred loudly.

Bill stroked the cat's head and tickled under his presented chin. He enjoyed that. But as friendships go, this one was brief. A piece of disregarded litter, caught in a blast of a cold breeze, caught his eye, and he leapt from the bench at pace, like a lion pouncing on its prey; he chased the wrapper in and around several headstones. "Pleasure knowing you!" Bill offered to the uninterested tomcat. The cat had other things on his mind now.

A buzzing sound. Or maybe a vibration. Whatever intrusion caught Bill's attention; his phone had received a text message. Opening the text app, he instantly saw Emad's name at the top of a list of more contacts, and old posts that he had deliberately didn't respond to. A facial image of Emad appeared in a small circle to the left of the message.

He opened it and read.

'Bill, my God! my God! I cannot feel sadder than I am now. My dearest, Laura. How on earth could something like this ever happen to a person as beautiful as a living angel? My heart breaks for you, my friend. If you had called, I would have come to your side. It's just so terrible. I honestly feel distraught at your loss.

'It was just today that Rev Hughes, I believe Laura's friend and retired religious man here in Malta, paid a visit to my office to tell us the untimely news. I tried calling you several times, but I understand how you must be. If you feel up to a meal and a drink, and a chat with an old friend, I am here for you. Come home to Malta. Emad xx'

There was a call from Rev. Hughes and Emad and several callers that withheld their numbers.

The retired vicar friend of Laura, who lives in Valletta. Bill never met the minister. It wasn't his subject. Religion was taboo for him.

He guessed Reverend Douglas McAuley had contacted him.

Laura had befriended both, so the connection was not surprising.

The message from Emad did penetrate his thoughts. Burdened with a payload of bereavement, capturing the very essence of his feelings, Bill knew that staying in Edinburgh at this time was not the best way forward. A change of scenery might be the action required. Shift his thoughts to the future. Step one turn off the auto-pilot, step two jump out from the cockpit, and change the current routine; this might change his life. He must book a flight.

Departing the following day at 7.30 am. The trip would take nearly four hours. Leaving a small note for his cleaner to wash the bed linen he had left strewn on the utility room floor and a letter of apology.

Chapter 19
The Flight to Malta

The flight left on time. An iced drink of gin and tonic was the choice of alcohol when the drinks trolley arrived. The laptop was open, and speedy fingers tapped continuously with only a few intermittent stops, and glaring errors deleted. Small, detailed emails sent to David Carson at Arran Dandelion; The Minister for his invaluable efforts helping with Laura's funeral arrangements, the Rev. Douglas McAuley; his Maltese solicitor, Andrew Attard; an apology for not taking his calls, and a thank you for kind-words-of-comfort, to Emad. And asking Emad for contact details for Rev. Archibald Hughes and his home address in Valletta. Culminating with a full-page letter, explaining why he hadn't phoned or made any attempt to contact Laura's cousin Jane Smith, at the Moulin Rouge wine shop.

He wrote a short letter but deleted it. On second thoughts, a personal phone call and a guaranteed visit to Pitlochry on his return would be the best approach. He felt ashamed at how his bereavement culminated to shunning dear friends and family from information on Laura's death. He realised, unlike Laura, he was blind to passionate feelings to close friends; or even strangers. His guilt allowed proof of this.

A text, sent as a reply to an earlier message received at the bar at Edinburgh airport, went to Monica Fenech, his housekeeper in Valletta. "The flight is on time. And in advance of my arrival. I appreciate the pizza in the fridge and the six bottles of Hopleaf. Your efforts are always appreciated. I'll call you tomorrow. Give Luke and the kids my best regards, Bill."

The text message was sent!

The rubber tyres made a braking noise as the jet touched down ten minutes early. From his window seat, Bill could see the spoilers on the wings deploy to reduce lift and transfer the aircraft's weight to its wheels, where the brakes are applied.

As the plane shuddered after touchdown, the reverse thrust began, as it slowed the aircraft fast. And within a few seconds more; the craft was taxiing along the apron to the terminal. An authoritative voice filled the cabin:

"Ladies and Gentlemen, welcome to Malta's Luqa International Airport. Local time is 23:20, and luckily, we landed ten minutes ahead of schedule. The temperature outside is an agreeable 14 degrees and not much cloud, so a pleasant end to the day. For your safety and comfort, please remain seated with your seat belt fastened until the Captain turns off the Fasten Seat Belt sign. This indicates that we have parked at the gate and that it is safe for you to move.

"Please check around your seat for any personal belongings you may have brought on board with you and please use caution when opening the overhead bins, as heavy articles may have shifted around during the flight." Bill remembered his first-ever flight to Malta, wearing the Biggles helmet and goggles, and receiving a set of wings from the Captain, but this was many years ago.

The luggage carousel started as he arrived at the luggage hall. The conveyor-belt spun out the baggage quicker than ever. Golf clubs, a wheelchair, a bicycle, baby strollers, many-coloured cases, bags, and holdalls, and two sets of skis? 'In Malta?' Bill asked himself. That thought soon turned to understand the possibility of returning residents who had spent time, in either Glenshee or Cairngorm; although Bill knew there were other fantastic ski opportunities in Scotland. He didn't ski.

His luggage was the second one on the conveyor. He has never been so lucky waiting for luggage. The sign near the suitcase merry-go-round gave information for two recently arrived flights sharing this point of extract.

Rome 23:00 landed
Edinberg 23:20 landed

Bill always smiled at the spelling the Maltese gave Edinburgh; 'Edinberg'. But, in a similar vein, Edinburgh, and other UK airports, used the name 'Valletta'. When it should be the Maltese spelling, 'Il-Belt'.

Pulling the wheeled leather trolley case through 'Nothing to Declare' at customs, Bill entered arrivals. A group of tour operators stood out from the crowd, wearing bright red uniforms.

Police officers watched from a distance. Private airport transfer drivers all dressed to kill. Looking like professional hitmen, held company signs with clients names written in black felt pen ink. The first one he laid eyes on was for 'Bill McKenzie.'

"Welcome home, Mr McKenzie. Let me take your case." The polite and professional chauffeur intimated. Bill guessed Emad had intervened by arranging this personal touch by sending a private transfer. He knew too well that the yacht business always used 'shuttle direct'. Of course, Emad was behind this. Bill was happy to take a taxi, but this was a subtle touch of politeness from a dear friend and he accepted the gesture with gratitude.

The drive was short; just fifteen minutes. Bill gave a sizable tip to the driver, and a broad sneer appeared on a slightly rugged face.

The door unlocked, his case pulled sluggishly behind him, the car disappearing in the distance, he entered, closed, and locked the heavy wooden door behind him. The 36 steps up felt good. He thought of Laura, his uncle William, and Aunt Beth. Memories all lost to time—memories of better days lay ahead he hoped.

The apartment was spotless. Monica had made sure everything was in place and as Bill would want it, and even more. There were fresh flowers in vases he had never seen before. A smell of a clean honeysuckle fragrance mixed with the flower scent, that added purity to the atmosphere. He felt at home. He missed Laura. Forget about pizza and beer.

Sleep was required.

Chapter 20
Archbishop Street, Valletta

Bill wakened to the sound of people chatting on the street below. It was Friday morning, and the time was 7:30 am.

Lying in an empty bed still strong with Laura's scent, and atop of her bedside cabinet was Langstroth's Hive and the Honeybee book sitting with a bookmark jutting out near the end of the classic beekeeping manual. Laura had told Bill that the book was the first constructive beekeepers manual. It managed to cover matters such as; hive construction, swarming, honey gathering plus many more subjects.

"It is as relevant today as it was 150 years ago!" Laura enthused. Laura was incredibly proud of how the honey business had grown. Reading as much of the history of beekeeping as she could get her hands on. Although Laura had read the book before, this time it revealed so much more.

But she would never finish it this time or any other time.

Bill picked up the book, removed the mark, and would, over time in Malta, promise himself to read it, from the first page to the last. The bookmark depicted a small boy wearing a flying helmet and goggles. That image brought tears to his eyes. He didn't know Laura had this. He laid the book on his bedside table.

After a long shower and a breakfast of two coffees, he picked up his laptop and rested comfortably on the brown leather sofa. He had several emails in the inbox.

One from David Carson at Arran Dandelion; his Maltese solicitor, Andrew Attard; And Emad. Which he opened and studied. He opened the email from Emad first.

"Hi, Bill, I hope you had a good flight. Likewise, I hope you liked the personal touch with the private hire? OK, the church is on South Street, about a

6-minute walk from your apartment. I can't believe in all your time in Valletta, you didn't have a clue where the church is?

"Forgive me, I took a small liberty and phoned him yesterday; he left his card at the office. And as your email stated, you are keen to meet this man; then I would advise you to head over to Caffe Cordina on Republic Street. He attends the café every Friday between 9–10:00 am. If you haven't eaten already, maybe you can, as you would say, kill two birds with one stone. I have already sent you a text with his mobile number and full contact details. Let me know if you need anything. Catch up soon. Emad."

Bill phoned the minister and agreed to meet for breakfast.

Hopping down the stairs of the apartment building, he felt a flow of dynamic energy surge through his veins. He felt good after a decent night's sleep. He did not have an outlandish dreamy link up with the stranger in Aleppo, he wouldn't know who the stranger is if he appeared before him. There was no recall. As with all his dreams, when he leaves the inter-connected realism, he forgets. It was just Bill, sleeping and dreaming as he used to do.

It was a pleasant morning. Bill loved Valletta. The leisurely walk gave him heartfelt images of strolls he took with Laura. But he never set foot in Caffe Cordina before. This will be the first-ever visit. But Laura, every Friday morning, went for a meeting with the church minister. Now he knew where they met.

The Caffe Cordina is a well-established, valuable and respected company with a long and prestigious history. An awning was already sticking out from the building in preparation of a sunny day.

Bill stepped into the air-conditioned restaurant and his face showed amazement; with his jaw dropping with the utter surprise of the scale and beauty of the place. In the Knights of St John, the Casa del Commun Tesoro; or the Treasury of the Order; was located here. Bill was amazed at the exquisiteness of the Caffe. The high-vaulted ceiling covered in paintings by Maltese artist Giuseppe Cali; gave the place a cathedral look or a chapel in the Apostolic Palace; or an opulent royal great hall. Bill was in awe at the sight of grandiose artworks the ceiling offered when the waiter disturbed his concentration.

"Good morning, sir, how can I help you this morning?" the articulate waiter said.

"I'm meeting a friend for breakfast. A retired minister called Archibald Hughes. Do you know him?" Bill inquired.

“Yes sir. The reverend Hughes always arrives just before 9:55 am. Please, let me show you to your table.”

The table sat under a winding stairwell. It resembled a banana sliced long-ways, connected to the 1st floor, bent underneath at a curved angle; and implanted into the marble floor tiles. Sitting underneath the yellow staircase, it reminded Bill of an aqua park slide.

The round marble table had two bistro seats. Bill pulled up a chair, and the waiter offered him a breakfast menu.

“Would you like tea or coffee while you wait, sir?” The waiter wore black trousers, paired with a black waistcoat, complimented with a black bowtie.

The bespectacled middle-aged man wiped the already spotless table.

“Coffee would be perfect, thank you.”

“You are welcome.”

The waiter left Bill to admire more of the café’s decorations.

The walls were panelled, and elongated mirrors were hung in portrait style to lighten the room with reflections from vintage wall lights and a central ceiling glow. He was impressed. He knew that this was the Caffe Laura spent lazy mornings having coffee with friends. Now he understood when she said she just loved Maltese Pastizzse and Qassata at Cordina’s.

“Bill!” a well-spoken voice said. “I’m Reverend Hughes. But please call me Archie.”

He laid the menu back on the table and stood to greet his fellow breakfast consumer.

“And me you, Archie. It’s nice to meet you.”

“Please take your seat,” the retired minister said politely.

They both made themselves comfortable. The Minister placed a briefcase next to his seat.

“Bill, I would like to offer my sincere condolences and I’m incredibly sorry to hear of your loss. Laura’s strength has left an indelible print on my life, and I’m sure others who knew her have similar feelings?

Laura was a special person. Our loss is heaven’s gain. Please accept my deepest sympathies at this sad time.”

The minister was preaching to a non-believer and called it quits before Bill got up and left. But he didn’t. He thanked the minister for his kind words. And added, “Laura was the churchgoer…I didn’t get into the religion thing.”

"I understand. I have family members that don't have a religious conviction. So you are not alone."

The waiter placed a coffee pot and cup and saucer on the table.

"Have your ordered, Bill?" Rev Hughes asked.

"Just coffee," Bill replied.

"In that case, I'll have my usual, Thomas, thank you."

The waiter turned his stared attentions to Bill and he ordered a cheese and mushroom omelette with white toast.

The conversation covered mostly Bill's loss. Rev. Hughes gave information explaining that Laura was an essential member of the church in Malta; and had been since 2001. The work she undertook on behalf of the church was without question, invaluable. Her fundraising was exemplary, as Bill understood. One part of Laura's church past that Bill never knew was that she worked close to one mission. Her contact with The Presbyterian Church in Aleppo.

The waiter returned with the desirable food.

"Your cheese and mushroom omelette; with white toast, Sir. And your usual, Minister. And of course; a pot of Earl Grey." He said, as he moved the items around the table like a chess player making room to find space to place the order.

The conversation touched many subjects, the retired minister was pleasant, courteous and likeable. Bill enjoyed his company. He understood why Laura was fond of this retired preacher.

Once the table was clear of empty plates and dishes and only cups and pots of beverages stayed in place. Bill raised a question he wanted answering.

"Can I ask you why you phoned me?"

The elderly vicar wiped his mouth with a paper napkin.

"I called you at home several times, but you didn't reply. Then I remembered Laura gave me your mobile number some time back, so I tried calling that number, but you still didn't respond. Later, when I received the tragic news of Laura's death from my dear friend in Edinburgh, Rev McAuley, I had to speak to you."

He looked forlorn as he recalled the news of Laura's death.

Bill knew the missed unknown calls on his mobile must have also been from Archie.

"I have prayed, the Valletta congregation prayed. Unforeseen death means that the start of the grief voyage is bright. You may feel in limbo during this time.

Maybe your life is put 'on hold', and you may feel as if you are working through everyday life motions."

Over his years of service, the pastor had preached faithfully to willing Christian believers and met many unconvertible atheists over his forty years of ministry. He knew he could not preach any words of wisdom to Bill.

He has said enough—time to call this service to a halt.

"Sorry, I got caught in the act of familiarity, Bill."

"Not so, minister. I understand Laura would agree with you 100%. Being pleasant and understanding means a lot. It's your job."

The minister picked up the briefcase that had waited by his side like a loveable dog.

"Did you know of Laura's connection with the church in Aleppo?"

Bill thought before answering the question.

The minister removed a large brown folder from the briefcase and placed it on the table. The case was returned to the floor. "No, Laura kept her religious relationships to herself. I knew she did some charitable work, most of which I helped with, but I didn't know she was involved in church related charities; that I didn't know about."

The minister shared more information.

"In our church, we have 'Missions' and Laura took one mission to heart. Toward the end of 2009, she contacted the church and befriended a young girl."

Handing the file to Bill. He removed the pile of paper and took an interest in the first page.

The page he looked at showed a photograph of a young girl.

"Laura had been in communication with the church in Aleppo over the possibility of adoption. I guess you never knew this?"

"No, no; however, we did discuss adopting.

"Yes, Laura told me," said the minister.

Bill was about to explain Laura's infertility. And the fact she wanted to adopt. "We spoke regularly about adoption, particularly in finding a child from a war-torn country. Laura felt these children experienced the full horror of war, and they deserved a better life; a better future. Whether it was rehabilitating ex-child soldiers in the Central African Republic, finding parentless children in refugee camps with no quality of life. She was adamant about helping children affected by conflict or war. She would mention getting medical supplies, water, food, even offer education. This was always a concern for Laura.

"But I never heard her mention this child. I didn't know anything about her," Bill claimed.

"It was a church member here in Malta that had friends in the Aleppo church. They knew the girl's parents before they were tragically killed in a vehicle collision. The family were elders of the Aleppo church.

"Both taught English at Aleppo university and with this, their young daughter spoke both Arabic and English from an early age. The girl corresponded regularly with Laura. Both hit it off almost immediately; as you will see from the correspondence. The church was keen for the girl to meet with Laura. She stayed with her grandmother, a woman named Sosa Der Kirkour, who was frail and in poor health. Then suddenly, it all went blank in 2012."

"Laura never mentioned any of this. I don't understand why this was kept from me." Bill thought he knew Laura, but this secret had set him back and took him by surprise. "Why didn't she speak to me about this girl? She never revealed any of this to me."

"What I gather was that after communication was lost, war broke out in Aleppo, as you well know. All church ties were severed due to the state of war. Only YouTube or social networks kept freedom of information flowing from Syria. Maybe Laura gave up hope. There was not much anyone could do then." The minister offered an answer but wasn't too sure if it was the correct one. Then he spoke again as Bill looked at the photograph of the young girl.

"This is where the story takes a weird turning, Bill."

"I received an email on my personal computer. The subject headline said: For Bill McKenzie. It was an email from Syria."

Bill looked lost and was bewildered by the vicar's statement.

The minister put a hand into his jacket's inside pocket and removed a piece of folded paper. He opened it. And read the email.

"Preacher, I hope you can help me in my search for a dear friend. I believe Bill and Laura McKenzie are members of the church you attend. We became friends back in July 2012. It's been a while since we spoke." Bill mocked faint laughter at him being mentioned as a church member.

"I am sure Bill is busy, getting on with his life, but as I don't have any information on his contact details, I hoped you could assist me with this matter. Please tell him I also met Raca Sana Sleiman. And yes! She does love cats.

"Currently, I am working with the White Helmet rescue teams in Aleppo. It is always dangerous, thrilling, and precarious to live on the edge of survival, as we do every day, to endure extreme conditions such as these is a task to which my colleagues become accustomed, but never accept. It is hell on earth.

"I have information on where Raca is living. One of my White Helmet brothers is a Christian, he knows the girl's family. He believes she still stays with her grandmother in the area of Al-Jedeideh. But this area in recent times is being fought after by all kinds, including criminal factions. I'm determined to help Raca and her grandmother. If you reach Bill. Please tell him; It's not necessary to have a religious belief to live by a moral code.

"It was signed by Farid Aboud." The minister waited on Bill's response.

"I have never met or communicated with this man before. But one name rings a bell. The girl's name, Raca Sleiman, Is she related to the old woman Laura connected with?"

Bill picked up the photograph and studied it.

"Raca, I know this name. I feel as if I have seen her before. And Fari?"

The minister looked at the email to get the name pronounced correctly.

"Farid, Farid Aboud."

"How on earth do I feel I know him? Because I don't. I have never corresponded with either, never seen these files before, not even communicated on social media."

The minister laid the email on top of the file.

"The email from Syria and Laura's death is dated the same time. I'm not one for believing in flukes or chances, even conspiracies, but sometimes life throws a curveball that catches us unaware. But it is most weird. The email arrived at 10 am on Thursday, 19 July 2019. And by checking the Edinburgh Newspaper headlines, Douglas sent me; whether it's a coincidence or not; the times are the same. An email from a stranger who asks for you by name. A person you have no familiarity with; is as strange as it gets. And I have come across many outlandish peculiarities in my time as a Church Minister. But this one takes the biscuit. Pardon for the idiom, Bill." He was keen to give more information on what he felt was peculiar and unexplainable beyond fiction.

The minister poured the last cup of tea, and Bill ordered a large latte. As the minister was about to continue with more curious facts, Bill intervened.

Bill wanted to explain his dream, his nightmare, and the mini terrifying sleep horror engulfed him on the night of Laura's funeral. Memories began to unfurl; latent thoughts became actual and recalled.

"I had a tormented nightmare. It was the day of Laura's funeral. I felt I was trapped. In an enclosed space, possibly under rubble. There were fires—much putrid smoke. Breathing was difficult. I…I felt pain." Bill stopped talking and looked at the photograph of the young girl.

"This young girl was in my dream. Raca…yes, Raca is her name. Her face was dirty, and her hair tangled and messy." Still staring at the photograph, he continued, "This is Raca. The girl Laura was in contact with. I am sure it is her." His mind was running overtime. More concealed memories flooded back, revealing more dormant dream facts.

"This may sound unnatural and unearthly, Archie." The minister smiled at the personal attachment Bill offered.

"I felt as if I was in another man's body, inside his mind. I could see through his eyes, I heard what he heard, and I also felt his emotions. A bomb had exploded. We were trapped together under rubble. We heard footsteps—tiny footsteps were getting close.

"Then a young girls face appeared at the only space available, just in front of where we were lying. She must have heard Farid's screams. She told us her name, she asked for Farid's name and told us she loved cats. But Farid asked her to find professional rescuers.

He wanted out of the grave. I wanted out of the grave.

She said she would get help, then she left. We thought she would leave without informing the emergency services. They wouldn't know where we were.

"Farid was in pain and needed her help. He shouted for the girl to return, but everything fell silent except for distant noise from other rescuers.

Then we saw two small brown lace-up boots appear, taking up much of the space he regarded as his only escape route. When a tiny hand reached down into his grave and dropped a wooden cross, held on a leather strap, well in reach. Still contained in this three-sided coffin, Farid reached out and grasped the cross.

"'It's for you, Farid," she said.

Archie was leaning over the table, searching through the pile of paper that sat near Bill. Picking a handful, he looked as though he was looking for a specific page, something that might add to this ever-increasing story. The page was found and handed to Bill.

Bill's head pulled back from the image he held in his hand. He glanced at the vicar, looking for help, hoping he had answers. The cross. The cross that Farid got from the little girl.

"How?" Bill looked stunned.

After scanning Bill's face for a reaction, the vicar spoke:

"Laura purchased the cross here in Malta. It was sent in 2011, I believe. There is a record of the parcel Laura forwarded to the church in Aleppo in the files. The package contained that cross. The girl you saw in your dream, Bill, is the same Raca Sana Sleiman The man you shared his terrible experience with is Farid Aboud; the same man that sent the email. I replied to him but got no answer. A church member that works in IT checked the computer and the system. He viewed the same result as me. When sending the email to Farid, it said *SMTP...Error: Failed to connect to the server.* I remember this because I must have tried over fifty times to reply.

"He explained that origination of the email was gone. There is no way now to source or contact Farid Aboud. But, in addition to all of this. Something so extreme and so different from any normality I can fathom; interpret this story's reality and find any form of credibility to this mystery. This fact lands head-on."

The minister leant both arms on the table, putting his face near Bill, intent on whispering the words, or pronouncing them, he offered an end to this whimsical adventure.

"The email was received on the date I mentioned. But...my friend from IT informed me that the email was originally sent from Syria in August 2015. No further details could be sourced.'

"Was the email copied and pasted?" Bill asked in the best technical way he could.

"No, Joseph is a specialist. He analyses and troubleshoots for a major phone company in Germany, and as they say, a whizz kid and tech-savvy; his words, not mine. Any problem regarding software and hardware, this is the person to talk to. He confirmed that the email was sent originally in 2015. And by whatever means of normality that exists. It was delivered to me at 10 am on Thursday, 19 July 2019. Where these missing years went; I don't have any answers."

"You are telling me that the email was sent in 2015 and just arrived recently?" A suspicious look appeared on Bill's face.

"I have only repeated what Joseph said. He could not give a reasonable explanation of why this happened or how it materialised. He is as mystified as you and me."

Bill paid for breakfast. The minister offered Bill support when he needed it. Both left on good terms. The sun was shining as they left the café, leaving much later than both expected.

Leaving Caffe Cordina, he walked briskly beyond Republic Square to head down the steep hill on St. Lucia's street on his way to the Sliema Ferry. Near the ferry terminal, at the foot of the steep walkway, he stopped outside Miceli's hardware store to send a text to Emad:

'Can we catch-up tomorrow evening? I have Laura's personal belongings to go through, and it will take time. I met Archie, the retired Minister, for breakfast at Caffe Cordina. You must try it. Now heading to Sliema to do some clothes shopping. And tomorrow at 9:00—I have the legal stuff to go through with Andrew Attard. I'll call you after the meeting, Bill.'

The ferry to Sliema was every thirty minutes, and he just managed to board in time. It was full of tourists and business people. He enjoyed the short trip.

Sliema was busy. Tourists, buses, cars, and delivery trucks swamped the main road near the harbour. He decided to take the burdensome and exhausting laboured walk up the hill on St Anthony Street. At the top of the thoroughfare, he turned right and passed and viewed the new apartments on Triq Tigne Street; on his way to The Point shopping mall.

An hour in and out of the mall, he collected new shorts, underwear, toiletries, flip-flops and sandals, T-shirts and polo shirts, and a new pair of sunglasses.

Carrying one bag in each hand; one being Laura's files. With difficulty, he managed to climb the steps to the top deck of the ferry. With his bags under his legs, he relaxed and enjoyed the trip. New sunglasses came in handy. It was a beautiful sunny day.

Chapter 21
Laura's Files

Barefooted, Bill sat cross-legged on the Persian rug in his apartment's living room on Archbishop street. He was wearing the new casual shorts and a black Le Coq Sportif T-shirt with white and yellow bands encircling his body. Black text, written boldly on the white trimming, said; La Grande Boucle—'The Big Loop.'

This marketing message sat below the triangular proud standing Le Coq, Rooster.

He had Laura's files spread over the floor. A bottle of Hopleaf Pale Ale was in his hand. It had a hoppy bitterness to its taste that Bill liked, and he supped a large mouthful.

Most of the correspondence Bill read, he saw his name mentioned. Laura did not just communicate on her own, and she involved Bill. All signed off: Love Laura and Bill McKenzie. He knew Laura had always wanted to adopt. They had discussed it and were due to start the legal process when they had settled in Edinburgh. Any literature from unknown sources might come as a shock. That would be a major surprise for him.

One email caught Bill's attention. It showed photographs and images of beehives. And bee farming.

"Raca, I will transfer money to your grandmother to help set you up with beekeeping. One hive is all you require to get started. There will be a beekeeping suit in the parcel with a round veil headgear to protect you. Remember, protective gloves are also essential. Once you have found your source of bees, then it is time to obtain your beehive. I understand that someone at your church can provide this.

Here is a list of what I will send you; The Beehive, a Bee suit, veil and gloves, honey extractor, Bee smoker, Hive Tool, Bee brush, bee feeders and a book called *Practical Beekeeping* by Clive De Bruyn. You will love beekeeping. Thanks for bee…ing sweet. Lots of love, Laura."

Bill wiped a tear from his eye and took a long swig of beer. He had seen enough. It is difficult enough meeting the solicitor tomorrow, but viewing her personal letters, and the thought she had behind them, was too much to take. He would pack them up and store them in the hall cupboard.

Another beer; then another, then another; then his mind proposed an alternative. *Let's do the thirty-six steps down, and ninety steps up the street. The pub is beckoning. Maybe Uncle William's ghost is pestering him to move so he can join him.* Once the strap of flip-flops was slipped between his toes, he closed the main door behind him.

"Now let's count. It's just thirty-six steps down, and ninety-four up the street." He tried hard not to lose concentration or be distracted by anyone he knew. He was counting each step as he went on his way to The Pub.

He chose a high stool at the bar. Ordered a large gin and tonic with ice. No lemon. No straw. He lifted his glass and said cheers to his uncle William; as he turned to see his Uncle's photograph on one of the walls. The photo of him with young Bill. Bill wearing a flying helmet and goggles. The words 'The two bills' were written on the picture and dated October 23rd 1978.

An hour passed having consumed more alcohol.

Bill was in no fit state to walk the steps down the street to the flat or one level up. But he tried. Staggering, smiling at the fact, by purchasing the Ollie Reed shirt. The black T-shirt was way too oversized for Bill. This version of 'The Pubs' illustrious and notable jokester and consumer of all things alcohol, that listed his last session of drinks he drank the day he died, was pulled over his head.

His stupefied laugh was loud as he pulled the bottom of the T-shirt by two hands, laughing at the upside-down writing; it was out of focus as he drew it up to his face. He read it out as if he memorised the fact. Tourists and locals laughed at his recital. Others gave him a severe body swerve.

So unlike Bill.

But sometimes, when life gets tough, the tough give in. He screamed the words aloud.

“Eight pints of lager; possibly more. Twelve double rums, and a half bottle of whisky.”

It took longer than usual. Finding the keys was as tricky as finding the lock. The steps up were awkward but manageable, and the metal and wood bannisters often provided assistance. The door to the apartment was not locked, which helped. As soon as his ablutions were complete, he staggered to the bedroom, aimed and struck his bed. He landed perfectly.

Chapter 22
Al-Jdayde, Aleppo
21 August 2015

Farid Aboud's apartment is in the Al-Jdayde district in Aleppo.

A video camera is running. Farid is talking and documenting an update on the Syrian conflict. In his city. In his district. In his street.

Day 1

He speaks to the video lens:

"It's 9:30 am. The war has finally arrived in my street. I can hear sporadic gunfire and loud shrieking voices. People are scared to leave their homes, we are all scared. It is a worrying time for everyone. We don't know what to do!"

He moves from the view of the lens, but his voice is still heard and recorded. The camera keeps filming as it's moved into a new position at the window. Filming soldiers on the street below. Farid describes the scene.

"There are armed men on the street, they do not look like Army. I don't want to move the curtains too much. I hear them talking. A pile of flour bags have been put on the street corner. It looks like a post of some kind; possibly to shield ballast and gunshots. It's a barricade. More militia is arriving here."

The camera is lifted from its location. Farid whispers now. The lens is used to sneak-a-peek view as the lace curtain is held back.

"One of the soldiers has got a megaphone. He is a leader, he instructs information.'

Farid stops talking and hopes the recorder picks up the soldier's speech. He isn't disappointed. It blared the soldier's voice loud. He pushes the camera further out the small space at the edge of the curtain. It points down to the street, two floors down and captures the Free Syrian soldier holding the bullhorn close to his mouth. He demands the opposition to surrender.

"Soldiers, come to us. Soldiers, leave your post and come to us! Assad will not help you. Come to us! We are all brothers. Allahu Akbar!"

Farid adds narration to the recording as the soldier repeats his demands.

"They look no older than students, just young men, possibly undergraduates with no war experience. I believe they are the Free Syrian Army. Just young naïve men fighting a brutal man's war. Not fighting under one flag but many different beliefs."

A gunship is heard hovering above local buildings. The rhythmic, pulsating thumping sound is primitive and exciting, as it flew over, and beyond Farid's street. A dipping, dropped-nose helicopter headed to a zone identified as hostile. Still visible in the sky, it now sat motionless in the air like a giant prehistoric hummingbird, flapping its invisible wings around fifty times a second, in preparation to attack its prey. It autorotated forty-five degrees, muzzle descending. Holding its stationary position as it awaited command information.

The Russian built Mi-24 was being used by Assad's regime. Farid caught the images on the camera. Recording the gunship in full action. The military helicopter viewing the scene as a predator would, holding its place in the sky, watching, and locating its target.

Bullishly showing its supremacy. The helicopter locked its weapons onto a zone that needed to be destroyed. Repeatedly firing a 12mm Yab-B minigun from a chin-mounted gun turret. And an ultra-powerful two-barrel 30mm GSh-30K autocannon, straddled along the right side of the cockpit, let go her overwhelming munitions. Hitting everything in its sights. To the pilot and his crew, this target was a local command centre and observation point. It had to be destroyed at all costs. It is war, and it's them or us. Shooting for over a minute, the result left the neighbourhood in total desolation. This gunship was designed to be a lethal killing machine. It did what it set out to do.

As the weapons became idle, the Russian pilot observed the devastation; admiring his work. Sitting in the kill zone, enjoying his artistry. His gloved hands pulling back the cyclic control to change the pitch angle as it flew from the scene. The pilot spoke, "Tsel unichtozena. Vozvrashcheniye na bazu. Target destroyed. Returning to base."

Smoke and dust filled the air as it swirled in the wake of the rotary blade as the killing-machine left the sector. Dirt and soil covered the damaged buildings.

The camera is refocussed on the street, and two soldiers are talking. The camera tilts to the right. Farid talks. He speaks softly to record his voice.

"The Government army is two hundred metres to the right. It must be the free Syrian army on my street. This place has become a place of interest to many factions. Everyone is worried. No one leaves their house. We are low on supplies. We don't want this war or any war. We need a peaceful life."

The camera is switched off.

Day 2

The camera is held in Farid's hand, which he turns to take a selfie of his face. He looks tired, exhausted, and afraid and hasn't eaten much recently. His food stock is low.

"I now live and sleep in the living room. It's safer here. The barricade below my window seems to be the front line. Possibly a checkpoint. I need to leave here, no one is safe!"

The camera is switched off.

Day 3

The camera is steady on a table, and Farid is at the far end sitting on a chair—sweet tea is being drunk.

The view shows his upper body.

"I have little or no food." He seems agitated and twists his head away from the camera lens when a loud bang attracts his attention. "The army is attacking the street from both sides. My building shakes with heavy bombing and shelling. We are all living under continual threat of injury or death. I can feel the anxiety from my neighbours and see the concern in their faces." He sits back, breathes lungs full of air. Pushes the chair back, walks to the camera and switches it off.

Day 4

The camera is filming the street again. Two soldiers are pulling a dead body away from the scene of action, leaving a bloody trail on the road. The television is on, some chat show, but the volume is low. Farid's voice is wavering. He is tired. He eats the fruit from one of the remaining tins he has left.

"The man that stood on the corner has been shot in the head. His friends are removing him. This is the epicentre of the war in Al-Jdayde." Multiple gunshots are heard and a rocket is launched in retaliation at the attacking force. Explosions are near his building. Shrapnel and other debris hit Farid's house. The window shakes but doesn't break. He dives for cover.

The camera is switched off.

Day 5

"Soldiers are dismantling the barricade. They are removing the flour bags." Several gunshots and grenade explosions are close—more chaos. There is much movement.

The camera is pulled into the room and is switched off.

Day 6

"Armed Forces are returning to my street. They are heavily armed; they have more firearms than the previous soldiers. They all have long beards. It is Liwa Al-Tawhid, the brigade of oneness, I have been informed.

"Television reports call them radicals. International broadcasters call them freedom fighters. I don't care what they call it, I refuse to choose any side. It's a lie that the revolution started peacefully. At least in my street—It began with a gun! It didn't start quietly at all. This will continue for a long time. I don't want to film war anymore."

The camera focusses on fighters rebuilding the flour bag barrier. Locals help them.

"It seems the neighbours work for both sides. Maybe they are scared. There is another group rebuilding the barricade.

The screen goes blank.

The camera is switched off.

Chapter 23
Valletta
The Present Day

Bill had a good night's sleep. No more dreams of Aleppo, though he did expect the unimaginable nightmare to raise its ugly head at some point; but today it didn't. His memory recollected all his previous experiences of being in Aleppo, sharing experiences with Farid Aboud and Raca Sleiman, and the reflections remained with him.

They were part of him now. It was if he had downloaded the data and stored it for future reference.

Andrew Attard waited in preparation at his desk, removing the glasses that were perched at the end of his nose; as his secretary announced Bill's arrival. He was standing and approaching Bill by the time he reached the desk. The secretary closed the door behind her.

"Bill, I'm so sorry for your loss. Please accept my sincere condolences. We are all stunned by Laura's death."

He shook his hand and hugged Bill as a long-lost brother would.

He pointed to a seat for Bill to make himself comfortable.

"Can I get you a coffee?"

"No, I'm fine, Andrew, thanks," Bill said, making himself comfortable in a sturdy leather tub chair.

"Well, this is business I never thought I would be doing." Andrew opened the file that lay on his desk. Removing the paperwork and sitting them on top of the folder. He rested his gold-rimmed glasses on the edge of his nose.

"Ok, Bill. The death certificate has been received so we can continue to read Laura's last will and testament." Andrew Attard picked up a two-page statement and stared between the paperwork and Bill.

The will was read thoroughly and, as Bill expected, it was straightforward and to the letter as they had agreed many years ago. Bill was preparing to offer his thanks then leave when his solicitor added.

"Bill, there is a subsequent addition to Laura's will. It was written on Thursday, 12 July 2018, it is by name a secret will and had been deposited in the voluntary court jurisdiction and stands up legally."

"We both wrote both wills back in 2002!" Bill sounded anxious and nerved by this event.

"It was handwritten and witnessed by Emad Naguib, Bill."

"Handwritten? And witnessed by Emad Naguib? I never knew any of this. Is this legal? Why would Emad have anything to do with Laura's will?"

"There is no obligation to inform a spouse if either is doing a will; both secret and public. This declaration was written in Laura's hand and witnessed by Emad Ammon Naguib. It is a legal document, Bill."

"Why Emad's involvement?" Bill was confused.

"I cannot answer any of this. All I can say is that this document is perfectly legal."

Bill was caught unaware and expected business to be easy. He didn't anticipate any modifications to her will. Why did Laura keep this from him?

"A holograph is sometimes better than type, and since it's in Laura's handwriting, it makes it legal. I will read it verbatim." Bill lurched uncomfortably back into his seat. Feeling unsure of this current event. He felt numb. He rubbed both hands over his face.

Andrew Attard cleared his throat and read the letter:

I, Laura McKenzie, being of sound mind and body, do now add the following to my last will and testament. I hereby bequeath to my husband, Bill , my shares in Valletta Yacht Holdings, and Arran Dandelion. My property portfolio, my bank accounts total to date at £3.86 million and all my personal belongings.

However, I would also like to bequeath all my shares in Moulin Rouge, Pitlochry, to my cousin Jane Graham. She deserves this.

Bill smiled and nodded his head in agreement as if he already agreed to this fact, accepting this was the proper and correct thing to do.

Andrew Attard continued:

In closure, I have set up a trust account of £250,000 for Raca Sana Sleiman. This girl was parentless and living with her grandmother in 2012. She and her grandmother were members of The Presbyterian Church in Aleppo. I was in regular contact with Raca, her grandmother, and the Aleppo minister to start adoption procedures as early as 2009; but lost all contact when the civil conflict in Syria began. Bill, I understand this may come as a shock, me hoping to adopt a girl, a girl neither of us had ever seen in real life, though I had seen photographs and received letters from her; but felt through prayer that she was chosen as our daughter. I realise this sounds crazy to a resolute atheist like you, but I saw this little girl in my dreams.

When a mission was set up to connect and out-reach other church communities, I chose the Presbyterian Church in Aleppo. We exchanged emails at first. Then viewing the excellent work, they were doing in their community. I watched a short video on their Facebook site. A young girl prayed for an opportunity to have a honeybee farm.

She was interviewed on the film and believe this or not; the little girl in the video was non-other than Raca Sana Sleiman, the girl I saw in my dreams long before any contact had been initiated. This was, to me, was a message from God almighty himself. Please forgive me for not telling you any of this Bill as I know we never kept secrets from each other, but this was different. You would have thought me mad, or possibly have an obsessive religious zealot as a partner. How could I tell you any of this? Me dreaming about the young girl I wanted to mother and raise as my child, appearing to me in my dreams before I ever knew of her existence?

Do you remember, we talked about adoption many times? I honestly knew this could be the little girl that would fit perfectly in our family. Emad had helped me search for this girl through his contacts. Syria has been at war with itself for many years, and any hope of finding her alive is remote, as I no longer have a connecting dream with her. I am lost as to where she is now or whether she is alive. But I never gave up hope of finding her and bringing her here, to live with us both.

This will also sound strange. One night in our apartment in Valletta, in fact, the same day you bought me the book called 'Practical Beekeeping' by Clive De Bruyn. Do you remember? I read it many times I know, but you told me you ordered the copy from Agenda Book Shop on Republic Street. I'm sure you remember.

He nodded in remembrance of when he bought the book.

Andrew Attard looked at Bill as if seeking confirmation his client understood the message. He continued:

We read in bed. You were reading 'Under the Dome' by Stephen King. I re-read Practical Beekeeping for the umpteenth time. Then it happened. I fell into a dream, a real-life fantasy. I was there, seeing life through the eyes of a little girl. At first, it was a dream, but it felt tangible. I saw the face of a young girl smiling back at herself from a mirror. A mirror in the washroom was my recollection. The young girls face smiled at her reflection. Then I heard voices. Male voices. The girl investigated by walking along the corridor then listening at the door where the sounds emanated from. The girl opened the door slightly.

I saw inside the room, through her eyes. It was just two men sitting near each other. One man using a money counting machine, the other looking at a small painting. I heard their voices in English. But somehow, I knew they were speaking in a foreign language. I listened and heard clear-as-day; what the men discussed. One man talked, the other listened, and I managed to recall every word said. I even wrote it down. These are the actual words.

"The icons are buried under the temple of the storm god in the Citadel of Aleppo. Near the Souk Al-Mahamasin, you will source Al-Zaki soap factory, which is easily recognised as you will see. Located in the basement's northern part, you will find a tunnel, a passageway that leads directly to the citadel. Eventually, you will find three shafts facing you. The one to the right is the option you must choose. There are several openings along this road, but you only enter the one with the Storm God's carving, Haddad; engraved on the wall.

"You will know which carving is Haddad, as he is holding a lightning bolt. Enter here. There are many steps down. The vault will be full of wooden cases. Look for the small box at one end. It is light, so move it to reveal another short shaft. Before you creep through this space, make sure you cover the entrance with the box. Do not leave any clues you are there. At the end of this move, you will find the Icons. Then, my friend, it is up to you to return the way you came. Take a head torch but use moderately. Only when you feel no one is near to see the light. It is dark down there, so don't be seen. Keep calm and collected. Don't lose your head. Because if you do, you will more than likely lose your head; literally!"

Precisely, word for word. Every detail mentioned; I could remember. Then Raca dropped a book she had held in her hand. Bending over to pick it up, her head hit the door which alerted the men. She ran. Ran when she heard men shouting orders. I heard footsteps and loud voices. Raca escaped by the way she came in; through the back door. She knew this restaurant. She used this facility many times. It was local, and the owners were family friends. Only stopping when she felt safe.

Then the door behind her, the door she just came through; opened and together we saw an armed guard, staring at us. He looked around the area, was happy that no men were involved, holstered a gun, and closed the door. I heard a bolt being shut. Behind me, behind Raca, a voice I knew immediately was her elderly grandmother, Sosa Der Kirkour, was shouting. 'Raca, Raca, come here. 'Come, Come!' She knelt as low as her frail body permitted. Holding both arms outstretched, Raca ran to her grandmother. We all hugged; which I know sounds absurd. Then we left.

Andrew Attard drank some water from a paper cup.

Now, this is where it gets weirder; that's if any of this story can get more illogical. There was an explosion, It was enormous.

We were lucky. Incredibly lucky.

Just as the blast happened, we fell behind a row of garbage bins. The bins sheltered us. Stinky, smelly bins that saved Raca and her grandmother's lives. It sounds apathetic how life can be saved, but these rickety old bins did just that.

Once to her feet, the grandmother held Raca's hand tightly and moved as quick as her osteoporosis bones allowed her. We only managed a few yards when Sosa, the grandmother stopped and raised a hand to her head. She was bleeding. Blood flowed over her face. She staggered and fell to the ground, which took her breath away. Raca told her to stay calm, she would get help. Moving over debris and rubble, taking short, careful steps to reach support; we heard voices; screaming voices; scared people; we saw dead people. Then blaring sirens were close by. Lights were flashing through dust clouds that shrouded us. Raca covered her mouth with a handkerchief. We listened to a voice together. A faint sound. A voice coming from below the rubble.

Raca walked over more concrete blocks, twisted metal fragments, even a plastic bistro table was moved to allow access to where the sounds emanated. As she bent down on the plastic table, she investigated a makeshift tunnel, and there was a man. Still partly hidden by debris and covered in wreckage. An imprisoned man. Caught in the explosion and held securely in this tomb. The man moved some materials to give a clear view of his rescuer. We heard the man breathing. He filled his lungs with air that flew into his enclosed space. Raca dropped onto a slab of mortar and crawled inside and got a full view of him. His voice was weak. But we heard him.

He spoke as if he had a dust-ball in his mouth: "Hello, I am Farid, can you help me, please?" He asked Raca her name. And she responded by doing so. He asked if she could go and get help which she did. But before any of this, she offered the man hope. She gave him a cross, not knowing his religious affiliation or his belief status; she did it for herself. It was the small wooden cross I had sent her. All of this is, to me, a miracle.

Believe it or not, this happened. If you listen to Andrew reading this, then I guess I am dead, but what you are listening to is real.

No longer living between real life and fake reality. But I would ask you to do one favour for me. Can you please, please find out if Raca survived the war? And I pray to God she did.

If you are successful in finding Raca, please give her a helping hand with her education, take care of her well-being, her future in your hands is a place that she would be safe and comfortable. I write this hoping and praying that Raca will be in your life as a daughter. A daughter I only knew in a dream. But the fact is she is real, and she can become the daughter we never had, a life that deserves a kind and honest future. Raca Sana Sleiman McKenzie sounds lovely, as I hope you agree.

I am so sorry for not telling you any of this, but madness is not the kind of thing I would ever want to be remembered by. Just one more thing, In the apartment, there is a small aluminium flight case beneath the floorboards, under my wardrobe, and inside you will find mum and dad's personal possessions; which I would ask you to keep and look after if you are OK with this? Also, in this box, you will find a small leather satchel. This contains letters that add intrigue to this mystery and another secret I had to keep from you.

I will always love you, Bill McKenzie, with or without a flying helmet and goggles. I will be with my parents and yours; until you appear in the future. Love as always, Laura x.

Andrew Attard had tears in his eyes and asked Bill to excuse him as he took a paper tissue from an open box to wipe dropping tears and blow his nose. He did both and made two loud honking noises as he cleared his nostrils.

"I'll send you copies, Bill. I will also contact the local bank and update the information they need." Andrew Attard was losing words which were generally not reasonable to solicitors, but they were friends for many years, and friendship had been close with both families.

"I need to wash my hands. I'll see you out, Bill." He cluttered the words into the best sentence he could, still reeling from reading the most heart-breaking letter ever. His wife Ġuża was a close friend of Laura's. They socialised together. They both loved the gym, had their regular girly nights out and enjoyed shopping. Always together in Valletta.

"Give Ġuża and the kids my regards, Andrew. I'll be in touch soon."

"Let's meet for a drink, Bill."

"Of course."

Andrew bypassed a question from the receptionist as he stepped into a washroom.

Bill was confused. His mind in turmoil. Laura's dreams were the events he had in his vision. All seen through the eyes of Farid. How could any of these apparitions make sense?

Bill left the office and headed out onto the street. He took time to inhale and exhale fresh air. Hoping to clear his head of the facts his dead wife informed him in her will.

It was 10:30 am. He needed strong coffee and time to contemplate everything.

Chapter 24
Flightover the Med

It was a perfect day for flying. An ice-blue sky with fluffy clouds passing far below. The sun highlighting the view beautifully. The Gulfstream G550 darted through the air at forty-five thousand feet; and moving at a speed of Mach .80.

Emad had a choice of eighteen seats but chose one near the flight deck. A single forward-facing position. He was drinking champagne. A stewardess arrived and placed a Maltese garden salad on the table that was unfolded before him. Freshwater was served, as was a top-up of Champagne. The bread was hot and smelled heavenly, and the plate of butter was ice-cold; just how Emad liked it. The jet was everything a businessperson wanted, and the interior held the image of a boutique hotel.

The panoramic oval windows, aviation's largest, provided the passenger-cabin more natural light to offer a more pleasant working environment.

All business communications he would need were available: Wi-Fi connectivity, satellite television, satellite phone, and widescreen High Definition monitors. Even fax and printing was available but rarely used. The galley had a microwave, an espresso machine and coffee maker, a high-temperature oven, sink with fresh water, and a well-stocked fridge. Emad told the stewardess that her services were currently no longer required. She could relax, read, or watch a movie, enjoy the flight as he told her. He wanted time on his own.

Opposite to where Emad sat, there was a high-gloss Assi walnut wood credenza. He opened a door on it and pressed a button that allowed a slow open drawer to move gradually till it unfastened fully; it held four bottles of wine. From left to right, sitting cradled on a velvet cushioned rack, was a:1960 Haut-Brion Bordeaux; a 1988 Mouton. And two bottles of 2008 Kapcsandy state Lane Cabernet California. Emad took a bottle of Kapcsandy from the case knowing it was one of his favourite wines. The wine was poured into a crystal glass—before swirling it, sniffing it, or tasting it—he just stared at it; giving the inky purple red wine a full examination before drinking.

Smelling the aroma of cassis, chocolate and espresso; an ethereal description he once read on this delightful Cabernet Sauvignon, and agreed with. Recurring thoughts remembering the quality of palate this wine created. A wine he knew tasted sublime. It had been identified as a monster of a wine…but Emad preferred his quote. *Fine art in a bottle*.

He had sent Bill an email before he finished his second glass. A good feeling encapsulated him and reinvigorated his morals, and a letter to his dear friend Bill, didn't come from the bottle; it came from his heart.

The Gulfstream G550 was two hours from landing at Adana Şakirpaşa Airport in Turkey. Emad now found time to chill-out and enjoy the flight.

Chapter 25
HMP Edinburgh – High-Security Prison
The Present Day

It was three a.m. when screams of terror came from Finlay McColl's cell located in Hermiston Hall. Several inmates shouted abuse at being awakened. It was dark, and most of the prison slept, but this evil killer stirred from a repellent nightmare, with the precise recall of the upsetting dream, wanted to be consoled. The hallucination was vividly realistic and disturbing. The message he received was intense. And he had orders to carry out; If not, he would suffer the consequences.

He saw a Vantablack sky open and reveal a space where extreme light originated in his dream. A long arm emerged from above, stretching, elasticated as it grew to capture a fleeing Finlay McColl, finally gripped by a gigantic skeletal hand that squeezed the life out of him, every breath, and disregarded his crushed remains at the gates of hell.

Was this divine intervention?

Whatever was happening to him, he wanted it to stop. He wanted it all to go away.

For once, this brutal, sadistic executioner was afraid. This was the third such nightmare he had. Yesterday, during his restless sleep, he had images that haunted him, and they lasted the rest of the day. He kept this first altercation with the slumber world to himself. Today's dream was different, there was a woman's voice demanding him to contact a minister: a Church of Scotland Minister based in Edinburgh. He didn't know which parish, but he knew the vicar's name; it was Reverend Douglas McAuley, and he wanted to see him now!

He had valuable information to give him.

There was an emergency alarm in each cell. And McColl pressed his one. The officers sitting at the island desk in the middle of the floor reacted.

"It's McColl! Go check it out."

McColl was screaming aloud and hitting the cell door.

"He is shouting for a minister?" one prison officer said.

"I didn't think he was the religious type!" The other officer, ready to respond, opened a sealed pack and removed keys needed to open McColl's cell. He took the steps up and along the corridor towards the cell. A kicking and thumping noise could be heard as the officer neared the lockup. The alarm had been switched off and the orange alarm light outside the cell went out. The prison officer raised a hand, looked through the spyhole and saw McColl slumped on the floor, holding his knees close to his chin.

"What the fuck!" were the words the officer used.

Finlay McColl's hands and head were bleeding profusely. The walls and floor are splattered with his blood.

"I need backup," the officer spoke on his radio, and within minutes, the duty manager and three other officers stood at McColl's cell. The big key was inserted into the heavy mortice lock, turned briskly and the door, a four-inch-thick metal frame, clicked opened. McColl, the forever evil and stubborn killer, sat on the floor, crying like a baby.

Unlike his usual staid demeanour, McColl had become a shivering wreck. He trembled as a child would after awakening from a nightmare, sitting stationary. Shaking uncontrollably as he cried.

"Please help me. Please help me!" he repeated in a low, wobbly voice. Tears flowed down his face.

For the first time since his incarceration, McColl was willing to do as the manager or officers asked.

With two officers helping him stand, he accepted their assistance, although arthritic weak knees added to the struggle, he managed to stand upright.

He had urinated himself. Fear-induced urination seemed to be likely as this man was scared, and when under stress, fight-or-flight response tends to kick in. Whatever scared him, it left him an emotional wreck.

McColl acted as gentle as a lamb and as timid as a mouse, as he walked voluntarily with the officers to the ablution area where they washed and treated his wounds. None of the scars was severe. Both his hands were wrapped in roller bandages. Trained in first aid, the officers applied skills to bandage McColl's hands on the inside of his wrists, below the bottom of his thumb and wrapped the dressing straight around each wrist. The dressing also covered his swollen and scuffed knuckles. The wound on his head would need to be cleaned with antiseptic cleaning products before a large plaster could be applied.

McColl, as the officers now viewed him, behaved childlike in his actions, innocent in his behaviour, by repeatedly asking the manager if he could meet a minister called Douglas McAuley. He spoke quietly, barely audible, almost with a sincere voice. The guards had never seen Finlay McColl behave this way. This is not the Finlay McColl they knew. Finlay McColl is Evil. Not a man that would show sentiment, divulge any form of grief, or interact with any soul, far less a prison officer. Yet he asked again politely.

"Can I meet Reverend Douglas McCauley, please?"

This man may have seen the light or turned to God. Or maybe one of his victims paid him a ghostly visit. But whatever scared him, it had left him petrified.

He pleaded to meet with the minister. The minister he only knew as Douglas McCauley. McColl would cause no more trouble tonight, he accepted the rule from the duty manager, that the minister would be found and granted permission to meet him, all of this would be organised first thing in the morning. He accepted this judgement. Back in his cell, Finlay McColl slept like a baby and had no more nightmares. The task he was given by the voice in his head had been accomplished.

Chapter 26
The Valletta Apartment
The Present Day

Bill sat on the bed and opened the flight case. He was looking over his in-laws, mementoes, and wedding photographs. Also, Laura's birth certificate, school reports, first Christmas card, and favourite teddy, 'Woody', were all found in the memory box. Additionally, top sports awards, a dried wedding bouquet, wedding cake toppers, the worn-out place setting for the bride and groom, and a copy of the marriage service gave Bill strong feelings. He lifted and opened an entire Daily Record Newspaper showing the front-page headlines: Tsunami toll rises as Pitlochry couple is reported missing. The paper was dated Monday, 27th December 2004. Bill remembered Laura's parents with fondness.

A few tattered photo albums of Laura's childhood were placed on the couch. Something to look at and reminisce later.

The leather satchel was small, it looked more like a man's toiletry Dopp bag. Bill shuffled to his feet and sat on the sofa. He unzipped the bag. Inside was a bundle of letters, held together with string, the top envelope had Laura's name and address as Moulin Rouge, 125b, Atholl Road, Pitlochry PH16 5AG; her parents' wine shop. There were three batches of letters. Laura had identified each pile by tying a tag to each bale. One, two and three. The documents had Edinburgh postmarks stamped near the queen's head. The first group of letters dated Nov 2001.

Removing the string from the stack of envelopes, he opened the first letter. An expression of disbelief grew on his face as he observed the handwritten letters. The sender used capped letters. The paper stated:

WE ARE GOING TO KILL YOU. WE HAVE ALREADY DESTROYED SEVERAL LIKE YOU.

'I have planted all my beauties!'

Bill opened the letters, one by one, lying them down and paid interest to the last sentence on each page. Some letters of these sentences were underlined and some only had words underlined. He copied the lines in order, by dates, through every sheet, hoping there was a poem, rhyming lyric; possibly a message. There was.

It was creepy and disturbing. *Why would Laura keep these letters from me?* he thought.

The last letter opened, with the tag line of 'To lay down your weary head' was signed—the only message with any valid signature—it was signed boldly and written by someone with beautiful penmanship. But an evil twisted mind all the same.

Finlay McColl

I have planted all my beauties
somewhere cold and grey
high among the pine trees
where you will lie one day

A grave awaits your body
Someplace among my dead
My child of wildflower honey
Let's rest your weary head

The hairs on the back of Bill's neck rose. He hyperventilated, felt anxious, and scared. He was nearly vomiting. What he read made his hands sweat. His eyes wandered and repeatedly blinked. His body was in fight or flight mode, his ability to focus was hindered, but he had to remain focussed.

He was reading genuine dysfunction and painful words, but the reality remained, he needed closure on all of this. What he saw chilled him. What his eyes connected with next, blew his mind.

On the last letter, under McColl's signature, it was dated as of 7 June 2019. The same day Laura died, yet this letter was delivered and received in November 2007.

"This cannot be real!" Bill voiced dubiously.

The date was purely coincidental. No way these threats could be conceived or created from behind bars all those years ago. The man is evil, but this is beyond the realms of nature, even for the likes of Finlay McColl.

He understood the first batch of letters was received in November 2001. The second in November 2004, and the last of the malicious threats on November 2007. Three years apart. All received in November. All Edinburgh postmarked.

Bill calmed down. Trying hard to forget these appalling transcripts. Forget all he had read or would remember, get this creep McColl from his life. Stop him from doing any more damage.

But why, Laura? Did McColl know of our engagement and marriage? Why the threats? Why not me? McColl must have known my existence through my parents, but Laura's death was an accident and could never be connected. How could McColl have been involved? The driver was never found or charged. We were in the wrong place at the wrong time.

This and other questions occupied Bill's mind. A bin liner sealed the threats, and they were placed on a shelf in a large walk-in cupboard in no time at all.

After a quick wash-down and hair reluctantly combed, an un-ironed T-shirt was thrown over his newly spruced head. A few overindulgent powerful sprays of a spicy wood cologne put closure to his evening's attempt at dressing.

Bill felt a few drinks were the order of the day. An eight-minute walk to the Trabuxu Wine Bar would be a welcome break; after the traumatic and challenging day he had; It would be the perfect distraction. The wine bar was Laura's favourite haunt, and it would be nice to acquaint himself with the classy bar again. A bottle of local Merlot would do wonders. He thought of a few of those delicate beauties as he strolled leisurely through the streets of Valletta.

It looked busy inside the wine bar, but Bill was lucky to find an empty table sitting on one of the well-worn steps outside the Bistro. A candle was lit and gave a romantic feel to the area, but he soon cleared his mind of any such emotion. Bill and Laura often planted themselves outside this establishment on many occasions. They always enjoyed the ambience on offer and the plentiful wine selection held in stock and always relished people-watching in the bar's colourful, vibrant environment.

Many happy memories existed here.

The glass was full of Marsovan, Cheval franc, a Maltese wine, as it landed on the mahogany table. Bill took the time to check his phone for messages. He had two. One was an email from Emad and the other a text message from Reverend Douglas McCauley. He tasted the wine and enjoyed it. There were two happy couples at the next table laughing and joking. At another table, a young man proposed marriage and produced a boxed ring from behind his back, which he presented to his girlfriend; and on cue, a bottle of champagne arrived to fulfil the celebration. The girl screamed in response, tears appeared and her hysterical reaction was to stand, jump and shout.

Bill raised his glass as did everyone else that witnessed this cute romantic love betrothal. The couple hugged and kissed to a reverberating hand clap. The attractive young woman wore a beige trilby hat over long blonde hair. And looked stunning in a floral print split thigh Bardot dress with original cherry-red doc-martin boots on her feet. She looked like every bit an American rock star. The young man was dressed casually; in jeans and white T-shirt.

An elderly couple walked past the wine bar without stopping. Bill thought he heard a Scottish accent.

Emad had sent an apology, knowing Bill would know his assistance to Laura. Helping her search for the little Syrian girl. He was right in his assumption. A full-blown apology and a request for forgiveness were highlighted in **bold**. He would be returning from a business trip in a few days and asked if they could meet up for a meal. Bill replied. He would look forward to catching up, and all is forgiven; of course, it is. The meal sounds great! See you soon. Bill.

The text from the minister was different. Unexpected and strange.

Text: Bill, I have just received a call from HMP Edinburgh. The serial killer Finlay McColl has requested me to visit him. This is the man that killed three young women back in the 1980s. I believe your mother was the QC in the case. The message I received from the Governor explained that McColl would only meet and talk with me. He would speak to no other. Can you call me when you have time? There is something I need to explain.

Bill was relaxed, he felt good, as good as he can be; and he was sure the wine helped with this mood swing. What he had read today, the fact that Laura saw the world through the eyes of a young Syrian girl, and he saw the same world through the eyes of a Syrian atheist; then it was highly likely, at some point soon, things would get worse.

If the minister was asking me to phone him, he must have a reason to do so. Whatever the motive, Bill was sure it could wait till tomorrow. Tonight was Bill time. The fourth glass of wine was empty, a full bottle had disappeared. He ordered another.

As the evening grew, more people were out and about, and the wine bar got busier.

Strait street was filling up with people of many different age groups. Some having a pleasant evening walk, others out for a meal and a drink, and many tourists discovering the surroundings of Valletta; Bill just wanted to drink in a social environment.

People came and went from the busy wine bar, everyone being dressed for a night out on the town. The chatter and laughter became louder as the drinks flowed. Blue smoke filtered through the air from designated smoking points. Music was playing in the background, and Bill heard an Abba song. A song he couldn't remember the name. Three tipsy women danced close to his table. Laura would have joined them, he imagined. They sang along with the lyrics and moved to the rhythm of the tune, he tapped his foot in time with the beat, but Bill still didn't know the song title. But as the chorus came and went, the women sang together, and the title suddenly hit him: "Does your mother know, Does your mother know?"

One of the pirouetting women, a slim twirling figure, lost her footing. The heel on her shoe missed the edge of the step, which threw her body twisting and turning, although she tried hard to remain upright and keep hold of her dignity; her balance was lost, and her frame fell cumbersomely at Bill. Luckily, he caught her, both hands fixed tightly around the slim waist, as she landed perfectly on his lap. She still held her wine glass, thankfully no spillage.

Apologies were made and accepted, an embarrassing giggle came from her mouth as she stood, shook, and adjusted her dress back into shape. And even in the low light, her face had turned red. She and her friends continued to dance as the musician played on. She raised her glass to Bill and mouthed the word "Sorry!"

Bill raised his glass and said, "You're welcome." She heard his reply.

–

It was much later. Trabuxu was still relatively busy, but the atmosphere had somewhat deflated when some lively and happy revellers left.

Only a few couples remained, they stood and chatted on the street. The young engaged couple had left an hour ago.

Bill had consumed his evening idly. He did enjoy observing individuals, how they interacted with each other, all enjoying a night out-on-the-town. Bill relished the vibrant atmosphere and would occasionally reminisce when he heard another memorable song playing in the background, a song that reminded him of being here with Laura. Bill got stuck in a chat with a holidaying couple from Chester. He kept the conversation limited and regularly lied to keep his private life safe, which he wanted to be bolted and secure; away from serious discussion.

Bill's explanation of sitting in a wine bar on his own, was finishing a day house hunting, looking for a second home was his excuse. A lame excuse but a believable story all the same. A way of diverting his real-life issues; he felt white lies was the perfect explanation to avoid revealing any personal details. He didn't want to go there. Although this fabrication of the truth fuelled the couple with added incentives to ask pertinent questions: *Have you found any decent properties yet? Are the properties reasonably priced? Which area do you prefer? What is the cost of living on Malta?*

He stood his ground amiably and batted every ball that came his way, keeping a friendly smile on his face as he portrayed a stranger caught in an uncooperative dilemma, not of his choice. After a few drinks, the couple moved on, wished Bill the best of luck house hunting, and hoped he found an apartment he liked. He felt guilty and stupid.

Trying to remain sober, Bill stood and gathered his thoughts, tucked his shirt into his trousers, and gave thought on working out the best route home possible. He left a substantial tip for the waiter. His movement, though drunk, didn't show much unbalance of dizziness. Stepping up the well-worn lime-stone steps carefully, treading along the frayed path of old long-lost footsteps, he soon reached the street he hoped would be there. It was. Thankfully. This is the correct starting point his churning mind acknowledged. He recognised the surroundings, and soon he was on his way and somehow, after a few minutes slow walking, he passed more groups of partygoers that stood near a bar on Triq Id-Dejqa; which was busy. A few hen nights and stag parties moved around this narrow street.

Each sharing tête-à-têtes with some intimate jovial connections beginning with some younger members of each group; as they headed off in the other direction to join a party at a club or disco or head home to their accommodation.

Further, along Strait Street, more people were eating and drinking. Passing the lively and ever-busy Tico-Tico bar, where music was playing but not too loud, trendy people grouped around tables, and soft lights lit the street. Bill had to squirm his way through the upbeat and enthusiastic crowd of beautiful people until he reached the end of the rabble. Consciously aware he lived a few minutes away, he made a concerted effort to move faster. His bed awaited him.

"Can I buy you a beer?" a female voice erupted near to him as he passed the gathering. Bill stopped walking. Slightly confused and disoriented, Bill scanned the group, hoping to see a familiar face.

The alcohol showed inhibitory impairment to his social and physical actions. His responses were low and unhurried, he looked around the gathering of people, and thought the voice came from the company near him. It was a narrow lane rather than a street. He should pinpoint the person that spoke; even if it wasn't directed at him.

He stared again but got no reaction. Just as he was about to move on, the voice spoke again.

"Over here!" the same female voice said. Which made Bill look until he saw a familiar face smiling at him. He focussed on a beautiful face.

And there she stood. The woman that had clumsily fell onto his lap earlier. Her two friends were in deep conversation with two flashy flamboyant men, who were trying to make a big impression. They were winning the women's admiration, but Bill thought of them as dull and boring twats. He didn't say that, but he wanted to, it was his impressions and all of that. They both exchanged names.

It was working for them but not Alessia. She looked bored. Bill watched curiously, but he did find the whole episode exciting, and Alessia caught his eye in a new way. An attraction that mutually crossed both his and Alessia's mind.

With his focus connected, he sobered to the best of his abilities or as much as the alcohol permitted.

"No more dancing?" Bill said, trying not to fall or stagger. He leant against the wall near the eatery.

"Maybe later. Let me buy you a drink." She showed a broad, red-lipped smile.

"Let me buy you one." Bill enforced his offer by catching the attention of a passing waiter.

They both settled on gin and tonic. Bill perked up somewhat and found a second wind that revitalised and energised him.

Time flew by. Alessia's friends had left with their two overbearing companions. Staggering along the street, laughing and giggling like school girls. Two seats had become available at a nearby table and they managed to grab them. The conversation was pleasant, and hilarity and exciting facts emerged as they both gave little personal details to each other. Bill explained his current life situation, and felt good enough to talk to someone from the female persuasion that had the heart to listen, and someone that also made him laugh.

He wanted the facts laid-out from the outset, and she retorted with her brief life story and her recent divorce. Her sudden flight home from Germany when her husband's lover had moved into their family home, and she had just returned to Malta at the appropriate time, a time when her elderly mother had recently become ill. She was settled now, starting a new chapter to her life, and running the small family shop in Valletta.

Talking about every topic under the sun, from Malta's football teams to the best cheese and wine partnerships. Merlot and blue cheese were mentioned, but neither had tried this mix, but Bill added a proposal that both would go fine with Scottish Oatcakes and a glass of single malt.

–

Alessia Grech was a thirty-five-year-old divorcee. Born and raised in Valletta. She spent most of her adult life in Berlin with her German husband, Kurt. Both working in his family business, running and operating a string of 'Kastanienbaum Kneipe's'; German for chestnut tree pubs; a traditional German tavern serving both food and drink. With all the establishments scattered around Berlin's city centre.

Based and living near the largest of the eight pubs, 'Kastanienbaum Kneipe No 1', located on Kurfurstendamm Avenue. A long boulevard considered the Champs-Elysees of Berlin.

It is lined with high-brand shop outlets, hotels and restaurants, fast-food outlets, and many fashion designers have their shops there, as well as many luxury car manufacturers showrooms dotted along the route. Life in Berlin was sleek and elegant and where the city provides a great work-life balance that finally allows its residents to engage in their interests and hobbies. There is so much to do, but it is also peaceful and quiet.

There are four lines of plane trees along the boulevard, and this avenue-of-trees runs for 2.2-miles through the city. It separates from the Breitscheidplatz, where the ruins of Kaiser Wilhelm Memorial Church stands, leading south up to the district of Grunewald. The family lived in a beautiful and expensive five-bedroom Reihenhaus in Duisburger Strasse; just a short walk from the Number 1 pub. Kurt Schneider, Alessia's husband, forever the Berlin playboy, and part of Berlin's high-society had been having a two-year illicit affair with a young Czech barmaid, who had worked part-time at one of his pubs. The girl was pregnant.

She soon basked in her glory, portraying herself as the future Fraulein Schneider, taking a repulsive and unusual step to move into the house before Alessia had packed her case. His parents, elderly and without grandchildren, sided with their only son and favoured the divorce. Settling for a financial settlement of €500,000. if the divorce was quick. It was. Alessia filled her personal belongings into several canvas and aluminium-built Louis Vuitton cases and flew to Malta within a week. This happened in autumn last year.

Chapter 27
Turkey
The Present Day

The burning rubber of the Goodyear tyres of the Gulfstream G550 hit Adana Şakirpaşa Airport's tarmac in Turkey ten minutes ahead of schedule. Emad felt refreshed, energetic, and prepared for the day early as the luxury jet taxied to a private hanger.

Emad's first vision was walking down the aircraft stairwell was a shiny black stretch limousine parked a few yards beyond, and a well-dressed man; waited patiently for his client.

Emad's second image was the man's face. Vanity or self-abuse had their share of practising or sculping this man's moulded look—a look the stranger liked. Lifts and tucks made his skin rigid, and porcelain teeth shone like beacons. His hair transplant didn't work, not yet anyway; bald areas had a harvest of follicles transplanted hoping to create a new hairline, which he wished, eventually, be full of hair regrowth. Part of his head looked like a newly planted wheat field.

His eyes had bright blue contacts that sparkled and were as blue as a turquoise Caribbean sea, that gave him a youthful and healthy look, and no visible lines or wrinkles could be seen anywhere on his head. Was this man a thirty-five-year-old fitness instructor, or a sixty-five-year-old self-indulgent narcissist? He guessed the second choice. A man that spends his money on his appearance is rich or full of his importance.

The VIP lounge covered all the formalities of handling control, passport, and customs, speedily and efficiently. Emad was soon on his way, leaving the airport and heading on the D-50 motorway at a top speed of 120km per hour, en route to the Luxurious Spa hotel of Gungor Ottoman Palace Antnkay Hatay; a two-and-a-half-hour drive. Emad had only heard reports on the hotel, all good ones.

He perused their website briefly and had a staff member book a suitable suite for his stay. He could relax here. The Spa Hotel is an ornate building on palm-scattered grounds with indoor and outdoor pools.

Time to relax, before the call of business, raises its head. And it would raise its head much sooner than he would ever imagine.

A few phone calls made, and a few received. Emad switched his handset off. Sleeping for most of the long drive.

Emad collected his briefcase and switched his phone on as the car arrived at the resort. The driver was quick to open the door. A tall doorman greeted him warmly, and a small tubby bellboy was already removing his luggage from the trunk and transporting several baggage items through the main entrance. The wheeled trolley squeaked as the boy pushed it.

Emad felt a fresh waft of air as soon as he set foot into the main lobby. With a face that would grow young gracefully, the respectful driver showed a full mouth of white teeth that promoted a stylish look as he followed close behind. He didn't talk; he watched Emad's every move. It was his job to protect his clients, and he was good at his job. Omar Faruk Kaplan is either a 30 or 60yr-old super fit ex MIT Agent, Milli Istihbarat Teskilati or the National Intelligence Organisation; Turkeys intelligence service. Working as a freelance bodyguard, Omar Kaplan, or as his nom de plume adopted—Cengar [(Jeng-a-where]) It's dictionary meaning is a warrior.

In contrast, it represented a regularly active person as a moniker. And this super fit man, a professional who took pride in his appearance, exuded confidence and control and always commanded attention. He was polite and humble and showed respect. What he offered was protection and escort services to an individual. As a freelance security specialist, he was open to all kinds of work. Anywhere in the world. But this man came at a cost. Wealthy businessmen like Emad can easily afford a man such as this when their services were required.

A .22LR calibre Beretta 71 was held in a shoulder holster tucked under his suit jacket. In his unmoving state, he stood a few feet away from Emad as the receptionist registered them both into adjoining suites.

It was noon, and it was hot.

Chapter 28
Valletta
The Present Day

Bill said goodbye to Alessia. They shook hands and kept their first meeting friendly, sociable, and not too serious. Bill was amazed to find Alessia lived just a few streets from his apartment. She lived above the shop, the beautiful and trendy; Kpiepel Redsky. A shop selling an assortment of both women and men's hats. Different types of headwear include; Fedoras, Flat caps, Straw hats, Baseball caps, Berets and Beanie hats, and many more designs from fashions worldwide. It is one of Malta's oldest hat shops that opened in January 1956. Devoted to providing the most extensive assortment of quality, stylish hats on the island. Their friendship would remain casual with no commitment. Tea or coffee or lunch was possibly acceptable, as they both saw it. Both agreed it was an enjoyable evening.

It didn't take long for Bill to hit the sack. While he was tired and drunk, his mind returned to Laura's letters, the grandmother's address still stuck in his mind. Next time he meets Farid, or if there is a next time, he can ask him if there is a chance of finding the girl or her grandmother. Just to know if they are still living in the area; or if either is alive. Bill placed the letter below his pillow. Weirdly, hoping the message would transport him back to Aleppo. And maybe the truth will raise its ugly head. He looked at the letter once more. It read: The house of soap, Al-Zaki soap, Al Qasilah Street, Aleppo.

The little girl's grandparents owned a successful Aleppo soap factory, producing soap for countries throughout the middle east and beyond.

They lived adjacent to the factory, where the famous soap was produced in millions of rock-solid blocks of the green hand-made, hard-bar soap; made from olive oil and lye, from which it is distinguished by the addition of laurel oil. More popularly known as castile soap. Although the origin of the soap is unknown.

Unproven claims of its magnificent antiquity abound, such as its supposed use by Queen Cleopatra of Egypt and Queen Zenobia of Syria, but with civil unrest and since Laura last made contact, it all may be gone now. But to find Raca, It was a chance, a very slight chance. However slim it was, and if he could contact Farid again. Then this may be the only chance to find her.

–

Slumberland arrived sooner than he thought. And his wishes were granted. In his new vision, he saw Aleppo, there was people screaming in terror and running from a scene of destruction.

Everyone was scared. Farid was frightened. Many were injured, the old and infirm lay where they fell, bodies with missing limbs blocked the road they approached. Farid Aboud was sitting on a wooden bench, in the back of an open-ended, canvas covered truck. Sitting opposite other rescuers, all dressed similarly. Black working overalls, rubber boots, each wearing a white helmet with a torch held to the hat's front. White dust and respirator masks rested on each of their chests waiting to be used.

There was no talking now. Work was the only thought on each of their minds. Saving life was their number one priority. These guys were arriving at a site of a recent bombing. A vision no one would ever want to bear witness. A Syrian army barrel bomb, a type of improvised explosive device made from high explosives, mixed with shrapnel and oil, had been dropped from a gunship.

The lorry moved slowly along the shoddily cleared roads close to the destruction site. It was a bumpy ride, running over stones and bricks, kicking rubble into the air; mainly hitting the ambulance behind them. "Can you hear me, Farid? It's Bill!" was the only words that came to Farid's mind. There was no response. Bill remembered Farid had to openly talk to respond, so he asked again.

"If you can hear me, can you rub your mouth with your right hand?"

Farid raised his right hand and rubbed his mouth to confirm they were together again. Bill was back as a guest, and Farid was the host. This time, together, they were embarking on dual education on lifesaving. Bill remained silent.

The small dilapidated serviced vehicles stopped short of the bomb-damaged area. Dust filled the space they entered. Devastated buildings faced them as they leapt from the van. The rescuers put respirators in place over their noses and mouths, and other rescuers met them—all arriving with the same understanding—to save any buried, living soul. A young boy walked from the scene, crying. His head was bleeding freely from an open wound just above his right eye. A dead woman lay near the boy. He screamed at the rescuers.

"It was the Russians. They killed my grandmother," said the tearful boy.

He sobbed, and a helpful paramedic ushered the injured boy to a nearby ambulance to clean his wound and inspect any other injury. The old woman had received horrendous injuries. Her head decapitated, her torso hanging by strands of sinews and torn muscle; both separated from her body by a short blast of fire from a 12.7mm Yak-B minigun on the bomb dropping gunship. Death to anyone caught in its line of obliterating gunfire. These death machines were killing civilians. They would destroy every living being in their sights, including innocent civilians. They always kill indiscriminately. Death was the game they played. A game with one rule; kill all opposition.

Civilian helpers were already on site, clearing heavy pieces of masonry, removing chunks of mortar, carefully getting rid of broken and burning furniture. They were stopping work every few moments, holding hands in the air to pass this message for other helpers to fall silent and listening for a noise, a cry for help, a baby screaming, a faint voice from a seriously injured person, a child asking for their mother. A dog barked in the distance. The red-furred mongrel appeared at the site of devastation and ran watchfully over the fallen buildings. It was looking for its owner. The work continued by clearing the mountain of debris in the hope to find survivors.

Crawling over the remains of a ruined house, a woman was frantically directing the rescuers to an area where she believed her daughter was buried. "Here, here! Please, over here!" she screamed. "My girl is here. Please, please help."

Navigating their way urgently over the insecure and unsafe rubble, they managed to unearth the child crushed under debris and clear her mouth of dust. One aid worker poured bottled water on her face, gave her a drink and told her to spit out. She could drink the next mouthful.

"We are coming, little girl. Don't be afraid," one rescuer told the child. "Praise God!" he added thoughtfully.

Bill viewed this scene as Farid was one of the participants waiting to rush the child to the hospital.

Within a minute, the team managed to free the girl. They were removing her from the rubble and carrying her alive, from the place of devastation. The child was passed along the line in a chain, which led the girl to Farid. He moved as fast as he could to rush the cruelly injured girl, whose left leg dangled from her knee, held in place with a slither of blooded skin, and hoped the hospital medical staff would do their job and save her life, and hopefully her leg. Farid applied a tourniquet to her thigh, and bandages held her loose leg together, and another sip of freshwater was given to her, which made her sick, spitting out black dust that filled her lungs' airways.

The girl's arms and face were covered in lacerations.

Her mother was uninjured, she followed Farid and her child, and they entered the ambulance together, leaving the ruined scene as another make-shift ambulance arrived to take its place. The remaining white helmets continued to search for more lost souls as they would for the next 20hrs; bringing small mechanical diggers in to help find buried people. They would save six souls and remove twenty corpses; one survivor was a new born baby.

Farid, the injured child and her profoundly concerned mother headed to the hospital in the Al-Safsafah region. A few miles away from the blast zone. The only hospital still operating in an area occupied by extremists and other religious groups.

The sad looking, undernourished mongrel dog that barked and appeared at the bomb site; continued to yell. It was a strange-looking dog, and as weird as it sounds, it looked as though it was a half fox and half Palestinian Pariah dog; beautiful but ugly. The determined mutt frantically clawed and scratched, and dug furiously at the debris, which made the curious humans assist her exploration into the mass of rubble. She refused to leave the site. She kept digging. She whined as she burrowed at the wreckage.

To support the dog, white helmets took turns burrowing to clear the dirt and remove big concrete blocks until a tiny gap appeared. They heard small puppies whimpering below where they stood. The mother dog had found her litter of four pups buried underneath the collapsed home of her owner. There was a cheer when the animals were pulled alive from the fallen house. The pooch and her puppies were safe, and soon she fed her hungry babies. An elderly man stood over the happy mother dog as she provided her litter with whatever nutrition she had in her, he beamed at the thought that animals had a strong family instinct even in war. Her once sad eyes now showed relief and contentment.

The dog's owner and his wife were later found dead. The dog and her puppies would join the elderly man and his family on the journey to Turkey, like many thousands of others fleeing persecution, violence, and war in the country, they were forced to flee Syria.

–

"It's not about the rights or wrongs, or even the curiosities of war that test every man's conscience. Whether part of one side or part of the other; or part of a bigger, more intricate clearer picture. A picture that allows everyone to stake a claim of their own choice; create their own destiny. In war, everybody loses. Its mutual suicide. And my decision is simple, I would side with no-one. Not the government, not the factions, not one of the fanatical religious rebel groups, nor the local criminal militia, and I stand by my choice. I fight no-one.

"Living under the restricted condition of war and saving lives in these extremities is always harsh. But people of peace often find themselves in this position. Living among the bombs, bullets, and shells. Law-abiding citizens always play an active role in these situations, and we suffer like everyone else. Those who kill in the name of war, not for order or justice, or giving hope to the masses, are for unjust, selfish causes.

"It's a crazy thing, war. I stand on no moral high ground, but I stand far enough away from the ground where evil and unjust men stand to fight. Living in peace and harmony kills no one. We just need to learn from our continual mistakes."

The video camera was switched off.

Farid had recorded another short film for his video diary. The day after another day of devastation. Three of his colleagues were killed when a gunship retargeted an already bombed school building. As soon as the white helmets resumed their search, waiting a period of five to twenty minutes, often during which first responders arrive, the military strike again. This time, killing over thirty civilian rescuers. And over twenty primary school children lost their young lives, due to indiscriminate bombing from a sophisticated army using murderous tactics and showing how disgusting and futile life is when human society becomes entangled in war.

Farid knew that Bill had at least returned to share his living reality. He spoke aloud.

"Ah! Bill, it has been a few years since we did this. Once again meeting in my mind and for you to bear witness to the atrocities that my countrymen and other disgusting mercenaries, repeatedly do." He said, sitting in his apartment on a sofa covered with red velvet cushions.

"It has been a long time for you, Farid, but for me, it has been only days," Bill offered within the mind of Farid, his host.

Farid didn't respond. It was crazy and surreal, so a few days or a few years didn't matter to him. He had no control over this connection, both men were veteran atheists caught in a world of fantastical things, some for power and others for religious reasons. And one of those things was real life. Neither would ever pray for guidance or peace. It was a prayer that started this nonsense in the first place. Strong-minded people with good-of-heart must always stand up to evil.

Farid stepped to the window and opened the curtain just enough to look out and see the rebels on the street. He spoke aloud allowing Bill to understand the current situation. Soldiers were both waiting for the action to begin. About a mile away, gunshots could be heard. "At this range, though, it may sound almost like somebody knocking on a table,"

"As you can see, Bill, nothing much has changed. Today is Wednesday, the 10th of February 2016. Many different groups control this area and surrounding neighbourhoods. Presently, we have Al-Qaeda and other religious assemblies fighting against the Syrian Army and fighting amongst themselves on the street below. The government forces are also deep into Aleppo. So whichever way we walk. We would pass any of the numerous amounts of willing killers. Do you know why you are back with me again, Bill?"

Bill had listened intently to Farid's statement; he, too, was surprised at the length of time that had passed since they had joined in real-time. But now they are part of the same function, together and sharing Farid's life in battle-scarred Syria.

"It's a very long story…but do you remember the little girl that discovered you after the bomb blast in Al-Hatab Square?"

"Yes, she found me and got help. It was our first meeting."

"I believe all of our meetings and close connections have a lot to do with her, I can explain much more details later, but at present, all I can say is that her full name is Raca Sana Sleiman. She is a local Christian girl from Aleppo, and I need your help to find her and get her to safety." Bill kept the information short and to the point.

Farid spoke to Bill as he returned to the sofa. He listened to Bill's request and would help if he could. He asked a question about the girl's whereabouts.

"Do you know where this girl is?"

"I have the address of the last place she stayed, but this was back in 2012. Her grandparents owned a soap factory near there, and It is the House Al-Zaki, Al-Qasilah street Aleppo. That is all I have. I'm sorry."

"Al-Zaki Soap. I know this place. But most of that area has been destroyed beyond recognition. But there are times when people return to the destroyed building and set up home again. This has been done by many people, regardless of how damaged the old houses are. She may be staying with friends or family."

"Is it feasible to check out the address?" Bill asked.

"Yes, it's feasible but dangerous!"

"Her grandmother is called Sosa Der Kirkour. It's her house in Al-Quasilah street," Bill said and mentioned further, "In a letter I recently read, the little girl, Raca, would often play in tunnels under the soap factory. So maybe she is hiding there."

"Maybe she did hide there. But I very much doubt if she could have hidden there for four years. There are still many people in the area, living a squalid life among the ruins.

Living daily with the threat of death. That area was bombed only yesterday, and we are due back today to assist with further searches. For some reason or another, I somehow feel obliged and happy to help."

"I thank you for your help, Farid."

"Don't thank me, Bill. Thank whoever paired us together."

–

Two trucks of white helmets arrived at Al Qasilah street, bringing medical evacuation, helping with the removal of civilians from hazardous areas, and provide critical life-saving services.

The recent onslaught to this district was a constant barrage of 160mm shell bombs, fired from a Russian M240 field mortar—a two-wheeled travelling carriage that is mobile and destructive; entirely focussed on firing, relentlessly, on the same concentrated area. Soviet 240mm Mortars were firing 130 kilograms of explosives anywhere from a range up to six miles. This region had been a base for a terrorist group, and that is why the government forces used so much indiscriminate firepower.

A target range, hit with success, over an expanse of fifty square meters, had been ruthlessly destroyed. The buildings were beyond repair, but this assault was relentless—intermittent bombardment over 48hrs. Presumably known opposition Headquarters, and terminating a viable, valuable infrastructure, to where the terrorists had a unified command and control structure deployed, was the attackers primary objective. All the rebels are gone now. Farid was sure the surviving ISIS rebels had disappeared into the mass of maze-like alleys, hidden tunnels, and other similar places to hide amongst the destroyed buildings. Preparing for medieval street fighting among the damaged buildings, narrow lanes, subterranean highways; when government forces eventually send in their ground troops, to begin the urban warfare. One way or another, they would live to fight another day; until they won or were annihilated. This was a fight to the death.

The Al Qasilah street intersection would leave a gap where other offshoots of opposition will fill and take over; regardless of the massive bombing campaign. Destroy the molehill and another two appear.

It is always that way.

Defenders have the advantage of historical facts of the district they protect, including an understanding with building plans and means of travel not shown on local maps. Buildings provide perfect sniping posts while alleys and debris-filled streets are ideal for installing booby-traps, or a unique, specialised place of allurement. There is also an advantage of moving from one area to another undetected using underground tunnels; where the defenders can operate further ambushes.

On the other hand, the attackers tend to be more exposed than the army defending, as they need to use the streets more often and would be unfamiliar with the defender's hidden routes. House to house fighting is always a requirement in civil wars. But it becomes a long drawn-out affair with many casualties on both sides.

In most cases, with street-fighting, hard-fought land gains are often followed by repeatedly losing the same land, and the battle restarts again.

But Farid had the feeling that the highly religious, fanatical insurrectionists would retreat and return another day. ISIS don't do running. Everyone is a martyr to their cause.

This recent damage happened over an already ruined Al Qasilah district. But the latest demolition was mainly on the road to look for the house; Al-Qasilah street, as Farid and his band of brothers moved at haste to search under the wreckage. As the rough and tumble convoy of two rusty old Nissan Vanettes, and a Long-wheeled-based Nissan Caravan Ambulance arrived at the scene, Farid was aware that Bill had again joined him. Now they both could search for Raca.

The street had lost all its buildings. Not one structure could be identified, even by a local. But Farid, in his wisdom, had looked over maps he had at home, and with some simple search of the area where he stood, staring north to the Aleppo citadel, he managed to place himself precisely on the spot where the house should be. Some buildings stood and looked intact, all but the loss of several walls. It looked like a movie set for a war film. Not a beautiful city as Aleppo was renowned. He was sure the edifice before was the place he sought.

What remained of the old apartment block was held together with hope—more than any strength of materials that stitched it together. The building was old, and one side had been completely blown off, he could see washing hanging from several windows about four stories high. Some apartments looked intact and gave him the impression that people may be living there. He would start his search here.

His fellow white helmets began looking around the area as civilians made their way from shelter to aid the cause of searching for survivors. Around sixty people, men, women, and children, joined the rescuers, actively working for the same goal. Although over two days of bombing, it was doubtful there would be any survivors—just dead bodies.

–

It was hesitant, unsure footsteps Farid took as he entered the wrecked apartment; the concrete stairwell was damaged in most parts, dangerous to tread, and challenging to walk on. Farid slowly but surely managed to clear two floors until he reached a point where the steps upward had disappeared. They were gone. He was now standing outside, open to the elements, with dangerous overhanging concrete walls dangling overhead. Some rubble collapsed above him, fell where he stood, and hit the ground below.

It was too late to look for another route, and a new way up had to be found, so he clambered over masonry that was loosely held together by rusty remnants of the metal rod rebar and mesh that once held the reinforced concrete together. Bill was more nervous than Farid; as his gloved fingers took a solid grip on the exposed steel framework, he managed with much effort to pull himself up and over to the third level. Bill was relieved. Farid spoke, "'I wonder how I get back down?"'

Bill remained silent.

Moving into the interior, the retained wall before them showed remnants of a room, a bedroom by the design of wallcoverings; suddenly, shattered brickwork threw splinters of slab and plasterwork around him. He dived into the open space, a few feet to his left. A sniper had taken a shot, and thankfully not a fully trained marksman, or if he were, he would be dead. But again, a white helmet was being targeted. People on the ground heard the shot and reacted defensively. The work below stopped, and everyone ran for cover. A marksman was testing his newly cleaned gun. Target practice, Farid thought.

Now running up stable steps, he reached a floor level facing two doors. He knew well that knocked doors may not always be answered, especially in Syria during this day and age.

He banged on the first door, partially open, and swung inward. He entered and took cautious steps eyeing every inch that came into his view but soon realised that this place was empty. The gaping spacious room showed him this. The apartment's far side was gone and was now part of the rubble lying on the street. He moved assuredly back to the landing, knowing too well that the sniper was still lurking somewhere in the distance and this time, his aim might just hit its mark. On the second door, he hit three loud thumps. Waiting for a moment, then repeated the noise by using the heel of his hand. Still no reply, he placed his hand on the door handle and was about to open the door when it swung inwards, and an older woman greeted him.

"Hello, can I help you?"

Farid was shocked when he saw the old woman, he was surprised that she looked unharmed, or had lived through the troubles to appear in such grace despite war's violence.

“My name is Farid. Farid Aboud. I am looking for…” Farid forgot the woman’s name. It faded from his memory.

Bill informed him, “Her name is Sosa Der Kirkour.”

“I’m looking for Sosa Der Kirkour?” Farid said with anticipation.

“I am Sosa Der Kirkour. How can I help you?

“I would like to ask you a few questions if that’s OK?”

“Yes, please come in.” she said without argument or reason.

The old lady walked back into the house and Farid followed. Walking along a short corridor and turned left into a kitchen come diner, that looked remarkably intact and undamaged; for the constant destruction, this area, and this building, in particular, had endured.

“Please take a seat, Mr Aboud,” the women said, remembering his name. Farid took a seat at the dining table in what was a large room. There were six matching chairs at a profusely inlaid Syrian Damascene rectangular dining table, where the legs are intricate in design with multiple inlays and boxwood line. The room looked grand—a better place than he had imagined. A Syrian carpet with a plush pile and a bold, decorative design, covered most of the wooden floor. An antique-styled Middle Eastern beaded chandelier swayed in the centre of the ceiling.

The room smelled damp, and heavy gold-coloured curtains swung at both sides of the main window, with yellow-lace-stained curtains covered the remaining glass. An L-shaped well-worn leather suite ran along two walls, and a matching tall, dark Damascene wall cabinet inlaid with mother of pearl proved that this apartment was a household of wealth. The dresser was filled with an assortment of porcelain figurines. It stood near the door.

Historical Syrian paintings and groups of family photographs were hung on most walls, and a picture of Jesus took centrepiece on the main wall facing him. A wall tablet was held on the back of the door when the old woman closed it. A senior Syrian proverb was carved into the hardwood plaque. It said: “Ejet el hazineh la tefrah, ma la2et matra7.” Farid didn’t quite understand the rhetoric behind the quote. But he had heard it before. The saddened woman came to a happy celebration and didn’t find a seat. What Farid thought it meant was: *When you finally decide to do something but have missed the opportunity*. He was correct with his assumption.

Farid was busy looking over the room, and admiring its precious treasures and hadn’t noticed the old lady re-emerge from a different place, which he soon gathered it was the kitchen. She walked to the table and placed a tray with a hot bowl of soup, fresh bread and utensils for Farid to enjoy.

"I…really." Was Farid's attempt at being polite. But he should have known better.

"Please, Farid. My Shurbat Addes is delightful. A recipe my mother gave me, from her mother before her. It will keep you warm inside."

Being polite and thankful, he ate the soup. He agreed with the old woman. "This is the best Shurbat Addes I have tasted in an awfully long time. It tastes wonderful. I am grateful for your generosity." He spooned the soup until it was gone but refused extras. While he was here for other reasons, the old woman asked him a question he would be glad to answer.

"So why are you here, Farid?" The old woman joined him by taking a seat at the opposite end of the table.

Farid wiped his mouth with the napkin he was provided. Crumpled the used towel in his hand and laid it on a small plate.

"I believe your granddaughter, Raca, saved my life in the bombing of Al-Hatab square in 2012. After the bomb exploded, I was entombed under much rubble, and thankfully, your granddaughter heard my calls for help. So, I would like to thank her, personally. To thank her for saving my life."

"Raca told me she had seen a man under the rubble. I'm glad you are alive and well. You are working for the white helmets now?"

The old woman's response was difficult for Farid to comprehend. She asked a question rather than divulge her grand-daughter's whereabouts which made Farid feel uneasy and somewhat perturbed. The old woman did not understand the circumstances. She was living in a war zone, in the centre of Aleppo, how could she treat life as if nothing has happened; especially under the current conditions of a civil war.

Maybe she had the onslaught of presenile dementia or Alzheimer's or perhaps the fact she was living in conflict areas where many people suffered depression, post-traumatic stress disorder, schizophrenia or bipolar disorder. With the woman being elderly, the burden of affliction rises with age. Possibly she was living in denial; protecting herself from the dangerous world that exists outside her home. A contradiction that can interfere with her ability to tackle challenges. Whatever the cause, she did show signs of some mental stress. Her body's defences kicked in gear, an automatic process known as the fight or flight syndrome raised its head, a reaction, or the stress response. She hid at home and thought all was well with the world. The world that she lived in was her perfect place of sanctuary.

"Yes, I joined the white helmets in 2013. I wanted to save lives. Your granddaughter gave me hope, and I wanted to do the same for others."

The old woman wandered off on another dialogue exchange, and away from the question Farid wished answered.

"My Sana loves my Shurbat Addes. Can you take a flask of soup with you? If you find her, that is. She will trust you if you offer her grandmother's soup. She will know that my soup cannot be copied by anyone. My recipe has a special ingredient. Her taste buds will identify my home cooking."

"To find her?" Farid asked. Bill remained silent but understood the situation Farid found himself. In a conversation with a sick old woman suffering from dementia. Her memory was deteriorating, her thinking, behaviour and the ability to perform everyday activities were failing, except for making soup.

"Raca has been staying with friends for the last few months, but Mithra returned to her, he wanted to lead Raca to the treasure. It is a journey she has longed to do for years."

Bill reminded Farid that Mithra was a cat, a ginger tomcat that he recently discovered information about. The old woman continued, "She went looking for treasure with her cat. The most beautiful, elegant and handsome tomcat you will ever see. A wise and mysterious cat."

"She went on a journey with a cat. Are you not worried about her safety? There is a lot of unsavoury people out there. There is a dangerous war in Syria, Mrs Der Kirkour. And your granddaughter is only…"

Bill promptly told Farid Sana's age, which Farid spoke it aloud, "She will be nine or ten."

"Don't worry, Farid. The cat will look after my granddaughter. Mithra is the storm God. He will protect her; he will lead her to the stolen artwork. He promised this. She must find the stolen art and return it to the rightful owner."

Farid thought the old woman had lost it; her mind had finally succumbed to the relentless battle against extreme confusion. She had lost her marbles. Even though he thought his uneducated diagnosis was a bit harsh.

Bill spoke for the first time.

"I know about stolen artwork, Farid. Raca overheard this information before the Al-Hatab bombing and Laura left me detailed notes on this. It's a long story, and one that you will realise is part of the bigger picture we are both involved in."

Farid understood Bill's support. He wanted details on Raca's status.

"Is Raca still in Aleppo?" Farid asked.

"Raca headed through the tunnels and is on her way to the Citadel," the old woman spoke reasonably. She honestly believed her young granddaughter was safe and on a journey of hope, with a mystical ginger tomcat. "The artwork is her route to freedom. Raca knows this," replied Sosa Der Kirkour.

"Where can I find this tunnel entrance?"

"It is close by. I can point you in the direction."

Farid said his polite goodbyes, thanked Sosa Der Kirkour for her hospitality and kindness and the superb-tasting Shurbat Addes.

"Please wait, and I will put some soup into a flask. Raca will be energised with my soup."

The old lady left the room, and Farid answered Bill's question about the soup. "It translates to red lentil soup, Bill. It's a delicacy here in Syria. It has many different herbs and spices, every recipe changes. But I must admit that Mrs Der Kirkour's soup is delicious. But what is all this stuff about stolen artwork?"

Bill was about to respond when Mrs Kirkour re-entered the room.

"Here is the soup for Raca, Farid," the old lady said, handing over a chrome vacuum insulated flask.

Farid put the warm container into the holdall that had been unstrapped from his back. He closed the bag, put his arms through the loops, pulled the straps over his shoulder and clipped the plastic buckle fasteners into place. He was ready to move on.

The old lady walked to the lace-covered windows and held back a small portion of the curtain so she could see outside. "Here, Farid. This is where you need to go."

Farid joined her at the window. Looking down to the street, he saw a white painted closed door, in a building that still contains the ground floor, with all the others above, in a derelict form.

"The entrance leads to our offices in our old Soap Factory. Once inside, follow the signs to the storage room, it is along many corridors, once you reach the storage room, there is another door, situated in the corner, behind a heavy metal cabinet, you will find steps that lead four stories down. This will take you to the place where the tunnels start. These passageways will take you to the

Citadel. This is where Raca and Mithra headed. She must find the artwork; she must leave Syria. Please help my granddaughter, Farid."

Again, he thanked her. He would do his best to find and help the girl. He gave his word. The old woman never crossed over the threshold of the front door. She gave Farid an alternative, safe route down to the ground level. She waved and wished him luck. The door was slammed behind him that made him jump.

–

Word spread that the sniper was dead, killed by a new group that moved in to fill the space. Rescue work had restarted. A group that wouldn't fire on civilians, thankfully. All of which was typical in Aleppo nowadays. The white helmets and civilians were working together, hoping to save lives. The badly demoralised ISIS-affiliated group would now retreat to another battlefront, with the ambition to find others with a similar belief, to join their cause. And in some cases make their captives join their struggle under the threat of death.

The bomb site was busy—people arrived from areas of shelter.

Bringing whatever food, and freshwater they could muster. Feeding and watering the angels that searched for life. They would keep working until all hope of finding survivors had diminished.

The door to the building entrance was stiff and jammed, but it was forcibly stuck agape with rubble and other forms of fragments holding it in position. Farid put his shoulder against the frame and pushed with much effort; the door moved inward a foot or so more, nearly enough space to squeeze his thin frame into the interior of the soap factory. As he attempted entry, he took time to look back at the first-floor apartment of Sosa Der Kirkour, and it was gone. The amazed, scared look ran the rule over Farid's face, and Bill also bore witness to the sight before them. A completely bombed-out apartment. Most of the walls was missing, a gap in the frame where the window once was—the window that he had glanced through five minutes previously—was bare of glass and missing. A portion of burnt lace curtain was all that remained.

A long oblong strip of lace hung from the long-gone window frame, fluttering, and flapping in the wind and making a snapping sound. The remainder of the apartment had been damaged many weeks previously, or possibly much longer. This was not a recent act of violence.

The door he pushed against had been stuck on a small wooden plaque wedged under the bottom sill. He removed it and saw an old Syrian proverb written on it: “Ejet el hazineh la tefrah, ma la2et matra7.”

Bill spoke, “The old lady’s wall plaque.”

Both stared at the bombed building.

“I spoke with Sosa Der Kirkour; she was as real as it gets, not with you in my head, that is too weird to fathom, but the fact is I sat in her home, talked to her, and ate her soup. She seemed genuinely alive and real. Not a phantom or a ghost. It seems that a force of some kind drives everything that happens to me nowadays, but whatever that power is, I don’t understand why it needs me. It is way beyond anything I can comprehend. No matter what happens next, however difficult life becomes, I will remain loyal to my atheistic view on life.”

“I agree. But the old woman also gave you a flask of soup. Check your holdall,” Bill offered. Believing that there was no flask now. It was part of a dream, possibly Farid had drunk polluted water which made him hallucinate, and Bill had witnessed the effects. The water in Aleppo had recent cases of typhoid and salmonella reported from drinking contaminated water. Bill wanted to say this but thought otherwise.

Farid had already taken moves to check inside the holdall. Removing it from his shoulders, ran the slider along the fabric’s full length, and with amazement, the flask was there. Just where he had placed it. Bill became aware that Farid had packed other items as if he was there when he loaded it; but he wasn’t. There were two bottles of water, a small black Ambertech torch, toiletries, a pack of Barazek sesame pistachio cookies, sunglasses, a bottle of hand steriliser and a Swiss Army knife and a physical, reliable and real, not an optical illusion; an insulating storage vessel holding red lentil soup. The vacuum flask obtained from a phantom.

“We carry on, Bill. I need to forget this nonsense; we must find the young girl. If she is two days ahead of us, she may well be in trouble. Or hiding.” Farid returned the backpack high on his back and made sure the shoulder straps were comfortable and tight. He pushed the door hard, and it moved far enough for him to gain easier access. After stepping inside, he struggled to close the door behind him. The journey was ready to begin.

Chapter 29
HMP Edinburgh
The Present Day

It was 11 am.

Reverend Douglas McAuley finished his half-cup of lukewarm, vending-machine coffee as he waited in the Multi-Faith Centre office at HMP Edinburgh. He spiritually prepared himself to meet the sociopathic serial killer, Finlay McColl. The evil murderer had requested this meeting and asked explicitly for Reverend Douglas McAuley by name. The minister only knew the infamous killer by reputation. They had never met.

The office door squeaked open, and an attentive officer appeared and held the door open.

"If you would like to follow me, Minister, McColl is ready," he said, showing the way ahead.

The minister dropped the empty, crumpled, ripple effect paper cup into the bin provided. The container was for recycled paper—the plastic bin with the green chasing arrow logo. Although this was his third, the coffee was acceptable, and the caffeine had increased his heart rate and respiration, and his disposition proved his anxiety levels had increased.

They both entered the religious room where McColl was already seated. The place looked like a church of sorts and was used for all religious prisoners. Which included Christian denominations, Jewish, Muslims and other world faiths or spiritual tradition; when inmates require solace, they could meet here.

The multi-faith-centre was used for interfaith dialogue and positive collaboration between diverse religious practices, spiritual, or even humanistic opinions. It was a large room, similar in size to a village hall, containing many seats, it was painted in light colours. It had a warm and welcoming feeling and a place where all religious denominations could enter, pray, or intermingle with others willing to participate in understanding each other's beliefs. If it only worked thought Douglas McAuley.

It appeared that sunlight was streaming through stained-glass windows, but there was no sunlight or windows in the room. A sign stuck on the back of the main door caught the minister's attention. It said: 'With God, all things are possible!'

Another officer who had escorted the prisoner here from his lockup stood near this door. The burly officer would wait and watch until the curious encounter was over, before returning McColl back to his cell, and would only intervene if the prisoner showed any sign of violence or violent aggression.

Finlay McColl slouched on a black plastic stacking chair with both hands resting flat on his thighs, he rubbed them on his trousers to remove excess sweat. He was wearing a green prison-issue polo shirt with HMP Edinburgh embroidered on the left chest, the shirt would possibly fit a man 42lbs lighter. Over a pair of dull-coloured jogging pants that matched the shirt, a fat belly hung. A pair of Adidas trainers without laces covered his swollen feet. On the toe of each shoe, his name was handwritten in blue ballpoint ink.

Unshaved for over a week, he had a beastly appearance, and his thinning hair was shoulder-length and greasy. He had a prominent bald patch on the middle of his head. His bloodshot and nearly closed eyes were yellow, and the skin around his eyes was swollen and puffy—a doctor had diagnosed a condition of jaundice. His bottom lip was swollen and had recently stopped bleeding.

The minister pulled up a similar chair, placed it near McColl, close enough to face him. They were three feet apart. Reverend McAuley held his small black leather-bound Bible on his lap. The minister had prayed and said another prayer in silence before starting the conversation. The younger officer that escorted the minister stood a few feet behind him. He would keep a close watch on proceedings. A defender of the faith, he smiled at the thought.

"How can I help you?" Reverend McAuley said while turning his head, hoping that both officers were watching. A morale boost engulfed him when he noticed they were.

"You can't help me, Minister. But I can help you!" Finlay McColl stared deep into the minister's eyes as if searching for his soul. It made the reverend feel uncomfortable and uneasy, but he had dealt with evil people in the past. McColl would be no different.

"OK…so how can you help me?"

"I believe if you look deep into someone's eyes, you can see a person's sincerity and truth. As if staring into their souls. Do you believe in God minister?" Despite the minister's unblinking eyes, he continued to look at him.

"Well…yes."

"You hesitated. Are you having issues with your God?"

"No! I believe in God. I have every faith in him." His response was weak and uncontrolled.

McColl's swerve ball caught him off-guard.

"Did you know that humans can suppress parts of the brain for analytical thinking and involve the elements answerable for empathy to believe in God. Maybe your God is in your head and nowhere else," he said, fidgeting in his chair as if moving in the direction of the minister. This movement made the reverend adjust his posture. McColl settled when the prison officers reacted and told him to remain seated.

McColl smiled at their embarrassing move. They didn't react to his foibles; they knew how he worked the system.

McColl continued, "You see, minister, or should I call you Douglas? I have had words with God. Not your God…but my personal God. And I was told things. Bizarre things." He paused.

The minister remained silent. Douglas McAuley was uncomfortable being in McColl's company.

Finlay McColl shouted forcefully, so the officers could hear his outburst.

"My God is a woman!" He laughed—a throaty laugh, with groans, pants and short snorts like a mud-rolling pig. The officer at the back wall moved hesitantly in response to the outburst. He would remain there. Close enough to react if any other problem arose.

McColl diverted his insensitive eyes to stare at the intruding officer who had stepped into his personal space. He held this gaze for a few long seconds. Before returning his constant focus of visual interest at the minister.

"Minister, my God mentioned you by name. She told me I was to help you…She told me to help your friend…Bill McFuckingKenzie. The son of the fucking bitch that so wanted me jailed—"

A prison officer interrupted, "Keep it clean, McColl!" voicing his authority. McColl didn't like the officer's intervention, he mouthed a conceited, arrogant smile that made the fearful minister clinch uncomfortably.

"As I was saying before I was rudely interrupted." He hesitated and spoke softly. "My God, my female God, has asked me to give you burial details of where all of my beautiful girls can be found. She wants me to confess my glory and release my beauties from their resting place.

"She gets mad with me, Douglas! Does your God get crazy with you? When she first came to me, I thought it was a bad dream, but there she was, every night, demanding me to reveal my secret. Tormenting me, intimidating me, threatening to kill me. Is it possible that God would want to kill one of her children?"

He tapped his forefinger on the temple point on his head.

"She screamed abuse into my head till it ached. I couldn't get her to leave me alone. My Deity is relentless, Douglas. My God wanted me to reveal the burial sites, so she could collect their souls. Not your concept of God, nor anyone's phoney God; It had to be my Divinity, asking me to surrender the truth, release their souls to her heaven, and I would live in peace forever." His lip was hurting as he raised his right hand to wipe his mouth using the knuckle of his forefinger.

He raised both hands and pulled his hair hard till it made him grimace. His demeanour changed. Leaning forward, he continued to talk. Both guards stood in preparation to react at a moment's notice.

"She must fuckin like you, Douglas. Maybe you should start praying to her. I will never understand why she never contacted your direct, it would have saved me so much lost sleep and causing severe excruciating damage to myself. My supreme Goddess commanded me to speak with you. Gods can demand things.

"I punched the walls of my cell and used my head as a battering ram on the door, just to remove her niggling voice, my personal God, with her relentless bickering from infiltrating my thoughts. She would not let me rest. Is your God like this? Douglas…" He stopped talking, he simpered and listened to the voice in his head; God was talking to him. The minister looked nervous, sitting close to and listening to a psychopath talking utter nonsense. If he was confessing to serious crimes, he should speak to the police. Or a Catholic priest sitting in a wooden structure, partitioned—where he could talk through a latticed opening to the holy man and ask for forgiveness. But this was Finlay McColl, and his penitents were not usual or customary.

"She said she likes you and wants you to tell your friend, your wealthy friend a secret message. Seemingly he is so desperate to know three little words. Bill

McFuckinKenzie. You know who I'm talking about. Tell him the words are Raca and Mithra. Whatever the fuck that means."

An officer again warned McColl over his abusive language.

McColl leaned in the face of the minister. Staring obstinately at his unique hairstyle, then pressed his full body, relaxed and supported against the back of the chair, and stretched his legs as if he were watching a movie.

"Do you have a pen and paper, Douglas? If not, you may forget what I am about to say." Reverend McAuley hastily put his hand inside his jacket and removed a biro. He found some crumpled paper in his outside jacket pocket. He scribbled as McColl spoke.

"NN57290, 55142. You will find my beauties there." He paused. He was listening to a voice in his head again. His head moved erratically; his face looked distorted.

His hands were banging his skull, a voice was screaming inside his head. The minister saw McColl's eyes twist and turn in their sockets, and he began to rock back and forth, making the chair scrape the studded industrial vinyl floor as he pushed his feet hard downward to make the chair move backwards away from the minister. He made low grunted animal type noises, and horrible green snot ran from his nose. It was with this move that he gained space. His time had arrived. He rose and attacked the startled vicar.

The officers also moved swiftly to restrain McColl, but before they got close enough to confine his actions, the prisoner had subdued the minister and looped both hands around his neck, pulling him close enough to speak into his ear.

"Minister, my God is your friend Laura McKenzie. She sends her absolute best wishes."

McColl, now tangled and tousled among multiple flaying arms, being pulled and tugged by keen, well-trained, determined prison officers; working hard to remove the serial killer from the solid grip he had on the petrified vicar. McColl had also snatched the preacher's Bible, and as it fell to the floor, McColl's foot launched it over to the exit door as another two officers arrived at the scene. One ran to help his colleagues; the other picked up the small Bible. The Bible was open, and a verse was circled in blue ink: Job 28-28.

"And to man, He said, '"Behold, the fear of the Lord, that is wisdom; and to depart from evil is understanding."

McColl was using every bit of his 20-stone blubbery frame to keep a tight embrace of the Minister, and by carefully pulling him closer, he forced an excessive full-blown head butt onto the nose of the cleric. His nose burst open, and gushes of blood poured from the wound. Internal nasal trauma had occurred when the cartilage and blood vessels had been damaged, and he would need Medical care urgently. McColl released the shaken minister but continued his wrestle with the officers.

Deeply shocked, Reverend McAuley covered his face with his bloodied hands, his eyes watered. Taking comfort in the disregarded chair, he wallowed in self-pity. Bruising soon appeared around his eyes. His face would be tender for several weeks. Possible treatment involved resetting the displaced bridge under anaesthetic. Although damage to the cartilage may cause lasting damage. McColl was soon restrained. Removed from the multi-faith centre and returned to his cell. A medic was called, and treatment adhered. Thankfully, his nose wasn't broken, but it would hurt. But not as much as his pride would. The ordeal was an extremely unpleasant and difficult experience for the minister.

–

Finlay McColl had given invaluable information that the minister recorded and remembered. He wasn't a priest, so there was no seal of the confessional; which is the absolute duty of Catholic priests not to divulge anything during the sacrament of penance. He was Just delighted that McColl had revealed where the bodies of his young victims were located. It was his Christian duty to contact the police and provide the evidence Finlay McColl gave him. He did, as did the prison authority, and the police duly arrived soon after. It was a brief meeting to provide just two letters and eight numbers; NN 5729 5514. The police understood that the letters and numbers related to an Ordinance survey grid reference location, and however far-fetched or reliable the evidence may be, they would check the site in any case. The minister did not pursue any charge of assault on McColl. He would never be released, so what good would another police charge do?

–

It took the police a few minutes to check the OS grid reference number online, with the code Reverend McAuley provided. The OS maps and Ordnance survey website gave them the exact location. Situated in Perth and Kinross, near

Loch Rannoch, above the Black Wood of Rannoch and around 372-meters above sea level, lay the possible burial site of one or more of Finlay McColl's victims. What amazed the police further; was how a fat unfit guy like Finlay McColl, even though he was a much younger man before his arrest and conviction; when the likelihood of these crimes was committed, could ever transport his victims to such a remote place. And why would a sociopath, who never spoke at his trial or confessed his crimes, would now spill the beans? None of this made sense.

The police took this vital information seriously, and the next day a small team was sent to take samples from the remote site.

Whether or not that this would lead to a more detailed search, or if any credence could be given to the rants and raves of an evil killer; or if this hunt would be a foolish and downhearted pursuit for something that is never attainable. They would be thorough in their examination, even although it sounded like they were being led down the garden path by someone who is mentally deranged and would belly laugh at the thought of wasting valuable police time.

–

The drive took over two hours. It was uneventful and tiring. It started raining after they left the city of Perth, but thankfully the scenery was a perfect antidote to snuffle any boredom the drive offered.

DCs Robert Thomson and Deputy DCI Trevor Stewart looked drained as they stretched their exhausted bodies as they left the comfort of the Black Audi A4 saloon, parked in one of the seven spaces in the car park of the Pitlochry police station. Located in a grey villa—typical of those house types in this part of the town, it sits back off the road with a large sign embedded in concrete, near the station entrance off the A924 promoting the police station. Pitlochry Community Fire Station occupies the same address.

DC Thomson stood straight, both feet rooted to the ground, filling his lungs with fresh air, he swept his arms outwards and flapped them like a bird. This physical exercise lasted no more than a few flaps. It was desperation and more than likely preparation; awaiting an opportunity to tackle his habit. A filtered cigarette was taken from a packet and stuck firmly into his mouth, lit while inhaling swathes of blue nicotine flavoured smoke he coughed several times in approval. It's a long drive without smoking, as doing so in a police car is a no-go. They both smoked and stretched their legs simultaneously.

A group of around ten constables emerged from the station; three of them had cadaver dogs on leads, all golden retrievers, all behaving well. One of the younger officers looked as though he was carrying a drone. The lead policeman who greeted their Edinburgh SCD superiors offered to take their luggage and personal belongings and place them in the back of a four-by-four Jeep. They would now become passengers. The journey to the locus would take just over an hour. There were 4 Jeeps ready and prepared for their arrival. All are full of items required for use at the site, including heavy hi-vis clothing and a few spades. Both Edinburgh cops knew that local knowledge would be crucial to this investigation and was glad to have local officers on board from the outset.

Both senior cops dropped their spent cigarette stubs onto the tarmac surface, and size ten shoes mashed the finished tar filled butts into the ground until they disappeared into tiny fragments.

DC Thomson repeatedly checked his mobile phone for any text messages. He had two. One was from his eldest daughter reminding him of his grandson's golf lessons that he promised. He replied with all caps: OF COURSE! C U SOON! And the other one was from his wife asking how his day was?

He replied: Busy, busy, busy. Call you tonight xxx

The mobile handset was placed into his jacket pocket then he spoke to the team that had gathered. 'Let's get this operation underway.' He stepped into the vehicle, followed by his deputy, and the convoy soon headed to Kinloch Rannoch , where they would be based.

–

DCs Robert Thomson got into the CID at Stirling and recently worked in Edinburgh in charge of the firearms squad. He investigated and responded to offences involving firearms, including potential hostage situations; or any armed robbery. Recently turning fifty, most of his adult life has been policing. Now into his third, and hopefully, last marriage, an expensive newly purchased house in Juniper Green was a debt he could ill afford but help from a large inheritance from his parents, this property would be the last big spend he would make.

It was a charming home set in the small village which was just over five miles south-west of Edinburgh city centre; it was his preference to work hard and play hard. A devoted father of three girls and two boys and four grandchildren, all from his first two marriages, he played golf when he had the time and liked watching foreign movies, drinking Scottish beer and babysitting. All his children lived within a few miles of his new home.

The journey north for both detectives was spent checking appropriate paperwork that would be used to meticulously record and retain every inch of evidence detected, making sure every angle was covered. No stone would be left unturned to do everything possible to solve the Finlay McColl murders; and would treat the location as a crime scene until assessed and determined by criminalistics, with the application of science. The information, despite coming from the mouth of a psychopath, had to be painstakingly verified and professionally endorsed. There were a few voicemails picked up and a few emails answered. Both detectives craved another cigarette.

Arriving at Kinloch Rannoch some forty-minutes later, a small hamlet that lies at the eastern end of the Loch with the same name. The convoy turned into the village square encircled by the 5-star Dunalastair Hotel Suites, where the detectives would stay during the investigation, and the All Saints, Scottish Episcopalian church, dating back to 1864, complimented the scene.

A few locals had noticed the build-up of the police and vehicles, and became inquisitive at the increasing police presence.

A young teenager took a video of police accumulation on his mobile phone, an elderly woman dog walker tried hard to stop her small white French poodle from incessant barking. She couldn't. The dog springing ahead of her and yapping excitedly until they were well over the ancient four-arch stone bridge that crossed the river Tummel and they had set foot on the southside of the river where the dog lost interest.

All four jeeps parked in any space available, one sizeable mobile incident-cum-office-vehicle took up much of the area outside the old church and sat near a bus stop shelter. Another two police cars were waiting for their arrival. Both detectives left the vehicle with lit cigarettes in their mouths. Taking time to remove each detective's luggage from the back of the car, the tall, skinny constable driver explained that this was also the hotel's location, and he'd check them in there. The wheels on the luggage trolleys made a clunky, rumbling sound as the plastic castors rolled over the patchwork of paver blocks.

"Is everyone here that needs to be here?" DC Thomson asked his lead officer, the officer he had just met from Pitlochry Station.

"Yes, sir," he promptly replied.

"Well, let's get this party underway," he said, exhaling the last of the tobacco smoke from his lungs and taking time to stamp on the cigarette butt routinely. A couple of strained guttural coughs followed, tucking his shirt back into his trousers, followed by a natural move that saw him straighten the knot on his nondescript black and grey tie. The car door was already open for him to enter.

Moving from Loch Rannoch, the team moved slowly over the narrow-arched bridge and took the right turn onto Bunrannoch place, leading to the south side of Loch Rannoch. It was a clear day. The sun shone periodically from behind scattered cumulus clouds that gave good news for the work ahead.

"Is that one of ours, Sir?" the driver asked.

"A helicopter would have been the perfect way for me to get to this site. Try and wave him down and ask for a lift."

Thomson's rude remark made DCI Stewart smirk, and his head shook like a car accessory bobbing head dog while his gaze remained on his mobile phone.

"It is heading upwards. Near to where we are due to work, in the vicinity of the locus." The young driver added further distraction to his curiosity. He tried hard to impress but got nowhere. No one answered or raised their eyes from their mobile phones.

The motorcade slowed, both Edinburgh officers' attention was awakened when the lead vehicle turned left from the main road and moved onto a dirt track that ran adjacent to the Dall Burn, and it was the first exit past the Dall estate. The way-ahead had a loose surface, and it was bumpy. The vehicles and their occupants were shuddering every time one of the wheels hit a pothole or ran over dislodged stones. It reminded the two Edinburgh detectives that they were driving over a washboard. Continual ripples on the surface that gave a very shaky experience.

It was a laborious and painful ten-minute trip through one of the largest ancient pine forest areas in Scotland, the Blackwood of Rannoch. When the track stopped, with no further vehicle access available, the jeeps were deposited at this point. There were no legitimate parking spaces here. Only DC Thomson, DCI Stewart, the local sergeant and the young Constable would search and locate the place they looked for. Constable Hope carried a spade and operated the GPS navigation system. He led the way.

What lay ahead was a gruelling walk over rough terrain, wellington boots were required as the land was soggy and wet. The vicinity had already been noted and organised for their arrival, so they were in the location they wanted, they just had to find the exact position. The handheld navigation system would accurately pinpoint the spot Finlay McColl offered as evidence.

It took fifteen minutes for the team to amble over the field, an open water area that has gradually vegetated into a quagmire.

There would be blueberry and heather and a smattering of bracken underfoot in the summer, but this was autumn, and the walk was slow and uncomfortable. They reached a locale called Lochan Rusg a'Bhiora. The young officer, carefully studying the GPS unit he held in his right hand, stopped suddenly, and said, "I think this is it. Yes, this is the position." He added boyishly, "And we are three-hundred-and-seventy-two meters above sea level. This is a great piece of equipment."

The officers avoided any response to his valuation as his left hand stuck the digging spade into the place he discovered. DC Thomson gave the command, and the young officer put the GPS tool into his jacket pocket and began digging. The police dogs were barking in the distance. They had remained with the convoy, out and about burning off some energy and stretching limbs and muscles that suffered fatigue due to the lengthy drive. DC Thomson felt likewise having walked with great difficulty over a watery swamp, stopping at times to heave a boot from the sludge mess it was caught in. A small drone flew overhead. It was noted that one of their officers was operating the sky flier. *Maybe he could find a more accessible and better route to this place*, DC Thomson wondered.

The team searching the place surrounded the position where the dig was, watched with curious stares, and waited in trepidation as the constable dug into the vegetation. Ripping a square foot of gnarled roots that held the top organic surface in-place. Once this large clump of entangled plant life was removed, the excavation was easy. The earth was stony-sandy soil, developed from reddish granite glacial till; with a layer of peat sandwiched below the surface undergrowth and leaf tiller. The clearing is dominated by moss and sedge. It is very, very wet. The officers felt they were sinking where they stood. Their boots making suction sounds as they lifted their trapped footwear from the bog; as grape treader's do as part of the maceration process when making traditional wine. Squish; squish; squish.

They could be grateful that there were no midges at this time of year. Wet, but insect irritant-free.

It took six spadesful of removed dirt to get a result. When a clunking noise proved, a metallic object had been hit and was of significant size. The find startled each officer. The young officer worked cautiously but eagerly continued with the excavation, clearing some soil from the object with the sharp edge of the spade, when a scared look appeared over his face, at what he discovered? His subsequent reaction was to get down on his knees, use his gloved hands to remove as much soil as he could, hoping this would give a better view of what remained half-buried.

"It's a metal tube. A canister of sorts." The enthusiastic young constable cleared more hardened muck from the object that showed a grey container lying horizontal and interred over a foot into the ground.

"That, my young fellow, is a time-capsule," was the response from DC Thomson. He made the young officer move aside and took several photographs of the item as it sat in-situ.

Assessed with a pocket tape measure, the cylinder measured 235 x 600 mm. The cylinder was a grey, rigid polymer tube, specifically designed for the purpose it was developed for, filled with mementoes of a time gone by; then buried. After lifting the tube from its burial place, DC Thomson, wearing black latex gloves, placed it on a plastic bag where it was re-measured and took more photographs. Deputy DCI Trevor Stewart was already taking notes as DC Thomson spoke in detail as he inspected the time-capsule. One end of the container had raised pre-cast lettering cleared of excess dirt. He said, making sure each verbal description to be recorded.

"The writing said: this is the graveyard of my beauties, Finlay McColl."

He ran the knife-edge several times around the ridge insert until the adhesive relented its firm hold and the lid popped open and fell to the ground. Each of the officers waited with bated breath to see what the capsule revealed, and their eyes homed in on the cylinder, expectant as a child would do ripping paper from a Xmas present.

"I am removing a clear plastic bag which looks as though it contains some paperwork and possibly, what looks like, the old type Polaroid instant photos that are held together with a rubber band." He placed the contents on the ground near the container lid. "There is something lodged in the bottom of the tube."

He stared into the tub and put his hand and part of his arm, which struggled to squeeze through the available space—fumbling his gloved fingers near to the end of the capsule, hoping to grasp the remaining item. Still searching for a hold, he could grip whatever remained inside. Once he got hold of the material, he jerked it free.

"It is a rag, possibly a handkerchief." He tugged and pulled hard on the item. It gave way, and he had his first sight of the tie-dyed fabric. It was placed on the plastic sheet, photographs taken, it was measured then documented. The brown parcel string that held it together was bound like a shoelace, and the parcel was opened to reveal a brown jiffy bag, it was addressed to: "The Pigs."

DC Thomson opened the envelope and removed the letter. He read it. But not aloud.

Dear Pigs,

Isn't it a fucking crime!

Do you know what I mean? Now you have all the evidence in the world which I am sure you could only have dreamt about having, but the thing is, you cannot charge me for any of this. The evidence I am about to reveal will take your tiny uneducated minds on the ride of a lifetime.

But before I begin, I hope you can regard me as a humorous and witty fellow human being in your heart of hearts and not see me as a flippant trickster twisting a sharp, jagged knife into the soft underbelly of the Scottish justice system.

Give honour where honour is due, my dear fellows!

This excursion, for you, will be a learning process.

I can fully understand if your thoughts on me are disgusting and nauseating, or even repulsive to a degree. But with this evidence—which I am providing free-of-charge—you will see that my time was not spent idly.

I am giving you indisputable proof!

What I do is an art, it's creative and imaginative; all of which results from originality of thought. I am a creator and a destroyer.

Way back then, when it all started, after my first kill, I found it energising to the point that it raised my state of being. Murder is intoxicating, rousing, and uplifting. And I must say that it is full credit to me for having such a strong character of mind to work meticuously, to generate such a premeditated legacy, that will last forever and give me a deserved notoriety.

Not delusional fantasies of power, or impotence, no, not that; just an obsession with lavish, extravagant activities my deadhead shrink would always offer.

In the end, however, she agreed with me.

I am the sole perpetrator of my own procedures. It is all my work. My creation. My authority. My way, or no fucking way!

However, not to be too offhand. I must also thank my beauties for playing such a lovely role in all of this. Without them, none of my creative art would be possible.

Just remember; the world is not a stage, it's just full of fucking actors, and I am one of the best.

My suffering pigs.

I will now be killed.

Up yours
Finlay McColl

DC Thomson bagged the letter into a tamper-evident bag and sealed it. He used a ballpoint pen to fill in the TEB label and handed it to his colleague. The message had a strange effect on him. Having read the gibberish of a madman first-hand, and having been a father of three daughters himself, he knew there could be multiple graves of someone's beloved daughters in the mud where he stood. He opened the large poly bag, removed the photographs which he handed to his colleague. DCI Stewart detached the rubber band that held the pictures in a neat bundle and counted each photo. Thomson stared carefully at the A4 sheet that wrapped the photographs, which he studied and scrutinised. Carefully studying the childlike drawing of rectangular boxes dotted around the sketch, intermittently averting his eyes between the drawing and vicinity where he stood, made his face turn pale, and an edgy look gave the impression that the muscles beneath the facial skin had collapsed and solidified.

"This is a detailed map of his burials," his inner voice said.

"Twenty-one photographs, Sir." The voice of DCI Trevor Stewart interrupted the moment.

Thomson didn't respond at first. He remained still and looked over the barren landscape. The other officers did, likewise, gazing at the chief, waiting on his response.

Then he spoke in a tone Detective Stewart hadn't heard before. The ordinarily robust and confident voice sounded distorted, even broken, as a grieving person would talk.

"Bag all of this and get the dogs up here. Gentlemen, we are standing in the middle of a graveyard."

DC Thomson gave his friend and colleague a glance and was about to speak with him. But his phone rang, and he responded by removing the gloves and answered it. The sergeant and the young constable worked together, collected, and bagged the items. They both looked terrified, a case such as this was new to them both.

Trevor Stewart contacted the officers based at the convoy who responded immediately. The dog handlers and the cadaver dogs were on their way over the harsh terrain, with the dogs eager to start the search.

DC Thomson answered his phone.

"Thomson. Yes…unbelievable…really? This is getting bizarre! I will need more officers to protect this site."

He listened again. And responded to the caller.

"Will do, sir; of course; thank you, speak later." He placed the phone back into his jacket pocket.

He told the sergeant and the constable to take the time-capsule and its contents back to the jeep and have the evidence logged, telling the young officer to stay with it.

The two detectives remained at the site. DC Thomson spoke directly to his colleague.

"I just learned that Finlay McColl is dead. His throat slit from ear to ear. But I didn't tell you that McColl signed the letter from the time capsule, saying: I will now be killed! And to add more shit to the fan, every national newspaper, central TV station and news corporation, in fact, every Tom, Dick and fucking Harry, received a letter this morning detailing every fucking move we made.

They knew we had details of McColl's victims. They had the same god-damn information—the supposedly unique ordnance survey reference point. So how the hell did this information get out? McColl didn't send any letters from prison. Does he have someone helping him? Is there a corrupt cop out there?'

"Or a deviant minister?" interrupted DCI Stewart.

"Well, whoever has spread this, it is up to us to shovel it up and move it the fuck out of here. We stay professional and get the job done."

–

The scale of the crime fitted no other in Scottish legal history. DC Thomson made several decisions to keep the mass grave sites securely protected, he had sought and received authority for the army to assist with the protection of the mass graves. A full team of officers joined the search for missing remains. Thirty forensic scientists, five forensic pathologists, plus a new group of forensic assistants made up a team focused on identifying the decomposed remains. police production officers and three police photographers worked the site in shifts, ensuring excellent care and attention to prevent cross-contamination between the burial places and systematically record the findings, and collect objects as evidence.

Archaeologists and pathological doctors working on all exhumations, as would the verbal historian or the social memory writer, work on what's left of a vicious killing spree of a madman. The digging teams used mostly photographic cameras to record evidence before the remains are removed, and during the identification process in the laboratory. Archaeologists and forensics will always say that "the dead speak." And they do. As one archaeologist said, "The dead don't bury themselves, it is up to us to discover the truth."

The other thing foremost in all the excavation team's minds is each victim's dignity and respect when carrying out the examination.

A whole range of equipment arrived onsite: including heavy diggers; ground-penetrating radar that used radar pulses to image the subsurface, and a magnetometer that worked particularly well over terrain covered with water; and metal detectors.

Metal detectors had become a popular way of detecting a burial place; inside the graves, they are often found metal belongings, such as buttons from clothes, jewellery, badges, or other similar metal items. Metal probes were used to survey natural compact disturbed soil. Near the mass grave site, on the old dirt track road, many metal-box storage containers held supplies, including in this group of amenities were toilet facilities and a portable canteen—which kept the team fed and watered. Ariel and satellite photographs were taken as the inquiry progressed. The forensic scientists would have their specialised tools and equipment once a burial had been located. Once the topsoil has been removed, the grave may then be probed by careful use of picks and shovels, and finally, with trowels and brushes.

In a portable office on-site, every part of the investigation was controlled and recorded on the HOLMES system,—Home Office Large Major Enquiry System

A computer procedure that every aspect of an enquiry is logged and ensured that no vital clues were overlooked. The system is a computer database that has been designed to aid the investigation into large-scale incidents such as serial murders.

Shortly after the initial find of the time-capsule, cadaver dogs paid interest on a piece of ground on the burial site's outer limits, beyond the plan that DC Thomson held in his hand.

The dogs are specially trained to track down the scent of decomposing bodies or parts, including bones, fleshy tissue, and blood. These remains can be buried deep in the ground but still reliably discovered. This grave, not one of the twenty-one burials drawn on the map DC Thomson held, was the first site to be excavated the following morning.

After a full-on twenty-hour shift, tired and weary, DC Thomson and DCI Stewart made the short drive back to the hotel, the beautiful 5-star luxurious Dunalastair Suites in the centre of Kinloch Rannoch. It was midnight when they entered the hotel, exhausted and suffering physical and mental fatigue, they collected the keys from a pleasant and friendly receptionist before heading off to look for their rooms.

Detective Robert Thomson was happily shocked at the room he received. Before arrival, he had predetermined a small box-type room, a curtained shower over a plastic bath with mouldy tiles surrounding it, an ageing tea and coffee making facility with UHT milk in small tubs and a slice of out-of-date shortbread. But this was different.

The first time he had ever spent a night in such luxury. A hotel in a small highland village could match any international branded hostelry in either Edinburgh or Glasgow. The look over his face was that of a more-than-happy customer, and soon the thought of bed and a decent sleep left his current thinking. A long hot shower in an oversized walk-in cubicle alleviated most of the day's stress, a white hotel bathrobe and slippers dressed him once dried. Even a vase of fresh fragrant peach roses gave an intensely refreshing, delicate scent that filled the room.

A comfortable double-seated sofa added cosiness to his overexerted body and dedicated the next hour working on his laptop. Thankfully, the hotel had high-speed fibre optic Wi-Fi which was as fast as it was stated in the hotel information. A few large glasses of McCallan 18-year-old whisky gave him further relaxation. He did the job he needed to do. Made a list what should be done in the morning and fell asleep on the sofa. Dreaming of all the dead women lying in wait on a small piece of land a few miles from where he slept in comfort. The full Scottish breakfast could wait. DCI Stewart enjoyed the same accommodation standards but ordered room service for a few cold beers. Both slept till 06.30 am.

Finlay McColl's life, trial, conviction, denial and unforeseen confession; he never gave the authorities suitable answers to the many questions they wanted answering. Yet, they realised one thing—always to expect the unexpected; and that realism struck home after the first grave was exhumed.

The remains were well preserved. The cadaver was not a victim of a murder many years ago but a casualty of a brutal and sadistic killer in recent months. The scene of crime officer gave an estimated time of death and burial around seven months.

These remains were presented which the soft tissue of the body was outwardly well preserved. The left leg was desiccated, and some parts of the body were covered with adipocere. The head, neck and upper torso and other details were all in the early stages of decomposition.

When the body was removed from the ground, it was fast-tracked to Edinburgh for a full post-mortem, this would take place at the city Morgue in the Cowgate. It was quickly discovered that the victim on the slab, a middle-aged woman, was non-other than the 52-year-old, mum-of-three, missing Edinburgh psychiatrist, Dr Emily Rankin.

Dr Rankin was the psychiatrist that had frequently evaluated Finlay McColl. The day of Dr Rankin's disappearance, her cottage in St Leonards Bank, Newington, had been burgled and her private files destroyed or removed. The police would now be searching for a new murder suspect other than Finlay McColl. All of the dead women were initially linked to McColl, but questions were now being asked about the murder of the Edinburgh psychiatrist. Did McColl have an accomplice or did some other evil sadist kill these women?

–

Many weeks passed, and the weather changed for the worse, but the police work remained constant and diligent. Apart from the twenty-second grave, Dr

Emily Rankin's burial plot, fifteen of the young women were identified relatively quickly with DNA and dental records. Most of the murdered girls were missing since the early part of the 1970s and 80s. Some were foreign students, some were seasonal workers from eastern Europe, and most likely, the unidentified Jane Doe were notably homeless or runaways without a stable connection with family or friends. Europol was informed with full details of the anonymous victims, and a dragnet stretched over many countries, hoping that identity could be found to give all the unknown victims; a name, and eventually, a decent burial.

Chapter 30
Aleppo

It was still Thursday 18 February 2016 in Aleppo, and Farid continued to participate in a shared life with Bill McKenzie—from his life in the future—ever-present and vocally rooted in Farid's conscience, both partaking in this dangerous, yet incredible journey through war-torn Aleppo.

They had entered the old soap factory, where the interior showed most partitioned walls and non-load bearing panels had collapsed, which gave the impression that it once was a much larger room. Some external light glinted through broken windows, but other than that, it was dark, but not dark enough to use a torch. The old factory had a damp and putrid smell of emptiness that made Farid shiver at what may lie ahead. They set out on this trip fearful yet hopeful.

After a journey that lasted several hours, a trek included walking along twisting dark tunnels and dank unused corridors, with hidden places and eerie disturbing distant noises that they guessed were from secret groups that shared the underground vaults. Eventually, they reached a location where Raca and the cat Mithra waited. It was as strange as it gets and weird, yet real and troublesome. It was if reality kissed the hand of mystery and magical fantasy. It was mind-blowing for both men.

There was no more conversation.

The sun was at its zenith when they surfaced from the underground maze.

Farid followed Raca and the cat Mithra through more ruined houses, across devastating gardens that once were colourful and luscious, and after a strenuous trip over more warfare wreckage, they reached a small courtyard. Well, it used to be. It was open at one side and had been hit by bombs on numerous occasions. But one structure, a two-storey building, stood relatively undamaged. Once inside, they travelled to the cellar, the door was open and a man stood awaiting to greet the traveller.

"Welcome, my friend, and thank God you arrived safely. I thought there was two of you arriving? Raca said two friends were coming?" Farid took the stranger's hand and shook it.

"Just me, I'm afraid. I'm Farid Aboud." He didn't want to try and explain that there was a living human being in his head. Raca didn't get involved in the conversation.

"Ah, I see. Well…pleased to meet you, Farid. I am Doctor Nabil Halif. Please follow me. There is a safe place you can stay until it's time to move."

A door at the far end of the room opened which the group moved through.

There was a further flight of stairs downward. It took a good few minutes for all to reach the bottom of the steps, with Doctor Halif carrying a lantern which illuminated the way. There were several routes at the bottom, shooting off in different directions, all intensely dark shafts into additional stillness.

"Now, before we move, I must say that what you are about to witness, this vision will be incredibly bizarre and outlandish. The first time I experienced this supernatural event, I fainted. Now, however, I accept that this is normal. And you will become used to this fact. I am sure."

The doctor finished his explanation as if he knew the newcomer had experienced many other strange activities himself. He wouldn't be here if he hadn't.

Doctor Halif stood as if preparing to perform a magic trick on stage. Raca approached with the ginger tomcat. The cat stood alone at the front of the group, sniffing and tasting the air, and its whiskers shook. By this action, it had chosen the middle tunnel from the five that were here. Barely visible in the light from the lantern, Farid used his headtorch to add to the brightness.

"That won't be necessary, Farid. Watch and see!" said Doctor Halif.

Mithra exhaled lungfuls of air and looked as though he had spat and blown out glitter dust that flew along the entire length of the vast expanse of greyness. Then, as if multi-coloured lightning struck, Mithra ran through the blackness, then all became light. The way ahead was daylight all but in a name. The group followed, and walked in awe, gazing at the twinkling lights' extraordinary beauty that gave the darkness a feeling of a stargazing sky. Glittering illuminations sparkled as if dispersing fairy dust; it was a strange magical powder that gave a mystical experience to what was already weird and carried no logic to either man.

Another shared experience of alchemy and trickery. Pseudoscience that does not usually sit well with either Farid or his mind companion Bill McKenzie. But that is their life now. This moment is not in their control. Wherever they found themselves, held in a magical realm of colour and light, and placed in a place of peace, they felt helpless but happy, but whatever contained them in this actual enchanting sphere, it was helping them. Not against them.

Chapter 31
Bill's apartment, Valletta
Present Day

It is known as "exploding head syndrome". Which sounds more painful and unequivocally vivid in its description than it is. It's only a condition in which an individual experiences unreal noises that are loud either when falling asleep or waking up. The noise may be scary, it may sound like firecrackers, a bomb exploding, a crash of cymbals, a gunshot, a police siren, or even a lightning strike. Also, although these sounds can be harsh and frightful, this condition doesn't hurt. It can cause confusion, stress, and happen frequently, there are many different opinions about its cause.

Some scientists believe it could be by sudden shifts in the inner ear, anxiety or trauma, or minor seizures in the brain's temporal lobe. But Bill was different, he was living two separate existences, his personal life; and the shared living dream with Farid Aboud. The sound appeared again that made Bill McKenzie awake suddenly, sit up on his bed and gather his immediate thoughts. It wasn't his mind; it was the apartments intercom system.

Buzz; Buzz; Buzz. The noise played further. Bill's mind was restarting, he was awake, and his Dreamtime had evaporated as his conscience roused into real life. Buzz; Buzz; Buzz. It rang loud and clear as his focus became sharp and realisation set in.

Bill was returning from a profoundly imaginative, realistic dream. Leaping from the bed, he ran to the hallway to answer the intercom buzzer system. He grabbed the handset and placed it to his ear.

"Yes?" he said inquiringly and sluggishly.

"I have a delivery for Laura McKenzie." The delivery driver urged.

Bill was lethargic but reacted in the usual way when deliveries arrived at the door. He pressed the entry button that made another buzzing noise; then this action allowed authorised access to the inner building, and Bill informed the courier he was on the 2nd-floor.

Signed and received, Bill wondered what the cardboard container held. It was a standard brown panel wrap box that he understood; typically contained a book—another honey bee biology book of some description. Laura was engulfed in the history of beekeeping and this would have been another addition to her collection. Bill placed the box on the kitchen table, returned to his room to shower, got dressed and had breakfast. His mobile rang when he stood daydreaming in the shower. He didn't hear it ring.

Breakfast was two medium poached eggs sitting on a bed of greens, roasted asparagus drizzled with hollandaise sauce and complimented with coffee and several ottijiet shortcrust cookies. These Maltese delicacies are shaped in a figure of eight, hence the name ottijiet. Possibly derived from the Italian word for eight. Bill could eat a full box at one sitting, and it was always his main companion to eat with coffee. Breakfast like this was a rare treat. He wanted a decent breakfast, so he created one of his favourite dishes, one he could eat at any time of the day.

Bill drank more coffee and examined the parcel.

It was a delivery from a Malta-based book publisher called 'Acutely Animus'. He placed the coffee cup on the saucer and began to open the parcel.

In the box was a letter, but Bill didn't want to read it, as he was completely engrossed in the small book he held in his hand. His fixated stare bore into the drawing of a little girl holding a ginger tomcat, both standing before the citadel in Aleppo. A bolt of lightning flew through the dark coloured sky, with the words embossed in gold on the cover, said: The adventures of Raca and Mithra. By Laura McKenzie.

Bill flipped through the book, the vivid images transporting him back to the dream-like world as much as the storyline. She matched the words with the illustrations well, and Bill was impressed with Laura's work. One of Laura's many secrets.

Bill had just awoken from a living dream he shared with Farid, and in this fantasy, he had met Raca and the Ginger tomcat called Mithra. All coupled in the same reverie and stuck in the cycle of life within the dark winding tunnels below the war-torn city of Aleppo. This book came as an additional shock. His dead wife writing and recording events he is currently experiencing in a deep sleep, penning, and producing a children's book about the events that had taken place several years past was another conundrum for his mind to evaluate. Based at a time when the Syrian civil war was well underway, and violence in the city of Aleppo was aggressive and destructive.

Bill took time to read the letter that accompanied the book. It was an informal letter explaining that the book was ready to publish. Additional information allowed Laura to comment on the style and format, as well as a private email address and mobile number for direct contact with the editor.

Bill picked up the book and read a few pages. The story he browsed held some facts he had already known. It was a tale of how a young Syrian girl called Raca Sana Sleiman had stumbled over a criminal plot, and how the thieves blackmailed the Aleppo museum for lots of money for the safe return of the treasure; and how Raca watched the thief count the ransom money, which the museum paid in advance for information on the whereabouts of three stolen ancient religious icons.

The museum official offered a briefcase full of cash; he, in turn, tested and checked the validity of a stolen piece of art. With the two men doing the deal in the privacy of a quiet restaurant in Al Hatab Square. The young girl overheard all of this. She witnessed the small bespectacled man with the case full of cash transfer the loot to another man; both stood talking in the hallway near the toilet facilities discussing their next move.

Raca was hiding in the cloakroom and listened to their conversation; she overheard the younger man say it would blow in five minutes and advised his colleague to be prepared to leave this area promptly. The illustration on the page shown the criminal's car driving away from the scene.

Bill was unsure if he should read on, what if the tale had a lousy ending, people he knew, such as Farid or Raca, being injured or possibly killed. His imagination was uncertain, but his mind decided that it was better not to view the future, keep faith with the journey he is playing a vital part in, let history reveal itself when the time was ready. He did flick the book over and look at the back cover, which made him feel gratified.

A young boy was running through a green field, wearing a WW2 Biggles flying helmet and goggles, with a Spitfire high above, heading in the same direction. It was Bill and his uncle William together again. Bill put the book in a drawer; he wouldn't contact the publisher. He needed to unfold his truth before publishing a book.

A buzzing and a vibrating sound told Bill his phone was ringing. He heard it this time. The phone was still attached to the charger, which he removed and saw multiple missed calls from the person calling. He answered, but the caller was gone. He had left a voice message, and Bill listened.

Hi Bill, it's Reverend McAuley. I sent you a text explaining that Finlay McColl, the Edinburgh serial killer, the man your mother sent to prison, was the same man that wanted to meet with me at HMP Edinburgh. I was asked to meet with him in prison despite never having met him or had any connection with him. I know perfectly well that none of this means anything to you, but when we met, McColl told me that Laura was his God, she was the harsh voice in his head making him confess to his buried victims' whereabouts.

McColl gave me an ordnance survey number; this information led the police to the exact place his victims lay buried. He also had a message for you…he said it was a message from Laura. However bizarre this may seem to me; it is only right that I forward this message. He said three words. ***Raca and Mithra****. Does this mean anything to you, Bill?*

The minister paused, then continued,

The story ends here, I'm afraid, Bill. The evil killer Finlay McColl was murdered the same day the police discovered a mass of graves at the location he gave them. I thought it was only fitting that you had this information. Although it was prophetic words of a mad man, I am sure Raca and Mithra were not his words but words from another source. For some reason or other, and although I can't fathom it out, I believe someone is working with Finlay McColl. The police released a statement confirming that one of the graves, at the mass grave site of twenty-one others near Loch Rannoch, was McColl's psychiatrist's remains.

Dr Emily Rankin had disappeared eight months previously.

There is no way McColl could have killed or disposed of this woman's body. Even for the fact she was buried among other murdered victims, in such a remote place, while Finlay McColl sat incarcerated in HMP Edinburgh, makes the finger of guilt point at an associate. Someone of trust to McColl. An accomplice that knew his burial site.

What makes all of this point to a partnership of evil, a devil on the outside is; that the police released a statement yesterday, that Gordon Leitch, the Psychiatrist that provided McColl with his initial psychological treatment when he was first jailed; was found buried in remote woodland in the Scottish borders. Finlay McColl had this Ordnance survey detail in his pocket when he was discovered with his throat slit. Discovering the truth in all of this may never be found, it is maze-like and full of anomalies in the complexity of the crime, that the greatest of consulting detectives, would struggle for any logical reasoning, to provide a solution to this scarcely believable criminality. A truth that may well remain hidden.

I will pray for answers, and I will pray for you, Bill. God bless.

I won't keep you any longer, but when you return to Edinburgh and if you need to talk, please do not hesitate to call me.

Bill sat and thought this information over and over in his head.

–

Bill was relaxed. He felt good, as good as he could be; possibly the drink he shared the previous evening with Alessia helped with this present mood swing. Where would this magical existence lead? Learning now that his wife had written and published a book about the adventure of a young Syrian girl and a mystical cat, the Edinburgh minister leaves a message that a serial killer revealed a piece of news for him; the exact three words;—Raca and Mithra. Laura saw the world through the young girl's eyes she had tried to adopt.

After her sudden death, Bill began to observe a similar experience, through an atheist's eyes like himself, all within the same storyline of events, during the same timeline. It was weird. It was so far-fetched that it might just be believable.

Bill would spend the day reading over Laura's letters; the written words she had received from a mad man and wondered if there were further links to all this craziness. Laura kept them for some reason, there must be more to this tale than meets the eye. It was time to study every letter from the first to the last.

Reading these letters concerned Bill. The fact that Laura could have kept such obnoxious and vile written expressions, written by an evil creature, was beyond belief. But after spending several hours examining each document, searching for a unique clue, or a significant revelation to unravel this troubling and ever-present mystery; none was discovered. None that was at least obvious or apparent.

Each letter never divulged further information that he had already extracted. Not seeing anything in writing could shed light on additional connections to his dreamlike out-of-body experiences. Bill looked at the pouch, the bag that had contained the batches of letters; before placing the letters back inside, he searched the interior. To his amazement, there was a zipped pocket that he had missed or overlooked previously. Inside this pocket, he discovered a diary. It was an envelope wrap journal.

The cover was detailed with hand-stitched edging and closes with a leather tie. Embossed in gold at the cover's foot was 'Laura's Notebook' and the date was Thursday, 19 July 2012. The leather tie was undone and Bill opened the book. The front page, as were all the pages, were faintly lined, buttery, cream-coloured. The first page was titled "Red Lentil Soup".

"Red lentil soup!" he roared. "The soup Raca's grandmother gave Farid. This is utter madness. Beyond anything I could gladly hold on to as indisputable fact or rationale."

Bill knew it would be difficult reading Laura's journal; it were her private moments recorded in her history. Whatever was going through Laura's head when she wrote this, it was about to surface in the mind of her husband. He started to read the journal. It felt as though Laura was speaking to him as he read each word.

If I could honestly speak with someone, someone as genuine and smart as Doctor Leitch, then I would be sure of receiving a rational reason for last night's nightmare. He was the incredibly talented psychiatrist I attended after my parents were killed by the Tsunami on 26 December 2004, and his help at this time was ever so valuable.

When my parents went missing after the Tsunami hit the Sri Lankan coast, I knew that I would never see them again in my heart of hearts. How could life be so cruel? This was when my disruptive nightmares began.

After their disappearance, I began to suffer severe nightmares. All the visions were about my parents being carried on an intense suction Tsunami wave train. Both thrown helplessly around turbulent seas, as clothes would tumble in a washing machine. Never getting free from the hold of the storm, as it held them tightly in the wrap of death, as nature turns beauty into cruelty, and dragging them deep into the depths of the Indian Ocean. My father always reaching for my mother's hand as they drifted further apart underwater, never grasping hold of her in a terrible struggle to survive. This was when I awoke, and always gasping for air!

My family doctor had concerns regarding my sleep disturbance and felt the underlying conditions were related to PTSD (Post-Traumatic distress Disorder) and advised me to visit a psychiatrist. This journal is, by all accounts, a lesson I learned from my sessions with Dr Leitch. This is my sleep diary I was told to undertake so my doctor could understand more about my sleep schedule, the issues influencing my sleep, and when nightmares occur. Every morning, I would record as much as I knew of the sleep rituals. And as the day ends, I recorded behaviours that could affect sleep, such as medication or alcohol.

Nightmares are considered a disorder if disturbing dreams cause distress or keep you awake. But whatever situation I found myself, whether drunk or sober, with medication or without, none of these activities mattered. These interactive nightmares continued to play a disturbing part of my everyday existence whenever they chose to integrate with my mental processes.

Suddenly, the nightmares about my parents stopped, then the nightmares changed to other realms of scary dreams. I was becoming haunted by real-life connections.

It was Friday 14 October 2005, during a walk on the beach at Lamlash on the east coast of the Isle of Arran, my life took another wayward turn. This is the extract from my pocket diary:

Today was superb for me, it was overcast with black clouds, and it rained. In fact, it poured. I am always determined to walk on a rainy day. Most people run for cover when it rains, but not me. If you desire peace during your walks, then, trust me, rainy days are the best. Left alone with your thoughts and able to de-stress when there are no other people out taking strolls. I always saved my best walks for the worst days of bad weather. I believe that the air is genuinely cleaner during and after heavy rainfall. Everything looks different on rainy days; whether it's the darker lighting, the mood, or the reflection of your image in puddles, it enhances me like no other day.

The rain remained torrential and unforgiving, and several thunderclaps banged before the sky lit up with umpteen lightning strikes. Strikes of light bolts originating high in the cumulonimbus clouds terminating on the ground, all hitting the Holy Isle. Folklore said a sacred site with a spring held to have healing properties is situated, and it lies some two miles over the Lamlash Bay. Flash, flash and flash, the lightning struck the island.

Only one delivery van passed on the main road near the beach and was heading in the direction of Brodick, an eight-minute drive away. The driver was cautious and drove slow and sensibly. The main road was flooded.

It was here, on this day, on the beach at Lamlash, I had an epiphany.

As the wind blew sheets of cold driving rain inward from the Holy Isle, I saw Mum and Dad, strange as this sounds, it was my dead parents; parents I hadn't seen since I dropped them off at Edinburgh Airport the previous year, walking on the beach, getting closer to me.

I understand and have long held the belief that grief has no compromise. I had been here before, but this was different, this was no illusion, I knew my parents, and they appeared as bright as an apparition could on such a day like this. My doctor once told me that grief can impact cognitive functioning and can mess with my appetite. Neither of which ever affected me. Of course, my parent's disappearance caused much pain and stress, but something new was a twist that physically changed my being. My life transformed instantly.

It still rained and didn't look like it would stop. My waterproofs didn't act or behave as the clothing label stated, neither did my wellington boots that were supposed to keep out the rain; my feet were wet. This weather was fierce and relentless. Then I looked at my parents; they had stopped walking. They looked as though they were waiting on my arrival, so I started to run. A slow run that was laboured and challenging in the severe conditions.

Other lightning bolts crashed onto the Holy Isle to add drama to my circumstance. Then, just as I approached my parents, the parents I had longed to hug and kiss, walked into the sea until they were submerged and gone. It was preposterous. This event was straight out of Hollywood, this should never happen. Maybe it was the weather that had beguiled my senses, threw my mental sensations up to the clouds and fired them back to earth with one-million volts of power. It was even more extraordinary when I reached the spot where my parents stood waving at me. The medal I won as a fourteen-year-old girl—a Scottish junior showjumping medal for finishing 2nd to my nearest rival and the fiercest competitor was lying on the sand.

'Life has a nasty habit of patting you on the back one minute, then slapping your face the next.' My father's profound words rushed through my mind as I picked up the medal I had long lost and forgotten.

The antique silver metal alloy medal had a clip ring holding a blue and white ribbon which was a replica; this couldn't be the medal I was awarded. I remembered throwing it into the River Tummel near my home in Pitlochry. I didn't accept 2nd best. I threw away a winner's medal opportunity when I hit the last fence, and this decoration was a reminder of failure. Yet, after closer inspection, on the reverse side of the picture of a horse and rider clearing a fence that was surrounded with an embossed laurel wreath, there was a small engraving. It said: "Never stop dreaming!"

I remembered father had this inscription done. It was meant to encourage me, but it didn't. I stopped show jumping, I never had the urge to compete and lose even at a young age. I didn't like losing. But there it was, sitting in the palm of my hand, my dead parents appearing to me in the strangest of places, just to present me with my childhood loser's medal.

I have had my share of occurring dreams over the years. The ones that tend to be utter nonsense and always weird. I would wake up and wonder, what the hell was that about? Dreams like the time I left the house, I would climb on the back of a fire-breathing dragon and fly around town. All of this seemed real and apparent. My home, the street where I lived, even the dragon seemed natural. But I knew it was all baloney. Reality drained the rubbish from my thoughts once I was awake and alert, then realism kicked in.

This supernatural manifestation of my dead parents was oh-so-different. It never gave me hope of transforming my deep-rooted religious belief. However, it opened my mind to further revelations that life could be much more than our living and breathing experience offers or how we view certain aspects of it. That first night, I slept with the medal under my pillow, and I saw visions, visions that were frightful, shocking, and repulsive; terrible images of murdered girls being buried in a shallow grave in a remote place.

This was a recurring nightmare, and not once did I see the face of the killer; I always saw these terrible experiences through his eyes, the eyes of an evil predator. I knew too well that veterans that had fought in WW2 battles such as El-Alamein, the D-Day landings, or any significant action contested, suffered severe trauma by reliving horrors they witnessed. But this was different.

I searched online for answers and found one quote best served my experience. It was a quote from the Swiss psychiatrist and psychoanalyst, Carl Jung: **Your vision will become clear only when you can look into your own heart. Who looks outside, dreams; who looks inside awakes.**

It soon became apparent that I was a crucible of truth, whatever I was dreaming, however harmful it was to my welfare, I had to continue to search for the truth. I understood that these nightmares were a symbol of fact, and it was me, and me only, that could bring honesty to the surface. That's why I accepted my dream condition, I just had to learn how to use it and not abuse my talent.

Carl Jung's dream theory is that dreams reveal more than they conceal. He also suggested that dreams are doing the work of integrating our conscious and unconscious lives. An idea he called: ***the process of individuation.***

A significant connection in this was that Bill's mother had helped sentence an evil killer to life in prison, and here was I now, apparently looped into the past life of a madman. Watching dead women being buried in shallow graves, I bore witness to these atrocities, these poor innocent women, their lives taken for no other reason than at the hands of a wicked screwball. It was challenging to comprehend all those images of violence in my dreams, I would pray nightly for a decent sleep. But I also prayed for a time to gather evidence on where these women lie and someday return them home to their loved ones. I knew they were victims of Finlay McColl; I saw tie-dyed material wrapped around each of the dead girl's necks. I had read the stories and watched the documentaries. He was evil personified.

One thing became clear—something I read online—that a dream with medals represents feelings of acknowledgement or a reward for an achievement. Feeling recognised for your talents or abilities. Feelings that you are the best at something. If I were 2nd best at show jumping, I promised myself, I would be the best at turning dreams into reality.

Bill continued to read Laura's journal. It was a sort of release in many ways, helping him understand the rhetoric behind such a realistic episodic journey he and others are taking. He also knew that at some point, whether it had a good or bad ending, all of this would end. Hopefully, and with much due diligence, it would end well.

Chapter 32
Escape from Aleppo
The Present Day

When the civil war violently started in Aleppo, Farid Aboud had several opportunities to flee for his life. But he chose to stay. He witnessed unimaginable horrors during this time, where an infinity of wasted life became a regular occurrence. It was his duty to save lives, not take them. Never in the name of God, not for any spiritual belief, or for someone's twisted hatred of human existence; or not being part of their persuasion or affiliation to a specific denomination, was an ideology Farid could never accept.

Farid chose to stay and help save lives. His time with the White-Helmets, a volunteer organisation operating in parts of opposition-controlled Syria, involving medical evacuation, metropolitan rescue in response to the bombing, and evacuation of civilians from dangerous areas, was valuable and essential. These rescuers saved many poor souls during the conflict.

The infrastructure of Aleppo was broken, freshwater was rare, and schooling was all but finished. Medicines were inadequate, and hospital staff made good with whatever supplies they could obtain. It affected everyone who suffered from the embargo and the sanctions imposed in areas controlled by the regime.

Farid's resolute stance on atheism and his scepticism of all things religious; would never falter or change.

In Malta's present day, Bill had awakened and had left behind Farid, Raca and Mithra in the tunnels under Aleppo, and didn't see the full extent of the miracle that happened. Mithra had blown a magical powder along the length of a dark tunnel, which means they entered a large atrium of a palace long forgotten. This palace looked as if it had just been built. It was so peaceful, there was no sign of violence or intrusion, and the bastion looked new.

It was a haven of sorts: a place to lie low or gain much-needed rest before continuing their magical journey. A few steps into the palace, there before him, Farid saw a maze of arches and domes that enclosed a succession of courtyards, each had its oasis, and rose petals covered each of the three garden ponds. This was crafted by wizardry, the cat Mithra had brought them here, and created this beautiful mirage. It felt unreal but appropriate, and if no outside interference could penetrate, this was an ideal place to rest. Even though it was make-believe, in his most in-depth atheistic views, this place was not real, but he would oblige to accept the position he found himself wherever it was. He breathed deeply, sending a message to his brain to calm down and relax.

Chapter 33
Flee from Syria

It was mid-morning, and the town of Reyhanli was busy. Reyhanli is an agricultural town in the district of Hatay Province in Turkey and is located three miles from the Syrian border crossing of Bab Al-Hawa.

It was 2013 when Reyhanli suffered a severe terrorist attack.

In May that year, fifty-one people were killed, and many more injured when car bombs were left outside Reyhanli's town hall and post office. The first bomb exploded, followed by another fifteen minutes later. Many people, including those attempting to help the injured from the first explosion, were caught in the second blast.

A traditional restaurant was near the roundabout next to a gas station on Ataturk Street.

It was here that Emad ate Pide, often known as the Turkish Pizza. It is a boat-shaped flatbread served with a variety of toppings. His cup was overflowing with hot Turkish coffee flavoured with cardamom; he had topped up his cup three times.

The mobile phone lying on the table received a message—a message brief and straightforward.

"Arrived. Waiting for the package. On my way soon."

The main door to the restaurant made a clicking noise as it opened that drew Emad's interest.

Two well-dressed men entered, both in their mid-thirties and chose a table near a window before the waiter could offer an alternative. They ordered coffee and refused the waiters offers of memorable meals. The waiter smiled but didn't thank them for the order, he didn't like rudeness.

Emad distinctly smelt the traditional lemon cologne both men wore. It nearly made him sneeze, the smell was overpowering, but more importantly, it scared him. Two men wearing the same cologne gave him the jitters; it made him believe that they were watching him, either professional assassins or government agents. He had dealt with many like them in the past.

Another obvious fact proved to him that they were too well dressed; both wearing Italian suits and handmade leather shoes. Usually, these agents will wear attire that matches the people within their specialty; and these two men were no different. Emad knew the form and knew these two strangers would not frequent this restaurant dressed like they were heading to a night at the opera. There was a possibility that his plan had been infiltrated. His demise would mean nothing to them, he knew that.

Emad had crossed the line on many occasions, but this was one line he hoped and wished, he could pass and complete. A mouthful of warm coffee crossed his lips when the waiter asked if he needed another refill. Emad declined and laid more than enough cash on the table that made the grateful waiter offer his thanks.

Other diners included and elderly couple having a marital dispute and made ludicrous hand gestures to prove a heated discussion was underway. An elderly bald man had his face engrossed in the sports newspaper AMK. The paper is officially an acronym of Açık Mert Korkusuz (translated: Open, Valiant and Fearless) but this suggested much controversy, as the abbreviation is commonly understood to mean a profane phrase in Turkey.

Emad walked unhurriedly to the restroom he had previously used when he first arrived in the eatery; he also noted an exit door that led to a backstreet lane. What alternative was there, he did not know the town, or acquaintances to call for help, he was alone and desperate to leave the restaurant and not have two assassins follow and kill him.

You say you should always listen to your heart and Emad was no different. His long business experience gave him an eye for standards and let him judge most things practical, and he knew these two stylish men were not interested in drinking over-cooked bitter house coffee.

He imagined two holstered guns hanging under the suit lapels. Escape was his best and only option.

As soon as Emad got past the first door, he ran for the exit and pushed the escape bar as hard as he could, he wanted free and out from the place where he felt and tasted fear. A smell of lemon zest was still in his nostrils. Looking backwards continually, making sure he wasn't followed, he found the street that led back to the main road. Managing a few steps, he heard a loud noise that sounded like the heavy doors opening and then clanging shut from somewhere behind him, a clatter of rubbish being displaced, bins being hit or knocked, yet no cries or moans were heard; but it made Emad stop and stare back to where he came from.

And as his eyes gained focus, his heart started to beat faster and harder than it had ever done. He felt his chest hitting his Luigi Borrelli shirt, and if it beat any more problematic, he was sure the pearl buttons would pop from the placket that held them in place. He shook where he stood, his mouth was dry, and his head hurt, as blood rushed through his veins that made his head throb and pulsate. Sickness was a distinct possibility.

The man who read the sports newspaper AMK, the older man from the restaurant, walked toward him, looming large as he got closer. He held a handgun with a suppressor oozing propellant gas that proved the gun had recently been used. Emad's scared look gave the shooter the impression he was looking after a child that had just been caught taking money from his mother's purse. The silencer was unscrewed and put in his jacket pocket, the gun reholstered and placed inside his jacket, then he spoke. "It's time to go!"

A stare back at the restaurant exit showed the same two men he felt were following him, lying dead among some disregarded food waste. They wouldn't smell too sweet now, he supposed.

"Who are you?" asked Emad in an anxious and apprehensive way, as the older man ushered Emad with a hand on his shoulder.

"I am a friend sent by Omar Faruk Kaplan, Mr Naguib. I'm here to protect you. We must move quickly, there will be more agents in this area soon."

No more words were spoken as the two men reached the main road where a Range Rover Sport waited. As soon as Emad and his bodyguard were on board, it sped off, spitting up dust and gravel as it headed for the Gungor Ottoman palace hotel. The supercharged 5-ltr engine purred on the journey that only took twenty-five minutes on the D420, the main highway in this region of Turkey. Emad remained silent in the rear of the luxury vehicle, and the man that saved his life sat chatting with the driver. The bodyguard made a few phone calls as the car drove into the hotel's car park.

The older man turned to face Emad. "This is yours, I believe," he said, handing over the mobile phone that Emad had left behind at the restaurant.

"Ah! I didn't know I had lost it. Thank you."

"You will go with my colleagues now. The package is due to arrive soon, my colleagues will take you safely to the airport."

Chapter 34
Disclosure in Malta

Early evening, Bill was taken from his Valletta apartment by force, under armed threat, with a Glock 36 pushed forcibly into his lower spine, driven without argument or struggle, to an unknown property by two henchmen. No one spoke during the journey, but the thug sitting in the back of the car next to Bill, continually checked his mobile phone for messages. Bill guessed he was sending and receiving funny text messages, as his eyes would light up, and he snorted like a pig after a message pinged into his WhatsApp messenger.

Although the guard was big and armed, Bill viewed him as nothing more than an overgrown blockhead and believed if he took an IQ test, it would come back negative, but he was the man with the gun and would likely use it. The blockhead had already covered Bill's mouth with silver duct tape that had been crudely wrapped around his head twice.

An annoying stout driver chain-smoked strong, pungent cigarettes and kept the windows closed. Every now and again, his stare would meet Bills in the rear-view mirror. The drive took around forty-five minutes.

The desired residence is situated in one of the most exclusive villa areas named Il-Qortin. It was snuggled above the expansive valley of scenic Mellieha, either classified as a large village or small town or an extended neighbourhood, in the Northern Region of Malta; and is home to one of the longest sandy beaches on the island.

The vehicle arrived at the well-lit driveway and cruised to a stop near two other similar cars. They all were black S-Class Mercedes Benz sedans.

The ugly guy pushed Bill forward when they left the car, forcing the Glock 36 somewhere into his back, repeating this irritating, childish aggressive sequence until they reached the main door of the building. At the entrance, Bill saw an oversized wall-mounted sign illuminated by soft wall lights that advertised three words: Das Verruckt Haus. The only words he understood were Das: the; and Haus: house. It was German. That much he did know.

This property's modern layout is typical for a 1970s Villa, providing an open plan living-dining area with superb panoramic views over the ocean from sizeable expansive floor to ceiling windows. There are five double bedrooms, four marble tiled bathrooms, a separate fully fitted kitchen: and a new butlers apartment in the basement level with an interconnected garage. The vast surrounding landscaped garden had matured Sandarac gum trees with a stunning heart-shaped heated outdoor pool, with views overlooking *Mellieha Bay.*

It features amazing architectural features, such as a glass colonnade and an enclosed courtyard garden reminiscent of ancient Rome. A state-of-the-art media room would pass for a CNN or SKY NEWS communication newsroom; accompanied with a modern Fitness and Sauna suite. In the basement, there was a full-sized snooker table. Further matched with a five-car garage and an elevator made from stainless steel and glass that served all floors.

Still being pushed in the back with the loaded Glock handgun. Bill skipped forward until he entered the main living room. It was an ample space containing two black leather sofas, three oversized Antonio Citterio Lifesteel armchair's dotted around the room, a piano black wall unit full of books and Dresden ornaments and figurines shared each shelf.

The windows were flanked by a row of Areca Palms—all of which stood higher than three metres, several different designs of Timothy Oulton floor lamps, and a wooden table with six seats surrounding it. Three modern glass, electroplated copper finish globe ceiling pendants swung over the tabletop. The lights glowed orange and covered the table in a fire-like wrapping. Beautiful peach roses filled every vase in the room, and four wall hanging baskets held the same colourful blossom.

At one end of the table, next to the window, sat a well-dressed gentleman, who remained silent. A wheezing Doberman slept at his side. Although it was dreaming, it stretched its legs as though it was running.

The stranger sat silent and oblivious by Bills arrival; he inhaled on a Cuban cigar and drank Louis X111 de Remy Martin Black Pearl Grande Champagne Cognac from a crystal balloon glass. Three armed guards stood around the room, watching the game unravel. The bully that kidnapped Bill from his house had already handcuffed his arms to the chair; and held the gun in a cross-arm grip just like James Bond as he stood a foot or so behind him. The pose was as close as he would ever be to being James Bond.

Bill's breathing was restricted, and he began to sweat profusely.

Bill's eyes were irritated as perspiration leaked into them, but his limited stare focussed on the man he knew as the boss, the owner of this property, the head-honcho, the money man; whatever his persona, Bill felt as though he had met him before.

Not meeting him in business or on a social level but felt a peculiar surge of Deja-vu shroud over him, he had an overwhelming sense of familiarity, being in his presence. It was an insecure feeling, Bill did not like this man, he had a bad feeling of being in the company of someone evil.

In his sixties, the stranger was over six-foot tall and slim built; he was skinny. Silver-white hair ran straight to his shoulders and had a neat centre parting with hair either side swept behind both ears. The unique and stylish pair of tortoiseshell glasses perched on his nose were Andy Warhol-fashioned Cutler and Gross bold-framed spectacles. A jade-coloured turtleneck pullover was accompanied by straight-legged white chinos and a pair of Christian Louboutin's Steckel stud-embellished black deck shoes with contrasting white laces were on his feet. And a chrome cross hung from a long chain around his neck. Finally, after prolonged inhalation of cigar smoke, he stared at Bill and exhaled the pungent smell that wafted over his face.

A low-pitched voice, soft in quality, being self-assured and confident without being antagonistic, spoke.

"You will be wondering why you are here, and more importantly, speculating who I am?"

Bill guessed the man had a German accent; although not fully visible as his English was near perfect.

"My name is Hector Doling. And you are here to discover the truth. You will have to bear with me as I tell you a short, yet significant story, and when I am done, I will welcome your questions.

"You are here for a revelation. A wonderous disclosure which I promise will blow your mind.

"First of all, I need to explain my academic background and how I reached my goal of finding the truth. A truth that can only define by challenging the materialistic model of reality. In many ways, it reminds me—in a small way—of Nietzsche's philosophy, which is his perspective view of the world and his thoughts of the truth and reality of the human condition. Nietzsche does not define, develop an idea, or compare facts, nor does he believe truth is waiting to be uncovered, exposed, or found. But that's where my reality differs. My process lies within the similarity pattern, which presents honesty beyond events and ideals. You see…I created a certainty within reality. I could control an army of minds. That is why my genius is beyond the fact of Frederick Nietzsche's ambition. And way outside the rubbish, he offered."

"He was lame, a paranoid and deranged weirdo that believed God was dead. How fucking delusional was he?"

Hector Doling paused briefly, then turned to face Bill, before continuing his verbal rant.

"Nietzsche, in his tortured wisdom, blamed the enlightenment and had eliminated the possibility of the existence of God. This, so-called genius, was a watered-down nincompoop exposed to the free absorbent minds of his sycophantic followers, that listened to every demented word he said and believed every bit of bullshit that left his mouth.

"He was the fool among the complex of his counterparts. Yet the socialites, the nobility, the intelligentsia and haut monde, all willing participants eager to accept his nonsensical gibberish as fact. Writing and lecturing to likeminded fools that were readily prepared to absorb his claptrap, which is synonymous with absurdity or the ridiculous, yet they found it all acceptable.

"Friedrich Nietzsche is the man that stated, 'Is man one of God's blunders? Or is God one of man's errors? I believe Nietzsche was one of God's mistakes!' The meaning of the word Philosopher states that it strives to know or know things better than most people. What fucking bullshit!

"I know for a fact that all mainstream scientists and academics will always protect their dogma. That is why they will never understand the truth. Even if it slaps them on the face. They work in the realms of belief, willingly learn what they have been educated, never question or demand answers to problems found, nor do they feel obliged to think outside the box. On all subjects, not just science."

Bill had never seen a tall man so lean in build. It was almost as if there was no excess flesh anywhere on his body. He felt like a student listening to a weird lecturer dispose of his feeling to a class full of non-interested students.

Doling stood and drank more cognac before continuing.

"Did you know Nietzsche suffered from psychiatric illness and depression? A gradual cerebral decline evolved and ended in profound dementia, and eventually became his own patient. How philosophical is that?

"And in the unconscious world of Carl Jung, now he is one mind too far. Jung was adored by the world of so-called leading minds, those speakers and critical thinkers that helped transform Jung's ideology. For what? I'll tell you what. It was for their own intentions. Those wishful dreamers accepted his wisdom with open hands, giving him infamous notoriety and a glorified status. I can be Carl Jung's most prominent critic, but generally, I am his biggest fan. His influence on modern psychology is untouchable.

"I give thanks for his concepts." He paused, then added, "Like introversion and extroversion and archetypes, and even advanced dream analysis and the collective unconscious. All of which I used as stepping stones to reach the pinnacle of my creativity.

"I studied works from other great minds; such as; Thomas Aquinas, Aristotle, Immanuel Kant, and Karl Marx, and mixed them, and to be honest, it got me fucking nowhere. Carl Jung was my inspiration, my bedrock, my motivation, and more importantly, my muse.

"It was then, I used my mind to create a new philosophy under his mental process, a new materialistic model of reality. I called this theory; Extra Mentem. It's the state outside of the mind of the creator—one person living in another existence or sharing a life. Of course, similar techniques have been used in the past, but my paranoid fantasy made my creation the best. You may have heard of one of my patients? Finlay McColl?"

Bill stared at Hector Doling briefly then looked away. Hector Doling didn't respond, he knew Bill McKenzie had information of McColl. This was a game he liked playing.

Doling continued, "Others with nefarious minds, that have previously attempted brainwashing techniques frequently fall at the first hurdle. But I was the one that found the trigger, implanted the seed, pressed the button, and fired the explosive. And it fucking worked. Everyone before me managed…some sort of technique to hypnotise a willing volunteer, but for me, Hector Doling…I could create a legion of distant soldiers, working to my command and orders, doing my dictatorial deeds to the letter. To you, I'm sure it sounds like a paranoid fantasy, but brace yourself, this ride is going to get crazy.

"My candidates were living robots and would work tirelessly, converting my projects into reality. The first opportunity to put my skills to practical use was in 1988. I chose a truck driver from many, a German haulage operator heading home to Koblenz, at the Motorway filling station Aire de Wasserbillig in Luxemburg, located under the state border with Germany. I only spent a few minutes in conversation with this man, chatting over a coffee about general mundane topics, then I applied my skill to hypnotise the overweight fool. I was sure his truck was full of Schogetten chocolate wrappers, as he scoffed two bars when we talked.

"I laid my plan of action there, and then, I didn't see any difference to his facial appearance, nor did I see a character change. He acted as if nothing had happened, and this is how I wanted it to work. As the fat driver left the café, he spoke and shook hands with other truckers, laughed and joked with staff, yet he was under my control and preparing to end his life. I ordered more coffee and waited for the event to happen. As I looked out the window of the roadside café, I saw the fat pig struggle to enter his truck and start the short drive to the Sauer Valley Bridge—that marks the point of the frontier between Luxemburg and Germany. I just needed to wait. Bide my time and trust my genius.

"After a few minutes, police sirens filled the air, quickly rumours began to circulate, and people talked about a truck driver jumping to his death from the bridge. It was true, I had offered my talent to the world, and the world accepted it. Mr Blubbery had parked his truck midway over the bridge, got out, walked to the edge, climbed onto the metal barrier, and jumped. He didn't hesitate, according to eyewitnesses, he just dropped, hit the water 320ft below and that was that. My God, how good did that feel!

"Since then, Bill, I have had bank managers steal money for me, a multitude of rich people bequest their lifesaving to my numbered accounts in Zurich, had contract killers kill my enemies. I operate for states and governments worldwide to offer unrivalled standards of assistance. I controlled professional sports stars to throw results, news reporters to spread fake news, I even have politicians all over Europe working to my demands and wishes.

"I am a master puppeteer controlling many. Yet, I wanted more, I needed to expand my portfolio. I have control of police and military officials throughout the European union, this is my safeguard in case anyone came snooping at my wealth, my empire, or dig into my life's work. Like most things, I needed to try new ideas and open an unbelievable criminal activity that would never be matched or surpassed.

"Unlike the superficial fictional celebrities like Ernst Stavro Blofeld, Fu-Manchu or Professor Jim Moriarty, no, I would strive to surpass any work these imaginary characters achieved. I would build a better mind than that of William James Sidis; who is reported to have had an IQ between 250 and 300. Yet, all this is nothing to what my genius accomplished. Never will I win prizes or honours for my work. I operate in the shadows, yet work in the open, although no one knows I exist, or applauds my virtuosity; I only suffer for my art but claim the benefits from it. Here is one of my work examples.

"I created twenty serial killers throughout Europe, one which you know well, Finlay McColl. Although of my twenty multiple killers, McColl is the only one that never killed. I created him as a patsy, the instrument of choice to take the full brunt of the law, and he played it perfectly. The McColl murders were done by a group of three mind-controlled automatons. One a solicitor, one a doctor and a Glasgow policeman. It was all so easy, Bill. And not one of them would understand what devious horrific deeds they did to each of these poor women.

"At this moment in time, five serial killers are still active in France, Germany, Spain, Poland and Ukraine. One phone call to each one, or a written word sent that they read, and it all stops. Why did I create all this murderous mayhem? The simple fact is I could, although playing games with the authorities is somewhat fun. I can do absolutely anything!"

"Here is another example of my power; If I broadcast an interview say, on Sweden's SVT, Sveriges första Kanal—a news channel—and speak the first four lines of the Swedish nursery rhyme Rida Rida Ranka, which is:

Rida, rida ranka
Hasten heter Blanka.
Vart ska vi rida?
Rida sta och fria

"With my voice broadcasting this simple rhyme, and if my targets hear this verse, it will set in motion numerous acts of violence. There would be shootings sprees in key cities around the country, arsonists would start fires in government buildings, rail networks will be targeted, and airports would be under siege.

Generally, I could create civil unrest that has never been seen before. I am my creation, a god within the detail.

"I am an obsessive enthusiast, my ideals work in a flawless state where everything is precisely appropriate. Perfection is a condition without culpability or weakness, failure is not." Doling made a point to Bill. And tried hard not to be trite or irritating when he offered a cliché.

"Bill, when you surf on boiling water, the first thing you learn to do is not fall off the fuckin' board."

Bill looked up and stared at Hector Doling and moved uncomfortably in the chair. Doling drank more brandy.

"There is one thing more about my creation that shows similarities with Jung's work. It is you and your late wife, Bill. You have all been on a dreamlike journey, you, Laura and Carl Jung. Seeing life through the eyes of others and playing a part in changing life's outcome. For me, it shows parallels and unbreakable connections, and I am sure Jung would love to have met you both."

Doling stood and thought before talking and drew information from his memory that Bill must hear.

"Whatever inspired Jung to write the red book is beyond me, yet I am fascinated by the links to your dream state of reality. You must want to know how I know about your dream state of mind?"

Bill's eyes looked nervously at Hector Doling, wondering where all of this was going and when, not if, the bully with the gun will use it.

"Come on, Bill, don't be so fucking stupid. You and your own personal Jung excursion. How suitable. I know that you and your late wife could live in the minds of other people.

"Something like that is way beyond my mind-control, and my abilities, sharing a duality is incredible and something I always strived to achieve. I could never create such an anomaly, not even with the help of Carl Jung. No one has ever matched this. So how did you and your wife manage this relationship?"

After drinking more brandy, Doling cleared his throat and spoke more efficiently. "When I first created Finlay McColl and his numb-skull cohorts, I worked as a clinical psychologist in Edinburgh, in private practice, empowering my clients to make decisions for themselves, and had others make my suggestions a reality. I put my Scottish protocol in place here, and it worked so well, I recruited more workers during my time in Scotland.

"Then, one day, in 2005, a patient came to me with a curious complaint. This woman, Bill, was your lovely wife, Laura. As a master of oneirology, which is the scientific name for the study of dreams, I had extensive knowledge about the functions of the human brain, as well as insight how the brain works during dreaming related to memory formation and mental disorders; but what Laura brought to me was oh so different."

"I had heard many weird and wonderful extensive clinical experiences during my time in psychology, but this revelation was godlike. Never in my time of the study, or in my knowledge of creating mind-control observances, did I ever expect a patient to ask me for help with what your wife was about to ask me. Her serious anxiety problems had started in 2004 when both her parents disappeared when a tsunami hit the Sri-Lanka coast. She lived with this incredible trauma. The grieving process takes time, healing happens over a lengthy period and can't be forced or hurried.

"I got your wife to fill in a questionnaire which is a general form for assessing somatic symptoms, anxiety and insomnia, social dysfunction, and severe depression, and so on. We talked, I listened attentively to her narrative, and I never for one minute thought I would hear what she presented. It was my fucking Eldorado, something I had chased forever, a person that lives in another individuals' reality, it is the holy grail of mind control, complete indoctrination. This was no thought-manipulation or mind-control, or hypnosis that I had perfected, this was different, this was a new realm of reality. How on earth could this young woman evolve such a god-like phenomenon?

"She claims she saw her dead parents while walking on a beach on the Scottish island of Arran. The spectres didn't talk, but they left her a present, a medal for show jumping which she won as a child. Returning a medal, Laura had discarded into a river when she was a child.

It was after this mystifying event with her parent's spirits, her dreams became a reality.

"Details that she regularly entered the sub-conscious of a particular person became a regular occurrence. But the person she connected to, had a connection to me, one of my workers under my influence and authority. Although Laura didn't know this, not at this time, she revealed the dream relationship was with Finlay McColl. She was scared, having joined the mind of an imprisoned killer, living with guilt by association, it was only inevitable she looked for professional help; and I was the person to assist with her dilemma.

"She detailed further familiar elements of her many shared dream memories with Finlay McColl as if reading from a diary, informing me that she continually asked McColl for information of the burial sites of his victims. Yet I was hearing her exposé, of how she became God in his head, how she became McColl's female God. Not asking for the truth but demanding it.

"I visited McColl. I had to hide all these killing facts deep in his childhood memories, implanted in forgotten recollections before his 2nd birthday. Deep-rooted in his sub-conscience, in a place he never knew existed or ever had, or ever would. Even her god-like intrusion could not make McColl disclose these facts. Only I could have McColl reveal this information. A trigger word is a post-hypnotic suggestion, that would open the door to offer disclosure, if I ever need to use this, or if I felt the need to send the dead women home to their loved ones; but I didn't see the point. They all lay still in my graveyard, sweet little dolls all neatly packed into a place of reverence, a home I made especially for all of them. It would have been such a waste of love.

"From that day on, I decided to work against your wife. She was trying to break into my structure, my limitless algorithm of lawbreaking, and if anyone ever did this, it could have many severe consequences for my ultimate design. But I could never allow or accept anyone coming in uninvited to my world. It belongs to me, and me only."

He continued, "That's when I had McColl's psychiatrist intervene, she was a friend that I could inform of McColl's disorder. She was my eyes and ears at face to face meetings. Communication between clinician and patient is the basis of psychiatric treatment, but McColl's clinician, Psychiatrist Dr Emily Rankin was someone I held under my spell. She was controlled by me and would keep me updated with regular reports on McColl's state of mind. She would have sessions with him, set his files into the profound recesses of his feeble brain, to prevent your fuckin annoying wife from gaining access to the invisible data I had implanted. She had to be stopped. It was if she inserted a virus into McColl's head and tried to find my truth.

"Bill, your fucked up little bitch of a wife gained illegal entry back into Finlay McColl's brain. Breaking every mental barrier I had put in place. She was searching his mind like a parasitic weevil, manipulating every part of his memory processes. This was not good!

"She transformed him into a nervous wreck, claiming she was his own personal female God, demanding him to surrender the truth. She worked his head so much his limitless capacity to hold carefully planted knowledge started to break down. During further meetings with Dr Rankin, McColl was leaking facts like a sieve, offering names, places, methods of killing and at that point I had to close the door the fat pig had opened and stuck his foot in. He was weak, he began to remember details of my killings, to unravel my truth that I wanted kept secret. This was now a problem. Your wife was interfering in my business.

"She ground McColl to a pulp, taking advantage of a broken spirit, it was relentless, it was stubborn and uncontrollable. I had to stop it. Dr Rankin heard McColl's confession. But I controlled her, this was never a problem, but I couldn't take the chance. She was an ultimate professional recording and keeping records, taking notes of her client conversations, and saved delicate client intel on a computer. If pushed, I was sure the bitch would break. Emily Rankin was a strong-willed character with an adept mind.

"But when she told me McColl had personally requested to meet a Church of Scotland minister, the person with no faith asking for someone of faith, I knew he had been broken. His spirit and whatever type of soul he had, both collapsed, deflating internally, at the hands of his female God: *your fucking wife*!

"Everyone that had an intimate connection to Finlay McColl needed to be suppressed. Your wife had to die; Emily Rankin had to die; Finlay McColl had to die; McColl's first psychiatrist Gordon Leitch had to die, each one screwing with my big picture. All were surplus to my requirements."

Bill was trying hard to scream, struggling tirelessly in the chair trying hard to get loose, to no avail, he wanted to kill Hector Doling, even if he took a bullet in the process.

Doling and his revelations were relentless.

"All those freaks that stuck their noses into my affairs have all been eliminated. That is the rules of my game."

Time had passed, and Bill was suffering fatigue, he was tired and severely dehydrated. He sweated out and needed water fast. Doling noticed Bill's lack of fluid and the signs that came with it. He ordered one of his thugs to offer water. He needed Bill conscious to hear his story. After a few gulps of bottled water, duct tape was reinstated around his mouth.

"Ok, where was I. Yes, I was about to reveal something much more enjoyable.

"When I freed the world of Dr Emily Rankin, I also took her diaries."

"I now had confidential records and files, hidden computer program archives holding secrets of many illustrious people and in possession of personal facts that could finish careers. Establish new money-making opportunities and much more intriguing fun games I could create. Still, my main attraction was this book," he said, placing his hand on a small leather book sitting near him on the table.

"The information from the book divulged so much. What astounded me most was that a female God was haunting Finlay McColl. Emily Rankin noted all of this information in her files.

"After all the work I had done previously, your wife entered McColl's psyche again. I spent many days trying to suppress his recollection, blocking and hiding information in his early baby memories; a place that the world's leading psychologists couldn't unearth. Sealed, locked, and protected from future busybodies, only to be released if and only when I decided the truth can be uncovered.

"But whatever I tried, your bitch of a wife squirmed her way into his inner self and unsettled McColl. She possessed him, tormenting his spirit, my implanted memories were being dragged out into the open, offering truths that should have lain dormant. But what surfaced was more momentous than McColl revealing the burial sites of some dead women. This was a crucial own goal scored by your fucking whore wife. For some weird and unbelievable quirk of fate, McColl picked up details from your wife's psyche.

"Through the link he had with her, he absorbed her living truths, saw images she had in Syria with a young girl called Raca Sana Sleiman. And one thing that may surprise you, Bill, during McColl's rants your name was mentioned. 'Tell Bill McKenzie three little words: Raca and Mithra.' And I believe you were also living in the mind of another living soul, in Syria, in fact, Aleppo. You were sharing real-time life activities with a man called Farid Aboud. And if my memory serves me well, you were a guest of Farid Aboud the day my bomb went off in Al-Hatab Square. How fucking impressive is that."

Doling told a guard to remove the duct tape from Bills face and allow him a drink of water.

"I believe you need to enter this conversation, Bill. Please feel free to make a comment or ask a question."

Bill responded almost immediately.

"You murdered hundreds of people. Men, women and children just to get involved in a civil war. You are sick."

Doling applauded Bill's reaction by slow hand clapping.

"Fuck me…how far are you from the maddening crowd? I would never do something as spontaneous as that, fuck me. It is so far from the truth. The dead were collateral damage, nothing more nothing less. Let me explain some of their finer details. If you remember your first acquaintance with your mind-share friend Farid Aboud, on the rooftop restaurant in Al-Hatab square in Aleppo, it was Thursday, 19 July 2012; and this was the day I was about to collect my prize. It is fuck all to do with any war or taking sides, the civil unrest was a welcome ally, I used Syria's instability to cash in my chips.

"Although I must admit it was a big bomb, the bomb had nothing to do with war, nor was it an attempt to kill a museum curator and his security team. He was in the wrong place, I'm afraid. But his death certainly added to the multiple reasons the law took into consideration when they initially worked the site. Detraction always helps. Smoke and mirrors and all that jazz?

"Anyway, the bomb was strategically placed to penetrate a sealed vault three stories down. This depository was a specialist storage facility, not known by the public and only a small hidden street entrance fifty yards away, could access be gained. Still, this point-of-entry was secured by highly trained armed guards. This off-the-grid bank is known by the criminal underworld as Madinat Khafia; the hidden city. Many dotted worldwide, all being used by Royalty, Governments, Power brokers, big corporations, famous and infamous and my likewise friends; those with a criminal mentality.

"Banks like these hold some of the world's best-kept secrets. Mysteries and conspiracies sharing the same room with gems and jewels, and those that kept their belongings in this place, would never, for one moment, believe that the level of security defending this treasury could ever be challenged. But they didn't know about the genius called Hector Doling.

"I needed access to this vault, and I took advantage of the Syrian situation. It's what I do best. With inside information, I had learned that the treasury was to be moved to a different location, the safety deposit boxes were dismantled and ready to be shipped from Aleppo.

"The owners of this bank have more influence than anyone would understand; they are the *power in powerful* and the *authors of the authoritative*. But like everything else in the magical world of Hector Doling, these men mean nothing to me, nor does their so-called fucking mandatory high standards. Setting the bar for privacy and protection, covertly offering a safe bank system for the world's elite, covering the underworlds reputation by safeguarding their ill-gotten gains. Hiding lies and truth in the same place.

"All I needed was to let these influential brain-dead bankers make their move, and when they did, my actions went into overdrive. My informant gave information that the deposit boxes were located three stories down but kept near the stairwell to the street entry point. The bomb would disable all security systems and block three escape routes, as well as all underground train systems operating on small gauge rail tracks. It all sounds far-fetched and bizarrely sci-fi, but one of these tracks runs from Aleppo to Om Al Toyour, 180km away on the Mediterranean coast. This at least will explain a little bit more of how powerful this bank and its owners are, and the people that use it. This is a very high-end institution.

Suddenly, BANG! My bomb went off and did more than I ever hoped. The explosion worked a treat. After a few minutes, my team, who were waiting in preparation a few streets away, all dressed as firemen and police, entered an inconspicuous door. It sat between a coffee shop and a pharmacy. This quiet lane led to a luxurious Hamman, or, in broader terms, a Turkish bath. Used by Aleppo's political elite, army officers, business people and organised crime lords, this was the main street-level entry point to the 'Madinat Khafia'.

"I had killers on the inside, and like many other places around the bathhouse, everyone had gathered near the Hamman exit, checking phones but got no signals, all petrified of what had happened outside. The explosion was so massive the baths shook and created severe internal damage. As my team entered the bathhouse, my inside killers had already begun to clear the place of witnesses. In total, we killed forty-six, lazy, overweight fat guys. The main reception door to the Madinat Khafia was at the rear of the plunge-pool, and that was coloured red by floating corpses, it was bolted locked and had extra security to reinforce its stealth.

"My team knew that enough force channelled in the right place would blast the door off its hinges. With several charges of PE4 plastic explosives detonated, they were in. Only one guard stood behind a desk asking for mercy, he was taken-out. The lift was non-operable. But the full metal industrial stairs was the way we wanted to head. The team killed the last of the guards and the place was cleared within minutes. All the loot we needed was sitting at the foot of the stairs.

Boxes and boxes of mysteries. All waiting for my unit to load and remove, through the only tunnel still operating. The bank did all the difficult work for me.

"A rail tunnel leading to a rural location to the west of the city was the destination of the stolen loot. However, I only wanted three small pieces from the Madinat Khafia plunder, three unique art pieces. The first one was a painting by Vincent Van Gogh called -The painter on His Way to Work, a self-portrait, painted in 1888 and hung in the Kaiser-Friedrich Museum in Magdeburg, Germany Nazi's stole the masterpiece. It has been missing since then. Some believed the Nazi's destroyed it.

"With my links to many minds, I managed to source this painting and other magnificent treasures such as A Portrait of a Man by Sandro Botticelli. Yet, another priceless artwork was stolen by the Nazi's from the Filangieri Museum in Naples, and finally, a priceless treasure by Johannes Vermeer. This painting disappeared in March 1990 from a Paris museum and never resurfaced until I repatriated the work. My collection requires it, so I took it. The owners would never divulge what I stole. They are criminals themselves.

"I'm not a greedy man, Mr McKenzie, I fully understand the importance of not being excessively cheap. Take what I want, then move on. It's as simple as that. Once I had my art repatriated, I also had safety box 88 removed; again, for my private home collection."

"You are evil!" Bill said, still looking dehydrated and uncomfortable in the seat. "You killed hundreds of people to get your hands-on stolen art. You are a low-life criminal. And you bring me here to hear your sordid story. It's pitiful."

Doling smirked, by smiling in an unpleasant way.

"If you remember back to that day, your mind-sharing partner Farid Aboud was having lunch with his friend Hasan Rahal? You know, the man that owned the cheese shop, the man that moved his family from war-torn Syria to a more suitable and peaceful environment and far away from the coming conflict. Didn't he advise Farid to do likewise? I can see it now, Hasan filling his mouth with overloaded spoonful's of Ful Medames, stuffing his already bulging belly with more food. Yet he was there on a mission, maybe he did try to help his friend, warn him of a bomb he was about to trigger."

Bill's attention was ignited, and his scared eyes focussed entirely on Hector Doling.

"Ah! The news you didn't expect to hear. Life has a weird way of showing up uninvited, Bill. Yes, that creepy Hasan Rahal was the leader I created to drive a dedicated performance within the group the bomb that killed his business friends, neighbours, innocent passers-by, the museum curator, his team of security, young school children and everyone else who shared my bomb site. I guess he had enough of selling cheese. Don't you think?"

"You are a deplorable example of a human being as well as being a deranged and demented psychopath."

"Of course, I am. Wouldn't you be if you had my intellect?"

Bill spoke petulantly, "You are a thief, a murderer, a control freak, and you bring me here to listen and bear witness to your nonsense, just because my mother helped put Finlay McColl in jail, or Laura helped screw up your masterplan. You are sick in the head!"

"If the world were full of brainless people like you, Bill, it would be a sorry place to live. Life needs people like Hector Doling, it would be so fucking dull and boring without me that's for sure. Look…if you honestly believe I had you brought here because of your fuckwit mother or bitch wife, you are far from mistaken." Doling mocked Bill by pushing his mouth upwards to make a clown smile. He kept the pose when he spoke, "I see by your facial expression that you still don't believe me. OK, I'll lay my cards on the table." The smile dropped.

"Let's have an open debate, a discussion to put closure on an issue that binds us together." Doling walked around the room, keeping in Bill's vision, and talked as a theatrical performer would.

Bill, I'm taking you back in time to 7 February 1942. Oberfeldwebel Erich Lux Doling, was a pilot in a Messerschmitt BF109, dogfighting in an aerial battle over Ta' Qali airfield here in Malta. But his rash, reckless and obstinate nature made him expose his weakness and fragility, more than required by good common sense. His plane was damaged, hit by a spitfire, and he needed to land. His foolish arrogance implies an eagerness to admit risk but not necessary irresponsibility.

"The Messerschmitt was struggling to stay airborne, and he had to use all his skills and training to avoid collision with dry stone walls of the many farms surrounding the airfield as he looked for a suitable place to land. He nearly made a safe landing by eyewitness accounts, touching down in a grassy field a mile from the aerodrome, but his plane burst into flames. It was a struggle, but my uncle was determined to escape the inferno. Luckily, he managed to exit the cockpit, moving diligently onto the wing and a few safety steps.

"That is when a spitfire returned to view the situation, and when the Brit saw his prey up close, the pilot fired eight machine guns bursts at my uncles crippled plane, hitting and killing him instantly.

"Killing a man that had survived a crash. Your uncle, Flight Lieutenant William McKenzie, was the fuckwit that acted like a Nazi rather than a British gentleman."

"The story you are trying to tell is wrong; I know this dogfight. I know more about the Siege of Malta than you would ever believe. The Messerschmitt, your uncle, flew had attacked the airfield to allow clearance for the impending bombing raid. There were many challenging fights in the area, and my uncle Bill did fight with a Messerschmitt, and yes, he hit the tail section of one, which made it lose control, and it struggled to stay airborne. Yet on its way down, your relative took time to off-load 20 mm cannon fire into a bus carrying sixteen civilians, the Mdina service to Attard, ten dead including three young children. You say my uncle was a coward. He was a damn hero killing an evil Nazi!'" voiced Bill in a vexed tone, his temper rising.

Doling made smiley faces and nodded his head from left to right several times. Like a puppet.

"Hilarious, Bill, and very fucking unpolite if I do say so. But I do enjoy the challenge. Let me tell you something about my uncle Erich.

"You may well believe you understand history, but my facts have been checked and verified; here is the truth. Firstly, my uncle was no Nazi. My mother told me he was as far from being a Nazi than Winston Churchill was. He was a classically trained artist, attended and studied at the Staatliches Bauhaus in Dessau in the late '20s. An artist, architect, and furniture designer, set to create aesthetically pleasing objects until Hitler and his cohorts put a stop to his artistic talents, and throw a swastika in the works of his bright future, as they would for millions of others. I dispute any connection or affiliation to Hitler's ideals. Art was his world; the war was just a disruptive problem to get through unscathed. But that wasn't to be; was it, Bill?

"My uncle flew over the bus, it was your uncle, in his Spitfire, that fired and hit the bus, as your crazed uncle went for the kill? He hid the truth from you, Bill. He buried his guilt!

"German archaeologists working for our family in the 1950s discovered the Messerschmitt fighter's remnants and forensically inspected it, it was soon found out and professionally observed, that both the guns had been hit by flack and spitfire bullets. In conclusion, there were no workable cannons in the BF109 just before crash-landing, this damage happened 20,000 ft in the air at the time of the initial battle. If you wish to angle another dig at my honesty, you will miss as always. I have the truth, Bill."

"You brought me here under armed threat to listen to a story from 1942? Is all this revenge for my uncle Bill's war heroics? Killing my wife and countless others because of family vengeance?" Bill was hurt and scared but spoke his mind and didn't understand why all the madness he had endured would end as part of a feud from World War 2.

"It is nothing to do with your uncle or mine, it's far beyond anything as trivial as that." Hector Doling laughed. "You are here to help me with the return of a particular piece of art. Art that I want. It was taken by your friend Farid and his child assistant Raca Sleiman in Aleppo. I only discovered this fact through McColl's link with your late wife.

"It was what the girl Raca revealed. Three religious' icons. Well, if they were available, I thought it only right I take them. That's why I need your help repatriating the art. I thought it would be a beautiful gift for a dear friend of mine."

"I haven't met Farid for a long time."

"Well, you can tell me the last time you shared life?"

Bill was tired and hoped giving information may be the factor that gets him released.

"It was 2016, in tunnels heading to the Citadel of Aleppo."

"Did they have stolen art with them?"

"No, I don't know anything about stolen art."

" You must have met Doctor Nabil Halif, Raca and the mystical cat, Mithra?"

Bill's eyes widened hearing Doling's words.

"The girl had this information, your wife shared details in her diary…oops! Yes, I admit that I've read Laura's journal. But come on, Bill, grow a pair, it's all about my love of art. Most people don't understand the intellectual qualities of art. Rich people purchase art for art's sake, tax reasons, or display their ability to afford such artistry. But all in all, they are Philistines, careless with money, and smugly indifferent to cultural values. Me, on the other hand, will always be concerned with matters of art and beauty, I am an aesthete, I have a delicate, refined sensitivity toward the beauty of art, and I will do everything in my power to save and collect all kinds of art."

"You steal art for yourself, that's not helpful if other people never get to view the items."

"Like your friend, Emad Ammon Naguib?"

Bill focussed his attention on Hector Doling. He made no further statement. The look on his face gave enough information on his demeanour, he was becoming more afraid. This man knew everything about him, it was if Doling had watched his every move since his childhood and held information on the fine details of his families existence.

Doling continued in his outlandish way, "Your friend and associate Emad Naguib had loaned three religious icons to a Syrian friend who unfortunately had them stolen from his house in the city of Jableh." He added, "Priceless Andrei Rublev's long-lost icons; The Nativity of Christ; Christ the Redeemer; and the Holy Trinity.

"It seems such a pity that such precious pieces of religious art should be shared like this. Passed indiscriminately between friends with no care or attention made to the wellbeing of such valuable antiquities. Your friend, Bill, is a moron and an untutored man, he is ignorant in the finer details of fine art, an unsophisticated boorish clown with no ideals on how art should be treated or admired. That's why I will take these icons. And give them to someone who cares."

Bill did not reply. He kept his stare on the sleeping dog.

Hector Doling took a phone from his pocket, a phone Bill recognised as his own.

"I have been in constant touch with Emad Naguib and his returning flight from Turkey. I wonder what goodies he will return with. Don't look so worried Bill, I have been checking your messages very carefully and the fool believes he has been communicating with you. Let me read the latest text:

Bill, I am returning from Turkey and should land within 1hr 30minutes, can we meet at The Phoenicia? I have great news and a pleasant surprise in store for you. Emad.

"I replied...Emad, can we meet at the Triton Fountain? I have a discreet meeting here which I can't divulge information on, and there is something important I need to show you. Exciting times, my friend. Bill.

"How amazing is all of this, Bill? Can you imagine, I get to have everyone attend and play my game, at my place of choice, and everyone abides by my fucking rules. It doesn't get much better than this, does it?"

Hector Doling walked from the table, heading for the exit and spoke one more time. He informed his security guard, “Unwrap him and get him in the car. We are heading to Valletta.”

Chapter 35
Escape Aleppo, Syria April 2016

Before leaving Aleppo, a doctor, with influential friends, had befriended both Farid and Raca, it was she that gave information on the safest route to Turkey. It was if they were agents in a foreign land being passed from link to link along the chain of freedom, by a string of aides, who fed and hid them and at considerable personal risk to her own life.

The passage to Turkey was codenamed 'Almashi min basatin alfakihat damiyat alraqs'—the walk of the dancing orchids—and had been used many times, especially after March 2011, at the start of the conflict. But it was a tried and tested escape line of resistance.

The organisation provided information on places to stay, where to go, and where not to go, produced new personal identities, their mobile phones were confiscated and luckily carried a cache of cash. They were informed to avoid taxis and buses and all kinds of public transport, and never, at any time, discuss their travels with strangers. All friends and family had to be forgotten and never contacted during the road to safety, or not until they were safely over the border.

Both had a transformation to their physical appearance. Before the journey began, Raca had her head shaved. She wore a hijab and plain dark clothes; that included a cosy padded hooded jacket over a warm fleece, a pair of walking boots and woollen gloves. Farid had grown a full beard which was black peppered with highlights of grey. He was given hiking clothes and boots, both carried backpacks with gratefully replenished supplies at each stopping point. It was a 30km journey, but on foot, walking on off-track roads, avoiding involvement with any trouble, would take them 4 days to reach their destination of Sarmada, a small town in the Harem district of Idlib.

Each of the four stopovers they would make during the trip was memorised, where to stay and whom to trust. No written letter or drawn plan of the route was permitted; any discovery of any such proof would have many people killed and 'the walk of the dancing orchids' compromised.

Farid retained details of each of the villages and towns where they would stay. Also, the names of friends he could trust, the roles they provided, and updates that would allow them to complete their journey. Helpers would resupply them with different clothes, new footwear, and new backpacks at each stopping place. And again, their physical appearance changed. This process was nothing short of professional; not one stone was left unturned.

A few guides called the escape route, Die Rattenlinnie—The Rat Line—which was Nazi Germany's system of escape for Nazis and other fascists fleeing Europe in the aftermath of World War 2, and this too was highly organised and sophisticated and operated by a powerful elite.

As they made their way over treacherous terrain and through frontlines of war, they knew the next day could be their last. But also understood their lives were in constant danger, being in the province with terror groups of over 30,000 rebel fighters where at least 10,000 are designated as terrorists; and, on their trail, was an extremist terror group hunting them down.

The journey west from Aleppo was difficult, they played the part of suffering refugees on many occasions, and in many respects, they were actual migrants themselves. However, their predicament was different, they were escaping a pursuing hunter, as they headed for the Turkish border. Witnessing many atrocities, that newsreels don't have access to, seeing the difficulty life, at times, must endure, and how hatred runs deep through the veins of people, individuals intent of destroying a historical past and obliterate any offering of a peaceful future.

Their escape to Turkey had been arranged by someone they didn't know. An influential sympathiser, and someone outside the Syrian conflict.

A wealthy benefactor capable of helping others escape from such a hot seat of war, an authoritative person who carries a lot of weight, and an individual with significant control in such desperate times is the type of character capable of laying such a pathway to freedom, under such uncontrollable conditions. Farid was grateful for any available help. Maybe it was his mind-sharing companion Bill McKenzie, that was orchestrating the route to freedom.

Farid made a big decision, by putting trust in others, in a land of no faith was a big gamble, but there was no alternative, this was the only way to go, and so far, it was working out well.

On the 10 April, they arrived at a refugee camp known as Al-Kamouna near Sarmada and is close to the Turkish border, about 40 kilometres west of Aleppo. It was a journey fraught with danger. The last day's walk through the open countryside from Tal Alkaram to Sarmada was strewn with armed bandits and belligerent militias. The trek included crossing large areas filled with landmines, often contending with the intervention of systematic bombing by the Syrian Government, and their Russian allies.

The Al-Nusra Front controlled the district, along with other affiliated Anti-Assad rebels. It is a dangerous place to live, but live they must, not at least with the evil forces surrounding them, but by avoiding capture and certain death from the killers that hunt them, which was also their main priority.

The camp didn't offer a hotel type welcome or a display an oasis of plenty. Still, they felt safe amongst the multitude, hiding amid the masses of displaced people, seeing how the exiles suffered from many clinical problems associated in this living environment. Farid kept Raca close, knowing women and girls were high-risk targets for trafficking and sexual abuse.

Keeping her safe by sharing a tent with two other families; families who willingly offered what little food they had; old bread and a smidgen of rancid houmous.

Thankfully, Farid shared what appeared to his fellow camp occupants as a feast; a pack of Syrian string cheese, pita bread and tinned fruit, and canned milk.

Up until now, they had felt safe and protected. Sarmada was a different prospect as many warring groups were located near the Turkish border. Regular bombings by Government and Russian forces had destroyed much of the town's infrastructure, making the town unreliable, with no public security to mention. The place was a hornet's nest, and everyone beat it regularly with sticks.

The Militia and splinter groups had become unorganised and erratic. They made the area vulnerable to other unknown groups entering the vacuum to fill any space left by weak or inferior led forces. It was bedlam and anarchy.

Continual bombings caused further problems.

One strike hit a safe-house they were due to stay, killing the occupants and their family. They were people that signed up to help with Farid's and Raca's move to Turkey, and now this evacuation route was delayed.

When word reached Farid at the refugee camp, a local tribal leader would soon find a new place of safety. To organise a new place to stay would take several weeks, and now Farid and Raca needed to remain in the refugee camp for the foreseeable future. More food, clothes, toiletries, and medicines, if required, arrived daily, all covertly delivered, secretly smuggled to the tent they now occupied. But this singled-out resource had to be concealed from other fellow exiles to the point that personal bodyguards functioned in the site to offer protection.

–

Twenty-five days passed and Farid and Raca had prepared to leave the camp. Any supplies they still had was given to friends and neighbours, they said their goodbyes and waited patiently at the edge of the camp, for the arrival of a vehicle that would take them to a safe place. Al-Kamouna was a small city of tents, queues and mechanical diggers scraping up new land for new arrivals, it was growing daily. It was a humanitarian nightmare, a refuge in a warzone. When it rains, the camp becomes a hellish swamp; it turns into a merciless desert when it doesn't. And today, it was a desert.

A local tribal leader, a powerful chief that still had a physical presence in Sarmada and held much control of local laws and political agreements in the region, would be their guardian and protector. A man that could safeguard their onward passage, keep them from the hands of the hunters that want them dead, and would take complete control of their destiny. It was his word of honour, 'Kalimat alsharaf.'.

–

Children's voices were first to react, screaming and pointing skyward. Frantic women joined the confusion, by ululating, producing high-pitched vocal sound resembling a howl with a trilling quality to express strong emotions of sadness and grief.

Men responded by shouting orders, asking for their loved ones to follow them to find shelter, or to lie down, to run, to hide, to pray.

A bomb dropped from a jet fighter, either Syrian or Russian, knowingly attacked the refugee camp. Two foreign TV crews captured footage of a jetfighter circling the site before dropping the barrel bomb and instantly reported the horrific news live.

Al-Kamouna camp had between 1,500 and 2,000 misplaced people, and like Farid and Raca had fled the fighting in the Aleppo and Hama provinces. Under disruptive chaos and confusion of the situation, Farid struggled to find Raca as he ran, helplessly struggling to discover her after the devastating destruction the bomb made. It was a wrenching scene of carnage.

The scene of annihilation was criminal.

Human body parts littered the ground. Severely injured individuals screamed in pain, and fearful mothers wept and prayed words to God.

Farid hoped that Raca was not a victim.

The second blast hit the camp's outskirts, where humanitarian volunteers had built a facility to assist refugees.

Farid was caught in the explosion. As a former white helmet, he should have known this unethical behaviour was a regular occurrence by Assad's forces. Still, he was a different man nowadays; he protected a young girl from militaries who wanted them dead. The explosion blew Farid several feet in the air, caught in a rainstorm of shrapnel and other debris, suffering severe leg injuries, with many cuts and bruises over his body. He was unconscious when Raca discovered him.

–

A noisy cockerel awakened Farid, it wasn't early morning as everyone would imagine, it was mid-afternoon, and the rooster's stubborn personality had him bullishly defend his territory. Perched on a small fence surveying his flock, Farid could see the bird through the large open door to his left, which led to a walled garden.

The alpha male consistently crowing sound established his dominance over other roosters and all his subordinates who is boss and control his harem of hens. The defence of holding his ground was admirable. This moment in time relieved Farid of the horrors his country was enduring. It was a near-perfect time to awake from a coma.

The bird's vocal sounds continued as Farid looked around the room where he lay motionless as a patient. It wasn't a hospital but had similar equipment that gave it that appearance, both his legs had thigh-high casts, and he grimaced when any slight movement interacted with the injury. It took another six months before

Farid would attempt walking. The severity of the damage to both fibula and tibia in both legs was horrific. In his comatose state, a skilful and experienced team of doctors, or surgeons, or possibly both, had worked wonders rebuilding his legs. He felt grateful but never had a chance to meet or thank his carers, it was his benefactor who once again saved his life.

Time passed, and healing proceeded, but his walking capabilities had all but gone. It took many months more of intensive therapy, working through the excruciating pain barrier of intensive rehabilitation, to stand without aid. His mind was always clear regarding the future; it was knowing that Turkey was the destination where he and Raca could feel safe and put closure to the craziness of war. During Farid's time of rehabilitation, Raca attended private school lessons.

–

Two years had passed since the camp bombing, and no militia group during this time compromised their safety. During this time, and unknown to Farid and Raca, several killers came to the town asking questions about their whereabouts. But almost immediately, they were eliminated, and their bodies were taken to a remote area and left to rot. There was a war on, and dead bodies did not raise eyebrows, either from the fractured police force or any official security organisations for that matter.

Word reached the Aleppo crime syndicate that the fleeing couple were hiding in Sarmada and had been in safekeeping for a lengthy period. The deaths of their hitmen proved that someone of power was offering a helping hand. The criminals hunting Farid and Raca needed a more subtle way of gathering information; utilising the skills of the extremists that held the region would be the best way to find the pair that stole their treasure.

–

Elbow crutches offered more support than a walking stick, Farid could no longer walk unaided, his legs gave him pain, and these supports assured he remained upright and allowed him to move sluggishly, but with certainty. The day of driving to Turkey had arrived; it was now or never.

At the Bab al-Hawa crossing, the border was still controlled by HTC—Hay'at Tahrir al-Sham, commonly known as Tahrir al-Sham, an active Salafist jihadist militant group, it was now time to be brave, and they had to act fast.

These radicals would kill first, then ask no questions later, and the word was out that the extremists were looking for Farid and his young companion. A sizeable bounty was on their heads.

A Volvo FH60 truck sat outside the building where they had been self-imprisoned for over two years. All the afflictions that went before them culminated in this chance, this one-time possibility of freedom; even though it would be the most demanding missions. This task would be difficult and dangerous.

Still, they had a mysterious backer and a driver that looked like a 1970s Italian hitman. And this hitman was Omar Faruk Kaplan, a super fit ex-MIT Agent and the bodyguard used in this region by Emad Ammon Naguib.

Kaplan was a professional in every meaning of the word; killing was not a pastime or leisure activity, it was a job, and it was a high paid job for the man that had reputedly killed over two hundred people.

A false bottom in the truck concealed a secret compartment where Farid and Raca would remain until their arrival over the Turkish border; it would take over an hour to get to their destination. Still, security was harsh and unsafe at the crossing, and likely to have thorough security checks on arrival. Omar Kaplan checked his phone and sent a text. He was ready to move.

The space inside the boxed compartment was limited. It was a tight squeeze and claustrophobic to most who used this way of escape. However, fresh filtered oxygen was pumped automatically into the box to provide a much healthier environment during their ordeal. It also helped to ventilate and cool the container. The heat at this time of year can rise to 80°F (ca. 27 °C).

The route had been used successfully in the past, so it must work, Farid hoped and prayed.

The journey could take longer than the hour projected, unforeseen developments such as heavy traffic, the vigilance of the terrorists that controlled the border, and the probability of corruption by those that held and operated this junction. At this border, every driver paid a bribe. The more money spent, the easier the task for a fast track through the border zone. Most of the time, the border guards would ask for money. Place a fifty Euro in the passport and smile. If not, they'll ask for it. If you refuse, you will wait for hours or possibly days.

In past crossings, travellers suitcases were opened and emptied onto the ground. It's no longer the case of offering a crate of Coke and a pack of cigarettes. The stakes were high and would remain so for the foreseeable future.

A bottle of water each was their only additional comfort. It was also necessary to remain silent at all costs, mostly when they stopped at roadside checkpoints. The laden pallet that covered their hidden box was a false load; it was light and easily removed by one person. Further real-weight pallets of agricultural farming materials were loaded until the trailer was full. The trailer wheels showed extreme load weight that the border guards would recognise, and hopefully, fool them into believing the truck was legitimate. The road ahead was busy, with many vehicles held in an inspection area, as the truck entered a parking zone near the international crossing point between Syria and Turkey. Men with guns were everywhere. After thirty minutes patiently, two guards waved the truck ahead; the driver produced the documents as requested. Tahrir Al-Sham extremists stood close to the driver's door, unwilling to engage in conversation. They talked, and Omar Kaplan listened.

A full complement of camouflage jacket and trousers gave them a uniformed look. Both wore military tactical vests with a fully equipped utility belt, with AK47 assault rifles swung over their shoulders. Bearded killers are wearing black beanie hats.

The largest of the two guards looked briefly at Kaplan's passport. The cash was taken and pocketed. He asked what he was transporting, and Omar Kaplan answered in fluent Arabic—; "Alnueaddat Alziraeia" [(agricultural equipment]).

The guard studying the passport showed a look of concern. Believing the driver's demeanour raised suspicion. There was no scanner to ensure the passport, visa, and other official documents were genuine. As the truck driver leaned out the driver's side window offering his best conciliatory smile, it didn't cut it with the border guard. Even the bright blue eyes and the black sowed hair implanted on his head confirmed the guard's thoughts, believing the driver was either a spy or a government agent.

Both guards whispered and discussed their misgivings. Just as the border guards were about to ask the driver to exit the truck, several mortar blasts landed near the main border offices a few hundred yards back in the distance. Shock set into the terrorists as further explosions occurred. They became confused. The terrorists, truckers and civilians ran away from the blast zones; the two guards spoke on a mobile phone and asked for instructions.

As they waited for a response, Omar Kaplan raised a Scorpion silent pistol and fired one shot into both the guards' foreheads before either could react. The 9 mm Kurz Browning bullets blew off the back of their skulls. A few more mortar shells landed to the column's rear, allowing Omar Kaplan to start the engine and move through the border crossing. As soon as the truck moved, several Tahrir Al-Sham extremists noticed the escape, and seeing two comrades lying dead, began firing shots, hitting all sides of the truck with a hail of bullets. The Volvo took a few minutes to drive the short distance into Turkey.

The alert Turkish guards knew of the Ex-MIT agent's arrival, and the vehicle freely passed the primary Turkish customs security area.

Allowing a clear road through onto the Antakya Cilvegozu Yolu highway, achieving an easy passage as the HGV drove unchecked through Turkey's Cilvegozu border gate.

After a thirty-minute drive, they reached the outskirts of Reyhanli where the truck was abandoned in an isolated industrial estate. Two men, assisting Omar Kaplan, rushed to the truck and moved fast to release Farid and Raca from the steel sarcophagus that held them securely for nearly two hours; they were severely dehydrated, the heat made them lose more fluid than that they put in. More water was offered and taken gratefully. A black Audi A5 waited as both were ushered into the revving car, at this time two other vehicles arrived at the industrial complex firing guns in all directions. Omar Kaplan returned fire, shooting a hail of bullets at the oncoming assailant's car, the driver was shot dead and lost control. The uncontrolled vehicle glided and hit a metal shutter of a business unit and blew up.

Kaplan sprayed the other car with gunfire from two Uzis. The automatic fire remained until the car slowed to a crawling pace, then stopped, venting steam from bullet holes that obliterated the bonnet—allowing the professional killer to spatter the vehicle with gunfire until his guns had expelled its munitions.

Every one of the hunters was dead at the hands of one man, one professional killer, Omar Kaplan. But he had been shot. Raca's view diminished; she watched as Omar Kaplan buckled and placed two hands over his stomach where blood flowed from his wound.

She watched as her defender collapsed to the ground, squirming in agony. His final stare was at the car that drove his two clients to safety; then, he stopped moving; his life expired.

Raca had observed and witnessed all this action from the rear window of the fleeing motor. It took a few seconds more before the speeding car hit the main road. The fleeing party arrived at Hatay Airport in 50 minutes, in a journey that would typically take 1 hour 14 minutes.

Chapter 36
Valletta The Present Day

A group of six men, Bill McKenzie, Hector Doling, and his gun-yielding accessories, arrived at the Triton fountain located on the City Gate of Valletta's periphery. The sculpture of three mythological Tritons held up a platter, and each face, of each Triton, being visible from the city gate. Hector Doling chose this angle as his podium to give his imminent speech, where he would stand on the outer concentric ring [(built from concrete and clad in travertine slabs]) to reveal to the world his gift of truth.

His final performance.

The water-showcase was spraying pulsating jets of water, coloured lights illuminating the classical fountain in its full circumference, in Malta's most famous Modernist landmarks.

As Hector Doling stepped onto the raised limestone edge, the water jets shut down, but the lights remained switched on; which guaranteed to highlight Doling's entrance, as a stage performer filled the spotlight. His sermon, a one-off Magnus opus, as he called it, could now be revealed.

In unity, two of Doling's hoodlums filmed proceedings on android phones.

Filming live footage. Using social media platforms, connecting to millions of eager viewers, *all possible*, unwilling guinea pigs, in Hector Doling's indoctrination of his unique masterly technique of total mind-control; that may set unprecedented turmoil throughout the world.

Bill was worried and scared. If Doling mentioned trigger words live, then all hell could break loose. Those innocent people under his spell could react in hateful, hurtful ways, and do unimaginable things.

But how can he be stopped?

The tough guy standing over Bill still held the Glock pistol against his spine.

Doling was mad, a psychopath with the qualities to turn the world in on itself. A creator of havoc, an evil administer of hate. But what hope was there? How on earth could this madman be stopped?

Doling spoke to Bill.

"I've just received several messages from some members of my audience tonight, all friends of yours, Bill. I took the initiative to invite them along to see my performance. I hope you don't mind?" He smiled at Bill, waiting for a reaction that didn't come.

"How fucking exciting is this, Bill?" Doling was energised by his performance.

Doling tossed Bill's phone at him, and he caught it. The guard behind him didn't flinch.

Almost instantly, as if waiting in the wings of a theatre, Doling turned to see the retired vicar appear before him.

"Ah! Reverend Archibald Hughes! How are you doing? And a warm welcome to Doling's asylum."

Hector Doling stared at the minister, and he waggled his right forefinger as in a naughty-naughty gesture.

"You have been a busy little bee, haven't you? Telling Bill all sorts of secrets, planting unjustified thoughts into his head: so much so that he doesn't know what the fuck is real and what is fuckin' fantasy. You are such a lost soul minister, moving between reality and mind-control, driving in the rain with no wipers, but thankfully all of this is all about to come to an end. Fucking with my vocation is not what I would say as being wise.

"Fighting my incredible power is something you cannot succeed in doing. Whatever you say, or do, is irrelevant. I control your every move. Why the fuck, would your tiny mind believe you could ever infiltrate my organisation. I don't need you sticking your fucking nose into my business. You are just a simple little pawn on my giant chessboard, not a fucking bishop or a king, only a tiny, nondescript, useless piece of shit. And for that, I need to show Bill what happens to those that fuck with me."

The bully with the gun brought the firearm into view, just to remind the minister that this was no game, he told him to stand next to Bill and remain silent. He did precisely that. Then, as If Hector Doling had rehearsed and stage-managed the whole scenario, Emad, Farid and Raca appeared at the fountain as if timed to perfection. Four more of Doling's security team emerged from the shadows, all armed and willing to use their guns and now participating in making sure no one moves or leaves the area. Many tourists, locals, and some people passing by stopped to view the gathering, believing that a street performer was about to begin his act; possibly a singer, someone who twists balloons, a mime artist, a juggler, or a person puppeteer. They would be right with the puppeteer; this madman played people, not dolls.

"Ladies and gentlemen, I divulge a truth, a truth so obvious that even the simplest of minds can grasp the ordinance of its structure."

Two curious police officers appeared at the scene and interrupted Hector Doling's speech, ready to check the orator's validity, and asked him to step down from the fountain ledge.

Doling became agitated, so he lifted his phone and used it. He sent a message to men under his spell, his control, his truth.

"Just one fucking press of a button, then the message is sent. Deal with this, you assholes!'

A speeding, off-road motorbike soon emerged near the fountain, the driver popping the bike on its back wheel and turning several wheelies. This erratic action got the police's attention; speaking through a communication device, the officer asked for backup. The biker subsequently drove off, raising the front wheel in a catwalk wheelie motion, one of the book's oldest tricks, heading for the Ponte la Valletta. The police officers became more concerned about the biker than the rants of a madman.

The rider's unpredictable behaviour disturbed them more; when the bike stopped at the entrance to the bridge, the motorcyclist raising an arm in the air, fired three shots from a gun; before racing off into the walled city. Avoiding scared people that ran and dived for cover as the dirt-bike flew past Freedom square onward to Republic street. Ten more off-road bikes immediately turned off the Great siege road, past the Phoenicia Hotel and headed in the same direction of Valletta centre. The police were in panic mode.

They needed assistance soon.

Many curious people arrived at Hector Doling's unpredictable seminar scene and watched the spontaneous outburst from the skinny man who looked so much like Andy Warhol.

"How beautiful is the vulnerability of the mind? Watch this, Bill."

Any words Doling shouted or messages he sent of any social media information he provided to receptive and vulnerable minds may create total anarchy. This madman was way out of control. What were the bikers going to do? They were armed; this could all get out of hand soon.

Doling cupped his hands around his mouth in a mocking fashion and shouted a few words.

These words were spoken in Maltese. "Orkidi tal-pupi jiżfnu!"

Bill didn't understand these words. But he reacted to the movement noise behind him; he turned his head. It wasn't the guard with the gun, and it was six couples waltzing as if attending Vienna's fabulously glamorous Opera Ball.

All pre-hypnotised for this one moment, a stage set -up for Bill and his friend's benefit. Yet another of Doling's mind-control additions.

"Wrap your left hand around the follower's right hand, keeping your elbow up at shoulder height. Keep your posture straight."

Doling sent another text message as the entertainment continued.

"And, just for you, Bill, the moment you and I have been waiting all our lives for, this spark will ignite the truth. Together, it's our moment of judgement. And finally, it is here. My gladiators are on their way!"

The dancing couples kept waltzing, turning, and veering away from the location.

Within seconds, everyone heard loud engine noises thundering through the sky.

"Feast your eyes on the sky above the city, Bill. Here is a reminder of our last judgement. I am Hector Doling, not God almighty, me and only me, that decrees the fates of all individuals under my illusion."

Bill and the group turned to look at the sky over the city. Doling raised his left arm and pointed in the direction of the city. And there, over Valletta, a Spitfire chased by a Messerschmitt BF109, zooming past on a low trajectory, making the crowd scream, and run for cover. The dogfight continued as both planes twisted, spun, and turned around in the sky over Valletta. Gunfire from two synchronised MG17s cannons fired quick succession bursts, and a short spurt from the single centreline Motorkanone gun riddled both tail elevators. Still, it didn't affect its evasion course as the Spitfire shot off in another direction away from the versatile predator.

Both aircraft, still in fight and flight mode, disappeared into the distance, just as Bill's Uncle William did back in 1942. But then, he was the hunter, not the hunted.

"I would suggest the odds are on the Messerschmitt winning this battle. What do you think, Bill?"

He continued, "In the long run, the machine becomes an extension of my mind, one machine against an enemy machine, both with eager pilots, each attempting to outsmart the other, both determined not to be defeated. The handling of the aircraft is vital, and of course, the Spitfire has the advantage in that department, but I believe that in this case, the Messerschmitt pilot is going to prove that his skill level has the power to win this battle. It is a kind of rerun of our private war. Don't you think?"

The two aircraft flew back from the Floriana district, just one hundred feet above the fountain, flying over the gates of Valletta, the spitfire weaving in a scissors manoeuvre, trying with urgency to escape.

The noise of short bursts of machine-gun fire echoed through the air as the fighters flew off into the distance, still in a dogfight.

The Spitfire at full throttle, this was something else—nothing compared to this—not even the Messerschmitt's Daimler-Benz engine that his uncle Bill told him sounded like a stone crusher.

Hector Doling got everyone's attention by clapping his hands, mocking his audience.

"How are you enjoying my show?"

Not one person reacted, no one that heard him talk could believe that one man could create such an ensemble of strangeness and something implausible to accept as accurate, but it was; In all its madness. Bill felt the staged aerial battle must be a show organised by the Maltese Government, or maybe a movie was being filmed; that's what the locals thought.

"Fine…if that's the way you feel, at least I'm enjoying myself. OK, Bill, Emad and Farid, my three wise men."

"Let me put closure on this. In my case, the end will justify the means, I have already enjoyed my last supper, and I now desire to close my book of truth with immediate effect. My Doling organisation, after many years of triumph and glorious success, now allows me to retire and withdraw gracefully."

Doling ran his hands through his hair.

Bill stepped towards the fountain, but the gun was forced deep into his back, and for the first time, the guard with the gun spoke. His voice was low and deep, like the American soul singer Barry White. He said, "Move, and you die!" and Bill believed him.

"And now, I introduce to you my Hungarian friend, Farkas Palinkas. Is this all getting too much for you, Bill? I understand your fragility, but if your mind is limited in collecting and retaining simple data, and I need to explain every move I make, it will get exasperating. You will need to listen better! This creep you call a minister, Reverend Archibald Hughes, is someone under my control. But like your whore wife, he thought he could fuck with me. But as I have told you before. No one fucks with Hector Doling!

"For fuck sake, Bill, I am everywhere! Do I always need to remind you how involved I am in your life? I have the power to do this." and he shouted the word, 'Vindiciae.'

Vindiciae was a trigger word. The minister, the Hungarian man called Farkas Palinkas, walked freely from the fountain, ambled 100 metres, like a zombie, to the Ponte la Valletta, watched curiously and uncomfortably by Bill; the man moved onto the metal barrier that spanned the bridge, put a gun to his head and fired. He was falling headfirst down to the Valletta ditch. People lost control and started screaming.

"Do I hear encore?" Doling said, raising a cupped hand to his ear.

There was much chaos at the famous landmark. Still, the police were preoccupied with arresting armed men on motorbikes to spend any time worrying about an outspoken simpleton speaking his mind at the Triton fountain. One officer ran from the city and looked over the bridge down into the trench.

Saying on his communication device: "A man has just shot himself and dropped into the Valletta ditch."

As Doling's game continued, two old wartime planes flew overhead toward Ta' Qali, the now abandoned WWII airfield. After the aircraft had gotten out of sight, a loud explosion was heard—possibly a crash—perhaps one of the planes had been hit and downed. "Are you still with me, Bill? Good. Now, This is what I call a fuckin' finale!"

Hector Doling raised both arms like wings, he smiled, then spoke, "The greatest secrets are always concealed in unlikely places. Just remember Bill, a secret will only remain a secret if you make someone promise not to reveal it. And, more importantly, a conspiracy, any conspiracy, is a fragile veil covering the truth. Keep this in mind!

"So now, I will unveil my truth."

His attention was drawn to the young girl Raca. The girl who had witnessed horrific scenes of horror and many atrocities in her homeland, Hector Doling and his extravagant charades didn't scare her in the least. She stood proud and returned Doling's stare.

Doling spoke. Raca mumbled under her breath.

"Raca, my little Raca from Aleppo, I must apologise for being rude and discourteous to you. I respect you very much and regret my behaviour wholesomely. I hope you can forgive me as my behaviour doesn't represent my true attitude. I won't make any more excuses or explain my reason; remember, I'm under no obligation to make sense to you. But if I may—your secrets are safe with me, and if I'm honest, I wasn't even listening."

His exasperated stare returned to Bill.

"I'd fucking kill for a Nobel peace prize!"

Doling rolled his head from side-to-side, cracking his neck muscles. And spoke again, "Now, Mr Bill Mcfuckingkenzie. My truth is a simple fact really. The fact is I have been fucking with you for an exceptionally long time. Read my fucking lips!" he said, pointing to his mouth.

Doling's thugs stood close to Bill and his friends, all ready to use their guns if necessary.

"It was me that killed Laura! The driver in the fast car, do you remember the registration plate. I thought it was a personal touch. LMD1E, Laura McKenzie, I Die! I see you didn't appreciate that. I did at least send flowers to the grave." Still staring at Bill, Doling wanted a reaction.

"Here's another one for you. I'm also the pathologist you met in the Edinburgh hospital morgue. Remember, you asked me about my unique name. You thought my name was unusual. Are you deliberately obtuse?

"For fuck sake, Bill. I gave you a fucking clue, and you still didn't solve it. Dirk Alleluia! The name on my security ID. It's another fucking anagram. Try it. It's an anagram of I KILLED LAURA!"

He added further abuse while laughing through his dialogue,

"Do you remember the boat at Cramond?

"I was the sailor on the "'Sana Miracle"' sailing from Cramond heading out into the Forth estuary. Come on, Bill, get your brain working! You waved at me. Fuck sake, you are so slow. My boat, the 'Sana Miracle'; it's another fucking anagram. An anagram of Raca Sleiman. Get with the programme, Bill.

"Gordon Leitch is an anagram of Hector Doling.

"Bill, you remind me of a steel ball in a bizarre game of pinball. I launch you into the game, use the flippers to knock you back into the turmoil of craziness, bouncing your tiny mind of the bumpers, getting caught in the spinning lane, held in a roller switch, and bungled upward by the slingshot. But tonight, Bill, you find the escape lane, find the escape hole; then leave the mad, mad world of Hector Doling. My job is to play with people's minds.

Doling paused for a moment. Then spoke directly to Bill.

"You must be wondering why you and your wife became such prominent fixtures in my life."

Bill so wanted to get his hand around Doling's neck and squeeze until the last breath left his lungs. He felt sick. He wanted to vomit.

"Bill, this is why you and your late wife meant so much to me," shouted Doling, He stood still, his arms raised high like he was flying; he called out louder, '*Rufus est mysterium lenticulae elit. Reveatum est*!'

Everybody heard a loud whishing sound, then a dull thump, as a snipers bullet, fired from a later discovered Israeli Gali sniper rifle; a 7.62mm projectile had entered the centre of his forehead and blew away the back of his skull. His sunglasses remained in place. The lone marksman fired from a few hundred yards away from St. James Counterguard on the massive pentagonal artillery platform, part of a defensive wall built-in 1640. A perfect headshot. But not an attempt to compare to the longest sniper shot ever; this honour goes to a Canadian trooper.

The sniper took out an ISIS terrorist near Mosul, in Iraq, with a McMillan Tac-50 rifle. Firing from a high-rise building, he killed the terrorist from 3,540mtrs, just over two miles away.

Doling stood still for a few seconds, rocking ever so slightly as an unstable statue would or a graveside minister. Eventually, his dead weight pulled him back into the outer part of the fountain. As dramatic theatrical performances go, this pompous, extravagantly histrionic display worked perfectly. As soon as Doling's body hit the water, the water pumps began to work. Bill thought Hector Doling would have approved, spitting his watery blood in a weird yet surreal colourful spectacle. More screaming people darted from the area, leaving behind the strangest and scariest night ever remembered in Valletta. Even Doling's security made good their escape.

It was time for Bill and his friends to move.

Emad nudged the group to the safety of the Phoenicia Hotel, he had pre-booked rooms for Farid and Raca, and they would head off for some long-awaited sleep-time. They had had a long and arduous journey over many years and escaping killers in Syria and Turkey was just half of it. Even tonight's obscure visual and graphic display did not come as a surprise. Raca had pre-warned Farid and Emad of this unusual activity and how it would play out. She knew the future; she had already seen it happen. They believed every word she said, the story she revealed how Emad would receive a text message from Doling (using Bill's mobile phone) and respond to such notices.

Raca knew the certainty of the outcome; every single part of Hector Doling's performance, every mundane task Doling made, was recognised.

She was lucid dreaming. In her mind sharing connection, Laura had spoken to her just after the explosion in Al Hatab Square in Aleppo in 2012.

She had been told of this day in Valletta, and how it would unravel. And the words Hector Doling spoke before he was shot, *Rufus est mysterium lenticulae elit. Reveatum est*, translated to *Red lentil soup is not a secret. It is a revelation.* However, all of Doling's insanity can be discussed tomorrow by Bill and his friends; the police would never know Bill's secrets of Hector Doling or Gordon Leitch for that matter; the future was all that mattered now. If the police asked questions, they would appear to deny any knowledge of/or responsibility for any damnable actions caused by Hector Doling. They were just innocent bystanders caught up in tragic events, as many were this evening.
Emad recommended a few drinks in the club bar, Bill agreed.

With one dead body floating in the fountain, another splattered in the Valletta ditch, and multiple crazed motorcyclists still leading the police a merry dance around the narrow streets of Valletta—by winding their bikes up and down around the old city. Tonight, created a severe convergence of unexplainable occurrences. The ancient Maltese city would take time to understand and comprehend what happened. And then, there was the unexplained two WW2 aircraft hidden somewhere on the island.

Chapter 37
The Oncidium Orchids Germany and Malta
The Next Day

Germany

It was 11 a.m. when the Embraer 190 private jet landed at Koblenz Winnigen Airport, situated close to the villages Winnigen and Güls, in the Rhineland-Palatinate region western Germany; a district renowned for superb wines. The aircraft taxied close to a private hangar at the edge of the runway. A well-dressed stranger disembarked and met a chauffeur—who stood at over 6ft—holding open the rear door of the lavishly expensive, Magnetite Black Metallic Maybach Exelero. A car worth over $8,000,000.

The stranger entered the car, slackened his tie and relaxed.

A warm sun shone through white-fluffy clouds, and there was little or no wind. It was a beautiful day, and the ride was pleasant.

The drive to Jäggerburg Castle took fifty minutes, passing Osterpai, Filsen and Kamp Bornhofen, before driving up the steep incline of the Burgenstraße to his home, which lies in the Nassau nature reserve and sits one-hundred-and-twenty meters above the river Rhine. Armed guards protect the castle. Two approached as the car slowed to a walking pace as it neared the main entrance; one guard saluted to the driver as he visually confirmed the driver and passenger. The driver had previously pressed a button on the car dashboard that sent an 'All-Clear' password to Castle Jäggerburg security, ensuring their arrival was without incident or obstruction. Besides, radioed ahead to inform internal protection, confirming the boss's arrival. All this action was viewed on monitors from a hi-tech security room in the castle cellar.

As the Maybach Exelero cruised silently to a stop near the castle's main door, the stranger was met by Ulrich, his forty-something-year-old chief of operations, a native of Prötzel in Brandenburg, Eastern Germany.

Ulrich Laundhart was the chief operating officer for his boss and was responsible for all business processes.

He was an ex-SOC German Kommando Spezialkräfte, (KSK). In his service days, he saw action in a NATO-led international peacekeeping force in Kosovo, fought with distinction during Operation Enduring Freedom in Afghanistan, where his unit was awarded the USA Distinguished Unit Citation. For his heroism, he was given a citation for allied countries and mentioned in dispatches. He is a grandmaster of the Thai art of Krabi-Krabong, which uses curved blades or single-edge swords for weapon-based fighting.

This multifunctioning man also flies aircraft and helicopters. As an orchid enthusiast, he cultivated and grew over two thousand different varieties of orchids at Jäggerburg Castle. Orchids constitute the largest plant family globally, with over thirty thousand types.

The overseer of the house was an anthophile, with a love of orchids, a floral aspiration—notably, a house favourite, a unique and stunning flower, the dancing lady orchid. Ulrich Laundhart made sure the main study had fresh orchids daily. And another string to his bow, a trained and knowledgeable wine professional, as a uniquely Master Sommelier, and one of one-hundred and three worldwide professionals who had earned the title.

The stranger handed Ulrich a briefcase and a parcel as they walked into the hallway.

"I would like Torsten to hang these pictures in the study and leave my briefcase on the desk, Ulrich", said the stranger.

"Very well, Herr Sulzbach. I will get this done immediately." In firmness of mind, he offered a choice of wine. "Today I recommend a bottle of Weingut Egon Muller-Scharzhof Scharzhofberger Trockenbeerenauslese Mosel-Saar-Ruwer, Herr Sulzbach."

"The vintage?" the stranger asked his servant. As they entered through the front door on the west façade, they pass into a grand entrance. The wallpaper is an Asian design. Hand-painted motifs and techniques formed a repeat pattern of wild animals, peacocks and birds-of-paradise among flowers and foliage. It was mostly gold and green coloured. It sparked as the sun shone through the open door.

There were Greek themes in the frieze on the walls and ceilings.

The white marble floor was littered with David Roentgen furniture of all descriptions. It was if the castle was a museum to the 18th-century German furniture maker. Roentgen's work's characteristic and ingenuity are the creative and convoluted mechanical devices that open concealed writing surfaces, drawers, and other hidden compartments in his beautiful household pieces. Used by Aristocracy and Royalty alike. This owner was more than a favourable fan of his work.

"It is a 2011 classic. There is a delicious fruity taste with a touch of sweetness and a delicate aroma with a hint of minerality. It is purely an excellent clean wine, Sir."

"I'll have it in the white tower, Ulrich; first, I need to take a quick shower."

–

Malta
The same day, 12.30

After lunch, Bill met Emad at the Bastion Pool Bar at the Phoenicia Hotel. Fresh coffee and tea was served. The pool area was busy with guests. Many were eating lunch. Others lay on sun loungers reading novels, a few tapped their feet to whatever rhythmic music played in their ears. Some slept. Little Raca splashed playfully in the glorious blue water of the infinity pool. She was watched closely by Farid.

A member of Emad's staff had provided him with a dossier, a confidential report from a powerful friend in the Maltese Government, it offered up to date information on all of Bill's questions. At least he hoped it did.

A look of bewilderment crossed Emad's face as he glanced at the report.

"Ok, Bill. This knowledge comes from a friend at the top of Malta's judiciary, a powerful man with powerful friends, in powerful places. This report is, as it stands, 100% correct. None of this information is public knowledge, and it must be kept under wraps." Bill nodded in agreement. Emad began.

"The house in Mellieha—where Doling held you captive—is owned by a man called Per Asplund, a Norwegian banker. And according to the police, he has been missing for over a week. The name of the house, as you enquired, is Das Verrückte Haus; it's German and translates as—The Mad House Or Crazy House."

He resumed with elaborate details.

"Asplund, in 2012, along with bank insiders and others in his criminal gang were able to steal tens-of-millions of Norwegian Kroner fraudulently; none of the money has ever been traced or found. A year ago, after a tip-off from an informer, the Maltese police started the arrest process and set in motion procedures with their Norwegian counterparts to instigate extradition for Asplund to face charges at Oslo's Supreme Court. He had been living a life of luxury here in Malta, under a pseudonym for years, and got away with it. Until now, that is.

"The local police believe he has skipped the island, or possibly in hiding in a quiet location waiting for the heat to die down. There is an intensive search at this moment in time.

"If he is still in Malta, they will find him. Whatever the scenario, the national criminal Investigation service in Norway, Kripos, is in the process of sending a team over to check the house and his personal belongings, under an agreement with the Government of Malta. This madhouse where Doling took you was never owned or rented by anyone called Hector Doling."

"What information do you have on Doling?" said Bill in a direct manner.

"I hope you are ready for this, Bill, but believe it or not…both bodies of Hector Doling and the other man…a man called…Farkas Palinkas…are gone. Taken from the Mater Dei Mortuary sometime between 2:00 am and 5:00 am this morning. There is no security footage or eyewitness accounts of how this was done. But by any stretch of the imagination, it was a slick, professional job."

"They even control body snatchers," Bill said under his breath.

"Hector Doling is, I'm afraid, a ghost. Under everyone's radar, a man living undetected with no criminal history or wanted by any police force anywhere in the world. There is no history, no written records, no TAX files, not even criminal records. In conclusion, he doesn't exist. He is a shadow. This man Doling, if that's his real name, is concealed in a deep swamp of a criminal underworld that has hidden forces in every walk of society, he is a bit player in a play of millions and it's unlikely his remains will ever be found."

He paused briefly as if he remembered a fact he wanted to add.

"And further to the weirdness of last night. The two aircraft that fought over our heads in a terrifying battle were found safe and undamaged, on the old Ta' Qali airfield. Landing on the part of what's left of the original airstrip. No pilots were discovered either. The explosion we heard, was part of an elaborate hoax, to let you believe that one aircraft crashed. A bit like the movies. Stuntmen and smoke and mirrors. An illusion, a costly deception indeed. And wait for it…all the motorbikes were found, but no riders!"

Emad laid the paperwork on the table. He wanted to confess something, he rubbed his right hand over his mouth and over the grey beard stubble in anticipation of Bill's adverse reaction to his upcoming disclosure.

"Bill, I know about all of the mind connections everyone has been living with. I too had a real-life dream connection with Laura."

Bill didn't respond. He understood that every one of his companions and confidantes would have been linked this way. That's how he saw the world now. His personal world!

"I was asked to help Raca and Farid escape from Syria. My contacts in both Turkey and Syria worked tirelessly to get them out, and thankfully we were successful." Smiling as he looked over to Raca and Farid at the pool.

"The last time Laura spoke with me was only last week. I thought it was a dream again, it was in many aspects, but it was genuine. You must understand this. Laura is dead, yet she was talking to me, showing me the truth as she called it?"

Emad somehow knew Bill understood his justification as if he had in-depth knowledge of the situation. Emad moved an empty tumbler on the table to rest both arms, folded. He leaned over the tabletop and closer to Bill.

"Laura told me a secret. It was a revelation of sorts, a disclosure that brought more danger than I would ever imagine possible. In 2010, I loaned three religious icons to a dear friend to hang in his house in Jableh, in Syria. It was more than safe. The property and the grounds had installed State of the art security, which was more than acceptable; the technology was just as proficient as the Louvre in Paris. I agreed to a year-long loan.

"But whoever planned and executed the robbery was ruthless. Not just intent of stealing my priceless art, the thieves murdered my friend and his lovely wife, stealing my priceless art, and if this was not enough, the house was set alight. These killers are cold-hearted and brutal, focused on seizing my artwork only, in the process they destroyed Nasrallah's private art collection worth over 1 billion Euros killing him and his wife for no other reason than theft of my artwork.

"But a miracle happened. When you and Farid joined forces, with mind sharing…you went looking for Raca. It was then that something peculiar transpired. Farid told me you both lost connection with each other under the tunnels of Aleppo. That's when Raca found the treasure. There were billions of gold bullion stored in caves and tunnel systems deep under the citadel of Aleppo.

"Raca had witnessed the thieves accept money for the return of the icon's just before the bombing in Al Hatab Square in 2012, at the onslaught of the Syrian civil war. A well-organised gang had the icons and were willing to negotiate their return. So, I asked my friend, Kamal Al-Maleh, Syria's Director-General of Antiquities and Museums, if he could take care of the business. He had at his disposal one of the world's leading experts on religious art, a curator at Aleppo Museum, the head curator of antiquities, Alem Najjar. If the Director recovered my art, I offered everyone involved to escape the coming war and fly them to Berlin.

"Najjar met the thieves, checked the authenticity of the specimen they provided, paid £100,000 in cash for information on the whereabouts of my icons, and an agreement was in place for further payment for their safe return. Najjar was in the car, ready to send a text, a password revealing a successful deal had been done when the bomb went off. And I don't need to remind you what happened in Al-Hatab square.

"During her expedition, Raca befriended a cat, a ginger tomcat named Mithra, whom she believes is a divine being, a God of storms, thunder, and rain. The cat seemingly created a haven, a place of sanctuary during the worst days of the war. A temple, underground where they lived, ate and slept in comfort as the war was violently fought above them. They remained there peacefully and without threat for weeks until it was safe to move.

"The treasure is safe, she said. Raca stated that the cat, Mithra, denies access to the treasure. If any person that tries to remove it is evil, they will fail, and they will die a tortured death. To retrieve the vault of riches, the person must be someone of faith, righteous, and pure heart. The treasure will remain safe under the city of Aleppo forever, and when the time is right, someone kind, someone who will spread the wealth among the people that suffered most, can enter and retrieve the fortune. Raca was one such girl.

"She didn't need the treasure that lay before her. None of the pots of stolen money or chests of sparkling jewels, nor the multitude of pallets stacked with gold bars or boxes full of bundles of notes, bonds or share issues.

She decided that all she wanted to recover was my three small icons. As Laura had asked, Raca wanted them returned to their rightful owner, and she did.

I now have them home and never for one moment did I believe they would survive the civil war.

"In all this madness, Bill, whatever we would call this miracle, a cat with a conscience, a God of some sorts, has returned my priceless work of art home to me, and strangely, Laura has her treasure too—Raca." Bill was shocked that Emad had his icons returned; he believed Hector Doling wanted them; he told as much; thankfully, he didn't get his hands on them. Emad spoke more.

"And, in some strange way, you have found a new friend in Farid, the brave man that took the same frightful journey as Raca, severely injured by a bomb, struggled to walk for many months, but still managed to get here. I know you don't believe in miracles or a divine spirit, but even you must think about how all this developed. You had a real-life shared reality, Bill; in principle, you were there in Aleppo with Farid.

"Being part of another human being, sharing life, feeling the same hurt and anguish as your host; both experiencing a connection, something like this has never been heard of before.

"Yet I experienced a similar joining of thought with Laura, as Raca did. We are a unique group of individuals, probably the first humans in history linked in this way. We overcame wickedness, battled hard against criminals using mind-control techniques and hypnosis. We wrestled through difficult times where we lost loved ones and friends, and most importantly, with the help of a brave young girl, we went on a courageous voyage together, helped by your friend Farid Aboud to bring closure to all of this. They survived and are here to tell their story."

"Doling may have powerful friends and allies, but he is dead now. No more threats of violence, no more crazy shows of power-loving rituals. It means we can all get on with our lives. We do not need to worry about Hector Doling anymore. He is the last of his type."

A well-dressed, bespectacled young man, in his early twenties, approached Bill and Emad, from steps that connected a garden path down to the outdoor infinity pool that overlooked the harbour.

"Bill McKenzie?" the young man inquired.

"Yes, I'm Bill McKenzie," said Bill warily.

"I'm here on an errand to deliver you a letter. I'm from Attard Azzopardi and Worley," said the young man blushing; triggered by emotions which sent blood to his face, causing his cheeks to turn red.

"And how do you know me, and know I would be here?" Bill was suspicious yet curious.

"My employers told me…It's been in our safe since 2012. I was told to deliver it today, at this place and at this time. I…I…don't buy it. I think it's a wind-up, sending me on a fools-errand, and if it is, I apologise. But I was told to deliver the letter and have you sign a receipt of delivery. I need to ask you to sign this book." The boy said handing Bill the envelope and offered a duplicate receipt book which Bill signed. The young man was nervous as he removed a copy for Bill, he wished him a good day and left.

"Another strange addition to all that has happened. The mystery deepens," said Emad.

Bill opened the envelope that had his name printed on it.

Bill recognised Laura's handwriting. His hand shook as he read it. He couldn't help believing that his world was unravelling into a weirder complexity of strange facts as the days moved on.

"Bill,

You will find this weird and odd, and as fantastically preposterous, but please bear with me. This will sound even stranger, but I am writing this letter in the year 2012. Why am I writing this? I write this because of events that happened to me then. Let me explain."

"This officer was none other than Oberfeldwebel Jurgen Lutz Sulzbach. He was the German pilot killed by your uncle William.

It's a puzzle; it's so extraordinary, trying to reveal these problematic facts, and the circumstances that have provoked all our lives, in a way we don't understand or fully grasp reality. Maybe Hector Doling was related to the pilot and wanted revenge in his weird way.

Doling was a leader, the head of a disruptive organisation, focused on immorality, extortion, murder, anarchy, and crimes beyond an average person's mental comprehension.

But, a few days before I died, I saw my funeral. I knew the burial was in Scotland but didn't know how I would die, but I didn't run or hide from the outcome, I had to live life as I had always intended, I had to be brave, I had to show faith, I needed to show spirit and bravery. I wouldn't let criminals rule my life, you know me, Bill?

I was influencing Finlay McColl, making him suffer and open his truths. I decided to fight back!

Before we left Malta and returned to Edinburgh, I had the most realistic lucid visual dream ever. It revealed everything to me. It was in the future, and I saw you being abducted from the apartment at gunpoint and made to listen to a tirade of nonsense from Hector Doling. Doling wanted you to be part of his game, a game which I saw and viewed the conclusion. As Doling said, 'his end game.' I knew then that it would all work out the way I prayed, everyone would be safe, and life could continue in the way we always wished.

The morning I wrote this letter, I took it to a local solicitor and informed him that it had to be delivered, on the day you receive it, which is today—delivered to you at the Bastion Pool at the Phoenicia. You would be sitting with Emad. I saw it all, Bill.

Hector Doling's criminal organisation is like a super ant colony, all connected by interlocking unlawful super-criminals, spread worldwide. All related to other supercolonies, which created a global megacolony.

This megacolony of crime represents the most dangerous organised crime syndicate the world has ever seen. I saw the prescience of everything, the whole structure of Doling's syndicate, and it was chaotic and deathly, and I am glad he is no longer alive.

He was bonded together by mind-control, a superpower of mental manipulation controlled by a supreme leader, the king of crime. And that man is not Hector Doling. Doling was a lone operative, managing and dictating his workers, building his criminal portfolio, to add to the all-powerful pyramid syndicate's prosperity. But like life itself, his corrupt structure was fractured by like-minded killers, and I played a part in his downfall; we all did. The door to his criminal world was closed and locked forever. His counterparts, his recruits, and contacts had to be eliminated by the collective. They closed ranks and completed the kill with immediate effect. The Overseer ordered Doling's death, and every one of his mind-connected associates would suffer the same end.

In total, 1,200 people of Hector Doling's corporate ladder were killed within 24 hours. I saw the vision.

I know you will find all this unrealistic and difficult to believe, but I got all these facts in my dream.

When the winter snow melts in Norway, near Straume, in the Vestland county, in a forest clearing overlooking the small town, the police will find three dead naked men, bound tightly, all sitting upright on three wooden kitchen chairs.

The bodies were seated in a triangular shape, each facing the centre of the shape, and where the dead men gazed, was an artificial stem of a white dancing orchid.

It is crude and disgusting in its method.

The dead men seated are Hector Doling, Farkas Palinkas and Per Asplund. This proves one thing, Bill, that this organisation is all-powerful and unstoppable. Workers who violate the rules, commit cowardice, mutiny, desertion, or work out with the structure are punishable through discipline. Decimation is the removal of a tenth in the Roman military discipline. The punishment given to Hector Doling's group is not so trivial. The high command destroyed everyone under the offender's control, as well as the chain of command.

All 1200 of them.

Hector Doling and his followers are gone now, as have the ones hunting Farid and Raca. It is not Doling, or cannon-fodder like him, that will end this secret criminal society. It is taking the head of the snake. But I am afraid the organisation's leader will never be discovered by me or anyone else, as this was my last living dream, and the facts I have, go no further.

I hope you will read my book, The Adventures of Raca and Mithra. And decide if it should be published? I now wish you all the luck in the world. I have one last treat; I just hope it works.

Remember Carl Jung's words, *Your vision will become clear only when you can look in your heart. Who looks outside, dreams; who looks inside, awakes*.

Tell Emad you are fine!

I love you forever,

Laura x

Bill was overcome with tears as he put the letter back into the envelope. Emad didn't want to intervene on Bill's moment, but he did speak.

"You OK, Bill?"

"I'm fine, Emad." Bill smirked, knowing Laura had also seen this brief exchange between friends. Bill was able to reflect on his moment when Emad left to join Raca at the swimming pool.

It wasn't long before Laura's last surprise was revealed-as the beautiful shape of Alessia Grech appeared at the table.

"Alessia, what brings you here today?" He offered, pleasantly surprised. His heart fluttered.

Alessia spoke before she pulled a chair and sat down opposite Bill.

"Today, a lawyer from the Valletta law firm Attard Azzopardi and Worley came to my shop delivering a package, I have never dealt with this firm previously, so I was apprehensive about wondering what this package contained.

The parcel contained this medal, a poster, and a letter."

Alessia produced the items on the table. Bill was perplexed and bemused.

What Bill saw was Laura's medal, the runners-up medal he had seen in many old photographs and knew the story of how Laura tossed it into the river. "The letter?" Bill asked inquiringly.

"Not so much a letter but a short note."

She opened the letter and looked at Bill, hoping for confirmation to continue, to read it. His silence approved this.

Alessia's voice was soft and delicate as she read Laura's words.

Dear Alessia,

I am writing to you today to explain a few details.

We are both caught in an inescapable network of affinity, bonded in a single thread of destiny, held together by Bill McKenzie. From the very moment you two met, I understood that you were also having real dreams of reality. You also saw the future!

I just wanted to take this opportunity to wish you and Bill every success in the world. I offer all my love.

Yours's forever, Laura.'

Alessia laid the letter on the table and waited for Bill to react.

"You had similar dreams?"

"It started the night we met. I thought it was just a nightmare, but it was more than that. The next night, the dream moved forward like a television serial, filling in blanks and making an accurate visual storyline. Giving me information on events taking place in your life, Bill. The dreams became relentless, like a showreel spinning out facts with intrinsic details, but Laura told me to keep out of the weirdness that was going on, her voice telling me not to get involved as it would soon be all over. After watching the TV news headlines last night and again this morning, it was as if I had known the whole story.

"I knew everything. Life and dreams are closely related and can, at times, make an imaginative thought occur to make a person have a sense of inspiration. To me, this was unimaginable but honest-to-goodness tangible.

"It was all real, Bill, and not a vision that I fully understood. I saw a real-life event unfold in my mind, my imagination. I saw clear moving pictures and words that were as clear as we speak now."

Alessia looked somewhat embarrassed and unsure how Bill would take her story.

Bill didn't wait too long to ask a question.

"I have had these dreams regular, Alessia; it is unexplainable what I have seen. And I guess that you have now had these experiences. What more did you see?" Bill asked.

"It's not what I saw; it's what Laura told me." Alessia paused again, but Bill didn't respond.

"It was a message from Laura. She told me my future; she told me about our future."

Bill still didn't react. He listened.

"I'm not overly religious, or do I believe what my dreams say, even if they appear real. But when Laura spoke, I listened to her every word. This morning, I got the medal and the letter, and if this didn't make me sit up and notice, nothing would. I believed the meeting of our minds was real; we did connect, even if your wife was dead. I would take her word as truth. Not Hector Doling's."

Bill realised Alessia was avoiding telling more. She didn't know where to start.

"Did Laura tell you about your future family" Bill interrupted Alessia's silence.

A look of bewilderment crossed her face; she fidgeted uncomfortably. After all, she had only met this stranger recently, had a few drinks with the man she sat with, and he knew about her real dream-sharing with his dead wife.

"Yes, she did, Bill, and you are the father of the three children. Laura told me their actual birth dates!"

Alessia was shocked by what she had heard from Laura and what she reiterated to Bill. The man that would father her three unborn children had the same information, and the same knowledge. She continued in an embarrassed, uncomfortable way, "You are the father of Alessia, Laura, and Bill Jnr. We get married in three months at the Scots Church in Valletta. Laura even informed me of my bridal party. Raca, as my bridesmaid, Emad, gives me away, and your best man is Farid. But it doesn't end there. We adopt Raca. Is this what you heard?"

Bill didn't answer, but he nodded in agreement. Alessia talked more.

"Laura even told me that both Farid and Raca have Turkish passports; they received Maltese visas at the consulate general in Istanbul. All arranged and covered by your friend Emad."

She spoke from her heart now.

"If I am honest, these words are words from your dead wife and not me, not my feelings or my emotions; it is Laura's explanation of the future. But since Laura told me we would no longer connect or meet in my dreams, our emotional relationship is broken and ended; I could return to normality. Sleep and dream as my mind saw fit. But I still had these living thoughts in my head.'

Bill remained silent and listened to Alessia's every word.

"A day or so, after returning from Berlin, I was struggling with how my life just blew open, and everything flew out. All alone, out of a loveless marriage, and now single and starting my life from scratch.

"I went for a long walk, I needed a coffee, and before long I found the ideal place to sit and think about my life. Our lives can be extremely demanding at times, and sometimes you need a break; forget your worries and be aware of the thoughts that are running through your head—thoughts…anxious thoughts about the future. All those memories, images of people I know, my father, whom I loved, what would he say about my current situation?"

"Then a beautiful woman pulled up a chair at the table next to me. We started chatting, and she, too, was out walking to clear her head. We joined tables and ate lunch, two strangers enjoying each other's company, two women with similar concerns, helping each other."

"There are moments in life, Bill, when you get to know someone, you realise that there is a bond. Something deep-rooted in each of us. It feels like we had known each other forever, as if we were long-lost sisters, meeting for the first time. We hit it off. It was the best tonic I ever had, and she agreed with me.

"We were due to meet when she returned from a short trip to Edinburgh. But this never happened. I didn't get the call. But what I never knew until this morning, is that my dear stranger, my mind sharing companion, my dream twin, was your lovely wife, Laura."

Alessia produced a photograph on her phone, a selfie taken at the café, a beautiful picture of two smiling strangers, loving life, and hoping to put their world to rights. Life was beginning to look bright, new friends sharing similar traits and ambitions. Two happy strangers now became friends.

"I don't know what to say now," said Alessia. Wiping tears from her eyes.

"Can I ask you out for a meal or a few drinks…maybe tonight, just so we can talk and go over all of this? It's confusing, I understand…but if you are busy, or have something better to do, or maybe…"

"Bill, I'd love to talk more over a meal. What about the place we first met, the Trabuxu wine bar? Do you know the night we met, I took my friends there only because Laura told me it was her favourite restaurant and that I would like it? She said she and her husband enjoyed the vibrant atmosphere, with great food and wine. Little did I know that the man whose lap I fell on was Laura's husband."

"I will book a table," offered Bill.

"No need to. I did it this morning."

Alessia removed a one-foot long cardboard tube from her bag and handed it to Bill.

"Laura told me to give this to you, Bill. It is a present for Farid." She smiled and offered her goodbyes, saying she needed to get back to her shop.

Bill took a poster from the cardboard tube, which revealed an Ali Farzat framed print. A caricature of a figure wearing an opulent military uniform, spoon-feeding his subject from a large cast-iron pot, brimming with medals. The political cartoon hung on the wall of a small cupboard room at the Museum of Aleppo. Although he didn't understand how he could define this nonsense, he did feel that these truths were the last pieces of a gigantic jigsaw, and hopefully, only a few missing parts remained. Let the picture be complete, he thought, but wondered what the final image would be?

–

Bill relaxed and enjoyed the sun, and another hot coffee was poured into the empty cup. He watched his friends loving life at the infinity pool. Emad chatting with Farid and little Raca frolicking in the water. It was an oasis of calm and relaxation, providing beautiful views of the harbour and the ancient city bastion walls. Everything seemed rosy in this garden.

The day moved on, and the temperature increased, the sky was turquoise blue, with no clouds to mention, and more and more sun worshipers arrived to enjoy the facilities; now Bill found time to reflect on recent events. As dreamers do, he thought over some parts of the journey he had been on, not trying to understand the essence of it but to generalise characteristics of the confusion he endured, hoping to find a truth that would suit his mental processes.

The number three came to the front of his judgements. Why this number? A voice promoted the word 'three' to his subconscious. Not a second person in his head but some procedure of his behaviour revealing secrets. The term appeared again—THREE!

Keying the question into his mobile phone—'Explain the symbolic influence of the number 3'—and a host of responses appeared on the screen.

The top choice was one that mentioned the number as Angel Number 3.

He opened it.

The number 3 represents the angelic realm, the 3rd heaven and the spirit world's energies. It mentioned the tri-power which can be considered as the third eye chakra. He read on. Many three's appeared with design or maybe purpose, on every page he looked. *It's just a number, a number like others that all have similar facts and meanings, it was nothing unusual in connection to his life, not now, not ever; it couldn't be.*

He came out of the search engine and began to watch his friends again.

As if a tap of influence offered a flow of information revealing more about three than he ever could have imagined.

As if his conscience opened a tap of influence, Bill's mind opened to a flow of information that revealed more about the number three than he ever could have imagined.

It gave knowledge that the world's most prominent religions have three as a united link, with focus on the world's three major monotheistic religions: Judaism, Islam, and Christianity. Likewise, Dan Brown, his writer hero, uses the triangle to represent three dimensions in his occult symbology

He used the triangle as a visual representation of the three-dimensions. And there is the masonic symbolism on the Dollar bill's reverse with the text: Novus Ordo Seclorum—New order of the ages. There are three dimensions: length, width, depth, and three parts to time, as we understand it: past, present and future.

Then more information flowed as more random thoughts and involuntary semantic memories rushed through his mind.

He soon forgot about the sunny day, the cloudless sky was no longer appreciated, the fun and laughter from his friends became a distant echo, he felt polarised from the crowd, and began to see the truth. He could never achieve a fact without the help of some power that influenced his being, his inner self. There it was, as clear as day, the number three was everywhere in his life story.

If he was speedreading an actual book of his journey, this number popped up repeatedly from beginning to end.

It was everywhere. *Three* linked to Finlay McColl.

The three murdered students, the three murderers that did the Finlay McColl's crimes, three unsolved murders in greater Manchester associated with the same killer, and three days McColl spent in hospital for a minor operation. McColl's three consecutive life sentences; and the three words he gave the minister; Raca and Mithra. And, of course, Laura's last three unheard words. He, himself, received three stitches in a head wound.

Then there was the honeymoon link to the number three: There were three yachts for Laura and Bill to choose from, with three folders; Emad had berthed the boats at the three cities in Malta. Emad reduced his new working partners for the yacht business down to three apparent candidates, and there were three guests in Emad's suite when Laura and Bill arrived to conclude the business transaction. And a fact that hit hard, his elderly uncle William marked with a 3-number-tattoo on his left arm.

Three letters: A.A.A. and, the inclusion of the Egyptian eagle of Saladin, etched above the text were visible on the yacht captain's polished buttons.

The Syria configurations added more complexity to the multiple connections to the number.

Further remembering three women in the restaurant in the rooftop restaurant at Al-Jdayde Hotel, Al-Hatab Square, three black security Limos, again in Al-Hatab Square. Then he saw a clear visual definition of three religious icons, and three initials hidden on the images, E. A. N.

More revelations appeared as if a video scrolled text before him.

- Curator Najjar was told once in the car's safety to text the code word 'THREE' to the Directors phone.
- The bomb in Al-Hatab Square had to blast and penetrate three stories, deep under the road surface, to reach the secret bank.

- Three art pieces were taken from the vault: The Painter on his way to work by Vincent Van Goch, a Portrait of a Man by Sandro Botticelli, and The Concert by Johannes Vermeer.
- There were three escape routes from the underground vault.

Then more information flooded into his senses, more and more three's came to view in this psychological mind-game that surfaced into his existence. Giving unrelenting knowledge of all that happened, in his actuality of time with Hector Doling.

- There was a vision of three cadaver dogs scouring the Kinloch Rannoch mass gravesite
- The Scottish police officer, DC Thomson, had *three* daughters.
- Dr Emily Rankine had *three* children.
- The crazed biker in Valletta fired *three* shots.
- Hector Doling titled Bill, Emad and Farid his three-wise-men.
- Progressus Trium, [Progress of Three] the Glasgow IT business that worked closely with Arran Dandelion. Owned by Glasgow business Guru, Gordon Alexander Morton.
- Hector Doling's finale took place at the *Triton* Fountain, and Doling shouted *three* final words: Red Lentil Soup!

But just as quick as the information filled his head, as dreams usually do, more three connections he discovered on his journey began to delete themselves; memories of these truths were disappearing as fast as they had come to him. He was flittering away as if sand in an egg-timer alleviated the facts one by one until his suffered mind could only gather and recollect recent memories.

–

Eventual Reality. The Final Image

At their first meeting at the Trabuxu wine Bar, there was an undeniable connection where two strangers instantly clicked. Not everything in life is seen through rose-tinted glasses, yet both openly took logic and threw it out of the window, along with the normality of tradition.

As Laura's future prediction said, they were married three months later. With the help of their lawyers, they set in motion an entire legal adoption process to become Raca's legal guardians. Farid had settled into a job at Valletta Yacht Holdings, Bill and Alessia moved into the Valletta apartment, and Raca had Bill's old room. Bill decorated the room for Raca's style of choice, pink and full of pictures of cats. A stray ginger tom cat entered their lives. Raca called him Thlatht, the Arabic word for three.

A long last friendship with Emad continued. He would remain a constant friend and companion to Bill and his new family.

Alessia was soon expecting a baby. It was a girl.

Germany
The Same Day and the Same Time

Showered and refreshed, the stranger dressed casually. Wearing black Tom Ford side stripe Shelton trousers, a cream Brunello Cucinelli (fisherman-style ribbed sweater) with a small upside-down triangle logo embroidered on the left chest, number 3 centred in it. Blue Santoni Croc Monk shoes were on his feet. The unfamiliar person was every bit of a man in sync with his sense of purpose. His aura gives off signals to that effect, and even the style of clothes he wore promoted class.

The turret room offers a distinctive space along with an abundance of light and air, through multiple windows and a door leading to a balcony.

As expected, the wine was sitting chilled in a bucket of ice, near his briefcase, both sitting on the executive desk, a stylish two-tone table in an oak finish; and near the antique studded brown leather executive seat. Opposite the desk, three new paintings were newly hung on the wall, and low-level background music played on a concealed music system. Richard Wagner's *The entry of the Gods into Valhalla. Das Rheingold, Act 11*, was playing. He began to hum along with the music.

He strolled unhurriedly toward the double doors and opened them wide, the fresh air rushed in, and he inhaled, filling his lungs with Frischer Deutscher Sauerstoff. Moans of gratitude left his mouth. The Rhine view showed the small town of Bad Salzig, situated on the river's west bank. The stranger stood on the balcony, arms out-stretched over the wrought-iron railing, viewing his kingdom from his tower that sat one hundred feet high in his castle fortress, perched on an out-crop sitting at 400ft above sea-level. The King was in his castle.

The metal and glass balcony doors remained open as the stranger re-entered his study, walking to view his recently acquired masterpieces. In a row, left to right, suspended on the wall were The Painter on His Way to Work by Vincent Van Gogh, A Portrait of a Man by Sandro Botticelli, and The Concert by Johannes Vermeer, depicting a man and two women performing music.

The stranger held his arms behind his back and viewed the art without talking; he leaned forward to see each one. He would never discuss, evaluate, or criticise any work of art in his collection. The man of wealth believed art transforms life. It envelopes those that see the higher good, with qualities such as power, beauty or faith. The cold stranger loved power, loved beauty, and most of all, he loved his faith.

Strolling back onto the veranda, he produced a mobile phone from his pocket, dialled a number and waited; the phone rang three times before the recipient answered. The listener didn't speak; the stranger said,

"I must congratulate you on the work you have provided my organisation. I thank you for your labour and obedient dedication, and as agreed, you are free." Then he paused, then spoke again. Loud and clear into the receiver.

"Rote Linsensuppe."

The crime lord ended the call and took a seat at his desk.

From inside his briefcase, he removed six red leather books he laid on his desk. Neatly piled, one on top of another.

One of Germany's finest, the wine was cold, served at its best temperature, perfect for releasing the most incredible possible aromatics in the glass without spoiling the taste. The bottle rim sat popped up proudly in a bucket of iced water as the crime boss moved to pour the wine into a magnificent yellow glassed Utopia Ruskin goblet; until it was full. The nectar was impeccable and flawless. It matched the standard of music and art, and the stranger relaxed; he was in his ultimate heaven. His tanned hands soon placed the goblet on the desk and drew his attention to the red leather books. They were diaries.

The top one was chosen and brought to view. It was smallish, embossed with a Nazi war eagle on the top half of the book, with the text embellished below saying: Volumen einer.

Relaxing back in the opulent chair, he picked up a disregarded cork from a 1982 bottle of Dom Perignon Champagne, which he sniffed contentedly for a prolonged period as if recalling fitting memories attached to it. By using a wooden honey dipper, he drizzled Arran Honey over a croute of toast and enjoyed its quality, which he thought matched his personality. Staring at the first printed page of the book with great focus, the reader, the stranger, the crime lord, Herr Erich Lux Sulzbach; or by his professional name, Omar Kaplan, spoke with a broad Rhinelandic accent, “Herr Hitler, tell me your secrets.”

Das Ende

Red lentil soup is not a secret. It is a revelation.

The upside-down triangle is female, lunar, passive and symbolises Mother.

3

The number 3 resonates with the Ascended Masters and indicates that these masters are around you, assisting when asked. The Ascended Masters help you focus on the Divine spark within yourself and others and assist with manifesting your desires. They allow you to find peace, clarity, and love within.

شوربة

,الأحمر العدس

Red lentil soup, or the Syrian pronounced, Shwrbt aleds al’ahmar, or the Anglicised name: Shurbat Addes:

Ingredients:

2 cups of red lentils (No substitutes!)
6 cloves of garlic
1 teaspoon of coriander seeds
1 teaspoon of salt
1 teaspoon of sea salt
2 tbsp of olive oil

The Beginning